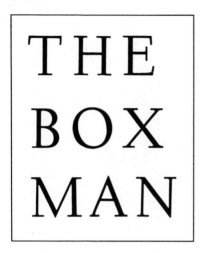

THE BOX MAN

A *Novel by* KOBO ABÉ

Translated from the Japanese by E. Dale Saunders

NORTH POINT PRESS   *San Francisco*   1991

Copyright © 1974 by Alfred A. Knopf, Inc.
Published by arrangement with Alfred A. Knopf, Inc.
Printed in the United States of America
Cover illustration: *Travelogue (1)*, by Zhang Yuan Fan.
Courtesy of College Women's Association of Japan.
Cover design: David Bullen

LIBRARY OF CONGRESS CATALOGING-IN-PUBLICATION DATA
Abe, Kōbō, 1924–
    [Hakootoko. English]
    The box man : a novel / by Kobo Abe ; translated by E.
    Dale Saunders
        p.   cm.
    Translation of: Hakootoko.
    ISBN 0-86547-461-3
    I. Title.
PL845.B4H313   1991
895.6'35—dc20   90-20845

North Point Press
850 Talbot Avenue
Berkeley, California
94706

The Box Man

CLEAN SWEEP OF UENO HOBOS
Check This Morning—180 Arrests

During the predawn hours of the twenty-third, the Tokyo Ueno Police began to arrest those vagrants trying to avoid the cold of the approaching winter by camping in and around the underground passages of the Keisei Line, Ueno Railway Station, Ueno Park, Daito Ward, in the hopes of preventing further shootings by the long-sought criminal no. 109. A total of 180 persons were arrested in the underground passages and behind the Tokyo Institute of Culture, located within the Park precincts. They were arrested on the spot under the Law of Minor Offenses (infringement of the prohibition against loitering and vagrancy) and the Traffic Laws (acts prohibited on highways). All were taken to the Ueno Police Station, where they were photographed and fingerprinted. Four, who complained of being sick, were sent to the hospital via the Daito Welfare Office; nine were sent to a home for the aged. Those remaining were released after signing an agreement not to relapse into vagrancy. An hour later there was every indication that almost all had returned to their former haunts.

My Case

This is the record of a box man.

I am beginning this account in a box. A cardboard box that reaches just to my hips when I put it on over my head.

That is to say, at this juncture the box man is me. A box man, in his box, is recording the chronicle of a box man.

Instructions
for Making a Box

MATERIALS:

1 empty box of corrugated cardboard
Vinyl sheet (semitransparent)—twenty inches square
Rubber tape (water-resistant)—about eight yards
Wire—about two yards
Small pointed knife (a tool)

> (*To have on hand, if necessary: Three pieces of worn canvas and one pair of work boots in addition to regular work clothes for streetwear.*)

Any empty box a yard long by a yard wide and about four feet deep will do. However, in practice, one of the standard forms commonly called a "quarto" is desirable. Standard items are easy to find, and most commercial articles that use standard-sized boxes are generally of irregular shape—various types of foodstuffs precisely adaptable to the container—so that the construction is sturdier than others. The most important reason to use the standardized form is that it is hard to distinguish one box from another. As far as I know, most box men utilize this quarto box. For if the box has any striking features to it, its special anonymity will suffer.

Even the common variety of corrugated cardboard has recently been strengthened, and since it is semiwaterproof there is no need to select any special kind unless you are going through the rainy season. Ordinary cardboard has better ventilation and is lighter and easier to use. For those who wish to occupy one box over a period of time, regardless of the season, I recommend the Frog Box, especially good in wet weather. This box has a vinyl finish, and as the name suggests, it is exceedingly strong in water. When new it has a sheen as if oiled, but apparently it produces static electricity easily, quickly absorbs dirt, and gets covered with dust; then the edge is thicker than the ordinary one and looks wavy. You can tell it at once from the common box.

To construct your box there is no particular procedure to follow. First decide what is to be the bottom and the top of the box—decide according to whatever design there may be or make the top the side with the least wear or just decide arbitrarily—and cut out the bottom part. In cases where one has numerous personal effects to carry, the bottom part can be folded inward without cutting, and, with wire and tape, the two ends can be made into a baggage rack. Tape the exposed part of the edges at the three points on the ceiling and at the one on the side where they come together.

The greatest care must be taken when making the observation window. First decide on its size and location; since there will be individual variations, the following figures are purely for the sake of reference. Ideally, the upper edge of the window will be six inches from the top of the box, and the lower edge eleven inches below that; the width will be seventeen inches. After you have subtracted the thickness of the base to stabilize the box when in place (I put a magazine on my head), the upper edge of the window comes to the eyebrows. You may perhaps consider this to be too low, but one seldom gets the opportunity to look up, while the lower edge is used frequently. When you are in an upright position, it will be difficult to walk if a stretch of at least five feet is not visible in front. There are no special grounds for computing the width. These parts should be adjusted to the required ventilation and the lateral strength of the box. At any rate since you can see right down to the ground, the window should be as small as possible.

Next comes the installation of the frosted vinyl curtain over the window. There's a little trick here too. That is, the upper edge is taped to the outside of the opening and the rest left to hang free, but please do not forget to anticipate a lengthwise slit. This simple device is useful beyond all expectations. The slit should be in the center, and the two flaps should overlap a fraction of an inch. As long as the box is held vertical, they will serve as screens, and no one will be able to see in. When the box is tilted slightly, an opening appears, permitting you to see out. It is a simple but extremely subtle contrivance, so be very careful when selecting the vinyl. Something rather heavy yet flexible is desirable. Anything cheap that immediately stiffens with temperature changes will be a problem. Anything flimsy is even worse. You need something flexible yet heavy enough not to have to worry about every little draft; the breadth of the opening can be easily regulated by tilting the box. For a box man the slit in the vinyl is comparable, as it were, to the expression of the eyes. It is wrong to consider this aperture as being on the same level as a peephole. With very slight adjustments it is easy to express yourself. Of course, this is not a look of kindness. The worst threatening glare is not so offensive as this slit. Without exaggeration, this is one of the few self-defenses an unprotected box man has. I should like to see the man capable of returning this look with composure.

In case you're in crowds a lot, I suppose you might as well puncture holes in the right and left walls while you're about it. Using a thickish nail, bore as many openings as possible in an area of about six inches in diameter, leaving enough space between them so the strength of the cardboard isn't affected. These apertures will serve as both supplementary peepholes and be convenient for distinguishing the direction of sounds. However unsightly, it will be more advantageous in case of rain to open the holes from the inside out and have the flaps facing out.

Last of all, cut the remaining wire into one-, two-, four-, and six-inch lengths, bend back both ends, and prepare them as hooks for hanging things on the wall. You should restrict your personal effects to a minimum; as it is, it's quite exhausting to arrange the indispensable items: radio, mug, thermos, flashlight, towel, and small miscellaneous bag.

As for the rubber boots, there's nothing particular to add. Just as long as they don't have any holes. If the canvas is wrapped around the waist, it is excellent for filling the space between oneself and the box and for holding the box in place. With three layers, divided in front, it is easy to move in all ways as well as being most convenient for defecation and urinating and for sundry other purposes.

An Example: The Case of A

Just making the box is simple enough; at the outside it takes less than an hour. However, it requires considerable courage to put the box on, over your head, and get to be a box man. Anyway, as soon as anyone gets into this simple, unprepossessing paper cubicle and goes out into the streets, he turns into an apparition that is neither man nor box. A box man possesses some offensive poison about him. I suppose there's some degree of poison even in a picture of the snake lady on a billboard or the bear man in a circus side show, but even so that can be canceled out by the admission fee. But the poison of a box man is not so simple.

For example, in your case, I'm sure you've not yet heard of a box man. Though there can't be any statistics, there is evidence that a rather large number of them are living in concealment throughout the country. But I've never heard that box men are being talked about anywhere. Evidently the world intends to keep its mouth tightly shut about them.

Have you ever actually seen one?

Let's stop fooling each other now. Certainly a box man is hardly conspicuous. He is like a piece of rubbish shoved between a guardrail and a public toilet or underneath a footbridge. But that's different from being inconspicuous or invisible. Since he is not especially uncommon, there is every opportunity of seeing one. Surely, even you have, at least once. But I also realize full well that you don't want to admit it. You're not the only one. Even with no ulterior motive, apparently one instinctively averts one's eyes. Yes, I suppose if you were to wear dark glasses at night or put on a mask, you couldn't help being considered some very timid creature or if not that, someone up to no good. All the more so then with a box man, who conceals his whole body; one can hardly object if he is considered suspicious.

Why, I wonder, would anyone deliberately want to be a box man? Perhaps you think it strange, but there are many amazing cases that explain why—trifling motivations that at first glance are not motivations at all. A is a case in point.

One day a box man took up residence directly below the window of A's apartment. Though A tried his best not to look, he did. No matter how he struggled to ignore the box man, he was very much aware of his presence. The first feelings that assailed A were anger and abhorrence toward a foreign body that has imposed itself, irritation and perplexity at having his territory encroached on illegally. But he decided to try and wait things out in silence for the time being. Anyway, he thought the neighborhood busybody, nagging about the garbage disposal or who knows what, would take action. But there was no sign that anybody was about to handle the matter. Unable to put up with the situation any longer, he complained to the janitor of the apartment building; but in vain. The box man was only visible from A's window, and anyone who could manage not to be seen would not deliberately move. As frequently as possible everybody pretended not to see him.

Finally A went to the police box himself. When the bored officer told him to fill out a damage report, A said that for the first time he experienced something similar to fear.

"Look here," the officer had snapped. "I suppose you made it clear he was to get out."

There was nothing for A to do but take action himself. On the way home from the police box he stopped at a friend's house and borrowed an air rifle. Once back in his room, he had a cigarette and calmed down; then he looked directly out the window, and as he did so the box man turned the observation slit of the box straight toward him. There were scarcely three or four yards between them. As if perceiving A's inner confusion, the box tilted, and the semiopaque vinyl curtain over the window divided vertically in two. From within, an indistinct whitish eye was firmly fixed on him. A felt a rush of blood go to his head. He flung open the window, and loading the gun, took aim.

But at what? At such close distance he might get the box man in the eye. And if he did that, it would only be trouble later on. It would be enough to shoot him somewhere else just to teach him not to show his face around here again. As A was speculating about his opponent's position in the box and the contours of his body, his finger, still on the trigger, began to grow numb and falter. It would be so much better if the fellow would vacate the premises because of a simple threat. He didn't want a single drop of blood left behind. But he couldn't wait forever. If a simple threat didn't work, it would be useless to try it again. He drew a bead. Again anger welled up within him. Time overheated, burned. He squeezed the trigger. The barrel of the gun, and then the box, made a noise like that of a wet trouser cuff snapped by an umbrella handle.

At the same time, the box gave a big leap. However inventively it may be used, corrugated cardboard is, after all, merely paper. Although it demonstrates considerable strength against general surface pressure, it is weak when stressed at a given point. The lead bullet must have bored into the fellow's body with great force. But neither the screams nor the jeers he had anticipated were forthcoming. Once it had leaped up, the box, again in repose, showed signs within of an extremely slow movement. A was at a loss. He had aimed several inches below and to the left of the line connecting the lower left and the upper right angles of the window. He estimated it to be about where the arm meets the right shoulder. Had he hesitated so long that his aim had deflected? But the box's reaction had been too great for that. An unpleasant thought occurred to him. The man in the box did not necessarily have to be facing front. The lower part of his body was completely covered with canvas, so there was no way to tell exactly what position he was in. He might have been sitting cross-legged, his knees on a diagonal in the box. If so, the bullet might well have grazed the top of the shoulder and hit the carotid artery.

An uncomfortable numbness formed an oval round A's mouth. Running steps in a dream. With bated breath A waited for the next movement. The box man did not budge. No, he had . . . he was clearly moving. The inclination was definitely increasing not so fast as the second hand of a watch but faster than the minute hand. Was he going to fall over? From the box came a sound like scraping on not fully dry clay. Suddenly the box man arose. He was unexpectedly tall. A heard a sound like that of striking a wet tent. Slowly changing his direction, the box man gave a low cough and stretched. He began to walk, swinging the box slightly right and left. The position of his hips was alarmingly toward the back, perhaps because he was bending forward. A thought the box had spoken, but he could not catch the words. When it got to the street that ran along the building, it disappeared around the corner in the same position. What disappointed A most of all was that he hadn't been able to see the expression on the box man's face.

Perhaps it was his imagination, but to A the surface of the ground behind the fleeing box man appeared darker than elsewhere. Five cigarette stubs had been snuffed out underfoot. An empty bottle was plugged with paper. Two enormous spiders were crawling about inside. One looked like a corpse. Crumpled wrapping paper from a chocolate bar. Then three large, successive blackish stains as big as a thumb. Were they blood stains? he wondered. No, phlegm or spittle doubtlessly. A simpered slightly as if in apology. Well, then, he had hit the target.

In about half a month, A had almost begun to forget the box man. But he was worried about using the shortcut to the station when he went to work, and to avoid the narrow lane, he unconsciously changed his route. Yet he still continued to look out of his window as soon as he woke up and first thing when he came home. If only he had not decided to turn in his icebox, in due course he would have been cured of this habit, but . . .

The new refrigerator, equipped with a freezing compartment, was normal enough, and it came in a corrugated cardboard box. Furthermore, it was just the right size. As soon as the contents were out and it was empty, A began to think of the box man. He heard the whipping sound again. He felt as if the air-rifle bullet had ricocheted from two weeks before. A was confused and decided at once to dispose of the box. But instead he washed his hands, blew his nose, and with great diligence, gargled repeatedly. The rebounding bullet flying about inside his cranium would doubtless set his brain functions askew. After observing the neighborhood for a while, he drew the curtains over the windows and gingerly crawled into the box.

Inside it was dark, and there was the sweet smell of waterproof paint. The place seemed very homelike. A recollection was on the verge of dawning, but he could not grasp it. He wanted to stay like this forever, but in less than a minute he came to his senses and crawled out. Feeling a little uneasy, he decided to keep the box for a while.

The following day, when he returned from work, A cut an observation window in the box with a knife, smiling bitterly, and then tried putting it on over his head like the box man. But he took it off immediately—he might well smile bitterly! He didn't understand what was happening. He viciously and resolutely kicked the box into a corner of the room, but not hard enough to destroy it.

On the third day he more or less regained his composure and tried looking out of the observation window. He couldn't recall what had surprised him so the evening before. He could definitely feel a change, but such a degree of change was desirable. From the whole scene, thorns fell and things appeared smooth and round. Stains on the wall with which he was completely familiar and which were utterly harmless to him . . . old magazines piled helter-skelter . . . a little television set with bent antennae . . . empty tins of corn beef beginning to overflow with cigarette butts . . . he was again made forcibly aware of the unconscious tension in himself by everything being so unexpectedly filled with thorns. Perhaps he should put aside his useless prejudice about boxes.

The next day A watched television with the box over his head.

From the fifth day on, except for sleeping, eating, defecating, and urinating, he lived in the box as long as he was in his room. Other than a twinge of conscience, he was not especially aware of doing anything abnormal. To the contrary, he felt that this was much more natural, he was much more at home. Even in the bachelor's life he had reluctantly led until now, misfortune had turned into blessing.

Sixth day. At length the first Sunday came around. He expected no visitors and had no place to go. From morning on, he stuck to the box. He was calm and relaxed, but something was missing. At noon he finally realized what he required. He went into town and bustled around making purchases: chamber pot, flashlight, thermos, picnic set, tape, wire, hand mirror, seven poster colors, plus various foodstuffs that could be eaten without preparation. When he got home he reinforced the box with the tape and the wire, and then, storing away the other items, he shut himself up in it. A hung the hand mirror on the inner wall of the box—left side toward the window—and then by the radiance of the flashlight he painted his lips green with one of the poster colors. After that he traced, in gradually expanding circles, the seven colors of the rainbow, beginning with red, around his eyes. His face resembled that of a bird or a fish rather than that of a man. It looked like the scene of an amusement park viewed from a helicopter. He could see his small retreating figure scampering off in it. There was no makeup so suitable to a box. Ultimately, he thought, he would become the contents that was right for the container. For the first time he casually masturbated in the box. For the first time he slept, leaning against the wall with the box over his head.

Then the following morning—just a week had gone by —A went stealthily out into the streets with the box over his head. And didn't come back.

If A made any error it was only that he was a little more overly aware of box men than others were. You cannot laugh at A. If you are one of those who have dreamed of, described in their thoughts even once, the anonymous city that exists for its nameless inhabitants, you should not be indifferent, because you are always exposed to the same dangers as A—that city where doors are opened for anyone; where even among strangers you need not be on the defensive; where you can walk on your head or sleep by the roadside without being blamed; where you are free to sing if you're proud of your ability; and where, having done all that, you can mix with the nameless crowds whenever you wish.

Thus it will seldom do to point a gun at a box man.

A Safety Device . . . Just in Case

Now I may seem to be repeating myself, but I am at present a box man. And for a while I intend to write about me.

I am getting along here with these notes, as I take shelter from the rain under a bridge. Overhead the Prefectural Highway Three crosses a canal. It is just fifteen or sixteen minutes past nine by my not too accurate watch. The dark night sky trails its skirt of rain low over the surface of the land. It has been falling since morning. Fishery warehouses and lumber sheds stretch away as far as the eye can see. There are no human habitations and no one passes by. Even the headlights of trucks coming and going on the bridge do not reach this far. A flashlight suspended from the ceiling lights the paper beneath my hand. Perhaps that is why the letters formed by my ballpoint pen seem almost black when they should be green.

The seaside smell of rain is quite like a dog's breath. The place is not all that suitable as a rain shelter, for the drizzle is directionless as if expelled from an atomizer. The bridge girders are too high. This entire location is unsuitable. Everything —being at a place like this at a time like this—is unnatural and not like a box man. For example, using an electric flashlight is a terrible waste. People like us, who live on the road, make do almost completely with items we pick up from the streets. It is an extravagance to use an electric flashlight only for the purpose of writing notes. With the number of new streetlamps there's plenty of light to read a newspaper while taking shelter from the rain.

Somehow it's been over two hours since I sat myself down in this spot so ill-suited to a box man. But I should begin with an explanation. Of course, no matter how diligent I am with my justifications, I am not confident of completely convincing you. Anyway you won't believe them. But the truth's the truth and that's that. This box of mine has been sold to someone. There is a buyer willing to pay fifty thousand yen. I'm waiting for her now to make the transaction. If you find it incredible, I too am suspended between belief and disbelief. There's no way of believing, is there. I don't understand the reason for someone wanting to pay out good money for an old worn-out paper box.

Why did I react to such a temptation when I didn't believe the buyer was serious? The reason is simple. There was no reason to be suspicious, that's all. It's just like being stopped by a shining object on the side of the road. My buyer was shining like a piece of broken beer bottle in the evening sun. One knows it is of no value, but there is nonetheless a strange fascination with the light refracted by the glass. One is unexpectedly made to feel as if one were seeing another time dimension. Her legs especially were as delicate and graceful as the rails of a railroad seen from an eminence, stretching away into the distance. Bluish, light steps where, like the open skies, nothing obstructs the line of vision. There was no reason for believing her, but neither was there reason to doubt her. It was as if, without realizing it, I had been completely disarmed by her legs.

Of course, I am remorseful now. Or rather it may be better to say that I am absolutely depressed by the premonition that I shall be made to feel serious remorse. A wretched feeling. No matter how I think about it, it is not like a box man. It is as if I have abandoned the prerogatives of a box man. If there is hope, it is so subtle as to be undetectable even with a high-energy analyzer. Is some transformation beginning to take place in my box? Perhaps so. On reflection, after wandering about this town, I have the feeling that the surface of the box has become fragile and terribly vulnerable. Certainly the town bears me some ill will.

Of course, choosing this place was partially the buyer's idea, even though I did suggest it. My danger is her danger. At the foot of the bridge stands a stone Jizo, the guardian of dead children, with a red flannel bib, apparently placed there in memory of some child who died by drowning. There is a recently painted white sign beside a flight of stone steps that leads down to a boat landing slightly upstream, prohibiting playing in the water. But fortunately the vinyl over the observation window has been moistened by the rain, and be-- cause of the faded matting effect, the visibility is enhanced. The concrete embankment along the canal cuts diagonally in bold relief across the window. The wan lights of a small freighter at berth, wavering fractionally against the current, spill over palely onto the sidewalk at the top of the embankment, and if someone were to pass by he would be as conspicuous as a spot of ink on clothing.

There! A cat cut directly across the pavement. A stray cat with a filthy matted coat. It is manifestly pregnant and has a bulging white belly heavy with its load of kittens. Its tattered ears bear the marks of fighting. And since I can distinguish such details, even as my pen glides along, perhaps I need not be neurotic. No matter what, the buyer, even if she wants to, won't be able to take me by surprise all that easily.

Of course, what I want most of all is for her to come here of her own accord as she promised. But as you see, too much is vague. I can't understand—fifty thousand yen for this box—and why would she want to negotiate in a place like this? There's no reason to believe her, nor is there any to doubt her. There's no reason to doubt, nor is there to believe. A slender transparent, ephemeral neck. Anyway there's nothing better than being on my guard. Hence my little safety device. If worst comes to worst, I intend to leave these notes as evidence. Whatever death I meet, I have no desire for suicide. If I die it won't be suicide even by mistake, but definitely foul play. No matter how much one rejects the world and disappears from it by getting into a box, essentially a box is di . . .

> (Stop. Out of ink. I get an old pencil from my
> bag. Two and a half minutes to sharpen it. For-
> tunately I have not yet been killed. As proof, I
> have changed from a ballpoint pen to a pencil, but
> my writing is exactly the same as before.)

Now what is it I started to write? The last thing I wrote was perhaps the first letters of "different." Perhaps I meant to write: "A box man is different from a vagrant," or something like that. Of course, as far as society is concerned they apparently don't distinguish very clearly between the two, as much as box men do. Indeed, they have not a few points in common. For example, not having an I.D. card, or a profession, or an established place of residence, or indication of name or age, or a set time or place for eating and sleeping. And then not getting your hair cut or brushing your teeth, rarely taking a bath, needing almost no cash for daily living, and a lot of other things.

Yet, beggars and vagrants are apparently quite aware of a difference. Any number of times they made me feel unpleasant. Sometime when I have the opportunity I intend to write about it, but the Wappen beggars are especially offensive to me. The minute I draw near the beggars' and vagrants' area they make me experience a reaction close to morbid nervousness that is a far cry from indifference. I am looked at with more undisguised contempt and hostility than by anyone who pays his daily expenses and lives at a recorded address. I have, in fact, never heard of a beggar turning into a box man. Since I have no intention of being a beggar, he has none of being a box man. Even so I do not intend to look down on them. Surprisingly enough, even beggars are a part of the environs that belong to the townsfolk, and when you become a box man perhaps you're below a beggar.

Paralysis of the heart's sense of direction is the box man's chronic complaint. At such times the axis of the earth sways, and one suffers a severe nausea resembling seasickness. But for some reason there is absolutely no relationship with the consciousness of being a social dropout. Not once does he feel guilty about the box. I personally feel that a box, far from being a dead end, is an entrance to another world. I don't know to where, but an entrance to somewhere, some other world. I say this, but the opening to that other world is not very different from a dead-end alley if I stifle my nausea as I examine the world outside my little observation window. Let's stop using the fancy words. I mean I don't yet have any desire to die.

Yet it's too late. Indeed I wonder if she intends to renege on her promise. I still have seven matches. Wet tobacco is absolutely tasteless.

Promises . . . promises . . .

To take away the bitter taste, a drop of whiskey. A little less than a third left in my pocket flask.

But it's all right if she doesn't come. Is breaking a promise anything to get excited about? I'll be a lot more amazed if she puts in an appearance as she said she would. What if she doesn't go back on her promise but sends a substitute in her place? And I'm positive this will happen. A substitute will come in her place. I have a general idea as to who that will be, too. In the final analysis they are both in it together. With her as decoy, the substitute intends to lure me under the bridge as a place of execution. Since I am a born victim—indeed, as I am a box man, which is the same as not existing, no matter how they try they'll never kill me—the role of killer automatically goes to my enemy. That doesn't mean that everything proceeds according to logic. I'm prepared to meet the attack. The wet surface of the slope is steep and slippery. Of course, when it comes to strength, I fancy he has something of an edge on me. I wonder if, contrary to my feelings, deep down I don't want to die.

Now, then, time and place are suitable to the victim. The speed of the tide is ideal too. A very old-fashioned thick-bodied bridge that spans like a last constricting ring the funnel-shaped mouth of the canal swollen at high tide with sea water. As the central portion rises in an arc to let ships pass, the girders from the area at the foot of the bridge are conspicuously high. Since I am a box man walking around with a waterproofed room on my back like a snail, there is no need to worry about mere rain blown sideways or the height of girders. Compared to a real room the weak point of a box is that it has no floor, I suppose. If the wet wind comes blowing up from underneath, it is hard to avoid, whatever I do. But you can think of it in another light: precisely because there is no flooring, I can sit close by the water's edge without fear of being flooded. Even if the water level suddenly rises, swollen at high tide by the rain, as long as it doesn't exceed the height of my boots I can always stand up and change positions. For those who have not actually had the experience, this will seem madly carefree. Besides from now on the tide will be going out. No need to worry lest the water rise more than it has. The black band of seaweed, as if drawn with a ruler along the base of the embankment now rotting from oil wastes, clearly divides the view into upper and lower parts.

A dark swell spreading out from somewhere has begun to erase the ripples from the surface of the water. Immediately downstream from the bridge pylons, large and small whirlpools, sluggish, like the melting of unrefined rice honey, gradually begin to form. They are actually rather small depressions; but wooden fish boxes, fragments of bamboo baskets, and plastic containers draw falteringly near, swirl suddenly around, trembling, turn over several times, and just as their speed seems to slacken, are all at once swallowed up.

Yes, indeed, in an emergency I shall join these notes to the wooden boxes and the bamboo baskets. The shadow of someone appears on the embankment; if it is not she, I shall immediately put them in a vinyl bag, seal the mouth after blowing it up, and wrap the opening several times with the thin wire that I have doubled. About twenty-two to twenty-three seconds. Then I shall bind red vinyl tape over the wire, leaving long conspicuous ends. I shall fix a stone, the size of a fist, to the tape by means of twisted paper. That will take less than five seconds. The whole business will take about thirty seconds. However long it lasts, it shouldn't take more than one minute. Furthermore, no matter how her substitute hurries it will take him two to three minutes to come down the stone stairway by the landing, cross the slippery stone slope, and get here. I have no fear I won't have plenty of time. If he shows the slightest strange behavior, I shall immediately throw the bag into the current. It should go pretty far with the attached stone. No matter how he tries to reach it, he'll never get it. The bag will head directly toward the whirlpools. If he's an expert swimmer I wonder if he'll plunge in and chase after it? No, an expert would surely avoid such recklessness. Even the passage of small boats is forbidden after the tide has begun to withdraw. But he will be aware of the whirlpools without reading the sign on the embankment. After faltering for a while, the bag will ultimately be swept out to sea. Then after hours or days the paper string will come undone and the stone will be released. The air-filled bag will easily attract attention with its red tape, drifting in with the shore tides.

Thus if the man who shot me were to appear right now, according to the contents of the notes up to this point, he will be the one who tried to kill me. Impossible. Even if I specify his name here on this page, I doubt I can get anyone to believe me. If I try to explain the motives, I will simply weaken the credibility of the notes even more. It will all sound like a lie. But I've got my wits about me. I've attached a black-and-white negative with cellophane tape to the upper right-hand corner of the inside cover. Perhaps it is not very clear, but it will constitute absolutely unshakable evidence. It's the back view of a middle-aged man hurrying off, hiding his air rifle under his arm, the muzzle pointed downward along his body. When enlarged, I suppose you will be able to distinguish the various features even better. He is poorly dressed, but the cloth is strong and of excellent quality. Yet the trousers are full of creases. His fingers are heavy and solid, but the tips are rounded and look as if they have never experienced work. And then the fancy shoes are most conspicuous. They are low shoes, like slippers, with the sides scooped out and the soles thin. He is in a profession in which he takes them off and puts them on more than the ordinary number of times.

These notes, if the finder so wishes, can make him a little fortune.

There! The whirlpools are beginning to swell. There is absolutely no need to worry about being seen. Heavy trucks piled high with frozen fish or pulpwood kick up the thick concrete slabs immediately above on the bridge, honking and crossing back and forth every few seconds; they are absorbed only in their own noise and are like blind beasts. This is an ideal place not only for the disposal of corpses but for living humans as well. And an ideal place for murder must be an ideal place to be murdered.

The lead in my pencil is gone. Come on, come on . . . I've had enough. Is she really going to come or not?

> (I can't sharpen the pencil with this rusty knife. Tomorrow, if I'm able to prolong my existence until then, I must get two or three ballpoint pens. The ones around the service entrance of the Middle School have the most ink left in them.)

Two or Three Additions Concerning the Photographic Evidence Attached to the Inner Cover

Time of shooting: One evening about a week or ten days ago (paralysis of the sense of time is one of the chronic ailments of a box man).

Place of shooting: The mountainside end of the long black wall of the soy-sauce factory (the shadow of the wall cuts diagonally across the foreground of the picture).

At the time I was just in the act of standing there relieving myself. Suddenly there was a sharp noise. It resembled the sound of a pebble kicked up by a truck striking the box (that frequently happened, for I often lay by the roadside). But no truck, not to mention any three-wheeled conveyance, had passed by. At the same time a sharp pain like biting down on ice with a bad tooth pierced my left shoulder, and my urine stopped flowing. Looking out the little hole in the side, I saw the sweeping branches of an old mulberry tree just where the curve began along the sweet potato field of the hatchery and where the wall of the soy factory ended and became a slope and the pavement gave way to a graveled walk (a part is visible on the left side of the photo). Turning away from the shadow of the tree (that is, as if to run away), a man was beginning to get up. He shifted a sort of stick about three feet long from his shoulder and put it under his arm, whereupon it caught the evening sun and gleamed a reddish black. I at once concluded that it was an air rifle. Without rearranging myself after urinating, I set up my camera. (To tell the truth, before I became a box man I was a photographer who had just become independent. Since I had become a box man right in the midst of my career, for no particular reason I still went around with a minimum of photographic equipment.) Changing the direction of the box, I snapped three pictures in succession. (I did not have the time to regulate the distance, but as the camera was set at $f11$ at one two-hundred-and-fiftieth of a second, it was more or less in focus.) The fellow sprang to the side, crossed the road, and disappeared from view.

Almost everything up until now can be proved by analyzing the film. But from this point on, nothing at all is backed by objective evidence. I expect that either you or the finder of these notes will believe my testimony and justify it on your own.

FIRST CONJECTURE CONCERNING THE TRUE CHARACTER OF THE SNIPER. I should like you to refer to the "Case of A." When someone is infected by the idea of a box man and tries himself to become one, there is a general tendency to overreact by shooting him with an air rifle. Thus I did not cry out for help or make any attempt at pursuit. Rather I thought that the candidates for box man had increased by one, and I experienced a feeling of closeness to him. Thereupon the pain in my shoulder receded and changed into a feeling of incandescence. From now on it was rather the sniper who must endure a pain a hundred times worse. There was no need to inflict any greater chastisement on him than this.

As I gazed at the deserted sloping road after the disappearance of the rifle man, I felt moist like a broken water faucet. The smoke that smelled like burnt sugar came from the soy factory and diligently filed away at the ends of the sharp shadows cast by the evening sun, dulling the angles. Somewhere in the distance, the monotonous grating of firewood being sawed. And still further in the distance, the lively sound of a racing motorbike engine. But after two or three seconds had gone by, there was no sign of anyone at all. Could it be that the inhabitants had withdrawn underground like grubs? A scene so calm that it induced an overwhelming desire to see a human being . . . anyone. But a box man's eyes cannot be deceived. Looking out from the box, he sees through the lies and secret intentions concealed behind the scenery. The scenery evidently intended to shake me up by pretending that this was a road where one could not go astray, intended for my surrender, but unfortunately I was not to be taken in. I just wanted to relieve myself at my leisure. The area around a station or a crowded shopping district was more suited to a box man. I liked the honesty of it. I felt at home with it— three or four straight roads pretending to be a labyrinth. For this reason I don't like provincial towns. Anyway there are too many sham straight roads there. Thinking of the confusion of the air-rifle man lost on such a road, I felt sentimental without meaning to.

As I pressed down on the wound, my fingers became sticky and covered with blood. Suddenly I was uneasy. It may be all right in one of the busier quarters of Tokyo, but in this commercial section of T City, there isn't room for two box men. If he insists on becoming a box man, it necessarily follows that a territorial dispute will be unavoidable. When he realizes he can't drive me out with an air rifle, it doesn't mean that he won't come for me next time with a shotgun. Was I wrong in the way I reacted? Frankly, fellows like him have tried to get on intimate terms with me any number of times.

One addressed me directly and even stopped me in the street. At the time, I looked back at him in silence from the crack in the inclined vinyl curtain. Anyone would have been non-plused at that. Even a policeman or a railway guard would have shrunk back. I wondered if I should have said something before I drove him to his air rifle.

BUT THE CONJECTURE HAS COMPLETELY CHANGED WITH A NEW CAST OF CHARACTERS . . . The new character in the cast came riding on a bicycle. As I was concentrating on the sham road, a voice suddenly came from behind me. "There's a hospital at the top of the slope," it said. White fingertips grazed the observation window, and three thousand-yen notes were tossed in. I felt like a mailbox and turned to see a retreating figure already some ten yards away. It was apparently a young girl whose low, rasping voice did not suit her. I had no time to point the camera in her direction, and she disappeared around the corner at the next lane. I had observed her for only a few seconds, yet I was quite taken by the movement of her legs propelling the bicycle. They were slender, but not too slender—light legs with a well-proportioned curve. The backs of her knees were glossy and beautiful like the inside of a shell. They were so vivid that I have no memory of the color of the dress she was wearing. But I wasn't necessarily dis-armed. If by that evening, the wound in my shoulder had not worsened, I probably would not have made it a point to go to the hospital at the top of the slope. Nor would I have realized that the air-rifle man (as the photo clearly showed) was in fact the hospital doctor and the girl on the bicycle, the nurse. Furthermore, quite naturally, I should not have been in the ridiculous situation of waiting for her—or her substitute—in such a dangerous place under the bridge.

But I just put another cigarette to my lips. Again and again I counted over the thousand-yen notes and, folding them in three, I dropped them into one of my rubber boots. They say that a wild bird that has been captured will refuse food and die of hunger. But the condemned convict relishes his last cigarette. I, who was no bird, leisurely lit the cigarette, reflecting that there was no connection between the rifle man and the nurse. It made absolutely no difference; the rifle man was the rifle man and the girl the girl. It was all right to assume that her hurrying on ahead was an expression of her delicacy, that she was simply ashamed of her charitable act.

But no matter how much I chain-smoke, the executioner will not wait. Indeed the time for execution is drawing closer. By dawn the wound in my shoulder had begun to fester and the pain had constricted me like an overly narrow rubber tunnel. When I slipped out of the box, I found myself at the hospital at the top of the slope. The bicycle girl holding a hypodermic needle and the air-rifle man grasping a scalpel were waiting for me. Rather than being surprised by this turn of events, it seemed that I had been expecting it from the very beginning.

After a while I awoke in a bed; the bicycle girl was peering at me and there was a heavy smell of disinfectant and vitamins. Apparently the white nurse's uniform had the function of stopping time. When time stopped, the causal relationship among things was naturally interrupted; and no matter what indecent act I might commit, I had absolutely no fear of being blamed. Unfortunately, as a matter of fact, I was not relaxed enough to try anything indecent, but with the box off, I experienced such a sense of release that it made me forget that I was showing my naked face. With each random detail I told her about myself she smiled encouragingly, a smile hewn of solidified air, so transitory and yet so defenseless, as if colored with a brush of light, that I had the illusion of having been made a confession of love to. Her face was so wreathed in smiles that it even made me forget the fact that her legs were quite hidden by the overly low hemline of her uniform. I beat my wings like a little bird starting to fly for the first time (clumsily, incompetently, yet in a daze). Then my wings took the air—now I'm going to fly!—and intoxicated with her airy smile, I felt that I no longer need return to the box. Before I realized it I was making a promise I myself did not understand, a promise to buy the box for her for fifty thousand yen directly from the box man. I had had an acquaintance with box men (quite naturally); I even stressed that I would sell it to her for nothing. I thought I had best inquire on the spot just what she planned to do with it. But I was powerless before her smile. It seemed foolish even to discuss the uses of a box.

As soon as I had left the hospital, her smile vanished. When I returned to the place where I had concealed my box under the bridge, I began to have stomach spasms and vomited for some time. It seemed that I had been drugged without knowing it. Though at last I realized that I had apparently been taken in, I could not hate her.

> (Here a score or more lines of marginal addenda. The writing and, of course, the color of the ink are all but indistinguishable from those of the main text.)

—I'm talking about the beggar who wore a box over his head, she said.

—I know, because I'm a photographer. A photographer's a Peeping Tom. His specialty is boring holes . . . anywhere. By nature a churl . . .

—A worn-out cardboard box . . .

—I thought perhaps it was a friend of mine. I guess I was wrong. But I can't claim to be completely mistaken. A fellow photographer happened to take a picture of the box man without realizing it himself. Then he got interested and ran around chasing him all over, but he didn't run into him again. Instead, he got interested in photographing the town. The seamy side of town that has an aversion to being seen . . . and since he took pictures of what had an aversion to being seen, he was obliged to do it on the sly so that he wouldn't be noticed. It suddenly occurred to him to put on a box and go around taking pictures in the guise of a box man. Since he himself had not seen the box man when he had been looking straight at him, nobody would take any notice of *him* with a box on his head. In effect no one did seem to notice him, and he was able to take as many pictures as he wanted. He became a fake box man and threw himself into taking snapshots of the streets. But just as he was acquiring some reputation among his fellow photographers he suddenly vanished. Since then he has not returned to his apartment. Rumor has it that he has become a real box man.

—I wouldn't mind how much I was seen.

—But this kind of seeing is like shaving something off with a knife, like tearing off the clothes you're wearing.

—A long time ago I used to do modeling.

—Seriously, I'd like to do whatever I can. But I can't do anything. It's exasperating, but about the only thing I can manage is to squint through the range finder and snap the shutter. And then float your transparent image in the developer. The yellowish-green bulb that resembles fluorite . . . the second hand of the clock in the darkroom that indicates the position of eight . . . the surface of the water-repellent photographic paper that gleams like an oily membrane . . . the faint outline that gradually appears . . . an outline from which another appears . . . an outline superimposed on an outline . . . at length the contours of your naked body, like the footprints of some criminal imprinted in my heart . . .

—I want that box.

DEAD BY THE ROADSIDE
Ignored by 100,000 People

About seven o'clock in the evening of the twenty-third, members of the Shinjuku patrol discovered a forty-year-old vagrant dead, leaning against a pillar in the underground passage of the West Exit to Shinjuku Station, Tokyo, where people returning from work and shoppers were coming and going. According to the information provided by the same officials, the man was five feet two and of medium weight. He was wearing a long-sleeved shirt with a floral pattern and work boots; his hair was in the mussy style of a vagrant. Besides a hundred and twenty-five yen in change, he had only several sheets of newspaper, which he perhaps intended to use to sleep on. He possessed nothing else with which to establish his identity, place of residence, or name. Several hundreds of thousands of passengers a day frequent the underground passage in question (Shinjuku Station Report), and nearby there were many people and a line of public telephones. According to eyewitnesses, the man had remained sitting in the same position since noon that day, but no one had taken any notice of him, nor had he been reported for the six or seven hours before the police found him. Further, the man was scarcely ten yards from the police box, but the officer on duty said he was not visible on the other side of the pillar.

Then I Dozed Off
a Number of Times

I wonder if you've heard about shellweed. It may be this grass with thorny leaves like twists of firecrackers that covers the whole rocky slope where I am now sitting.

When you smell the fragrance of shellweed they say you dream of being a fish.

The story should be taken with a grain of salt, I feel, but it's not implausible. As shellweed prefers swampy land containing considerable salt, naturally it grows readily at the seashore, and it is not particularly surprising that there should be a tradition of its odor producing dreams of fish. Furthermore, according to one explanation, the alkaloids in its pollen bring about a floating sensation that resembles dizziness; and since at the same time it irritates the respiratory membranes, it is also possible, apparently, to have the hallucination of drowning in water.

But if that were all, it would not be particularly surprising. What's worrisome about a shellweed dream is not so much the dream itself as the problem of awakening from it. With a real fish there's no way of knowing, but they say that the passage of time that the dream fish experiences is quite different from when it is awake. The speed is remarkably slower, and one has the feeling that a few terrestrial seconds are drawn out to several days or several weeks.

Nevertheless, thanks to the strangeness of the dream scenery, one at first takes the utmost delight in the lightness of one's body, subtracted as it is from gravity, sporting among the undulating seaweed in the shadows of rocks, passing through strips of light limned by the lens of the waves, chasing after schools of trusting fish. As one is light oneself, one feels as if the world itself has become buoyant. One is completely liberated from bodily afflictions caused by gravity—drooping belly, stiffness of shoulders and neck, pain in the knee joints, falling arches—and one frolics around as if one were at least ten years younger. The lightness intoxicates the dream fish like alcohol.

But unless the fish is real, every case of intoxication sobers up and ultimately palls. In the sluggish flow of time, boredom soon becomes unbearable. It should not be too hard to imagine the feeling of irritation the completely bored dream fish experiences, the lack of resistance as if its five senses were numbed. Soon the free lightness of substance gradually begins to pall. One's whole body is wrapped round and round, as if forced into a restrictive garment in the shape of a fish. The soles of the feet send out feelers, seeking the sense of resistance they are used to when walking on land. The joints begin to recall fondly the heaviness of the various tissues and musculature that govern them. There is an unreasonable desire to walk. And suddenly one is amazed to realize that one lacks the legs necessary to do so.

But legs aren't the only thing lacking. No ears, no neck, no shoulders, and more than anything else, no arms. An inexpressible sense of deficiency. Quite definitely because the arms have been torn off. No curiosity can ultimately be satisfied unless one can check by touching with one's hands. If one wants really to know another person, if one does not know him with one's fingers, push him, punch him, bend him, tear at him, one can scarcely claim to know him completely. One wants to touch, to pass one's hands all over him. The bag of scales is insufferable for the fish. It strains to tear it off, but all it can do is to open its gills wide, raise its dorsal

If you intend to proceed beyond here, you
either have to go over the fence or around it to
the right or left. Since this area is the middle,
whichever way you go around it takes the
same amount of time. When walking, it
usually takes a day and a half, but if you rest
on the way it takes more.

fin rigid, and trail a cord several inches long of pepper-colored excrement.

Writhing in a pain that floods to the very tips of its toes, the sham fish suddenly arrives at the fatal suspicion that he is perhaps fake. The instant doubt begins, everything becomes very strange. When one has the body of a fish, without any vocal cords to begin with, to say nothing of hands or feet, one is plagued in one's use of such words. Double perception is as irritating as an itch.

Perhaps all such happenings are dream sequences.

Nevertheless, the dream is too long. It has been going on for so long that one can no longer remember when it started. However protracted, one will supposedly awaken from it sometime.

To ascertain that one is dreaming, the first thing—and it's reliable, for I have tried it several times myself—is to give the back of the hand a good pinch. But unfortunately a fish doesn't have nails to pinch with, nor a hand to pinch the back of. If that doesn't work, you can jump heroically from a steep cliff. That too I remember having succeeded at any number of times. Certainly if a fish is capable of that, there's no particular inconvenience in not having arms or legs. But what kind of a fall would a sea fish have?

I have never, of course, heard of a fish falling. Even a dead fish floats to the surface. It's much more complicated than a balloon falling in air. As far as the descent is concerned, it's a reverse fall. A reverse fall . . .

Indeed, does such a way of waking from a dream exist? I suppose a fish may well drown in air by falling in reverse, upward, toward the sky. The danger of death is the same. It's the same as a fall on land, and one of necessity awakens from the dream.

Yet once having pushed his thinking this far, the fake fish, with a timidity unexpected in a cold-blooded animal, still hesitates. They say that when one is able to realize that one is dreaming one is already near the end of the dream. The fish has done all he can do to wake up, and although it is waiting a while longer to see just what will happen, it will not influence the outcome.

The fake fish decided to wait. His very determination touched with the pallidness of the sea seemed to have paled.

Days, weeks passed, and the time had come for the fake fish to reach his decision. A storm had broken. A great tropical storm bore down, causing the bottom of the sea to tremble. Great waves rose, making the timid and indecisive fake fish demonstrate what little courage he had. But he was in no hurry to die. He simply gave himself over to the movement of the waves.

Suddenly a wave crest like the blades of fifty electric saws marshaled horizontally bore down on him. Sweeping the fake fish before it, it broke momentously against the cliffs and tossed the fish high into the air. And the fake fish drowned in the atmosphere.

Now I wonder if he awoke from his dream. No, one does not have a shellweed dream so casually. It is altogether different from an ordinary one. As the fake fish died before awakening, he could not expect to awaken from his dream again. He still had to go on dreaming until after he died. Ultimately the dead fake fish apparently would exist forever as a fake fish, as if it had received the latest freezing treatment. They say that among those fish tossed up onto the seashore after the storm there were not a few unlucky ones who had fallen asleep suffocated by the flowers of the shellweed.

But for some reason I have not yet become a fish. I have apparently dropped off any number of times, but I am still the box man I was. On reflection, a fake fish and a box man don't seem conspicuously different. The fake me becomes something not at all myself when I put on the box. Perhaps I who have been immunized against being something fake no longer possess the capability of having the dream of a fish. No matter how many times box men keep awakening from their dreams, they apparently end up being only the box men they always were.

The Promise Is Fulfilled, and a Letter with Fifty Thousand Yen Covering the Cost of the Box Was Dropped from the Top of the Bridge. This Was Barely Five Minutes Ago. I Attach the Letter Herewith.

I trust you. No receipt is required. As for the disposal of the box, I leave that up to you too. Before the tide goes out, tear it up and throw it into the sea.

. . .

Something strange has happened. I have read and reread her letter. Can there be some other way of interpreting it? At this point, I can only give a literal explanation. I try smelling the stationery with green lines that has been folded in three. It simply has the faint odor of disinfectant.

I assumed arbitrarily that the doctor would come. My various strategies all presupposed an attack by him. However, she herself was the one who came. Yes, she herself came. She came herself. She herself . . . the reason is quite unclear . . . oh, it's clear enough . . . she was simply carrying out her promise. I wonder why I am upset? Didn't I quite expect betrayal on her part? Perhaps so. A betraying woman like her quite suits me. I'll indeed be at a loss if the promise is kept. But just a minute, perhaps I have committed some important oversight. For example, I might well try rethinking her position . . . and her role in the affair.

> *I don't think there is any point in continuing writing. Since I have neither killed nor been killed, there's nothing further to explain.*
>
> *A letter adrift in space . . . address unknown . . . shall I tear it up and throw it away?*

Calm down now. Look here, fifty thousand yen. But since I have the money, simply disposing of the notes isn't enough. She wants me to dispose of the *box*. With the fifty thousand yen, its ownership has already passed to her. If I intend to respect her will, I suppose I shall have to dispose of it as I promised. Even so, I don't understand. Who in heaven's name would stand to gain by my doing such a thing? Fifty thousand yen just to throw the box into the sea—it's too much money. Am I so offensive? I must not flatter myself; by rights the motive must be something more practical. Some more matter-of-fact reason so that she should not feel she has lost something even in paying fifty thousand yen.

I don't understand it at all. It is just as well that I'm in a fog. I wonder, should I insist on returning the fifty thousand? She is sorely mistaken if she thinks I'm not capable of doing it.

But such an interpretation doesn't hold. It's a plan she divised so the doctor wouldn't get the box. For some reason he wanted it very much. Perhaps at first she too fell in with his plan. Or else was pretending to. But as the time to carry it out at last drew nearer, her doubts began to grow. Whatever she thinks, she can't believe anything good will come of it. But no matter how she remonstrated with him, the doctor turned a completely deaf ear, and in the end she could do nothing but oppose him. Fortunately the box man seems to have an uncommon affection for her. If she leaves the disposal of the box up to the box man himself and he disappears, whatever the doctor may think up, she will be able to contain him before he does anything.

Indeed . . . somehow I feel it makes sense . . . the box may perhaps be worth fifty thousand yen, depending on the doctor's reason for acquiring it. The circumstances are totally different, depending on whether her motive for interfering stems from her own selfishness or from a desire to protect the doctor. But I recognize that at least there is a conflict between them. And if that's true, then it's not a bad sign.

However, I do not fancy disposing of the box as she wishes. I still know too little about her to trust her. At least I had better put off disposing of the box until I check her real motives once more. I have the right to do that much. And then, frankly speaking, I am dissatisfied. It's fine that she herself put in an appearance, but it was altogether too businesslike. She didn't even come down the embankment. When she had sped past the "No Playing in the Water" sign, mounted on a bicycle made of some light alloy and equipped with five-speed gears—illuminated by the lights of a freighter, her raincoat gleamed as if gilded . . . through the fabric the outline of her body was clearly visible . . . and then the movement of those calves and knees which so disarmed me—she had gone out on the provincial highway, ignoring the frantic signals I flashed with my flashlight. After a while a trembling circle of light came slipping over the surface of the ground about two yards ahead of me. It was the beam of her flashlight shining between the balustrades of the bridge. I couldn't very well look up, it is too awkward for a box man. Then there was a sound, and not far from the trembling circle of light something fell. It was a vinyl bag weighted with a stone. In it were the letter in question and five ten-thousand-yen bills rolled up. She went off without doing anything else. While she had come as close to me as could be, she had gone off without saying a word. The movement of her calves disappeared into the darkness, the glitter of the wet raincoat vanished, and last of all the red taillight of the bicycle faded away. When I had read the letter and counted the bills, I suddenly began to hear the sound of drizzle, which should not have been audible. Perhaps it was the blood coursing in my head.

Fifty thousand yen. I should like to tell her alone that for the person paying out perhaps it is an extravagance, but for a box man it is a paltry sum not worth accepting. Generally people know too little about box men. They take too casually the meaning the box has for a box man. I'm not bluffing. With pure bluff alone, one can't go on living in a box for three years. They say that even in the case of the hermit crab, once it begins its life under its shell, the back part of the body, being covered by the carapace, becomes soft and thus breaks into pieces and the crab dies if forced out. A box man can't very well take off his box and simply return to the

ordinary world. When he takes it off it is to emerge into another world just as an insect metamorphoses. I secretly expected
that my meeting with her would provide that opportunity.

From the human chrysalis that is the box man,
Even I know not
What kind of living being will issue forth.

In a Mirror

The rain had turned to a light drizzle, but the wind had
risen. With every sigh of the breeze splashing drops flew
like the waving tentacles of a jellyfish. It was quite impossible
to see through. However, perhaps because of the placement
of the buildings, only the red gate light of the hospital at
the top of the slope that was my destination was always
and from everywhere visible. It was enveloped in dark green
and seemed like a stain in my eyes. I had taken the road any
number of times, but this was the first time I had walked
it wearing a box. Considering that, it seemed terribly far.
Usually when I was in the box, distance was seldom a serious
obstacle.

When anyone comes into contact with the scenery
around him, he tends to see selectively only those elements
necessary. For example, though one remembers a bus stop,
one can have absolutely no recollection of a large willow
tree nearby. One's attention is caught willy-nilly by the
hundred-yen piece dropped on the road, but the bent and
rusty nail and the weeds by the wayside may just as well not
be there. On the average road one usually manages not to
go astray. However, as soon as one looks out of the box's

observation window, things appear to be quite different. The various details of the scenery become homogeneous, have equal significance. Cigarette butts . . . the sticky secretion in a dog's eyes . . . the windows of a two-story house with the curtains waving . . . the creases in a flattened drum . . . rings biting into flabby fingers . . . railroad tracks leading into the distance . . . sacks of cement hardened because of moisture . . . dirt under the fingernails . . . loose manhole covers . . . but I am very fond of such scenery. The distance in it is fluid and the contours vague, and thus perhaps it resembles my own position. The scenery has the gentleness of a garbage dump. One never wearies of looking at such a view as long as one is peering out from a box.

But the effect of the box was reduced to nothing as I took the rising road to the hospital. The red light remained far off in the distance. A stain the color of blood deep within my closed eyes. The road was of gravel, and the space at my feet was not so dark as elsewhere. This scenery seemed to urge people to keep going, its details were all abridged. After that, a dimly white sky (clouds were beginning to cross from the west). Perhaps it was because the night was too dark (hence I abhor the night). It might also be, perhaps, that my destination was too well defined.

Despite all of that I shook my box and continued doggedly walking. But the box could not make time along the road. Since the ventilation was bad, I broke out in a sweat. Even the insides of my ears itched with the dampness. As I leaned forward, the box tilted, and there was the sound of it striking my hips. The very fragile sound of something made of paper.

Suddenly I heard the violent breathing of some beast. A huge growling mongrel brushed against my knees with its shoulder, and ran off at once. His wet back appeared to be dyed red. When I raised my head, I saw the red gate light.

The mist peeled away and a closed iron portal came into view. There was a special bell for night use painted with a phosphorescent color. I didn't want to ring the bell and have them open the door. Nor did I want to come face to face with the doctor. Stepping over the hedge, I entered the garden.

The dog had arrived before me and was waiting, but he made no pretense of barking. I had won him over by giving it some food beforehand. A light was burning faintly in one window. A luxuriant tangle of weeds twined around my feet. Apparently the remains of an old flower bed. I stumbled over the edging stones, and the dog, misunderstanding, frolicked around me. When I stood still and took a breath, sweat poured out and ran into my eyes.

Her room was in the back of the building, second window from the left. She had dropped the money to me less than an hour ago—possibly she was still awake. Even if she had dozed off, it would only be a light sleep. I need have no concern that she would set up a din on waking up surprised. I wanted to have a serious talk with her (even through the window, if that were possible) return the fifty thousand yen, and get her to cancel the promise I had made to throw the box away. Depending on her attitude, it was conceivable that I could assist her in another way.

But I wondered why there was a light in the window facing the garden. Over there was the waiting room, next, the examination room, and further inside that I assumed were the examination instruments. Twelve o'clock had come and gone, and I thought that one way or another they had forgotten to turn the light out, but for some reason I was uneasy. To be on the safe side, I decided to have a little look.

The window was rather high and the lower half was frosted glass. I could see only the ceiling. The light that came from below what seemed to be a floor lamp spread out diagonally in a parabola toward the inner part of the room. In order to see more, I needed something to stand on. It was out of the question to turn on a light and look around. Fortunately I remembered I had put the rear-view mirror from my car in my tote bag. I had had the feeling that it would come in handy and had stashed it away instead of tossing it out. After wiping off the dirt, I held it up diagonally and peered into it from below. Stretching my one arm and looking up through the space in the narrow window was laborious work. But my labors bore fruit. Contrary to my expectations (I had assumed that top and bottom would be reversed), I was able to view everything at an almost perfect angle.

The first thing I could see was an electric table lamp sitting on a corner of a big work desk. Then a large, whitish expanse. As I held the mirror stable, the white separated into walls and a door. Walls and door were old, and the several layers of paint could not conceal the scratches on the surface. The typically high hospital bed in the corner by the window was, of course, white too. The bookcase, crammed with old magazines and books, was painted white like the rest, but was somewhat less fresh. The room was simply spacious and without interest on the whole, though there was a stereo set beside the work desk; it was apparently the doctor's sitting room–study.

Indeed, the room itself was of little importance. When I put my recollections in order later, such was the arrangement. There were two people in it. I was completely fascinated by them. Other things were merely the reflections of mosaic fragments, compounded, as in the eye of some insect.

One was the girl, and since it was in the same building as her room, it was natural for her to be there. She was stark naked. She was standing facing me stark naked in the middle of the room, and she was talking to someone about something.

The person who was being addressed was a box man. He was seated on the edge of the bed and was wearing a box exactly like mine. From where I was, only the back and the right side were visible; it was a cardboard box, exactly the same as my own—from the degree of dirtiness to the remains of the printed letters giving the name of a commercial product . . . to say nothing of the size. It was a fake replica of myself, imitated by design. And inside . . . the doctor, I presumed.

(Suddenly it occurred to me. Somewhere I remembered having seen exactly the same scene as this.)

Alone in the room with the naked girl . . . it was as if I could vividly feel her nakedness with my hands. But when . . . where? No, I must not be deceived, this was not a memory but a hallucination stemming from my desire. I could not believe that I had come visiting like this, that my objective was simply the repayment of the fifty thousand yen. Somewhere in my heart I must have secretly wished for this scene really to materialize. Yes, seeing her naked . . . stripping her naked body even more bare until I could see a nakedness beyond mere nudity.

(Marginal note—red ink: Why do I persist in staring like this? Perhaps because I am too cowardly. Or perhaps because I am too curious. When I think about it, I fancy I have become a box man just to go on being a voyeur forever. I want to spy on all sorts of places, and the box is a portable hole that occurred to me under the circumstances, it being impossible to punch holes throughout the world. I also feel like running away and also like pursuing. Which is it to be?)

My desire to spy on the girl was clearly beginning to exceed the capacities of the box. I have the feeling that my mouth is packed full with distended and aching gums. But I alone am not to be blamed. She too had dropped an indirect hint. Aside from the fifty thousand yen paid by the doctor for the box, she suggested a special bonus from her to me as a photographer.

When my shoulder had been treated I tried patching together the story of her life, which she told me in bits and pieces: Until accepting her present position as apprentice nurse, she had been a poor art student (let's not ask whether she had any talent in these circumstances) and made a living by posing for those who belonged to privately run art schools or amateur art clubs. (She said it had left a bitter taste, resembling regret.) Two years ago she had had an abortion in this hospital (she was beginning to exist for me physically). Her convalescence was not satisfactory, and while she was in the hospital free of charge for about three months, a nurse who had been working there left, and the girl had taken her place for no particular reason (an aspect of her personality irked people and was hard to understand). She was busy with her work, but then she was assured of all her treatment in payment for it. As long as there was no special emergency, she had enough time to paint her pictures in the evenings and in her time off. But income aside, the modeling she had done before was apparently the work she liked best. It was not because she could take it easy, she insisted innocently. And while it wasn't especially pressured work, it had been tiring, and one needed stamina. She had said that the excitement of exposing her naked body as a model was the spice of life and inspired in her the will to create. (I considered that wrong. Incidentally, pictures of her are completely nonrepresentational and have no connection with any model.) She spoke as if she would still be doing modeling if the doctor had not strongly objected.

However much she was interested in my profession as a photographer, this was an obvious provocation. From the air-gun bullet that had come from the wound in my shoulder and from the way my hair was raggedly cut, she must have already guessed that I was a box man without his disguise. But I had overlooked her pretense. I had the feeling of licking her wound with the generosity of a protector. At such times a discharge came from my eyes. I braced myself, determined to break her with my own hands before she was broken by someone else. Teeth sprouted on my upper and lower eyelids. At the wild idea of nibbling at her, my eyeballs flushed hot and I got erections.

In a sense, this wild idea materialized. The naked girl . . . I who spied on her . . . I was indeed watching the naked her. But it was a conditional nakedness. It was a nakedness already looked upon by someone else, and that was the fake me. Far from being satisfied by seeing her naked, my jealousy increased because someone else had seen her. When one's throat becomes dry, it serves no purpose to be shown a picture of oneself drinking. At the same time as I was looking at her, another I was looking at me looking at her. I recalled a dream in which I had writhed desperately as I floated near the ceiling and looked down on my own dead body. I was ashamed and laughed scornfully at myself. The strength left my arm, the mirror tilted wildly, and the room flew off. I shifted it to my other hand and this time rested the edge of the mirror on the windowsill to keep it steady. When you're thirsty you can't help running in the direction of illusory water, even though you realize it's a mirage.

The two were facing each other separated by about four paces. Her attitude was relaxed, and to my regret I could not detect the slightest antagonism between them. I wondered if she had already reported on what had happened an hour ago. Supposing that the two were in league with each other, they would really be laughing at me. A foolishly honest box man who had only been waiting to be tossed fifty thousand yen like a reward to some dog, spending as he had promised a half day watching the whirlpools under the bridge . . . box head . . . toilet box . . . sheltered man in a box . . . box juggler.

But on the part of the naked girl I could feel not the slightest malice or machination. Though I experienced a sense of humiliation as before, no feelings of hatred welled up in me. I intently followed on her heels. My water jar that had been stolen by the fake box man. Her naked body was far more charming than I had imagined it to be. It was natural; there was no question of my imagination being able to catch up with her actual nakedness. Since this nakedness existed only while I was looking at it, my desire to see it became poignant too. Since it would vanish the minute I stopped looking, I should photograph it, or get it down on canvas. The naked body and the body are different. The naked body uses the actual physical body as its material and is a work of art kneaded by fingers which are the eyes. Although the physical body might be hers, concerning the proprietorship of the naked body, I had no intention of retreating in impotent envy.

Her naked body was supported by the left leg, as if it were floating lightly in water. It was as if a mysterious cord stretched straight from the tips of a magician's fingers. The toes of her right foot were placed over the instep of the left, and the bent knee opened slightly outward. What, I wondered, attracted me so much about that leg? Was it that it suggested the sexual organs? Judging from the cut of clothes today, perhaps one could consider the reproductive organs belonging to the legs rather than to the trunk. But if that were all, many other legs are more sexy. When one lives in

The last freight of that day had started out
from the sectional branch line to the main
line, listing far toward the outside and making
the switches creak. Absently watching the red
taillight, the trainman saw a cardboard box
fall to the tracks and tilted his head in perplexity.
The box began to walk.

a box, one looks principally at the lower half of people, and it's the legs one is familiar with. The femininity of legs, whatever you say, lies, I think, in the simple fluidity of the curving surfaces. The bones, tendons, and joints are completely fused in the flesh and have no effect on the surface. Certainly legs are much more suitable as covers for the sexual organs than as instruments for walking (I am not being sarcastic, there's no need for that; it is natural that a cover be needed for such a precious vessel). Eventually you've got to open the cover with your hands. Thus the charm of feminine legs (and he who denies that charm is a hypocrite) can only be tactile rather than visual.

However, I don't mean that her very visual legs are masculine. A man's legs, thanks to having continuously carried weight against the pull of gravity, are knotty, and the deeply imbedded joints spread horizontally; they are practical mechanisms for walking. But no matter how one searches, one can find absolutely no visible traces in her legs of the effort she expends to support her weight. To make a venturesome comparison, her legs are the pliant, fully extended legs of an adolescent before he has undergone a change of voice. Things that suddenly incite longing in a man exhausted from walking: for example, the lightness of a bird . . . the sensation of walking free from gravity. Willful legs that do not continually go against gravity like those of a man nor give up walking like those of a woman. A hasty retreat—the same as sex—is liable to provoke pursuit. Sexual attraction is not particularly lacking in her legs (even coverless sex is provocative enough). But even if I find my way to her sex, I feel that somehow there's something more to it. I wonder if I have discovered the ideal legs in hers or whether I am trying to fit her legs to the ideal.

White globular forms tilted diagonally. Compared with the legs, the buttocks as you might expect are tactile.

Perhaps it is because the center of gravity lies in the single deep crevasse. The raised right hipbone juts out, describing a smooth curve like that of a bird's breastbone. A faint smoke wells up from the crotch. Its tip, like a shadow, is subtly teased by the wind. But when I looked at the soft light hair on her head, and saw that it wasn't moving in the slightest, I realized that the wind was blowing only below. I assumed the fan was poorly regulated; and the cool air flowed along the floor. The hips had a tendency to draw back, and the stomach filling out generously gave the feeling of being terribly defenseless. The shoulders were bent far back, and the neck rising perpendicularly from there supported a head bent forward as if a hinge had come loose. It was an altogether relaxed pose, but I had the impression that a slender steel core passed down the middle of her. The right arm was positioned in the vicinity of the navel, the left near the solar plexus, and her position was such that she seemed to be embracing herself. Since her chest was stretched back, her breasts seemed smaller than they actually were. Under them were red marks left by the brassière. There was a line above the hipbone too, that was apparently left by her underwear. It would seem that not much time had gone by since she had taken them off and thrown them aside. The clothes she had removed lay in lumps at her feet. On the nurse's white uniform the tiny black undies stretched out like a dead spider.

She lightly bit her underlip. But spreading wide to both sides, it escaped from her teeth. Seeing her full-mouthed smile, I felt my heart cut by the blade of a faint sadness. Her raised eyes, filled with coquetry, looked up at the fake box. He apparently said something (obviously it was a random remark), and the girl raised her face and said two or three words in reply. The muscles of her back stretched like a steel measuring tape. She rose on tiptoes and began walking in the direction of the box. "You're going wrong!" I shouted involuntarily in my heart. My diaphragm stiffened, like wet leather, my breath shortened, and my face with lines of sweat spilling down from my hairline resembled the stripes on an overripe melon. She took something from the box. It was a glass with some beer still in it. I did not at all like her drinking from the same glass as the fake box man. All my muscles were ready to break through the windowpane and jump into the room, but because of her betrayal I knew I wouldn't do it (an example of a box man-like excuse). Some way or another she had drunk down about half of the beer with an awkward movement of the mouth as if she were sucking up spaghetti. She returned the glass to the box, and, swinging her body, she took several great steps backward. I was relieved when I realized that the fake box man had not left his box. The tension that reached from my shoulders to my hips relaxed, and I made a noise like the tearing away of something pasted. She returned to her former position and was saying something rapidly. Suddenly she shut her mouth, looked up at the ceiling, and began to pass her two hands over her hips. Again the box man took over the initiative of the conversation, which she apparently didn't find very interesting.

Abruptly pivoting on her heels, she turned her back. Then all at once she dropped to all fours on the floor, placing her elbows and knees together and assuming a posture in which her hips jutted up higher than the rest of her. The direct light that did not pass through the shade of the lamp made her seem exaggeratedly tactile and globular. Her breasts were a lid on the inside of the inverted triangle formed by her trunk, thighs, and upper arms. My whole body began to wither away, leaving only my eyes. The fake box man, bending forward, swayed slowly back and forth.

Suddenly the ground at my feet surged up as if it had been kneaded, and, losing my balance, I sank to one knee.

I still had enough wits not to make any noise. But it wasn't the surface of the ground that was heaving; the dog, bored, had squeezed himself in between my knees. It was difficult to chase it away quietly. I couldn't make any noise, and I couldn't let him bark. But he continued to grow more and more excited, and with all his strength, he thrust his nose like a piece of wet soap between my legs. It evidently intended to get into the box with me. Having little choice, I punctured a small hole in a can of beef and after letting him sniff the gravy and lick it, I flung the can as far away as I could. I knew the poor thing would be wrestling with the can until tomorrow morning.

I hurried back to the window. The surface of the mirror was smudged with my fingers. I hastily wiped it with my shirttail and set it up again. The scene had changed completely. Fortunately what I had been so apprehensive about had not taken place at all. The fake box, neither torn up nor broken to bits, was still sitting in the same position on the edge of the bed. Of course, even wearing the box, he might have been able to take advantage of her. If he had bored a hole for his penis and was prepared for some unnatural positions, it would have been possible. But to do that he would need her cooperation, and that would take a good deal of time. Had it taken me that long to chase the dog away? I wondered. Perhaps it had, but anyway she was no longer naked. She was smoking a cigarette, leaning against the work desk in the corner of the room. Even the buttons of the too-long white uniform were carefully buttoned, and her legs could no longer be seen. With her legs invisible, she seemed strangely distant, another person. About a third of the cigarette was consumed. Tired, forbidding eyebrows. An enema syringe peeked out from the pocket of her white uniform. Her slender sinewy fingers were encircled by the rubber tube of the syringe, and her fingernails bore a silver polish. It was unbelievable that she had been naked a few minutes before. Or was it that everything had been merely a mirage in the mirror?

From somewhere beyond the shrubbery came the sad breathing of the dog pounding against the ground with the can gripped in his teeth. When I rubbed my neck, lumps of dirt kept coming off. And as I gathered them into patties, I was terribly depressed. I seemed to be somehow profoundly hurt by what in fact had not happened—the scene in which she was violated by the box—something I didn't want to happen, something that absolutely couldn't have happened. Perhaps it was because I have all too often been outwitted.

Rubbing out her cigarette, she nodded her head, scratching inside her ear with the little finger of her free hand. When the light from the lamp struck her straight on, the space between her two eyes opened up, and she appeared slightly walleyed. She laughed only with her mouth, showing her teeth suspiciously, whereupon her face turned into that of an obstinate child. When she closed her mouth, shaking her head slightly to the right and left, the lower projecting lip was unexpectedly voluptuous. Then slightly shifting the upper part of her body, she adopted the stance of kicking an invisible paper balloon. She crossed the room toward the door. When she began to walk, I saw that it was indeed her. There was a giddy lightness to her body. And I wondered if this most familiar sense of weightlessness was a sense of falling. The fake box man crawled down from the bed. Without even looking back, she pulled the door knob, and swinging around the door, disappeared on the other side. The box man who tried to chase her resembled an insect whose limbs had been torn off. Except for the fact that he was not wearing rubber boots, he was my mirror image, even to the canvas around his waist. The door closed, and the box man came to a halt. Evidently he did not want to pursue her too far. Shaking the box, he changed directions and came shuffling back as if his underclothes were wet. I could see the front of the box. The hanging vinyl was exactly the same color and arrangement as my own (other than that there was not a single little hole in the box—not even a penis hole).

Nevertheless, it was an elaborate reproduction. It was overly elaborate for ordinary purposes. What was he hatching up? Judging from the present state of affairs, no matter how determined I was to return the fifty thousand yen, it looked as if it wasn't going to be very easy to get him to agree to it. From the instant I took the money, the right of being a real box man had shifted to the other party, and perhaps it was I who had become the fake. My shadow came and went with the tottering steps of a toy robot following the diagonal across the room. It was not very pleasant to see my image in the mirror, ignoring my will, moving around as it wished. Stupid man! Why didn't he take the box off right away? Perhaps he was drunk. If he continued like that, he wouldn't be able to get out of the box at all. Well, if he didn't want to leave it, that was just fine too. If he wanted, I could just as well get out of my box instead of him. I felt that leaving the box was a possible course of action. Perhaps, if I dare engage in wishful thinking, her original objective in dreaming up this deal was to confine him to the box. Then she would be free. How would it be if I used this as an opportunity to sever all connection with my box?

I decided for the time being to leave. There was no merit in simply hastening the conclusion. If I just made up my mind, I could remove the box at any point. After taking my time and getting my feelings in order, it might be just as well to come again tomorrow. Before leaving, I decided to have a peep into her room. I crossed over the gravel path that led to the entrance (being covered with dirt, it made no noise). Turning the box sideways, I pushed my way into the thicket of asters as tall as a man. A cleavage like the inside of a convoluted shell flickered in my eyes—perhaps it was due to some association of ideas that came from the intense fragrance of the grass. Perhaps it was the hollow under her armpits. But the back of the building faced northward, and all the windows were small and high. Her windows especially were cut off by heavy curtains and I could barely distinguish any light, but I had not hoped for anything more. Not yet ready to give up, I kept waiting for something, concealed under the eaves. The wind shook the gutter, making great drops fall down, and my box resounded like a bass drum. But there was no reaction from her room.

Of course, it was nothing at all to get out of the box. And since there was nothing to it, I felt no compulsive need to leave it. Yet I wanted someone, if possible, to lend me a hand.

Three-and-a-Half-Page Insert on Different Paper

(It's not only the paper that's dissimilar. For the first time a fountain pen is being used, and the writing is clearly different. If in time someone makes a clear copy in a new notebook with other notes, they should simply standardize the paper and the writing. There's no need to worry about the difference in writing and in paper now.)

—Well then. Now what? (said the doctor).
—I'm thirsty. (she complained).

—There's a crack in that glass.

—I don't care.

—Well . . . ?

—I took them off . . . just as I promised.

—I'm asking about the light.

—Is this all the beer there is?

—I'm interested in how dark it was as you were taking your clothes off.

—It was pitch black. It was so dark it took me a long time to unfasten my brassière.

—There's no relationship between the light and the brassière. Anyway you can do that by touch.

—Well, I suppose so, but . . .

—Let it go. And then what?

—He lost patience and insisted on helping me unfasten the brassière . . . he wouldn't listen.

—Strange.

—Why?

—It was pitch black, wasn't it? How did he know you were having trouble with the brassière?

—Oh, he just knew . . . some way or other.

—Then you did get him to help?

—Not at all.

—Why?

—I made a promise, didn't I, absolutely not to let him touch me? Besides, see how long my arms are. I can shake hands behind my back.

—All right. So then you took off your clothes in the dark, and after you had finished, you turned on the light. Is that right?

—Yes, I think so. . . .

—Well, what about the shot?

—I gave it, of course.

—Naked?

—You can't break the capsule by feel.

—Being naked's enough. It's ridiculous to go so far as giving a shot naked.

—It comes to the same thing, doesn't it?

—There's a big difference.

—Don't raise your voice so.

—Listen to me. You're a lot more frankly naked when some of your clothes are off than when they're all off. The same logic holds true for shots. A naked body doing something is more completely naked than a simple nude. You can't get away with saying you didn't know it.

—I realize that. I'll be careful from now on.

—Try repeating what happened in order once more from the beginning.

—So I took off my clothes, turned on the light . . .

—Before that, the light was out, wasn't it?

—So I turned out the light, took off my clothes, turned on the light, and then gave the shot.

—Pretty amazing. During all that time you didn't say a word . . . isn't it?

—I don't mean that . . .

—We're going to be in trouble if you abridge whenever you want.

—He didn't say anything important. It's true. I recall we talked about the weather . . . as he patted my hair like this . . .

—You promised not to let him use his hands.

—But it was only my hair.

—It's the same thing . . . anywhere . . .

—But he just happened to touch my hair just by chance, and . . .

—Don't shield him.

—It was just when I was leaning over to turn on the lamp by the pillow.

—The lamp?

—He asked me to.

—What?

—There are places you can't see very well with the light coming only from above.

—Drop it there. There'll be no end to it if you spoil him so much.

—You're right. I'll be careful.

—Then what did he say?

—He said it looked like rain . . . since my hair was winding into little curls.

—You were just wet with perspiration.

—Yes, I was dripping.

—But just a minute. Before his weather report, you were asked to put the light on, weren't you?

—Yes, the light came first.

—You're not reliable.

—I'm sorry. I'm already exhausted. I'm not suited to this sort of thing. Look, my legs are trembling as if I'd got on top of an electric washer.

—Well, come over here. My lap's better than any washer.

—I'd like a smoke.

—Smoking late at night makes your skin rough.

—It's better than being naked.

—You're exaggerating. Don't go thinking a fellow like that's a man. Being naked in front of him is no more than taking your panties off in the bathroom.

—You, Doctor, are the one who's concerned with my nakedness in front of him. You ask too many questions.

—I only want to know the truth.

—I'd at least like to forget what's over.

—Apparently there are things you want to forget at any cost.

—Unfortunately they're nothing you imagine, Doctor.

—If that's true, fine.

—It is. First he wiped away the eye mucus and made me take all kinds of poses; he watched me as if he were on a treasure hunt. But the shot began to take effect at once, and the look in his eyes gradually became strange. In less than five minutes he was staring at the fluorescent light and seemed quite oblivious of me.

—It's all right to let him dream the way he wants.

—But last of all he made me give him an enema.

—An enema?

—It was too much. The same question over and over. I wondered if he would never tire of asking. Imagine it . . . he asked me to check to see whether he had an erection or not. I was so annoyed I fooled him and told him it looked about eighty percent up. Immediately he got angry. He told me to stop talking nonsense, that he should know best about himself.

—If he knew, he didn't have to ask you, did he?

—Then he began badgering me. When he smelled my perspiration he apparently got an erection, so he told me to get more to the side.

—Don't joke. What part of the castrated pig was up, I wonder.

—Well, he wasn't up. He began to cry instead. I was amazed. Or maybe he was pretending to cry. When I looked closely I could see he was crying, but only by the set of his mouth and his voice. And then . . . what halitosis! As long as he was badgering me, I could stand it only by holding my breath. He was apparently rather excited. He said he couldn't stand looking up my crotch when I was on all fours.

—Did you go so far as to do that?

—Not at all. It was the fault of the shot. I just stood there stock still. And he just imagined what he wanted. But it's strange, isn't it. Maybe that's hypnotism. He wasn't actually seeing me, yet just by thinking that he wanted to, I somehow came to have the impression I was being seen. From the moment I thought I was being seen by him all my strength suddenly left me, and I was unable to give up imagining I was on all fours. The blood left my buttocks, and they grew pale and numb. I had the feeling of turning into a stone.

—What about the enema, then?

—Oh, that was later. Suddenly just when he stopped crying, he let out a scream like a patient with a heart attack, saying to hurry up, that he wanted nitroglycerine.

—A weird fellow.

—All the same, he didn't have an erection, but apparently there was some reaction. He ground his teeth and panted, and when I listened closely I could hear him saying, "Thanks . . . thanks."

—Why didn't you refuse the enema?

—You yourself said not to take it seriously, didn't you?

—Quite true, quite true.

—Please, let me rest. I wanted you to tell me that all this was unimportant.

—Well, let's take a pause here. Don't just stand there . . . come over here. Take off your stockings.

—I'm not wearing any stockings.

—Hurry up, come on. . . . What sort of pose did he explicitly want you to take?

—Turn off the light. . . .

In Which It Is a Question of the Sullen Relationship Between the I Who Am Writing and the I Who Am Being Written About

The naked girl on all fours. The inverted triangle formed by her torso, her thighs, and her upper arms was burned deep into the backs of my eyeballs; and wherever I looked a flesh-colored openwork forever overlaid my field of vision. The pores of my whole body opened their mouths at the same time, and tongues dangled limply from them. I was nauseous . . . abnormally tense . . . from lack of air. I had not had enough sleep either.

Nonetheless, when and how did I get to this point? Apparently I'm deceiving myself. Eighteen minutes past three. Now I'm here at the municipal seaside bathhouse facing the Port of T across the harbor. A deserted sandy beach where hermit crabs crawl noisily about. A soaked green triangular flag flapping round a bamboo pole. No matter how much of the way back here is downhill, I couldn't possibly have just come rolling down. I must have had some purpose, whatever it was.

As a matter of fact, it was right here that I had made my preparations a week before to go to the hospital to get treatment for my wound. It's an ideal place for a box man to leave his box unnoticed. I wanted to clean my underwear and my shirt, shave, and wash my hair, to say nothing of my body. I was free to use the hydrant at the station or the boat landing, but the crowds came here late, and if I choose my time well I can take it easy and use the shower in the dressing room without being questioned by anyone.

I really don't have to hide. Just a moment ago, I finished doing what I had come for. I had cleaned my underwear, shaved my beard, washed my hair and my body. To avoid catching a cold I withdrew temporarily to the box until my underwear and shirt were dry, but this was purely to tide me over, and I intended to leave it presently. Yes, I had the impression of being already half out. You don't need any particular resolution to scratch where you're bitten by an insect. The exit to the tunnel was visible right there. If the box is a moving tunnel, the naked girl is a dazzling light flowing in the entrance, waiting intently to be seen. I think that surely here is the opportunity I have been waiting for for three years.

Furthermore, I unexpectedly met the fake box man. My replica was fixedly staring at the girl on all fours with her rump high in the air (defenselessly waiting to be seen). So far I had not felt that the box was all that unsightly. What was disagreeable was the recurrent dream where I became a ghost, and hovering at the ceiling, looked down on my own dead body. Could I still have a lingering attachment for the box at this point? Far from that, I was already thoroughly bored with it. A tunnel is functional only because it has an exit. It makes absolutely no difference if I tear these notes up and throw them away as soon as I finish this last line here. . . .

It can't be very long since I began living in a box. I once saw a broken and empty cardboard box roughly stuffed

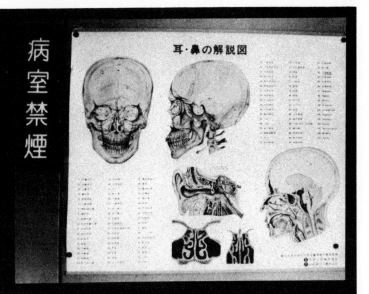

病室禁煙

耳・鼻の解説図

I am now looking around the inside of the box . . . a cube slightly more spacious than my own capacity . . . cardboard walls tanned by sweat and sighs . . . graffiti inscribed with a ballpoint pen all over in small letters . . . reverse tatooing . . . a not very prepossessing personal filigrain . . .

into the narrow space between a public john and a board fence (perhaps around some outdoor parking lot). The box with its resident gone was like a deserted house. The aging process had apparently been rapid, and the box had weathered to the color of withered grapes. But at a glance I was able to distinguish that it was the discarded skin of a box man. There, where it appeared half torn away, was what remained of the observation window . . . the curled vinyl curtain was still pasted on. On the sides the protuberant clusters of little holes for hearing were all swollen like some skin disease. I tried to strip away the surface. It sounded like adhesive plaster tearing off, and the inside of the box was visible. I instinctively inserted myself into the space and concealed this sloughed-off skin from the gaze of those passing by.

On the inside of the box, like a handprint impressed in clay, the traces of the life of the former occupant (let us give him the name B for the moment) were vividly and negatively etched. There were the traces of the cheap chopsticks he had used to strengthen the torn places by attaching them with insulation tape, and clippings of nude photos, now faded and bearing stains the color of bird droppings. There was a red cord to tie to the trouser belt so that the box would not shake; a little plastic box was located underneath the observation window. Further, traces of numerous graffiti covered the entire surface. Large and small white rectangular spaces outlined the spots where such things as the radio, the bag, and the flashlight had formerly been suspended.

My strength drained away and I felt cold. I had the feeling of witnessing the opening of the sarcophagus of B's mummy. I quivered. I had never contemplated my own (my box's) death in such a form. I intended to vanish naturally—when the time came—like a volatilized drop of water. But this was the real world, not imagination. How in heaven's name had B met his end?

Of course, it did not necessarily follow that the death of the box was exactly B's physical death. Perhaps he just passed through the tunnel and threw the box away. The corpse of the box became a butterfly (if a butterfly is too romantic, then a cicada will do, or a May fly), the cast-off skin of a chrysalis that has flown away. I wanted to think it was possible. If I didn't, I couldn't have been able to stand it. And to do so I needed proof. I concentrated my gaze on the graffiti all around, searching for evidence. Unfortunately B apparently regularly used a felt-tip marker, the ink of which was water soluble, and deciphering was nigh impossible. There was a cover on the little plastic box. If there was some clue it would surely be in there. When I wrenched off the incrusted top the hinge split open. Inside were two ball-point pens, a handleless knife, a flint for a lighter, a crystal-less watch with only the minute hand, and then a small notebook with the cover missing. The first page of the notebook began in this way. Fortunately I copied it on the spot on the inner side of my box (at the time there was still a lot of blank space left), and I am able to quote it exactly.

> "His concern was excessive. When he was absent from his room even a little longer than usual, he worried lest in the meantime the room might not have disappeared, and he could not go out in peace. Gradually his proclivity to stay at home grew worse. It got to the point where he would shut himself up in his room, unable to take a step outside. In the end he died either from hunger or by hanging. Of course, I hear that no one has as yet identified the corpse."

When I tried turning the next page the notebook fell apart between my fingers like a soaked biscuit. With it my evidence crumbled away too, and I was still unable to assess the significance of the crushed and empty box-corpse.

Now should I bid goodbye to the box? But my underwear and my shirt for some reason were taking a long time to dry. The rain had lifted, but because of the moisture-laden, low clouds they were long in drying. Fortunately I felt fine there naked in the box. Perhaps it was because I had carefully cleaned off the dirt, but the various parts of my body felt strangely fresh, and I even experienced an actual longing to embrace myself. But I did not intend to stay like this forever. I hoped the morning calm would end soon.

The dark, wet sky and the black sea fused at eye level. The water was much darker than the sky. A deep black like an elevator falling. A bottomless black that you could still see even if you shut your eyes. I could hear the sea. I could see the inside of my own cranium. A dome-shaped tent whose inner struts are exposed. Exactly like the inside of a dirigible. My complete lack of sleep sends my blood pounding. I wanted to sleep. I wanted to sleep at least two or three hours before leaving the box. I tried shutting my eyes even tighter than they were. Waves became visible. Waves in regularly receding, gradually narrowing parallel lines kept rolling ceaselessly toward the open sea. There were a front and back to the successive waves, and the front part glinted slightly. As I leaned forward, trying to see through them, my right and left eyeballs popped out and dropped straight down. And from where they had fallen a wisp of smoke came wafting up. As the eyeballs bounced against each other, they kept rolling between the waves. I felt nauseous. I opened my eyes. Sea and sky stood still, blackly, and everything was as it had been originally. I was miserably small on the hard, wet sand. Apparently I could only wait with my eyes open until I was overcome with sudden sleep.

But even if I can't catch a nap, I must, under any circumstances, begin the planned course of action when the time comes. After disposing of the box that I have taken off, I shall visit the hospital again at precisely eight o'clock. Since outpatients start coming at ten, I shall anticipate as much extra time as possible before that. However, if I am too early, I will incur their displeasure and that will cause problems. Eight o'clock is a good time, and I won't disturb them while they are still asleep. I estimate that I can get them to spare me a couple of hours for negotiations, though I can't go so far as to say that that will be sufficient. It's possible that I could get them to take the day off from examinations and to make them accept going on with the negotiations. At any rate the negotiations will take plenty of time . . . but what negotiations . . . ?

> (Let me put this down before I forget. A clincher has just occurred to me that I should like to use when I see her. "I don't want you to laugh or get angry. I don't care about others laughing or getting angry, you're the one who's important.")

Now calm down. Let's go for broke. If I manage without a breakdown in the negotiations, I imagine they'll come to an agreement, and if they don't there's nothing to do but break off the negotiations. Rather than worrying about the negotiations, what is important now is to calculate the procedure necessary to arrange things so that I can be there at eight o'clock. I say arrange things, but there is nothing particularly troublesome. If I tear the box up into three or four pieces and fold them up, it will be ordinary trash. That will take scarcely five minutes at the most. Even if I liquidate my possessions, in any case they are articles of daily use for a life on the move, and they won't amount to much. For example, this plastic board that I am using now as a pad for my notes. It's simply a piece of rather thickish board, ordinary, milky white, sixteen by eighteen inches, but it is an absolutely essential item that I cannot do without in my life. First of all, it replaces a table. A stable level surface is necessary at all costs for eating and telling fortunes with cards. It also becomes a chopping board when I cook. It's a shutter against the rain over the observation window on winter nights when the wind is strong, and on summer evenings when there's no breeze at all it conveniently takes the place of a fan. It's a portable bench for sitting on the wet ground, and it becomes a perfect worktable for undoing the cigarette butts that I have collected and for rolling them again.

Of course, as it is, it has taken time and trouble to cull out my personal possessions as much as I have. When I first started living in a box, there was a time when I was quite unable to abandon the common idea of convenience and stored away willy-nilly things I didn't even know how to use, not to mention those articles that seemed as if they might come in handy. My baggage was endlessly increased with various items: a tin can on which were embossed three Technicolor nudes holding a golden apple (surely that would serve some purpose), a precious stone (perhaps an ancient implement), a slot-machine ball (it would come in handy for moving heavy things), a *Concise English-Japanese Dictionary* (indispensable sometime, one never knew), a high heel, painted gold (the shape was interesting, and it might be used in place of a hammer), a one-hundred-and-twenty-five-watt, six-ampere house socket (it would be a problem if it wasn't around when I needed it), a brass doorknob (attached to a string, that could be a dangerous weapon), a soldering iron (surely useful for something), a key ring with five keys (it was not impossible that sometime in the future I would come on a lock one of them would fit), a cast-iron nut one and five-eighths inches in diameter (suspended from a string, it could be a seismograph and would also be handy as a weight when I dried film). When it got so that I couldn't move for the cramped quarters and the weight, I was at last vividly aware of the necessity of throwing them all out. What a box man needs is obviously not a seven-appliance, all-purpose knife but some device that uses a single safety-razor blade for any number of purposes. If the article is not used at least three times a day, it should be disposed of with no regrets.

But there's a limit to throwing things away. It takes work to store articles too, but the effort required to throw them away is still greater. If one does not somehow hold one's possessions down, one is on tenterhooks lest they be blown away by the wind. For example, could a person who habitually used a small radio—a portable FM with quite good sound—dismiss it as trash just because he wanted to make his burden lighter? I, however, was able to do even that.

Indeed, I would certainly tell her about the radio. If the necessity arose, I should like to tell the fake box man too. Before the negotiations, I would like those two to understand clearly what sort of opponent they are dealing with.

—You're wondering what I have come for so early in the morning. (I address myself exclusively to her; as for the doctor, let him stay in the corner of the room with the fake box over his head just as he is.) I'm taking a simple stroll. A morning walk. It would be hard to draw the road up the slope from the soy-sauce factory, it's so dispersed, but I like it. What's the name of that ancient tree with the profusion of small leaves on the way? When the triangular hospital roof here came into view beyond the tree leaves, I became strangely nervous. It's an atmosphere where strange machinations are going on, with the small, high, painted windows in the cracked mortar wall. Don't you believe me? Then let me put it this way: there is no particular reason, I came just because I wanted to. You still don't believe me? Do I look as if I want that much? I was born with this face, and there's nothing I can do about it. It's a real handicap to have a face with shifty eyes. But look here, these fifty thousand yen . . . (saying this, I throw them onto the examination table . . . not too hard, but just hard enough). I took them for the time being, but I have not yet decided to accept them. Right now I'm seriously thinking about it. But don't worry, I disposed of the box as you ordered. So we're even . . . no, I'm the one who's owed something. How about it . . . how does it feel living in a box? (As I say this, I suddenly look in the window of the fake box, and without giving him time to answer, I immediately again turn toward the girl.) Now I'll get right to the point: I'd like for you to listen to a story about a radio so you can know what sort of person I am. Yes, a radio. Actually I was terribly addicted to news for a long time. I wonder if you see what I mean. I couldn't stand it if there weren't fresh news reports coming in one after the other all the time. Battlefield situations go on changing minute by minute. Moving picture stars and singers keep marrying and divorcing. Rockets go shooting off to Mars, and a fishing boat sends off an SOS and blacks out. A pyro-maniacal fire chief is apprehended. When a venomous serpent escapes from a load of bananas and an employee of the Ministry of International Trade and Industry commits suicide and a little girl of three is raped, an international conference achieves great success and ends by collapsing, a society is formed to breed sterilized mice, a child is discovered buried in cement at the construction site of a supermarket, the total number of deserters from troops throughout the world sets a new record, the world seems to be boiling over like a teakettle. The globe's capable of changing shape the minute you take your eyes off it for even a second. I took seven different newspapers; I set up in my room two television sets and three radios; when I went out I never let a portable radio out of my hand, and when I went to sleep I left the earphones plugged in. I got different news reports on different stations at the same time, and there could be special news broadcasts at any moment. Timid animals keep too close a watch around them, and gradually like the giraffe their necks stretch or like the monkey they become incapable of coming down out of the trees. Don't laugh. For the one afflicted it's serious. He spends the greater part of the day just reading and listening to news. Angry with the weakness of his own will, still with aching heart, he is unable to separate himself from the radio or television. Of course, I was very much aware that no matter how much I went rooting around for news I wouldn't necessarily come closer to the truth. I realized that, but I couldn't stop. Perhaps I needed the news form, which is summarized in clichés, not truth or experience. In short, I was thoroughly addicted to news.

One day, however, I suddenly recovered. A trivial event, served as an antidote, so really trivial that I myself inclined my head in disbelief. It was—where was it indeed?—oh, yes, at one corner of the wide sidewalk between the subway station and the bank. During the day few people pass that way. A middle-aged fellow who at first glance seemed to be a white-collar worker was walking in the most ordinary way right in front of me. Suddenly all the strength left his legs, and he moved as if to sit down, but fell on his side, and lay motionless. I had the feeling he was playing a game of big bad wolf with a child and had been shot. A young fellow with the air of a student, who was passing by, looked at the fallen man amused. "My God, he's dead!" he said. I remember that he looked up at me shocked with a wan smile on his lips. I paid no attention, but he reluctantly went to use the telephone at a tobacconist's two or three stores farther on. Being a professional photographer—well, I was, merely to the extent of getting a job once or twice a month making commercial samples of insert advertisements—I at once set up my camera and tried focusing it from all sorts of angles. In the end I changed my mind and did not take a picture, but that was not because I was especially grieving over the corpse. It was because I realized at once that it would absolutely never become news.

Dying is, of course, a kind of transformation. First of all, the skin suddenly pales. Then the nose thins, and the jaw withers and gets smaller. The half-open mouth resembles the edge of a tangerine skin cut open with a knife, and the red artificial teeth of the lower jaw begin to jut out from the opening. Further, even the clothes that are being worn change. What appeared to be of very high quality turns before one's eyes into cheap goods, showy but worthless. Of course, such things are not news. But it would seem that for the dead man in question whether it's news or not has nothing to do with him. Supposing one is the tenth victim that had fallen into the hands of a much-wanted, fiendish killer, I don't suppose he would devise a particularly different way of dying. The dead person has changed himself, but the outside world has changed too, and things cannot change any more than they have. It's such a great change that no news, however big, can match it.

No sooner had I realized this than my thinking about news suddenly changed completely. How shall I say . . . ? Slogans won't do the trick: "You too can stop news-watching." But I think you understand . . . somehow . . . why everybody wants news the way they do. Are they preparing for times of emergency by knowing in advance the changes taking place in the world, I wonder? I used to think so. But that was a big lie. People listen to news only to feel reassured.

Because however great the news of catastrophe they hear, those listening are still perfectly alive. The really big news is the ultimate news announcing the end of the world, I suppose. Of course, everybody wants to hear that. For then one does not need to abandon the world alone. When I think about it, I feel the reason that I was addicted was my eagerness not to miss this ultimate broadcast. But as long as the news goes on, it will never get to the end. Thus news constitutes the announcement that it is still not the end of the world. The following trifling clichés are merely abridgments. Last night the greatest bombings of North Vietnam this year were carried out by B52s, but somehow you are still alive. Gas lines under construction ignited and eight persons received serious and light wounds, but you are alive and safe. Record rate of rising prices, yet you continue to live. Extinction of marine life in bays by waste products from factories, but somehow you survive everything.

—Now what were we talking about?

"You were saying, it seems to me, that you were bored listening to news," she said, rearranging her legs (apparently she was quite aware of where my interest lay) and lighting another cigarette that she had put to her lips.

From her side the fake box man added, in a muffled voice, "I don't understand at all. What's the use of introducing yourself the way you're doing?"

—What I'm saying is that there aren't any baddies among those who don't listen to news. (I rejected the doctor's words highhandedly and did not break my smile in the girl's direction.) I have no intention of changing things here arbitrarily, for not believing the news is, I think, not believing in change.

"Nevertheless, isn't it illogical?" interrupted the fake box man in an unexpectedly abrupt tone.

"What's illogical?" I said.

"I mean the fifty thousand yen. You took the money provisionally to buy a box, because I thought you were on intimate terms with the box man. It would indeed be illogical if you thought you could keep it or not."

"Stop twisting things," I said, flinching from the unexpected counterattack. "You already know very well that I'm identical to a box man."

"No, I don't. . . ."

"There's no use lying. I've proof." I inhaled slowly in order to calm down and then exhaled. "That morning about a week ago when I came to get my wound treated, you already saw very clearly that I was a real box man. My poorly trimmed hair . . . my sandpaper face covered with razor scars . . . although I smelled strongly of soap, bits of skin like dandruff continually peeled off on my neck and shoulders."

"But they say there are a lot of eccentrics among photographers, don't they?" she observed lightly as if pointing out a blunder in a game. Could it be that in the last analysis she was in league with the doctor and had simply taken advantage of me?

"But at the time—you admitted it yourself—it was an air-rifle bullet that was stuck in the wound in my shoulder."

"A lot of people around here have air rifles. Weasels apparently have easy pickings in the chicken houses."

"When I was hit, a thoughtful witness who happened to be present told me about this place. She even gave me the price of the medical treatment. Three thousand yen, in bills that smelled a bit of disinfectant," I said, staring deep into her eyes. I could not believe that she would betray me so easily. Hadn't she clearly promised to be my model? She said that when she modeled and felt the eyes of an artist on her she became supercharged. She had indeed been provocative then, but now she was temporizing in front of the doctor. It would be anything but desirable here to have the doctor get up on his high horse. By pushing her too far it was conceivable that I would worsen her position. "Some girl in a miniskirt riding on a new-style bicycle . . . perhaps it was a girl. Unfortunately I only saw her retreating figure, but the legs were terribly beautiful. They were legs that once seen were unforgettable. When you go on living in a box for a long time, since you naturally see only the lower half of those going by, your eyes become trained to see legs and only legs."

I had the feeling that her cheeks filled slightly with a certain smile. But it was the fake box man who laughed.

"Surely there's a big difference between wearing a box and looking at one."

"Let me remind you that I haven't yet completely renounced my rights of ownership."

"Indeed. There's a big difference," the fake box man repeated reflectively in a calm voice. "Last night for the first time I spent the whole night in the box. I understood the difference very well. No wonder one is ready to become a box man."

"I have no intention of holding you back by force."

"It's quite natural that you shouldn't."

A chuckle infected the fake box man's happy-go-lucky voice. It was both friendly and sarcastic, and I did not like it. It was as if it was out of tune. I felt rather that from the beginning I should have treated him as a fellow box man. Surely there was nothing at all to get excited about. If I were to broach the subject of advice for a box man after he goes out into town, such as methods of procuring foodstuffs, little-known but good places to find slightly used articles in relatively good shape, ways of obtaining long-distance free travel, or the whereabouts of at least seven fierce dogs to avoid within the city, then we should talk this thing over more calmly. But being in his presence was uncomfortable. Even though I realized that he was a copy of myself, I was embarrassed and shrank from doing so. In a situation like this perhaps I should have challenged him with my own box on. I shifted my attack to her.

"If it were up to you, what would you do? Would you keep him in check or would you let him do as he wished?"

She looked up at me, leaning lightly as she was against the corner of the examination table. As the corners of her mouth were drawn up, she seemed to be smiling, but her eyes did not smile at all.

"I simply think that if we suddenly gave out a tab indicating there was no examination, the patients would be inconvenienced."

That would be quite true. A sly answer that might be interpreted in a number of ways. But for the time being I suppose I should be content with that much. Now I only had to wait for the fake box man to make a statement.

The box, making a sound, drew my attention and leaned over as if to show off. The vinyl over the window separated and an eye looked out. An eye that simply looked, expressionless. An insolent eye that forced on me the role of being seen, but of not seeing. I wonder when he learned such a technique. It goes without saying that the model was myself. I was depressed. I was being seen, but was the one seeing too.

"No matter how much we exchange words, it's useless," said the fake box man in a small voice that was ill-suited to his appearance. "Anyway you wouldn't believe it."

"What?"

"You won't believe that I am going to leave here instead of you. In your heart you want that to happen, but you won't believe that I will."

"But you have no intention, actually, of leaving."

"I've prepared a little compromise plan." Clearing his throat, he continued in a lower, more obsequious tone. "For example, how would it be if we tried it this way? What about you making yourself at home in this house? No matter what relationship you establish with her I will absolutely not interfere. I will not interfere or meddle with you or cause you any trouble. But I want you to accept just one condition. I want you to give me the freedom of watching you. Just watching. Of course, wearing the box the way I am. Exactly the relationship that stands between the three of us now. I'm just asking you to let me watch from a corner like this. When you get used to me, I'll be just like a wastebasket."

Somehow I had the impression that I had had the fake box act in my place and made a proposition that I myself had formulated. When I stealthily stole a glance at the girl, she had begun concentrating on a stringless cat's cradle, rapidly moving the fingers of both hands. Slowly she shifted her legs. The hem of her pressed white uniform separated and knees peeped out and made me feel as if I should like to touch them with a finger on which saliva had been applied. Perhaps she was naked under the white dress. The rubber balloon I had swallowed, that had some device for making it swell and which I knew nothing about, I suddenly felt expand in my stomach. Nevertheless, I wondered if I would have the courage in front of the fake box man to ask her to strip off her clothes.

"There's nothing to hesitate about," continued the fake box man encouragingly. "If you pay no attention to a box man, he's just like wind or dust. I myself had an interesting experience in this respect. When I developed a photo I had casually taken, right there in the picture was a close-up of something quite unexpected. A man with a cardboard box over his head was nonchalantly walking by. Since I'm no expert like you, the camera was anything but sophisticated.

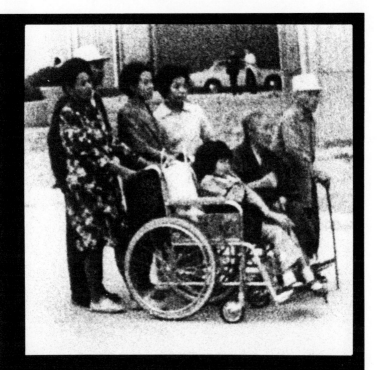

In seeing there is love, in being seen there is abhorrence. One grins, trying to bear the pain of being seen. But not just anyone can be some-one who only looks. If the one who is looked at looks back, then the person who was looking becomes the one who is looked at.

I wonder just what I intended to take a picture of. This happened some time ago, but I think it was the scene of some funeral. I had decided to take pictures of the funeral of a patient that I had treated myself . . . as remembrances. Even so, I was surprised. I should have seen him with my own eyes since he was so close. Yet I have absolutely no recollection. If a ghost is something that is not visible, yet which one has the impression of being able to see, a box man is just the opposite. It was since then that I began to be interested in box men. When I keep my eyes open to see if I can spot any, sure enough I see them roaming the streets, looking just the way the one did in the picture. But on the several occasions while I was observing them, I noticed that no one paid the slightest attention. It wasn't only my oversight. For example, suppose a box man goes up to a greengrocer's display. He stretches his arm out from a hole like this and begins pilfering stuff right and left in the area. Of course, only cheaper things without a price like tomatoes or milk or fermented soy beans. However, the clerk, dealing with a customer right beside the box man, far from scolding him, pretends not even to notice —pleasant, isn't it? You know what they say: 'Sweep the dust under the carpet.' Packing oneself up like baggage and walking about is an insult to the world and goes beyond just being strange behavior. Or was it so harmless an existence that one could overlook it by merely wishing to? You should be able to ignore me too if you want to."

The fake box man's words trailed off, and he stopped talking; I heaved a long sigh. As a condition perhaps it wasn't so bad. I more than anyone else knew full well that a box man lived a harmless existence. The location of the hospital was inconvenient, but since establishing himself the doctor had surely put aside a little nest egg; and then the very inconvenience of the location would serve to put a distance between us and the world. In the final analysis the question hung on her attitude alone. If she would only agree then perhaps the three of us could really make a go of it. No, no, not three, two and a little more. Treating him as a wastebasket would be stretching things, but if I considered him as a monkey I could keep him in a cage in my bedroom.

"Then it's all right with you?"

"With me?" She glanced quickly back at me and then just shifted her gaze toward the fake box man. As she did so, I felt a sharp jealousy at the smile that she let spread over her face. "It's beyond me. I'm not good at answering when I'm made to take responsibility. When I try thinking about it I'm always doing something strange like dropping a pair of scissors on my foot or sitting on a glass. I wonder what time it is now."

"Twenty-four minutes to ten," replied the fake box man, speaking rapidly, and I was made to feel guilty as if I were being blamed for my indecisiveness. She went right on, as if to press me.

"How old are you . . . really?"

"According to the official record twenty-nine, but actually thirty-two or -three, I guess."

Carried along, I answered in spite of myself, but apparently the question had not been what she really had intended to ask. Before I finished speaking, she had already turned her back to me and begun setting the instrument desk in order. Had she expressed without words that they had not yet decided on canceling examinations? Surely, arranging the instruments was a very normal thing to do. But she didn't seem all that serious about what she was doing. She simply appeared to be pushing the instruments and the glass containers here and there with her fingertips like model cars. Should I consider this a negative agreement? I wondered. If she did disagree, she would say so in so many words.

The fact that she had shown concern about the time could be an attempt to push me toward a decision. In short, I had the feeling that if I came to a definite resolution everything would be all right. If only I were to say the word and ask her to strip, at once the scene would change: two or three seconds of frantically unbuttoning the nacre buttons of her white tunic . . . and there she would be, naked before me. From where I was standing barely three yards away I could smell the very odor of her body, depending on the air currents in the room. But then would I be able to play, as they expected, the important role they had assigned me?

> (An unpleasant recollection suddenly occurs to me. It concerns the student entertainment program in primary school. I was generally not popular and was thus assigned a trifling role, perhaps because no one else wanted it. It was the part of a horse by the name of Dunce, but for all of that I remember romping around in the greatest of high spirits. However, when it came time for me to go on stage, the short lines I was to deliver at only one point during the play would not come no matter how hard I tried to get them out. When I gave up and started to leave the stage, my classmate who played the role of the horse's owner, in an excess of anger, gave me a boot in the pants. That made me no less angry, and I kicked him back, whereupon he fell, struck his head on the floor, and lost consciousness. I have no recollection at all of how the play was subsequently discontinued. But it was soon after that that I became terribly nearsighted and squeezed some glasses out of my miserly parents. Myopia developed because I deliberately used to read books and magazines with fine print in dark places. I just wanted to run away from seeing and from being seen.)

I am quite aware of my own ugliness. I am not so shameless as to expose my nakedness nonchalantly before others. Of course, I'm not the only one who's unsightly: ninety-nine percent of mankind is deformed. It is my contention that man did not invent clothing after losing his hair, but that his hair atrophied because, aware of the unsightliness of his naked body, he tried to hide it with clothes. (I know very well that such an explanation goes against fact; yet I do believe it.) The reason men somehow go on living, enduring the gaze of others, is that they bargain on the hallucinations and the inexactitude of human eyes. By putting on clothes that as much as possible are identical and by having similar hairdos they manage to make it difficult to distinguish between one another. If I don't give a straight look, then the other person won't either; and one ends up leading a life of lowered glances. Thus long ago the punishment known as the pillory used to be used, but it was said to be too cruel and was discontinued in enlightened societies. That the act of spying on someone else is generally looked upon with scorn is because, I suppose, one does not want to be on the side of being seen. When one cannot avoid being seen it is common sense to demand compensation. As a matter of fact, in the theater or in the cinema usually those who look pay money and those who are looked at receive it. Anybody would rather look than be looked at. The fact that they keep on and on selling endless instruments for "looking"—radios and televisions—is excellent proof that ninety-nine percent of men are aware of their own unsightliness. I became nearsighted of my own accord, frequented strip houses, became an apprentice photographer . . . and from there it was but a step, and a most natural one, to being a box man.

> (Some marginal notes again in red ink. As for the
> existence of exhibitionism, I certainly have no bone

to pick with the claim of the author who considers visual rape to be a universal tendency in man. Time and again, exhibitionism tends to be confused with excessive sexual desire unsatisfied by the normal sexual act; but in fact there are many cases where it is overrepressed sexual expression. One patient, for example, made the following confession: His first condition for making the exhibitionistic act more effective is that the person he intends exhibiting himself to be unknown and of the other sex. Second, a fixed distance must be kept between him and the other person, and the relationship of seeing and of being seen must not be broken by approaching too close. Third, the two parties must not be able to distinguish each other's face. As a concrete case in which the preceding three conditions might be fulfilled, the patient suggested something like the inner courtyard of a girls' dormitory where there are numerous thickets. The tendency toward exhibitionism indicates that while the patient had a strong interest in the opposite sex generally, he had a morbid sense of shame concerning them individually, as they actually existed. According to the author's argument, this is the patient's realization of his ugliness. Further the patient said the following: In order to reach orgasm by the act of exhibitionism he would imagine receiving a sexual stimulus by the other party's seeing his sexual parts. If the other party clearly manifested her disgust that put a wet blanket on him, but to have her show curiosity was also irritating. To have the other party pretend that she didn't see him was by far the most stimulating. It was clearly a desire to have the other party participate in his exhibitionistic act as a visual rapist. Exhibitionism is merely the act of visual rape reflected in a mirror.)

"You're a vacillating fellow," said the fake box man, speaking rapidly in a tight, hard voice. "I would jump at the chance . . . something's wrong with you . . . such good conditions . . ."

"I hesitate because you get in my way."

"Ah . . . I see."

"Since I've had experience myself with being a box man, I think I know somewhat more about them than you. The reason the world ignores box men is because nobody understands who's inside the box. But your true colors are perfectly clear. I even know your way of looking at me. I don't like being stared at. I don't like it at all."

"But that's why I paid fifty thousand yen, isn't it?"

"I got used to looking, but I'm not yet accustomed to being looked at."

The fake box man swayed. After once bending diagonally forward, he arose with surprising agility. The back of the box rubbed against the wall and made a tawdry sound peculiar to dry cardboard. After all, something fake was something fake. It could not be compared with a genuine box long in use.

"Let's stop the idle talk now," cried the fake box man unsuitably cheerfully, stretching his legs. His bare limbs were sinewy and white and conspicuously hairy. I wondered if he were wearing no trousers. "I'm not exactly hungry, but *l'appetito viene mangiando*, you know." Then calling the girl's name, he ordered, "Come on, show him what you look like naked."

I was confused. Over and above the fact that she had suddenly been ordered to strip, I felt perplexed that she should be called by her own name. I hesitate even writing her name here and now. I am made to realize anew just how irreplaceable she is to me. Since she was the only person of the opposite sex that I had happened to meet, although that was pure chance, and since I had no one else to compare her with, one pronoun by which to distinguish the sexes would be plenty for me.

"Right now . . . right away?"

There was no particular hint of disapproval in her voice as she questioned him in return. She didn't even appear puzzled. Her answer gave one the feeling of caressing the curve of an egg with a palm smeared with facial cream. The way things were going now she would definitely be naked. I was nonplused, but I kept my mouth shut. My lips were paralyzed and I could not get a word out.

"It doesn't make any difference to you, does it?"

"No, but . . ."

A brief, businesslike exchange.

"It seems to me there were some matches over there, weren't there?"

Urged on by the fake box man, she slipped diagonally in front of me and crossed the room. Her gait was that of a small precision instrument that did not make one feel any wasted energy. She took a box of matches out of the pocket of her white tunic and flipped them with her finger-tips into the fake observation window. Suddenly I smelled her fragrance. It resembled the breezes flowing in from the fields of peanuts that one smelled on the seashore. The skin round my heart rippled. Was it jealousy directed against the fake box man? When she had turned adroitly aside and returned to her original position, she suddenly began un-buttoning the buttons on her white uniform. At the second button she casually looked at me. As the look was extremely light—it was as if it could float in space for a half day like that—far from averting my gaze, I managed to return her glance without blinking (this was important: if it was she looking, no matter how much she looked I had almost no feeling of being looked at). A light was lit in the lamp of her expression. The line of her eyebrows softened faintly, and her teeth were visible between moist lips. It was an open expression. Were the doors open for me? She went on . . . the third button. Then the fourth. If she really tries to understand me completely, if she intends to catch me with the posture she showed to the fake box man last night, then surely I need nothing like a box. Others' unsightliness should be invisible to those who have no unsightliness of their own to hide. If a box man is a specialized voyeur, then she is a born victim of that voyeur (the only worrisome thing is why the doctor, faced with this aspect of her, was made to feel he should live in a box). Then the last button. . . .

Fortunately she was not at once naked under her white uniform, and I finally regained my composure. A blouse of orange silk fitted close to her skin. There was a line of tiny buttons of the same color, like grass seeds. A short yellow-ocher skirt held at the side by three black buttons about three-fourths of an inch in diameter. I heard the sound of a match being struck in the box. I had assumed that the color of her skin was on the light side, but in contrast with the shade of her skirt it was rather swarthy. Yet her fingers, poised on the buttons of the skirt, were definitely light. As I looked I could no longer tell, actually, which was true. Her fingers once poised on the skirt, hesitated, changed their mind, and shifted to the grass seeds on her blouse. Ah ha, of course she should start from there. As for me, I wanted more time. I began to smell a cigarette. For example, she whom I had happened to meet the week before—she who unsuspecting as a child had wiped away all my debts like some high-powered, all-purpose cleaning device —if it were she alone it was possible that I might happen on her again somewhere. In any case I would apparently have the opportunity of meeting the one whom I had spied on last night, she who was so tolerant of others' unsightliness, who was like a device for freeing me of desire that made me forget my sense of inferiority like a drug or alcohol. Although it was a fact, it was difficult to believe at a moment's notice that the two had come together in a single personality. Of course, as far as she was concerned, I did not yet know her well enough to be able to express any opinion that smacked of criticism. What use was it, I wondered, for the right eye to know about the left? The essential thing is trust where very naturally one shares concern with another, where one can observe things without any particular consciousness. She undid the third grass-seed button. Under her blouse she was apparently naked. Although I could smell a cigarette I could not see any smoke. It was wrong to smoke like that. In the meantime smoke suddenly began to waft out from the cracks in the box and from the observation window, filling the inside so that anyone in there would not be able to keep his eyes open.

"Are you about ready?" said the fake box man triumphantly. "Look, she doesn't pay any attention to me at all."

The girl smiled slightly as she undid the fifth button. It was a faltering smile. There were still seven grass seeds left to go.

"It's all right if you want to take pictures."

I was taken by surprise. To be sure she had promised to model for me. Even though she had stripped, there was no reason for me to do the same. I had nothing against taking my clothes off, but there was no need to do so on the spot. I seemed arbitrarily to be worrying unnecessarily. In an effort to ease the awkwardness of the situation I reached into my tote bag (it was in the basket I put my clothes in when I took them off), which contained my camera, but in the end gave that idea up. If I set my camera up here and now, I would be tacitly recognizing a life in common with the box man. That might be better than stripping my clothes off, but after all it was like handing over a passkey to my private room.

"This background is impossible."

As she undid the seventh button, she twisted the upper part of her body and looked at the wall behind her. The neck of her collar opened and I could see her brassière. It was a dark gray with exposed seams like those on a rugby ball. Indeed, perhaps the setting was tasteless. There were a glass case and lines of sterile instruments. A very narrow examination couch. An enamel washbasin supported by slender, curved, metal legs. And then a weird mechanical seat that resembled a dentist's chair, but that somehow had a different feeling. That was what made it interesting. There was an eroticism in this assortment as in pictures of hell. I supposed then that if I had plenty of film and when the sun moved a little over to the south, I should ultimately not be able to resist the seduction of taking some pictures.

"If you wish we can shift places. I'll go over there," said the fake box man obligingly.

"No, no, that won't do at all. I'll be against the light."

Quiet! Quiet! If I talk here I'll end up by confessing. Her fingers went to the ninth button; if she undoes the remaining three buttons the blouse will slip off.

"From what I have observed about you, you would prefer more direct action than just taking pictures," he said with false vivacity. The fake box man began to putty over the space left open by my silence with random chatter. "If I had the choice I would prefer direct action too. Let's stop saying she doesn't excite us. You can take pictures any time; it's like being told to hold off at the crucial point. You don't have to pay any attention to me. I long ago waived my rights to her. It must already be about a year now. . . . Our affair began with her coming to have an abortion. After the operation was over, as she had no money, she asked me unexpectedly to let her pay me back by working. With that innocent face . . . I was surprised . . . but anyway at such times one comes to a decision amazingly fast . . . surprisingly so. Properly, I did not inquire into the name of the man or about her relatives. I tried to hold her by ignoring her past."

"If you had asked me, I would have told you."

"I don't particularly mean I intentionally didn't ask."

"Anyway I was glad you didn't."

"The nurse who had been here up until then didn't put a very good face on it. She called you a saucy minx."

"How did *you* think of me?"

"At first I thought you were terribly suspicious of people. Then I thought you were perhaps overly trusting. You do everything so impulsively. Furthermore when you're scolded you at once admit your mistake with equal simplicity. You seem to believe that just by recognizing your errors any misdeed is erased."

"Was I all that bother?" Her fingers were poised on the last button.

"No. Everything's erased. When I think back on it now my intuition not to try to question you about your past was pretty good. And knowing you, you could have taken to your heels without leaving a trace . . . even if you had walked on freshly fallen snow."

She laughed briefly with the tips of her tightly pursed lips, and when she pulled the tails of the blouse, which she had finished unbuttoning, from her skirt, she let it slip to her fingertips and flung it with two fingers onto one end of the examination couch. A number of narrow pleats gathered at the stricture of her waist as she twisted. Although she did not appear to be especially thin, the layer of subcutaneous fat seemed scanty. That set up some association of ideas, but what was it now? Oh, yes, the feel of the soft chamois skin that I wiped my lenses with.

"But we were able to get along rather well, weren't we?"

"We did too well!" said the fake box man in a nasal voice, scornful of himself. "But I'm an easily satisfied rascal. I arbitrarily assumed that I had the power to keep her. I'm the weird one. I would shave twice a day, morning and night. I acted like a seducer. Further, since our relationship was one of doctor and a patient who had come for a D and C, we could talk about her uterus and her clitoris as if we were discussing the ripeness of figs in the garden. Our relationship after that went like Newton's apple . . . and the law of gravity. The nurse I had had up until then promptly upped and left."

> (There is a marginal entry in red ink and an arrow marks the insertion between these lines.
> "I didn't know the nurse who left was your wife, for heaven's sake."
> "It wouldn't have made any difference if you had. She was thoroughly fed up with her part.")

"I don't like to see anyone hurt."

"Hm. I wonder . . . When was it that I asked you . . . ? If it were established that the world were going to end, I wanted to know if you would spend the last moment together with me. You answered that if you could you would like to spend it alone looking at the sea."

"Liar! I must have said I'd like to be with as many people as I possibly could . . . someplace like a station, a department store . . . a bustling place."

"It comes to about the same thing."

"I can't believe that the world will come to an end so simply."

"Anyway I've got you to pay what you owe me. You don't owe another yen."

The yellow skirt became a tube and slipped to the floor at her feet. Standing over it on her left leg, she hooked it with the tip of her right foot and propelled it lightly into the air. The skirt described an unexpectedly heavy movement and fell to the floor on the near side of the examination couch. The buttons clicked against each other, making a sound as if someone were treading on little mussels. Incredibly tiny sheer blue panties cut into the flesh of her hips. She bent her legs slightly and put the flat of her hands on the outer sides of her thighs. It resembled the posture of one about to dive into water, but there was a more comical feeling to it. One by one her movements made creases in space, brought about a chiaroscuro, created currents, and carved out a whole new world. I was stricken by a wretchedness as if suddenly catching a cold. It was a kind of feeling of jealousy at seeing all these things for the first time.

"Just a minute," interrupted the fake box man just as she put her fingers on the band of her panties. She stopped moving, looking somewhere into the distance beyond my head.

"Say, you're almost not looking at her at all. After all you're the one she took her clothes off for. Use those eyes of yours, man, and feel her up. Do you know those figurines made of white rice-flour paste? That's the feeling I get from the stretch from her neck to her arms . . . it's a flowing sensation as in the elongated paste just before it gets hard. But what I like best is the curve that runs from her waist to the swelling of her buttocks. Somewhere a little something still remains of a girl's body before she blossoms into womanhood."

"Well, as far as I'm concerned, I like her legs best." As I said this, my jaw suddenly stiffened and my teeth ground together. My eyeballs were heavy, and I was unable to raise my eyes to her face. What, I wondered, would her expression be now? Nevertheless, I was suspicious about the fact that there was no sign of cigarette smoke rising from the box, nor did the fake box man even begin to cough. "But I don't understand . . . well-shaped legs, poorly shaped legs . . . it's like being forced to read a foreign language I am unacquainted with. Why do I cling so to legs? I myself find it strange."

"It's because they're closest to the sexual parts."

"I don't agree. If that were true then any leg would do the trick. I wonder if it doesn't have something to do with flight, running away. I am tempted to chase after legs that look fast for running away."

"Pretty far-fetched, don't you think? She's not running away, she's waiting. Shall I tell you what's wrong? You're too far away. Since you won't try taking a half pace forward, you can't even lift your face. And I'm going to tell you just why you can't take that half step forward." The fake box man cleared his voice and left the corner where he had been standing; he shifted his position to the tip of the isosceles triangle whose base formed the line connecting her with me. "Fish, birds, animals—all engage in strange courtship ceremonies before mating. According to specialists, it's apparently a modified form of attack and threat. All living things have their individual area of influence, and they demonstrate an instinctive reaction in attacking any encroaching invader. But mating would never come about if you based yourself on the single principle of attack no matter what. Since coupling is the contact of epiderms, it will never take place unless somewhere the boundary lines are broken or some door is opened. Therefore, in mating, by a modified movement or gesture that at first glance resembles attack but that somehow is different, a technique is born

When I look at small things, I think I shall go on
living: drops of rain . . . leather gloves shrunk
by being wet . . . When I look at something
too big, I want to die: the Diet Building . . .
or a map of the world . . . or . . .

by which the protective instinct of the other party is scrambled or made to relax. It's the same for humans. We talk about romance, but this is after all merely aggressive instinct camouflaged with makeup and feathers. Whichever it is, it doesn't change the fact that the ultimate purpose lies in breaking down and disregarding the lines of demarcation of a given area. From my own experience the line in the case of humans seems to be located at a radius of about two and a half yards. Courting is good, making the other party hesitate with sparkling beads and all that is good; anyway when you get through that line of demarcation you have already taken possession. At this very close proximity it is difficult rather than easy, as one would expect, to distinguish the true character of the enemy. Only touch and smell are of any use."

"When all's said and done, what do you mean?"

"If you take a half pace forward, you'll be right on that line."

"So what?"

"You're a vacillating fellow, aren't you. You've gone to the trouble of getting the girl to make you out a *laissez-passer* over the demarcation line, haven't you? If you go another half pace forward, like it or not, you will be asked to present that *laissez-passer*. It's a free pass, of course. Naturally when you use it, you at once waive any pretext, any right to go back to the box. You're frightened of recognizing that. You're marking time because you're afraid. You've got her tied hand and foot, there, see? You've sealed off time."

When I considered what he had said, I could see that it was quite true. She had made almost no movement from the tentative position in which she had poised her fingers on the elastic of her panties. Her eyes, vaguely fixed in space as if seeking something beyond my head, remained wide open like artificial ones.

"What's wrong?"

"Ah . . . 'There's no villain among those who hate news'? I wonder," snorted the fake box man, slurring the ends of his words. "Aren't you, who don't believe in change, being inconsistent? You're afraid of getting what you yourself asked for, and so you're stopping time."

"Such a feat is impossible, I should say."

"I read the story of the fellow who stuffed his mistress and lived with her that way. He says that a stuffed mistress is a lot more faithful than a real live one and a lot more sexy."

"Unfortunately I don't have those tastes."

"That's perfectly all right. That's the conclusion we have come to, isn't it? Anyway the only thing that's clear is that you don't want to get out of the box."

"I've told you, I disposed of the box before I came here."

"Well, then, let me just ask, at this very moment what are you doing and where are you doing it?"

"As you yourself can see. I'm chatting with you . . . here."

"I see. If that is true, who is writing these notes and where are they writing them? Then it wasn't someone writing in a box by the light of a naked bulb in a dressing room by the sea?"

"Oh, that's something better left unsaid. If you talk about it you yourself will admit that you two are merely figments of my imagination."

"Hm . . . I wonder."

"It's indisputable."

"Of course, only one of the three of us really exists. The one who is in fact continuing to write these notes. Everything that has happened is merely the monologue of that someone. Even you must recognize that. At the rate things are going, this someone intends to go on writing forever and ever in order to cling desperately to the box."

"You're too suspicious. I'm just waiting for my underclothes to dry. As soon as they are, I intend to leave at once. I scrubbed myself so hard that when the wind blows on my skin it tingles. I've just stayed in the box to get out of the wind for a while. There's no particular reason for me to have any lingering affection for notes like these. I'll stop at once. I'll make this the last line I write."

"When your underclothes are dry do you really intend to come to see us?"

"I say I made preparations to visit you, but from the first I arranged for very little baggage. Strictly speaking, I need just one thing in order to get out of the box. But it's indispensable. I can't leave the box if I don't have it—do you understand? A pair of trousers. If I were just in trousers, somehow I could go out into the world. It would make no difference whether I was naked from the waist up and my feet bare just as long as I had trousers on. Otherwise if you go walking around the streets without trousers, no matter how new your shoes and how elegant your coat, it's enough to raise a big hue and cry. Enlightened society is a kind of trouser society. Fortunately I have made provision for what is to come and have prepared for future use a new pair of trousers only. When I came for treatment last week I was wearing them for the first time. If you use them as padding at the ceiling of the box, they don't get in the way. And then a professional camera . . . and other things not especially important. If they're troublesome I have no regrets about tossing them out. No, I don't have to throw them away, I can turn them over to you. Toiletries, safety-razor blades, matches, paper cup, earplugs, thermos bottle, a rear-view mirror for a car, waterproof rubber tape . . . paregoric, eyewash, Mercurochrome, and so forth, but these may be omitted since you're a doctor and already have them . . . six photos cut out of Volume Two of A *Collection of Modern Nude Photographic Masterpieces* and a tube for looking at them . . . as far as instructions for use are concerned, you'll understand as soon as you try using it . . . and then, besides a pocket flashlight, a ballpoint pen and other sundries like a plastic board or a ring of wire and items of daily use it is difficult to describe. They seem to be trifling things, but they form a necessary and efficient living set endorsed by the experience of box living. I do not mean to put you in my debt, but I think this set a suitable parting gift for a new box man. And then it would be well perhaps to have a miniature radio for a while at first. Aside from being afflicted with total news addiction as I was, one is periodically overwhelmed, until one gets used to it, by an unspeakable sense of loneliness."

"Really, when do you expect your washing will be dry?"

"It's just stopped raining and the air's pretty moist. They're half dry, and when its gets light and the direction of the wind changes it won't take long."

"Then you mean that it's still dark where you are?"

"See there, there's something flashing around the horizon line and the sea. The squid boats are heaving to, I expect. It's just about time for them. It'll be light soon."

"I don't care if your clothes aren't completely dry. Put them on anyway, don't be persnickety. Even the urine-stained shorts will dry by themselves while you've got them on. If you don't hurry up, we'll get tired of waiting."

"I feel as if I've caught a cold. Perhaps it's because I haven't had enough sleep, but my feet feel hot and I'm having chills. It feels good when I bury my legs in the sand, but it's cold. Maybe I took too long in the shower. When I went to your hospital last week, my wound was hurting me terribly and I couldn't wash thoroughly, but I intended here and now to get completely rid of the three years' accumulation of dirt. I used up a whole new bar of soap. I just wanted to show it to you, it was special soap. I had plenty of time, or rather I suppose the work at hand tended to absorb me, because during this week I had many things to think about. I tried sculpting her torso. Just a woman's torso, because it was quite beyond my capabilities to make it look like hers. I put some nostril hairs at her crotch, and though I tried to sculpt her absolutely realistically, frankly it resembled a frog more than a woman. Well, aside from the shape it was now in, the soap was a good brand and of the best quality. First I wet myself completely in the shower, then soaped myself all over, and scrubbed myself hard with my underwear in place of a washcloth. Then after I had scraped away with my nails until I hurt, I showered off. When I had repeated this four times, the darkish rinse water turned clear. The fourth time I washed my hair, a lot of what seemed to be bubbles began to rise. But after that everything went wrong. What I was looking forward to was the sensation of passing my fingers over a polished glass after having taken a long bath and got rid of the grease. It wouldn't work. In the meantime the soap had wasted away and could no longer be used, my arms were heavy and would not rise, and my whole body smarted as if a thin layer of skin had been stripped off. I felt like retching. Anyway perhaps it was an error to try to get rid of three years' worth of dirt with just one cake of soap. Perhaps I had become a pile of dirt, except for my bones. As soon as I flopped down exhausted on the sand, I heard from above me what sounded like a gravel truck falling down. It was nothing. Only the motor to the pump. I was defeated. If I took another three years, with the brinish water from the well dug directly on the seashore, I would never get the soap off."

"Which one of us will give up first? The one who

wears out talking or the one who wears out listening?"

"Ah! I've finally come to realize who you really are. I thought that the way you expressed yourself was simply too clever . . . a simple product of imagination. Saying you were not a product of my imagination would not particularly raise you in standing. This examination room itself, including yourselves, is the scribbling on the walls of my box. Simply scribblings. Judging from your box, you can't imagine it, I suppose, but there's a difference between a genuine and a fake box. I am now actually looking at that closed-off room big enough for just one person. The inside of a face that no one can imitate since no one can see it, a collection of graffiti written compactly all over the inner cardboard walls tanned by three years of sweat and sighs . . . this is the story of my life . . . there is a sketch map of the town for the purpose of collecting foodstuffs as well as memoranda for the purpose of these notes. Besides all this, ciphers and diagrams the sense of which I myself do not clearly apprehend. Everything I need is here."

"What time is it now by your watch?"

"Ah . . . eight minutes . . . of five."

"You started writing on the beach at exactly three eighteen, didn't you? It's a weird watch. I figure that since you began, only an hour and thirty-four minutes have gone by."

"It would be better for you not to forget that you are merely my scribblings. You say that I tend to cling too much to the box? As soon as I dispose of it as you advise, you too will completely disappear with the scribblings."

"You're rather an optimist."

"And thanks to you I rather dislike myself."

"See . . . the pages of your notes come to fifty-nine. Fifty-nine pages in an hour and thirty-four minutes. No matter how you look at it, that's impossible, I should say.

How many times did I warn you? You're too long-winded. I'd like you to remember what you've done up until now. How many pages could you average an hour? Normally not even a page. When you were writing at your fastest the best you ever covered was four pages. And they were written in a horrible scribble."

"There have been times when I could write more."

"Well, then, shall we compromise and say that you can write five pages an hour? Fifty-nine pages divided by five makes eleven, leaving four. Eleven hours and fifty minutes, shall we say? Since these are your last pages, it comes roughly to twelve hours, wouldn't you agree? A total of twelve hours of constant writing without food or drink. If you began at three in the morning, it would be absolutely impossible for it to be now something before three in the afternoon."

"May I remind you that these are my notes. Whatever way I write them it is purely up to me."

"Perhaps it is, in certain circumstances. Maybe, for example, you wrote all this nonsense for some reason I don't know. Or maybe over twenty-four hours went by while you were unconscious. Or maybe the rotation of the earth was put out of kilter by some natural calamity. But if you go so far as to claim that, then I can set forth a completely different hypothesis. Yes, quite different. There's no need to claim that you are the author of these notes. Because there's absolutely no problem even if the author is someone other than yourself."

"Stop these false charges. I am actually writing. The seashore's dark and enveloped in the smell of the sea. Right overhead tiny insects swarm like smoke around the naked, filthy light bulb in the bathhouse. For some reason when they fall on my box they make a sound that resembles raindrops, so I realize they're larger than I thought. Now I put a cigarette to my lips, strike a match, the flame lights my naked knees, I approach the burning tip of the cigarette to my knees and look—I clearly feel the heat. These are realities that no one can doubt. If I were to stop writing here and now, no other character, not another line would appear."

"Hm . . . Then perhaps someone different is writing in some other place."

"Who?"

"Me, for example. . . ."

"You . . . ?"

"Yes, perhaps I'm the one writing. Perhaps it is I who am going on writing as I imagine you who are writing as you imagine me."

"What for?"

"For indicting the box man. Maybe I'm trying to impress on people that he really exists."

"That's an unexpected turnabout. If we suppose that you are the author, then the box man becomes simply a figment of the imagination."

"Well, then, suppose I am trying to impress on you the fact that he doesn't actually exist in order to prove his irreality."

"Ah, indeed. I wondered if that weren't it. I had a premonition. But no matter how many tricks you try, they are destined to be futile. Because I have material proof. Yes, perhaps I should have warned you ahead of time before entering into negotiations. If you know that I am not unarmed, even you won't act rashly. No, I have no intention of putting that proof to bad use; if I had I would have done so long ago. If only you would show your sincerity. I'll give you all the material evidence later."

"I'm sorry, but I've no idea what you're trying to suggest."

"Please. I feel quite dizzy from lack of sleep just doing

nothing. Well, then, let me tell you. Who was it, I wonder, who shot me with an air rifle? I've got my eye on someone."

"A lot of people have air rifles in this neighborhood. The weasels apparently wreak havoc in the chicken houses," she suddenly said again, repeating the same excuse. Creakingly, somehow time began to move. I did not wish to hurt the girl, but I found it unpardonable that she should side with the fake box man.

"Unfortunately there's unshakable proof, you know. The instant I was hit, I at once snapped the shutter—a professional reflex. I saw the developed picture that very day. I had made a good shot. It was a back picture of someone busily going up the sloping road, concealing a rifle by trying to fit it to the length of his body under his arm. The way he cut his hair, the new made-to-order suit fitted to his round shoulders, the conspicuous wrinkles in his trousers, nonetheless of the best material, and the distinctive low shoes like slippers." Then my tone changed to a plain and simple one, and I addressed myself exclusively to her: "Shall we play a little guessing game? Some profession where one is constantly taking off and putting on shoes, one where there is often the opportunity of sitting in Japanese fashion, one belonging to the financially upper classes, one where one can wear one's hair without worrying what others think. What would you guess? I don't think it's all that hard. Anybody would immediately think of a doctor on house calls, wouldn't he? Furthermore, it happens that the mounting road I photographed was right next to the soy factory at the foot . . ."

At this point events suddenly took an abrupt turn. The fake box man—the fake box man who until then had stood straight upright merely expressionless, harmless, like a trash can that had sprouted legs—began to shake his box awkwardly, making an annoying sound. The vinyl curtain over the observation window separated, and from within a long stick was thrust out. It was an air rifle. Aimed straight at my left eye.

"Stop it!" I parried in a casual tone, half jokingly. "I seem to have a touch of phobia for extremities, a weakness in me. So pointing at me like that . . ."

"Won't you show me the film?"

"I didn't bring it along. It's my only trump that will guarantee me an equal right to speak."

"Search him!" the fake box man urged her in a shrill voice.

She hesitated. Entreatingly she looked up at me. With her hands clasped at her breast and seeming to push up the collar of her dress, she began to shift her balance forward. Whereupon the front of her white ironed tunic (had she put it on sometime without my realizing it?) gaped wide open. Only the topmost button was fastened. Under the white dress she was naked. I had half expected that, but I was taken by surprise. The nakedness under the white garment gave the feeling of a nakedness stripped more naked than ordinary. The white dress was not a white dress, but had turned into the ceremonial garment of a sacrificial victim. The strong curved skin surfaces, uniformly taut, were suggestive of some strange machine I did not understand. The narrow jaw and the roundness of her belly alone did not suit her and were childlike. I wracked my brain. As in someone else's brief-case, the disorder in my head was extreme. Her left leg moved forward, trying to support the leaning weight. At once my field of vision contracted, and I felt aggressive. I myself did not understand why.

"All right, I'll do it myself. It's not worth bothering yourself with." I went to the box in the corner by the door in which I had put my clothes when they were removed, opened the neck of a mountain-climbing bag (probably an American Army surplus item), and fished out a stuffed toy crocodile. "As far as I'm concerned I'm lucky just to find that you feel guilty. I had the feeling your conditions were simply too good to be true."

The crocodile that I took out was a little less than eighteen inches in length, the circumference of the torso sixteen and a half; it was a toy crocodile painted green with inset plastic eyeballs and fangs, a warty back, claws of light brown, and a red, snapping mouth. Anyone looking at this merry, overly innocent doll would surely have his fighting ardor dampened. A child's toy usually makes the average adult lose his hostility unless he has a morbid dislike of children. In view of my psychological tendencies, this was not an ordinary doll. The crocodile was a blackjack that I had invented. I do not refer to cards, but to the blackjack, the deadly weapon that has gained notoriety by being favored principally by the Mafia and the secret police. I take the shavings and spongy filling out and usually carry around just the outside bag, but this morning I had a premonition and in advance stuffed it with sand from the beach. If you take hold of the tail end and just give it a shake, you feel how really dangerous it can be. If you strike with all your force you crush the skull. Of course, there's no need to go about things so enthusiastically. You can attack someone fatally and yet leave no outer wound; that's the good feature of the blackjack. When you've finished using it, you unfasten the end and scatter the sand that comes out around the garden. If there's any trouble it would never occur to anyone that a crocodile skin could be used as a dangerous weapon.

Pretending to give the crocodile to the fake box man with some reluctance, I struck from below at the end of the gun barrel. The destructive power was unimaginable from the speed. The rifle barrel bit into the upper frame of the window, and the box jumped. An angry groan came from the doctor, who had been taken by surprise. At the same time I heard the sound of air escaping, as if someone had driven a nail into a bicycle tire. The bullet had gone up toward the ceiling, but the sound of it hitting could not be heard. I wrested the gun from his grasp. The doctor, not to be out-done, thrust his arm out the observation window. He clutched my right cheek like a rice cake, and with unexpected power I brought the sandbag crocodile down on my oppo-nent's farther shin. There was a damp and heavy sound as of a hatchet biting into unseasoned wood. Uttering a shriek, the doctor drew his arm back into the box. I broke out in sweat at the vociferations that ran the gamut of the vowels. I began striking at the head at the top of the box to try to make him stop and then paused. I did not want to hurt the box. I con-tinued to beat at his farther shin, this time taking more care (I would be in something of a fix if he were able to remain in the hospital under the pretext of broken bones). The doctor squeezed himself up into a small ball and became perfectly passive like the wastebasket he had said he was. If he had not groaned like an empty pipe, I should never have thought a man was hiding inside the box. At first I looked at the box expressionlessly. The wan ten-o'clock sun flowing in from the window melted into the white of the mortar wall, filling the room, and in it the box seemed like a scooped-out hole.

Supposing that it is not I who am pushing on with these notes now (I too cannot help but recognize the contradiction in time that has been pointed out by the fake box man), and whoever it may be, I think he has an extremely stupid way of advancing the story line. If he has come this far the next scene can only be one thing in any case. I turn and look at the girl. What attitude does the author intend to have her take now? Depending on how she reacts to me, the outcome, how-ever pleasant or unpleasant it may be, will make clear what I have gained and what I have lost by giving up the box. For example, is she going to accept me like that with the buttons of her white dress unbuttoned, or with them buttoned up? No, it is hardly suitable to make the buttons the measurement of her attitude. But out of amazement she may forget to button them up, and on the other hand she may well button them up once to accept me formally and not abridge the ceremony of unbuttoning them. Thus as long as I stay beyond the two-and-a-half-yard line as I am, it will surely be easy to read her expression. If an unconcealable look of relief shows through her tense expression, that will mean that her relationship has, from the first, been one of estrangement with the doctor and that I will rescue her from his high-handedness and restraint; but if, on the contrary, she is afraid of accepting me, that will show that the two have been accomplices from the beginning and that I shall have to escape from this tiger's den.

Enough. Whichever it was it was indescribable ridiculousness. The objectionable thing was not so much the lack of logic but rather the fact that in all these happenings everything was so smooth. The truth was more fragmented, like a picture puzzle with many pieces missing and filled with flights of imagination. Although I am perhaps not I, was it necessary for me to go on living and going to the trouble of writing these notes? I may seem to be repeating, but a box man is an ideal victim. If I had been the doctor I should have at once offered a cup of tea. Being a doctor, it would be easy for him to slip in a drop of poison. Or . . . perhaps . . . had I already been made to drink the cup of tea? I wondered. Perhaps I had. It was possible. Certainly there was absolutely no proof that I was still alive.

AFFIDAVIT

All statements made are truthful. Since you ask about the corpse washed up at T Seaside Park, I make herewith a detailed deposition of my own volition, concealing nothing.

Name: C.
Permanent address: Omitted.
Profession: Doctor's assistant (orderly).
Date of Birth (day, month, year): 7 March 1927.

My real name is C, but the full one I use when I practice medicine and the one registered at the Bureau of Public Health is the name of the army surgeon who was my superior officer when I joined the colors as a medical corpsman during the war. I used it with the permission of the officer in question.

I have never yet been condemned for crime to penal servitude nor have I even been questioned as a suspect by the police or the public prosecutor.

I have never been a public servant nor have I ever received any decoration, relief funds, or pension.

I am still unmarried, but in point of fact, concerning my family, until last year I have been living with my common-law wife, Nana, who helped me as a nurse in my work and was in charge of all accounts. Originally Nana was the legal wife of the army doctor whose name and identity I borrowed while I was practicing, but since I was cohabiting with her with the doctor's understanding and approbation there was never any trouble. Until last year there was no conspicuous disharmony between Nana and me, but when I hired Toyama Yoko as a new apprentice nurse, Nana was not happy and suggested we live apart. I agreed, and until now that is what we have been doing.

During the war I discharged my military duties as a medical corpsman, and, putting that experience to good use, I engaged in practice on my own. I enjoyed a good reputation among the patients, and I have never requested instructions or help from a regularly licensed doctor. My special proficiency lies mainly in the area of surgery such as appendectomies. If I am blamed for illegal practice I shall reconsider using another's name; I shall make amends to the world and promise never to engage in medical work again.

Now I shall discuss the corpse, the cause of whose death is unknown, that you ask about. . . .

The Case of C

Now you are writing.

A dark room where the lights have been turned off with the exception perhaps of the lamp on the worktable. At just this instant you raise your head from the affidavit you are in the act of writing and have just drawn a deep breath. When, in the same position, you turn your neck diagonally to the right, a thin line of light runs over the right edge of the desk. It is a beam seeping in under the door from the corridor. If someone were to pass by, like it or not, his shadow could not help but be inscribed on that line. You wait. Seven seconds, eight . . . there is no sign of anyone.

On the old white door the layers of paint cannot conceal the surface scratches. Staring at the door, you think of many things. What is that sound that catches your attention now? Is it only your fancy? Yes, you hear it . . . there . . . that's it . . . from a different direction. You look around at the window. A movable house of cardboard precisely modeled on the one worn by the box man on the bed next to the wall. Has the real box man at last taken it into his head to come? No, the interval between footfalls is too short. It is not a dog either. Perhaps it is that chicken. It is that weird hen that sometime learned to walk about at night. Every night she wanders around here, searching for food. Is a night-prowling chicken an extremely strange phenomenon or not? Since it can monopolize all the night insects that crawl out unafraid, there is plenty of food and it should be well fed, but it is thin and sickly. If one finds oneself with exceptional talents one has to pay unexpected compensation (you seem to be taking a lesson from the chicken now).

You try lifting to your lips the half-drunk glass of beer. You decide to stop with just wetting the tip of your tongue a little. The beer is completely flat and undrinkable. More than four hours have already passed since you sat down here. Although it will soon be the end of September, the weather is depressing. You stop the sweat that flows from the hairline at your forehead with some cotton soaked in alcohol and moisten your sticky lips with saliva, but you cannot very well turn on the fan or the air conditioner. You must not miss hearing whatever footfalls there may be. You have become terribly suspicious.

A thick slab of glass lies on the desk. On it the half-written affidavit. The affidavit concerning the incident that has not yet taken place and that we are sure will. Pushing it

The white tiles are bespeckled with spots the color of dried leaves, and notched in them are grooves to prevent slipping. A thin line of water undulates gently along the grooves. For a moment it forms a little puddle, then begins to flow again, and disappears under the door.

aside, you open a notebook. Quarto size, lined with orange-colored horizontal lines . . . This is surprising; I did not know that you had even prepared notes exactly like mine. You absently turn the cover. The first page begins with the following sentence:

> *"This is the record of a box man. I am at this time beginning to write this record in my box. I am in a cardboard box that fits over my head and covers me completely to the hips.*
> *"That is, at this point, the box man is my very self."*

You flip over more than ten pages and open to a clean one. Grasping your ballpoint pen, you assume a posture for writing, but changing your mind, you look at your watch. Still nine minutes until midnight. The last Saturday in September is just coming to a close. You rise from your seat, pen and notebook in hand. You walk to the bed. You tilt the box over diagonally and crawl in, bringing it down over your head from the back. You present a figure seated on the edge of the bed with the box over your head. Apparently you have become rather used to getting in and out of the box. You adjust it so that the observation window is directed at the lamp on the desk. But there is not enough light to take notes. You switch on the flashlight suspended over the observation window. Making the plastic board you have provided into a table, you begin taking your notes on that.

> *"The following is a summary of the incident: The place is the city of T, the last Monday in September . . ."*

You evidently fancy to begin recording the past events of the day after tomorrow when nothing has yet occurred. What is the hurry? Or is it that you are backed up by your considerable self-confidence? Since you are trying to establish a chronology of actions that you describe in the past tense, evidently those actions had already been going on when I began reading these notes. You already were aware of the results of those actions, though I was not, for you could make an educated guess. But I should like to read right on in your notes. I cannot believe that there was any other clear purpose for the action than to bring death.

You begin to write.

> *"On the outskirts of a little frequented seaside park, an unidentified body was washed up. The body was wearing over its head a box made of packing cardboard, secured by a cord tied around its waist. Undoubtedly it was a box man who had been wandering about the city lately and who, by mistake, had fallen into a canal; the body was swept by the tides onto the beach. Other than the box, he had no possessions. The result of the autopsy made it possible to set the supposed time of death about thirty hours previously."*

Thirty hours previously . . . you were very decisive about that. Let us suppose for the moment that the time of the autopsy was early in the morning of Monday. Going back thirty hours from then puts us at precisely the present moment. At the latest it will be within several hours from now. You too have evidently made up your mind to face death. When you hastily close your notes, you slip off the bed and kneel on the floor. You shove the box, which has dipped forward, off toward the back. The things inside the box knock against each other and set up a din. Confused, you hug the box to you, looking over your shoulder. You look up, straining your ears to catch any noise beyond the walls, beyond the ceiling. Fear paints a streak of varnish down your face. The varnish is evidently quick-drying, and the surface of your face is covered with crepelike wrinkles. You are much too nervous.

Why can't you be more practical? You can only do what you can no matter how you try.

You straighten up and face the door. You begin to walk. You hold your elbows close to your sides; and your fingers, all together, slightly bend inward. You take three steps and your strength leaves you. You change directions and go in front of the desk. Seating yourself, you hold your head in your arms. The notes that you have placed between your elbow and your side slip noiselessly onto the desk. And then time indolently goes by as you think.

You are now staring at the edge of the thick glass plate on top of the desk. A pure blue that doesn't belong anywhere, that has no feeling of distance between its two surfaces. An infinite greenish blue. A dangerous color, filled with the blue temptations of flight. You drown in the blue. When your body sinks out of sight in it, you look as if you will go on swimming forever. You recall the many times you have had this temptation. The blue of the wake welling up from a steamship propeller . . . the stagnant water of an abandoned sulphur mine . . . blue pellets of rat poison that resemble jelly candy . . . the violet dawn that one sees, waiting for the first train with no place to go . . . it is the colored glass of the spectacles of love distributed by the Suicide Aid Society, or if you wish, the Spiritual Euthanasia Club. The glass is tinted with the thin membrane of a wan winter sun that a skilled technician strips away with great care. Only those who wear these glasses can see the terminus from which the one-way train sets out.

I wonder if perhaps you are not too engrossed with the box. Perhaps you are poisoned by the box, which is merely a means. I hear that the box is indeed a dangerous source of blue.

The color of rain that gives beggars colds . . . The color of the hour when the store shutters of the underground passages are drawn . . . the color of the graduation watch forfeited to the pawnbroker . . . the color of jealousy broken on the stainless steel sink of the kitchen . . . the color of the first morning of unemployment . . . the color of the ink of a useless I.D. card . . . the color of the last movie ticket the candidate for suicide purchases . . . the color of the hole that has been eaten away by hours of such strong alkalinity as anonymity, hibernation, euthanasia.

But by shifting my gaze only a few inches, you are already outside the hole. No matter how serious you pretend to be you are after all a fake box man. You can't stop yourself from being what you are. You are now looking at a calendar from a pharmaceutical company, that you have laid under the plate glass on the desk. Monthly slogans are printed on it: to the left, "The Season for Vitamins and Cortisone Products"; and to the right, "September and the Lack of Harmony of the Autonomous Nerves," between which is inserted the trademark representing a cream-colored Hippocrates surrounded by some Latin aphorism. The red letter in the left corner attracts your glance. The last Sunday in September. The day immediately before when the drowned man in a box is scheduled to be cast up on the outskirts of the seaside park . . . the next day . . . no, it's already today by a few minutes. No matter how you pretend not to see them, the already printed letters do not disappear. It's the same as your chronology written in the past tense. You place your two spread hands separated by shoulder width on the edge of the desk. Yes, that's fine. By shifting your weight forward and supporting yourself on your elbows, you are able to rise easily. Once things are started you cannot stop.

Nevertheless, it's that unfinished affidavit that annoys me. I beg you to destroy it and throw it away before you leave your seat. If things go as planned, such an affidavit will be a useless white elephant, and if they don't, the situation will be a lot worse than the one you describe in it.

AFFIDAVIT—Continued

Now, concerning the incident of the corpse you ask about, I can tell you with certainty that the body is that of the doctor-captain whose names I borrowed in order to practice medicine. The reason why I call him doctor-captain is not because of his old rank but because I used the title for so many years half jokingly and it became a habit with me. Permit me to call him in this way. There was the danger of suicide from sometime past with the doctor, and I am deeply sorry that I was remiss and unable to stop him before anything happened. I regret that very much. I beg you to give me the opportunity of explaining the situation.

The year before the end of the war I was assigned as an orderly to the army doctor in a certain field hospital. Since at the time the doctor was absorbed in his research on producing sugar from wood, I had to take over a good half of the examinations and treatment of patients. Fortunately my memory was good and my hand more than averagely dexterous, and under the guidance of the doctor I was able to perform quite complicated operations. Let me say a word about his research: during the war there was a great shortage of sugar, and sweets were very precious. If he were able to extract sugar from wood, that would be a discovery of world-wide import. The doctor noticed goats eating paper, the raw product of which consisted of wood, and thinking that there must be some active enzyme in the goats' intestines that broke up the cellulose into starch, he devoted himself night and day to separating and extracting it.

One time, I don't know whether it was because he was infected by the goats' intestinal bacteria or whether he was poisoned by tasting the processed wood, the doctor had the misfortune to fall ill. It was a strange sickness: he ran a high fever for three successive days, and after that in three-day cycles he experienced severe muscular cramps accompanied by spasms and nervous disorders. The doctor himself was unable to diagnose his case, and his colleagues gave up on it too. Since then, every time I have the opportunity I watch for literature on the subject, but as yet I have no indication even as to the name of the sickness. As I had long felt kindly disposed toward the doctor, I did my best to care for him. The condition of the sick man seesawed, and there was no satisfactory progress. I still regret to this day that unable to stand the sight of his suffering and in view of his persistent pleading I began to administer drugs to him daily. By the time the war ended, he had already developed symptoms of addiction. However, I did not leave him, and we were demobilized together. ·

Even after demobilization, I worked along with the doctor to open a clinic and participated as his assistant in both management and practice. Of course, his illness took no turn for the better, and outside of giving me instructions by means of medical charts the fact was that he was personally incapable of giving examinations or treatment.

Since you ask, I should like to tell you without

covering anything up why I dared to continue to perform illegal medical activities, knowing they were illegal.

First of all there was the necessity of replenishing the doctor's drugs. At this point there was no question of higher or lower rank between us, nor was I at all coerced by him. It was something I did out of a feeling of friendship, spontaneously, and I think that I should hold myself totally responsible. To your question of whether one should not pay special attention to the treatment of drug addicts, I should like to answer in the following way. The treatment of the doctor's drug addiction—he was different from the usual patient—was extremely difficult, and further the actual rate of recovery from addiction is pretty close to zero. While I realize that giving drugs is euthanasia over a period of time, I did not have the courage to abandon him.

Second, I cannot deny the fact that my livelihood was guaranteed under the cloak of the doctor's qualifications. But I did not take advantage of his weak point, his drug habit. The accounting was all in the hands of the doctor's wife, Nana. Only later did Nana and I become intimate, but even so the doctor was afraid that I would abandon him, and he constantly resorted to strong pressure on Nana to establish a relationship with me as a device for keeping me from leaving. This type of persecution complex tends to be frequently observable in the later stages of drug addiction. Third, my realization that daily my reputation was increasing and that my skill was beginning to be recognized was one of the reasons why I dared to continue my practice. Of course, there is no objective measurement by which one can precisely appraise the techniques of a practicing physician. Indeed, I continued, I suppose, because I did not have a strong sense of the crime of charlatanry. What's more, my interest in medicine was gradually growing, and I diligently and ceaselessly absorbed the latest information in medical books and specialized reviews. I considered that twelve years' experience and a conscientious and inquiring mind gave me a confidence in myself that went beyond having or not having a license. In point of fact, I was frequently amazed, when I examined patients that came to me from other hospitals, at the irresponsible and mistaken diagnoses of those doctors who had graduated from the university but who had been poor students there. However, I don't mean to excuse my own offense by that. Whatever my reasons, it is not permissible to infringe the law.

An important turning point occurred in the eighth year. Until then I had got the doctor to take charge of outside contacts such as attending medical meetings; but gradually his abnormal speech and conduct began to be obvious, and abuse and defamation of him, including the suggestion that he was mad, began to get back to us. In addition, since we were being investigated because of the excessive amount of drugs we were using, I also felt in danger; and after talking things over with the doctor we closed the clinic and moved here to this city. That is the course of events up to the present.

But because of this situation, the doctor's mental state grew worse and worse, he became weary of life, and an inclination to suicide became obviously pronounced. At Nana's suggestion we stopped having him appear in public even for outside events and decided that I should register myself as him. Although there were some formal modifications in our setup, the actual situation remained unchanged, even the doctor was in complete agreement with the plan. Fortunately the patients' trust in me was strong here too, and even if my guilt were confirmed I can say that I was confident there would be no damage suits filed nor would I be prosecuted. If we suppose that an injured party that is not aware of being injured is not an injured party, I should like to say that neither was I, who had no sense of having inflicted injury, a person who had caused damage; but for all of that I do not think it is right to break the law. Since I receive protection of life and property as a citizen of the state, it is not possible for me to go against the law.

Now we come down to last year. I have already described how I engaged a new apprentice nurse and how this became the cause of my living apart from Nana. But I report all revenues and expenditures to her and continue to recognize her rights as co-manager. Furthermore, as Nana has recently opened a piano school and is coaching students in the city, after more details on the situation from her I should like to request that you recognize that there are no errors in my statement.

Now no immediate reason occurs to me why the doctor fled the hospital and chose the path of solitary death. He used a room on the second floor; but since he went to bed and got up at varying hours and frequently used the emergency stairs to come and go as he wished, it is impossible to assume responsibility for all his acts. I must tell you of a little dispute that occurred recently. The doctor developed a morbid preference for sweets under the pretext that he missed his old research where he produced sugar from wood. When I tried to curtail his hunger for reasons of his health, he became exceedingly angry. But I cannot believe that that was the cause of his death. Since the corpse was wearing a cardboard box over its head, it is conceivable, I think, that he did not originally intend to die. It is possible he simply slipped during his walk on the embankment still wet from the rain of the day before.

Further, you ask why he was wearing cardboard over his head. I have absolutely no idea. For several months derelicts have been wandering around town wearing cardboard boxes, and there are witnesses too; if you ask whether the cardboard wasn't the doctor's disguise, I cannot go so far as to deny the possibility that he had so dissimulated himself without my knowing it. The doctor seemed to believe that along with his name, address, and license, he had handed me his personality and had become a nobody. Since he also fell into extreme misanthropy, it is not incomprehensible that when he went out he felt like trying to hide himself by wearing a box over his head. As the findings of the autopsy made clear, the scars from the hypodermic needles on the inside of the arm and on the thighs had already formed scabs. When addiction progresses as far as this, it's not worth, I think, being particularly surprised at such eccentric behavior.

There are eyewitnesses who saw a box man enter and leave the hospital; from their testimony and from the scars made by the shots over a long period of time, his connection with the hospital is under suspicion. As a result of that, I have been summoned. Without the eyewitness, the box man would have been disposed of as simply an unidentified body, and I must say, I would find it most regrettable if there were a hint of criticism that I was continuing in my illegal medical practice and not telling anyone. Both the nurse and I had promised not to visit the doctor's room unless he rang for us. Any number of times until now, more than half a day has gone by without our being called. It was only late Sunday night, when we did become suspicious, that we checked the room. I was firmly resolved that if he did not return by dawn, it was absolutely unavoidable to file a search request with the police even though my illegal medical activities would be exposed.

It was the doctor more than anyone else who was strongly against my giving up my medical work. On the one hand, he plied me with flattery and even threatened me with repeated suggestions that if I gave it up he might commit suicide. It's already common knowledge how very cunning and reckless a drug addict is in getting his hands on drugs. Indeed the doctor's suicide would be very troublesome. First, even though I might draw up a death certificate, it would have the same name and surname as mine, and I could scarcely present that to the government office. Repeatedly I had had to entreat the doctor respectfully to put aside the idea of suicide. He, on the contrary, wanted even greater quantities of drugs; his highhanded directions to let him admire the naked body of Toyama Yoko, the newly arrived nurse's apprentice, and to have her give him an enema naked caused me considerable concern. But I didn't necessarily bear him any bitterness. Since those who are sick suffer pain that those in good health do not understand, I consider that they should always be treated with sympathy.

As the doctor had long since come not to need me, I too from now on had no obligation to go on deceiving the world by continuing to engage in illegal medical practice. Illegal medical practice causes trouble for the patient, economically and physically. It was the doctor's view that if there was no claimant there was no crime, but I considered that being a fake doctor did constitute a crime, and I gave a lot of thought to the subject. I should like to use this opportunity of making a clean breast of everything and put paid to the heavy responsibilities I have borne in my heart for so long.

The above is all true.

The Executioner Bears No Crime

You have apparently decided at last to take some action. The vague metallic sound I hear now is that of a syringe being placed in the sterilizer. I could distinguish that noise alone from any distance. Like a sand rat that catches the scent of water over six miles away.

To go on . . . The skylight on the stair landing seems to be rattling in the wind . . . there's no mistake . . . it is the sound I can hear only at those times when the door to your room opens and closes. I can hear . . . the sound of your bare feet treading cautiously along the corridor of plastic tile. You are coming slowly along at the rate of about one step every second. Of course, your head is completely covered by the box. With the eleventh step the sound changes, and you seem to be treading on wet mats, and now I imagine you have just placed your foot on the stair. You are mounting, one step, and then another, and gradually your pace slows down. Soon you arrive at the landing and stop for a moment, whereupon you shift your box half around and look up. Following the banister along the corridor on the second floor, you come to a small room at the very end set back the depth of the stairs. The door is varnished cryptomeria boards, almost indistinguishable from the walls and extending the full width of the narrow passage.

Mortuary.

The room is not treated differently because it has dead bodies in it; it is inconspicuous out of consideration for the feelings of patients entering the hospital (or of those who have been there for some time) who are especially sensitive to death. Furthermore the emergency exit is nearby and it is convenient for carrying out the corpses.

Of course, I am not yet a corpse. I am not all that perky, but still I am not a corpse. The reason I who am not dead am in the mortuary—for your sake I should stress this strongly— is not particularly that I am receiving the usual treatment accorded a dead body but that I requested being here. I like this room. That there are no windows more than anything else suits my present mood perfectly. Lately the regulatory function of my pupils seems to have noticeably declined, and daylight makes my eyes tingle as if irritated with sand. Further, I have completely lost human defensive reactions such as feelings of anger, discontent, and hatred and feel very much at home in this room proportioned quite like a coffin . . . the depth being two and a half times the width.

Since you have come to this room you seem motionless. Just as I look for signs of you on the other side of the door, so you too look for signs of me, I suppose. If the door is aware, it is surely having a big laugh over us. However, I understand your feeling of hesitation. No matter how much sympathy you have for me, you must under any circumstances perform the duties of executioner. It is natural that you should be heavy-hearted. Even I, if our places were switched, would tremble and hesitate. Moreover, the one whom you kill is well aware of being killed. You don't look as if you could chatter casually with the one you are cutting up and who is aware of being killed. I wonder if you will feel more at ease if we engage in a debate on death than in small talk. It probably won't work. A debate is even more grotesque. However, as we exchange looks in silence, soon the covering of our nerves will wear thin and produce a short circuit that will burn us badly.

The best thing for you is that I be fast asleep. The best thing is to send me quietly into that other world while I'm asleep. But the light slap of a drug-addicted patient is something you are quite aware of. Though he is drowsy all year long, his sleep is not deep. You are not so foolish as to expect me to sleep soundly. Actually, like this, I'm awake. I am sitting up in bed, and my pen is running right along. I'm wiping away the secretion in my eyes with boric acid, and this is a condition you don't want me in. But you may be at ease. Before your hand touches the handle of the door . . . as soon as you show signs of moving a single pace from there . . . I intend to pretend I am sleeping. You obviously will see through this pretense, I dare say, but you will be more at ease than if I really go to sleep. If I really go to sleep, there is the danger of waking up, but you don't have to worry about that when you feign sleep. Anyway before that I shall drop the notes on the floor and attract your attention and let you know that I am in a consciously feigned sleep. The principal offender in killing me will always be me; you are no more than an accomplice. I have absolutely no intention of pushing the responsibility off onto you alone. Since any time's as good as any other, I want you to begin. Even at this very instant, it makes no difference. The moment you take action will be the end of these notes.

If you wish, I shall leave something like a little posthumous memorandum for you. I think there's no absolute necessity for it, but just by chance it may make you feel better. Yet it's ridiculous to be accused of the crime of helping a suicide.

Here is a town for box men. Anonymity is the
obligation of the inhabitants, and the right to
live there is accorded only to persons
who are no one. All those who are registered are
sentenced by the very fact of being registered.

As with a knitted jacket, everything comes undone from a truly trifling rent. It may be well to cut out the following few lines (seal them up in a vinyl bag so they will not get wet) and fasten them to the fingers of the body. Just a minute. No, not to the fingers but somewhere where it would be easy for the corpse to tie them on himself. Oh yes, what about placing them around the neck in a ring? No, since we want it to appear to be an accidental death, until the investigating authorities, who are suspicious, get here, I should perhaps hide them somewhere in this room. In a pipe coupling of the bed, which will be discovered at once with a little effort, but which at first glance is not obvious. The rest of the notes cut out are, of course, to be incinerated.

> *I personally chose death. If the findings suggest murder, it will all be the fault of my clumsiness. . . .*

No, to make this too apologetic is not wise. Indeed, I may sow the seeds of suspicion if I do. It is better to be more straightforward.

> *I have resolved to die. Let's stop the hypocrisy of hope at this point. Toffee feels pretty hard until you put it in your mouth and suck on it. But you want to crunch it to pieces at once. A piece of candy once broken will never again return to its original form.*

Do I look as if I still have some lingering attachment to life? In spite of myself, my real feelings come out. But worry is useless; no matter how attached I am, attachment is merely that. My reason understands very well that I should not go on living any longer. It's amazing that I should still have my reason. But this reason is as fragile as a castle of sand by the seaside that the rising tide begins to wash over. Another two or three large waves and it will disappear without a trace. At once I change my mind, and greedily I feel like beginning to resist death. First I shall woo the girl boldly, and if I am refused (and refused I shall be), I shall kill her and over a period of days I shall enjoy eating her corpse. This is not a figure of speech; I shall literally put her in my mouth, chew on her, relish her with my tongue. I have already dreamed time and time again of eating her. I won't cook her too much; underdone is fine. She is submissive, and even when she turns into meat, her smile will be unquenchable and she will have a taste somewhere between veal and wild fowl and will be utterly delectable. Apparently my sentiments toward her have been boiled down and now converge into appetite. If my appetite has increased to the point of devouring her, like it or not, I cannot avoid clinging to life. And so, while my reason remains, somehow I wish to wind things up. Of course, suicide is an honorable act, and as long as it is an act, it will not become reality by reason or aspiration alone. A little attachment, a little appetite, become pretexts for hesitation. While my reason is awake, I can manage not to pretend to brush aside at least your helping hand. So I beg of you, won't you please lend me a helping hand while I'm asking for it? It's both for your own good and for mine.

What's wrong? What are you so slow for? I promised that I would pretend I was asleep, didn't I? If you don't hurry it up, I'll turn into a piece of wood or a stone. I suppose you've gone off while I wasn't aware of it. (Probably not. You couldn't be more stealthy than when you came.)

"Are you there? If you are, answer me. What about just coming in?" I tried calling through the door, straining my swollen vocal cords to the utmost.

There was no answer. There was not even any sign of movement. Only the still of night became a pain that was like the striking of an iron plaque, rebounding against my eardrums. Had I been wrong? I wondered. The sound of the rattling skylight over the stairs and the creaking of the corridor as if a wet mop were wandering along were conceivably due to the suddenly dry wind that came blowing down from the mountains after three days of continuous rain. Furthermore, the circumstances were such that I could simply not avoid coming to a hasty conclusion. After all, tonight you did not send her to me. Her naked body should have been an absolute bargaining point for extending my life, for as long as I see her I will not commit suicide. It will soon be ten days since you began preparing the box (my coffin), and since she has not shown her face, there is nothing to do but accept the fact that the preparations are at last completed and the sentence of death has been handed down. Even though the signs beyond the door led me to a hasty conclusion, your coming was a matter of time.

After a while the door opens quietly but surely. At once I pretend to be asleep. Since there is no one other than you who can open a door so quietly, there is no need to take the trouble of checking. I go on feigning sleep. To get used to the stench here, you hold your breath a moment. Before beginning to breathe in, you swallow your saliva. A lump of ice as big as a thumb caught in your breast shifts an inch or two lower. You set a plastic water container on the floor and, as you take off the box, look around the long, narrow, windowless room and are again struck by how much it resembles a coffin. For light there is only a single fluorescent thirty-watt tube concealed in the ceiling. A sticky ribbon for catching flies, camouflaged as an artificial rose, is suspended at one extremity of it. In the very middle of the room, immediately below the artificial flower, like a core, is the iron hospital bed. Looking as if I am about to fall out of it, I am asleep like so much gelatine.

With each breath the aftershock makes me quiver like a melted ice pack. My body is like a slice of unsold skate on a fishmonger's counter. The front of the night kimono with vertical stripes is open, and on my stomach, the color of boiled asparagus, is a towel with a flower design faded from too much washing. The two legs that protrude from under the towel show sparse hairs and are moist like freshly skinned squid. Although I try to expel the air I inhale through my nose from my closed mouth, my lips tremble like thick rubber valves. Methane or ammonia crystals cling to the rubber valves and glitter like a dancer's tights. Every time I sleep, my internal organs fall into decay little by little. In speed of decomposition, I would not lose out to any dead body. You hold your nose. Tears come because decomposed substances of oxidized sweat burn your eyes. You can't endure it any longer. Haven't I been saying all along that there's no need to endure? Just think of a murderer as someone who checks the progress of decomposition—and it's true.

You try giving my shoulder a little poke. I continue pretending to be asleep. You wrap a piece of rubber about my upper left arm. With a scalpel you lightly cut the inner side at the elbow and probe for a vein. Since the skin has formed a thick scab, you cannot very well insert a needle directly. The flesh is white and only a little blood comes out. Grasping the vein with absorbent cotton, you thrust in the needle. Darkish blood flows back and is heavy on the inside of the syringe. The plunger is pulled fully out as far as the twentieth notch, but inside there are only three cc's of morphine hydrochloride. You undo the rubber around the upper arm and inject the three cc's. Even if I were to awaken during the process (I cannot awaken since I have been feigning sleep from the beginning), you can think up any number of excuses for vindicating yourself by saying that I am getting morphine only because my breathing is so difficult or some such pretext. Instantly my breathing quickens, my relaxed expression becomes even more relaxed, and around my mouth the signs of death appear. You push the plunger down further. Only air comes out. The exposed part of my vein dilates like a fish bladder. You pull out the needle, paint the wound with a binding agent, and press down hard on it with the flat of your finger. As there is no need to be concerned about cure or worry about festering, I shall ignore the rather rough handling. Besides, perhaps I am already deep in a dream. Having a couple of fingers chopped off would feel just about like munching on a very peppery Vienna sausage, I should think. Suddenly my breathing changes drastically again. It becomes rough and quick, rumbling in my throat like a cat snarling, and then it cuts off once and for all. In a dream I am standing at the entrance to a city with no shadows; here there are constructed numberless arches that radiate light. When I rush through them laughing madly, my body floats gently in the air. My shadow vanishes and with it my weight. While the I who is in bed at the time grinds his teeth, the lower half of my body springs up high (like a fish yanked out of water). It makes the bed grind its teeth along with me. A thousand springs, each with a different tone, split open like dry wood in a bonfire. The grinding merges into the dream, echoes from one to another among the forest of arches, and begins to play a funeral dirge for me. As I fly round and round with my arms clasping my knees, I am terribly cheerful and a little sentimental. I see a close-up of her sobbing for me. The smell of winter becomes her, as it does a young larch. When I stretch out my fingers, a hole opens in the air and becomes an anus. I am suffocating. When I open my mouth my tongue flips far out because of the extreme negative pressure on the outside and will not return to its original position. Just as I am on the point of inserting my erect tongue into the anus of air, the dream darkens, comes to a standstill. And I die.

.   .   .

You come creeping up over the dead me. In your arms you hold the water container. You sit with your buttocks on my chest and your weight causes me to expel my breath. And the end of my breath changes into a sound like the cracking of fish eggs . . . *phut* . . . *phut* . . . After constricting my lungs, you put a large funnel to my mouth and pour in the contents of the tank. At the same time you raise your hips and decrease your weight on me. The tank contains sea water. Little whirlpools dance on the surface of the water in the funnel. The hole gets clogged with scraps of seaweed. When you clear away the refuse, there is a sound like sucking on a decayed tooth, and perhaps the sea water overflows from my mouth. In such a case, it is well to raise your hips more rapidly. When you have fully raised them, the two-quart container is about half empty. With this, preparations for making the body look as if it has met death by drowning are complete.

> (Of course, you can't very well deceive the official autopsy. In order to hand down a finding of death by drowning, at the least, sea plankton must be detected in other organs besides the lungs. Sea water contained in the lungs alone would be a very strange trick and would doubtless engender suspicion. And once there was suspicion, in due order my corpse would be a nest of misgivings. There are certain physical signs that cannot be overlooked, no matter how bloated the body is by water or how much the fish have nibbled away at it: the irregular clusters of scars over which corneous tissue has formed stretch along the arm down to the wrist and along the legs to the back of the knees. To anyone it is clear at a glance that this is a drug addict, and what's more one who has been making

daily use of drugs for a very long time. If there were a steady underground channel, that would be different, but in a small provincial town like this not many are able to go on procuring supplies of drugs to the point of having so many scars. It might be a terrorist who plays on the weakness of some doctor. Or if not that, the doctor himself. In point of fact, statistically, according to occupation, those who have some relation with medical treatment show the highest rate of becoming addicts. Of course, you are in a bad position, for you have been investigated concerning the amount of drugs used. I think I understand your desire to begin practicing writing an affidavit. But anyway it's too late now. What you can do now is to see to it that the rest goes without a hitch. Come, come, it's all right, everything's sure to be fine. I have just thrown a wet blanket over you, but there's no possibility of a hitch developing now. You must have already reported the existence of vagrants with boxes over their heads to any number of policemen, and the wasteful use of national budgetary funds for legal inquiries concerning dead vagrants, no matter how they die, is prohibited.)

Now the last stage. It is considerable work to carry me down to the bottom of the emergency stairs. I imagine it is really a heavy task for you who are so slight. And then when you lift me to your shoulders, perhaps I puke up some of the sea water from my compressed lungs and get your collar wet. It would be best to take the towel I wear at work and put it around your neck. Then you go back to fetch the box. While you are doing it, don't forget to dispose of the sea water left in the container. A trifling oversight can cause unexpected and fatal results. Then you put the box over my dead body and attach it to my waist with the rope to secure it. This bit of work had best be left until after you load the corpse into the bicycle-drawn trailer. It will also be better to put on the trousers and boots before putting the box on. With that, preparations are all completed. The only thing left to do is to leave. To be on the safe side, don't you think you'd better drape a towel over the top? No, a white towel would only be conspicuous. Furthermore, there's really no danger of running into anyone on the way. Of course, even if you do, you can just get off the road and let them go by. It's downhill all the way, the trailer's axle is well greased, and you should be able to move easily and quietly. But watch out for dogs. You're in trouble if that spoiled mutt follows you. Make sure you chain him up before you set out.

Now as for the place to throw the body, I should like to suggest behind the soy-sauce factory that the two of us decided on before. I can't say that the ground's convenient for hauling a trailer over, but the cliff falls perpendicularly right down to the water, and the fact that anything would most certainly be swept away by the currents makes it an ideal place for throwing a body. While you are doing this, it is already after half past one. At the latest the business will be cleaned up by three. If you don't finish by then, the outgoing tide will have passed its peak, the current in the canal will come to a stop, and you won't be able to finish things tonight. If you put off unpleasant things until tomorrow . . .

(a sudden, unexplained interruption)

Another Insertion . . . the Last

Well, now, the time seems to have come to clarify the real situation. I intend to take off the box, reveal my face, and let you and only you know just who the real author of these notes is and just what his real objective has been.

Perhaps you will not be able to believe me, but there is absolutely no falsehood in what I have written. Products of imagination perhaps, but no falsehoods. A falsehood deceives and makes one stray from the truth, but imagination can be a short cut leading one rather to the truth. We have already got to within a pace of it. Everything will suddenly become clear with a last little correction.

Of course, I am under no obligation to confess the truth. In the same way you are under no obligation to believe it either. This is not a matter of obligation but clearly one of actual advantage or disadvantage. There is no advantage in deception. I don't want to talk about some detective story that can have a variety of solutions.

Of course, I feel that lately the signs of the times are more and more going in a direction unsuitable to detective stories. As I write this, the way in which the installment-plan system is expanding, for example, occurs to me. Just as there are almost no more people who are afraid of shots, contrary to times past, now there are few who shrink from installment buying. But with installment buying one mortgages everything, one exposes oneself, one's work, one's house to securing the money borrowed. Almost everyone has a good name and a reliable profession to be able to obtain clearance, and quite naturally roles for criminals and detectives are very few. These days only a guerrilla or a box man would want to cover up his identity to the extent of refusing the convenience of installment buying. But I am that box man. A representative of anti-installment-ism. Even if I am against the times, I should like to end with a clear solution: the denouement of these notes.

Now I wonder just what you think about euthanasia. For your information I shall cite the official precedent handed down by the Nagoya Superior Court in February, 1955.

EUTHANASIA IS PRACTICABLE UNDER THE FOLLOWING
CONDITIONS:

1 When a sick person has contracted an incurable disease and is threatened by imminent death;

2 When the pain experienced is obviously unbearable;

3 When the object is the elimination of the sick man's pain;

4 When the person in question is fully lucid, gives his consent, and specifically requests euthanasia.

5 If there is ample reason for approving such a step, any medical intervention is to be performed by a physician.

6 The means of causing death should be morally appropriate.

In my own opinion the text of this legal precedent clings somewhat too much to physical dimensions. From the standpoint of human interpretation, I think it is too timid, too conventional. Sometimes there are cases where sickness of the mind and the suffering of the body are equally appalling. But at this point such matters are unimportant.

What I wanted to say is just that if one has to do with people who live where the law does not apply, then all murders there are euthanasia. The murder of a box man cannot be a crime any more than killing on a battlefield or punishment meted out by an executioner. For the sake of experimentation, try applying to a box man the clause about the sick man in the above legal precedent. I'm sure you understand that like the enemy soldier or the condemned criminal the box man too leads an existence in which, legally, from the beginning, his very survival is not recognized.

Thus rather than asking who is a real box man, it would be better to ascertain who is not a real one; that is an easier approach to reality, I think. A box man has experiences that only a box man can talk about, adventures that apply to him alone, that a fake box man can never tell.

For example, the first several summer days a box man experiences on becoming a box man are the beginning of his ordeals. A feeling of suffocation makes him want to scratch out his memories with his nails. But if it's only the heat, one feels one can somehow still put up with it. If worst comes to worst, one can go to the entrance to a building facing an underground passage and get the outflow of the air conditioning. The uncomfortable thing is the sticky sweat that has no time to dry and builds up layers of dirt. They constitute only too good a culture for bacteria, yeast, and mold. Below the layers of fermented dirt the sweat glands stop breathing, panting and gasping like dried mollusks at low tide. The itching of disintegrating skin is more difficult to stand than any visceral pain. Stories of torture where one is covered with tar or where some dancing girl painted with gold dust goes insane are very meaningful to me. The whiteness of fruit from which the skin has been peeled away with a knife flickers radiantly before my eyes. So many times I have thought how I would like to strip off my own skin including the box the way one peels off the skin of a fig.

But in the long run, my attachment to the box won out. After four or five days, perhaps my skin had become used to the dirt, but I experienced almost no discomfort. Or perhaps my body, as far as the skin's rate of breathing was concerned, had adapted itself to husbanding the amount of oxygen consumption. If that were true, then I who had originally sweated profusely at this summer's end had come to sweat but very little. As long as one sweats he is a fake box man.

While I am about it, let me write about the Wappen beggars. That's the most unpleasant person a box man can meet. Doting old beggars all covered with insignia and badges and toy decorations like fish scales, with little flags bearing the rising sun sticking out of their caps like birthday-cake candles. One came after me shrieking every time he saw me. Once I was unable to avoid his surprise attack, for being used to ignoring him, and was inadvertently off my guard. Emitting senseless shrieks, he swept down on me and thrust something in from above the box. Later, when with difficulty I had driven the beggar away and drawn the object out, I saw that it was a little flag with a rising sun that had graced his cap.

I was profoundly disturbed. Another few inches to the side, and the haft might have pierced my ear. After that, with Wappen beggars only, I decided to strike first, though I don't usually. Thanks to that I have been able to get the hang of throwing heavy things from the box. In the first place (in case one is right-handed), horizontally on the inside you bend your right arm, that goes out through the observation window, using the elbow as a fulcrum and twisting the upper part of your body including the box to the left. Following your body back, you extend your arm firmly in the direction of the objective. Essentially it's a discus throw without the running. You can't claim to be a real box man unless you can deal with Wappen beggars.

But usually a box man's days, after he goes out into town, pass tranquilly. There are almost no incidents that merit the name. One's self-consciousness and diffidence toward others at most last only two or three months. Clinging to one's outward appearance interferes with living. No matter how much one may be a box man, he cannot very well stop such daily functions as eating, defecating, and sleeping. For sleeping and evacuation, one doesn't choose any special place, but that will hardly do for eating. When the foodstuffs on hand are exhausted, like it or not, one can't very well not bestir oneself. If you want to get food without paying and without causing trouble, the first thing is to go foraging for leftovers. And for that you naturally turn in the direction of the busier areas of the city that have both abundance and variety.

Foraging for food has its own knack to it. But the situation is different from that of vagrants and beggars, who have gradually got used to the circumstances of foraging; not anything will do for a box man just because it is edible. It's not a question of luxury but of a sense of hygiene. It doesn't necessarily follow that leftovers are unclean, but one way or another the impression they make is not very pleasing. One is especially disconcerted by the foul odors. Over a period of three years, in the final analysis, the stench was the only thing I was never able to accustom myself to.

I remained unaccustomed to the smell because of the disagreeable feeling produced by tastes that did not match. Fish have the smell of fish, meat that of meat, vegetables that of vegetables—everything has its own individual smell, and when we confirm the quantities as they mix together in our mouths, we are at ease and satisfied. If we expect fried shrimp, we are nonplused at the taste of bananas. A piece of chocolate is disgusting if it has the taste of fried clams. All the more then, there is no way of equating a given food to the smells of leftovers that are mixed together at random. Even if one understands this situation in principle, psychologically it is quite unacceptable.

Now the first step in foraging for food is to look for those items which as much as possible are dried and odorless. However, these are surprisingly troublesome. Leftovers thrown out by restaurants generally fall into two categories. The first are those goods that easily deteriorate, that do not keep well; and from the standpoint of quantity these are overwhelmingly the most numerous. Inedibles (used chopsticks, wastepaper, broken dishes, and the like) are placed apart, and the edibles are gathered in great plastic containers, which are picked up by the trucks from the hog farms every morning. The second category comprises those items that have a definite shape and cannot be served again to one client after the preceding one has left—for example, bread, fried items, dried fish, cheese, pastry, fruit, and the like. They would seem to be common enough, but no matter how you hunt you cannot find them. I wonder if it's because they can be used again since they do not rot easily even though they are divided into pieces. Indeed, if you break up dried bread you get breadcrumbs, and you get delicious stock from plain fried fish and chicken bones.

I'm sure I wrote about this before, but a box man can easily obtain food from store counters. He doesn't actually need to resort to foraging for leftovers. But it does provide a good opportunity to get accustomed to the town which you really have to do in order to enjoy life as a box man among the crowds. When he's used to the town, wherever he is, time begins to describe concentric circles around the box man as the center.

The false goals of those
Who have kept running, but
Who have never caught up—
The night stadium . . .
Where the flag still flies
But that both umpire and spectator
Have long since forsaken.

One is absolutely never bored, for the background goes by swiftly; but the foreground passes at a snail's pace, and at the center things are perfectly still. Anyway it's the fake box man who's bored in his box.

Now I'd like to have you think about this. Which one of us was not a box man? Who failed to become a box man?

The Case of D

D was a boy who yearned to be strong. Often he would pray to be stronger. But he didn't know how to increase his strength. Suddenly it occurred to him one day: he decided to try and construct a kind of periscope out of plywood and cardboard and mirrors. At either end of a tube he placed two parallel mirrors inclined at an angle of forty-five degrees, by which his eye shifted to the further extremity of the tube held horizontally or vertically. He attached paper hinges especially to the mirror situated at the upper end, and by manipulating a cord from below he had a device where the angle could be altered considerably.

For the first test, he decided to try it out between the fence and shed of a neighborhood apartment. It was a place that he had discovered as a child when he still used to play hide-and-seek; a narrow space set at a blind angle with the street and, of course, the side of the apartment. When he crouched down he could smell the odor of mouse droppings mixed with the smell of wet earth. First, supporting his two arms on his knees, he pressed the body of the periscope firmly to his forehead. Gradually he tried pushing the upper end above the fence. The street was a steep slope, and even the pedestrians who were quite tall did not come to the height of the wall there. Furthermore, since the footing on the slope was not very secure, very few people paid any attention to anything above eye level. Reassuring himself, D calmed his fears, but when he saw the vista of the street reflected in the mirror in which he was looking, he was terror-stricken. He had the impression that the whole view had turned into eyes that reproached him. Instinctively he ducked his head. As he did so the tip of his periscope struck against the fence and simply broke off with a wet thud like the squashing of an orange. He repaired it with cellophane tape as he wiped away the sweat that pearled on his face.

The second time he continued watching in defiance of the vista that bore down on him from the eyepiece. When he once tried returning the pressure, his tension too simply began to slacken. When he realized that there was no reason to fear anyone's looking back at him, his sense of guilt vanished at once, and the vista began to change before his eyes. He was vividly aware of the change in the relationship between himself and the scene, between himself and the world. It would appear that he had not indeed missed his first objective in constructing the periscope.

There was nothing particularly novel. Every detail of the scene was pervaded by a soft but penetrating light, and everything that struck the eye was velvety smooth and graceful. Anything that might cause feelings of hostility was completely erased from the pedestrians' expressions and from their actions. Nowhere was there a cross or faultfinding glance to be seen. The rough edges had been taken from the various projections and depressions that made up the view—street signs, telephone poles, walls, and concrete pavement. The world was filled with a softness as of an early Saturday evening that would go on forever. He looked playfully at the street beyond the mirror. And the street returned the smile of the amorous boy. Just by looking at it, the world was happy for him. In his imagination he put his signature to a peace treaty between himself and the world.

Thoroughly encouraged, D, who had become courageous, peered at the street, shifting from place to place. The street too did not challenge him. As long as he looked through the periscope, the world was unconditionally magnanimous. One day he artfully thought up a little adventure. He decided he would try peeking at the toilet of the place next door. It was an independent cottage a little way from the main house inhabited by a lady instructor in gymnastics at the Middle School. Perhaps she did not actually live in the cottage but, simply taking advantage of the fact that it was soundproofed, from time to time played the piano there. He was not very clear about that, nor did he particularly try to find out.

But once the thought of spying on her occurred to him, he had the feeling that he had been thinking of it for a long time. He even felt that all his efforts had been in preparation for that. The cottage came flush to the fence and directly on the other side of it was his little study that had been made independent by partitioning off the end of a corridor. Thanks to this position, the sounds of flushing water in the toilet were clearly far more audible, far nearer, than the muffled voice of the piano, whose high notes were deadened by the soundproofed walls. As a matter of fact the sound of the piano and the noise of flushing were not audible at the same time, but in D's head the lady teacher's favorite piece, which was sweet and sad and which she always played last in her practicing, and the sound of rushing water mixed with the swirling air in the white porcelain cavity overlapped in a seemingly meaningful way. At the mere thought of a human presence in the neighboring toilet he had the impression of smelling steaming urine, and the accustomed melody was enough to make the sinews of his back twitch with sensual desire.

According to reconnaissance that he had previously carried out on the sly, there was a narrow opening for sweeping out the dust at just about floor level. If that were open, there would be no problem; but if not, the only thing left was to peek in through the vent near the ceiling. It would be difficult to see through, but it would be absolutely reliable since there was only an insect screen, for the ventilating fan had been removed (it was doubtless out of order). But as much as possible he liked to peek into toilets from below. By simply imagining the act of peeking, a squirming living cream fell into his eyes.

According to his reckoning up until now, the lady teacher next door finished practicing the piano sometimes about five o'clock in the afternoon and other times about eight. The probabilities of her going to the bathroom after practicing were greater around eight o'clock. But as far as he was concerned that time was inconvenient. Since both his parents were at home, it was difficult to go out into the garden. At five o'clock his father would not yet have returned home, and his mother was liable to be out doing the shopping for the evening meal. If he was going to carry out his plan, five o'clock was decidedly the time. As it was still light, there was the danger of being discovered by the teacher, but then he could only have faith in the periscope. By observing the town from various places, he had gained absolute confidence in managing the instrument. Furthermore, once he had made up his mind, the impulse to peek covered his hesitation like a thick coat of primary color.

When he got back from school that day, in order to ensure his freedom around five o'clock, he made up some excuse to delay his mother's shopping. About four forty, after he had made sure that the practicing was over and that the usual final piece had begun, he at last got his mother out. After slipping on a pair of canvas gym shoes with the backs trodden down, and with his periscope under his arm, he sneaked out into the garden. Contrary to what he had imagined, the periscope would not reach the little window from this side of the board fence. Being caught in the act of peeking on *this* side of the fence might be rather more sticky. He felt that the chances of being challenged would be less by getting on the other side. As long as he didn't expressly inform his victim that he was peeking . . . as long as his victim, even if she was aware that she was being spied on, kept on pretending to take no notice . . . he vaguely expected that a kind of collusion would arise between the person being spied on and the person spying. He certainly could not consider that the timid and reserved confession of love that peeking is was all that censurable.

D slipped under the board fence and came up on the other side. It was more damp than the garden of his own house. The space between the building and the fence was scarcely two feet wide, and it was rare that anyone entered; spongy liverwort formed a thick covering. Slipping in sideways, he crouched in the space between the toilet and the fence. He was lucky. The edge of the dust opening was open about two inches. Naturally he used the periscope horizontally. His breathing quickened and his chest hurt. Leaning back against the fence, he closed his eyes. After taking a breath, he adjusted the periscope and took his position. First of all, the porcelain toilet bowl came into view. It was not white as he had imagined it, but a baby blue. Yet the floor was of white tiles, and rubber sandals painted silver stood in a line. No matter how he adjusted the mirrors, the field of vision just shifted right and left and he was not able to establish the necessary angle. He must be calm. Since he was using the instrument horizontally, he would have to revolve the tube so as to see up and down. The walls were plyboard printed with wood grain.

It seemed to him that time passed extremely slowly. The music too today seemed especially long. His whole body felt warm, and his breathing sounded like a whistle. His cranium opened with the pressure, and his eyeballs flew out like cork bullets. His mother would doubtless be coming back soon. The pretentious rhythms of the piano attacked the joints of his knees like some nervous disease. He was carried away by a compulsion to enter the house, to destroy the piano.

Nevertheless, the music somehow drew to an end. Soon came the several final bars he was accustomed to . . . then the final drawn-out chord. D told himself not to expect too much, that to anticipate success the first time would be too presumptuous. Since the temperature today was high and the day dry, the number of times one urinated would necessarily be proportionately fewer. Yet, he could not but be expectant. D began to quiver. He could not get enough air through his nose alone. He left his mouth open, and his whole body was pulsating like a pump.

Suddenly a voice sounded next to his ear.

"And just who are you? What are you doing? And don't try and get away. If you do I'll report you."

He cringed. He was pinned to the ground. He had no strength to shift his glance in order to see from what direction the voice was coming. His gasping breathing, he thought, was like the red, lighted end of a sparkler dangling at the end of its paper string.

"Go around in front and come in through the entrance." The voice was not all that threatening, and that was a relief. "All right . . . get up . . . quickly now." Quite definitely the voice seemed to come from the toilet. But he could see no one. From where and how, he wondered, could he be seen? "Don't forget that weird piece of machinery there. Go directly round in front. The door's not locked, and you can come right in." Was she going to finish urinating, he wondered, or would she stop now? The position of his periscope was definitely wrong. "Do you understand? You're not to run away. Now go around in front right away, and no loitering."

It looked as if there were nothing for him to do except do as he was told. It certainly seemed out of the question to take to his heels. If he interpreted the warning not to run away as meaning that if he did not she would not report him to the school or to his parents, then whatever his punishment he had best get it over with here. In the state of mind of a lamb being led to slaughter and clutching his periscope that had proved useless to his breast, he circled the building and proceeded in the direction of the entrance. The door, which had always suggested to him the sensation of touching folds of flesh, had now changed to a feeling of concrete.

Immediately inside the door was a spacious music room with a piano. He saw the sound-absorbent wood dotted with holes that gave him an itchy sensation just looking at it. On the floor lay a green carpet. At the same time as he closed the door behind him another inner door opened, and the lady instructor entered. Behind her came the sound of flushing water. She had evidently finished urinating after he had been discovered. In a corner of his conscience her white buttocks projecting into the toilet bowl overlapped with the swirl of the flushing. Since he could not raise his face he experienced an oppression as if he were face to face with her naked buttocks.

"I'll lock the door," she said, going around in back of him, and there was the sound of a key turning over.

"You're not ashamed, are you?"

"Yes, I am."

"Your voice is beginning to change. What you did is natural, I suppose, but I hate dirty acts. You are probably ashamed, but I am a lot more. To the extent you're embarrassed you make me feel embarrassed too. What are we to do? If I gloss it over, you'll just repeat the same thing. . . ."

"No, I won't."

"I wonder."

"I really won't."

"But even so, I can't very well let you go completely unpunished, can I. I think it would be best to make you experience the same feelings that you caused me."

The lady teacher turned to the piano and suddenly began to let her fingers run over the keyboard. It was a section of the piece she habitually played last of all. It was splendid, like piled marbles, quite different from the sound audible through the wall. It was like a silken flag softly streaming in the breeze. Increasingly D thought himself wretched and dirty, and finally he was unable to stop the overflow of tears.

"What do you think of this piece?"

"Oh, I like it."

"Do you really?"

"I like it very much."

"Do you know who the composer was?"

"No."

"It was Chopin. Wonderful, marvelous Chopin." Suddenly she stopped playing the piano and stood up. "Well, then, take off your clothes. Strip naked. I'll go in the other room."

D did not at once take in what she had said. Even when the lady teacher had withdrawn, he simply remained standing absently for some time.

"What's wrong? Why are you so slow?" came her voice from the other side of the door. "I'm looking at you right now through the keyhole. If you really think you embarrassed me, you can surely do what I ask."

"What am I supposed to do?"

"But I told you! Take off your clothes. Since you put me in exactly the same position, no excuses now."

"Won't you forgive me?"

"Certainly not. Would it be better if I reported it to your father or your mother?"

D was defeated. His stomach sank to his bladder, and his chest seemed to become hollow. He didn't particularly dislike getting naked. Concerning that point, in his own way he assumed that they would come to a mutual understanding. But he was not at all self-confident. If he were to strip, like it or not, he was sure to get an erection. Would the lady instructor ever pardon his reacting like that? he wondered. It was unbelievable that she would. She would get angry and this time would certainly not overlook his offense. Or if not that, she would hold her sides with laughter. Whichever, he was too miserable. Since he realized that he was so wretched, he wondered if his erection would not go down a bit. But it wouldn't work. Just by thinking of being naked he had already started to get a hard-on. Even while he was being laughed at, his erection would keep on growing.

He resigned himself. Braving his own ugliness, he took off his coat, stripped away his shirt, and lowering his trousers, he was stark naked. He was firmly erect. Yet there was no reaction. Beyond the door everything remained perfectly quiet. It was not simply that there was no sound, but a hush like some substance was cowering there. Her gaze, turning into black light, came piercing through the keyhole. From his field of vision the color vanished and there was only chiaroscuro. Sensation vanished from the soles of his feet.

As he tottered along he began to pass water. It was not urine, but a seminal emission. He could not stop himself once he had started. He fell on his knees, and covering his face with his hands, he pretended to cry. There were, of course, no tears. In an instant his viscera dried up like a beach at dawn.

"Do you understand now?" Her voice on the other side of the door was dry too. He nodded. Indeed, he understood very well. He understood profoundly, more than his nod to her indicated, more than he himself realized.

"You had better go home now."

The inner door opened a crack, and the key to the front door that came flying in fell soundlessly to the floor. It was a door he could have opened without a key from the inside.

.   .   .

The door of the hospital that I finally reached is locked, and a card announcing that there are no examinations today has been hung out. In the back the friendly dog sniffs hoarsely through its nose. I ring the bell. Being impatient, I push on it without letting up. There is an indication that someone is coming. Suddenly the door is flung open, and the girl with wide-open arms hastily invites me in. She walks away toward the inside as she says something quickly. I do not really catch what she says, but apparently she is grumbling to herself, mistaking me for the fake box man (or the fake doctor). The best thing is to correct this sort of misapprehension at once. Coughing, I begin to explain.

"I'm not the doctor. I'm the real thing . . . the genuine article. The former photographer who was waiting under the bridge last night. . . ."

With parted lips she quickly scrutinizes me from top to toe. Her expression is vague with surprise.

"I'm in a quandary," she says. "You didn't keep your promise, did you. Take off your box right away. Maybe you don't know it, but . . ."

"Oh, yes, I do. You're talking about the doctor. I saw him a little while ago in the street."

"Take it off . . . please."

"But I can't. That's why I came running in such a hurry."

"That won't work . . . not at the point we're at."

"But I'm naked. Stark naked. After I saw you at the hospital I took a shower at the bathhouse and was waiting for the underclothes I washed to dry. I've got to put something on before I can leave the box. I planned to come here after disposing of it. Because I want you to see how I keep my promises. But I fell asleep. I slept so hard it was like being rolled over and crushed under a construction roller. Furthermore, I had a series of dreams, and since I could not sleep in them, although I remained lying down until a while ago, I'm still suffering from lack of sleep. But when I opened my eyes, my underclothes and trousers that had been hung out to dry had vanished. What a mess! I had the impression that near dawn I had had a dream in which a lot of children raced around with a flag attached to the end of a pole, but perhaps it wasn't a dream but actually happened. When I thought about it I had the feeling that it wasn't a flag but my trousers. I didn't know what to do. Somewhere, somehow, I had to get at least some trousers. I would find some trousers, any old rags would do. As I thought about it, I headed in the direction of the town, whereupon a box man, exactly the same as I, was walking in the area at the end of the embankment. Too late, I thought. I had no time for trousers. I had to get to the hospital."

Suddenly she begins to laugh. Supporting her body bent double on her heels, she shakes with laughter. At first the laughter is unpleasant and jeering; but in the midst of it the sting leaves it, and it turns into amused laughter. She finishes laughing, relaxed, and her tone changes to a cheerful and friendly one.

"I don't mind if you're naked. A promise is a promise."

"I'm sorry. Can't you lend me some trousers? Any old ones will do."

"Well, then, I'll strip too. Anyway you mean to take my picture, I imagine. We don't have to be shy, do we, with both of us naked?"

"There's not much point in seeing a man naked, is there?"

"Oh, you're wrong," she replies expressionlessly, beginning at once to take off her clothes. Blouse . . . skirt . . . brassière. "I don't like that box. I can't stand it another second."

She stands without reserve before me naked. About her lips there is a touch of teasing. But in her eyes lurks dark entreaty. She is naked, but she doesn't seem to be at all. Being naked suits her too well. But that is not true of me. The lower half of my body, particularly, that peeks out from the box is exceedingly comical, I imagine. "Close your eyes a while. Turn in that direction."

"All right," she says, her voice filled with laughter, and turning her back, she leans her shoulder against the wall of the corridor. As I take off my boots, I have the feeling that my whole body is shaking slightly. Quietly I extricate myself from the box, noiselessly approach her from behind, and put a hand on her shoulder. As she does not try to resist, I reduce the distance between us even more. I tell myself emphatically as I do so that I must forever maintain this closeness.

"Is it all right? What if the doctor should come back?"

"He won't. He doesn't even want to . . ."

"The smell of your hair is so good."

"What a beautiful, firm ass . . ."

"I confess . . . I was a fake."

"Ssh . . . don't say any more. . . ."

"But these notes are the real thing. They're the will the real box man gave me to keep."

"You're all sweaty. . . ."

> (But there's no need to apologize. Writings left behind by the dead can't always be taken at face value as inevitably relating the truth. Those who are going to die have jealousies and envies that are incomprehensible to those who remain. Among them are those perverse ones whose hatred for the empty promises of "truth" cuts to the bone and who at best nail the coffin lid on with lies. One can't very well swallow the bait whole by just claiming it is the writing of the dead.)

In His Dream the Box Man Takes His Box Off. Is This the Dream He Had Before He Began Living in a Box or Is It the Dream of His Life After He Left It . . . ?

My destination was the house located at the top of a slope at the exit from the city. After having traveled far and wide in a horse-drawn carriage I have finally just arrived before the city gate. Judging from the length of my voyage, the house is probably at the entrance rather than at the exit of the town.

Furthermore, the horse-drawn carriage is only a manner of speaking, for the vehicle was drawn not by a horse but in fact by a man wearing a cardboard box over his head. More precisely it was my father. Father was already over sixty. Naturally he had certain conservative aspects, and since he wholeheartedly refused to break the custom handed down from ancient times in the village that at a wedding the bride must be met with a horse-drawn carriage, he himself had gone out to do so, taking the place of the horse. However, so as not to cause me embarrassment he had hidden himself in a cardboard box. It was also out of consideration for the bride lest he shock her.

Of course, if I had just had the money to hire a horse-drawn carriage, my father would never had had to go to such extremes, nor would I ever have asked him. However, it would be simply too bad to give up the wedding because I could not pay the fee for the carriage. Indeed, I could only depend on my father's good offices.

But my already sixty-year-old father was not after all a horse. Since he was panting up a rough, sloping road, his progress was not one tenth that of a real horse. Nor could I very well get down and push from behind; the carriage crept slowly along. Time alone went wildly by. Furthermore, with the merciless jolting there was no reason for me to be blamed if the demands of nature finally reached their limit.

The carriage stopped. Father undid from the box something that looked like a leather belt (I don't know its name) that attached to the horse's belly and, looking up at me from the open observation window in the front of the box, smiled weakly a wan, exhausted smile. I smiled back at him stiffly, and slowly crawled down from the baggage cart. I said a carriage, but actually it was a baggage cart. There was no agreement that it shouldn't be a baggage cart, and after I got married I could do with it what I wanted. Breathing hard, I ran shufflingly to the side of the road, at the same time opening my fly. As the pressure drained from my belly I experienced in a profound feeling of liberation as if I were flying away over some distant range of mountains.

"Chopin! What a thing to do!"

From behind me came Father's perplexed cry. I had been too careless. Between the bride's house and the road stood a great thicket of palms, and I was sure that I was completely screened off by them. But my bride had tired of waiting. Apparently she had caught the sound of the carriage from a distance and had come out right to the roadside to welcome me. Out of timidity and constraint she had concealed herself, ironically, right behind the palms that served as a shield for me. Our gazes crossed. It was certain that she saw my penis. Her white garment fluttered between the branches, and I could hear her light, running steps and the sound of a door being slammed as with a wooden mallet. Everything was lost. As I crossed over the wavering rope stretched between hope and despair, my breast aflame, and as I was about to reach the opposite side in just one more step, the ax had fallen. I was profoundly disappointed.

"You're her guardian, Father. Do something, I beg you."

Tears of resentment came welling up. As I sobbed compulsively, my urine still kept flowing. It dug a hole in the ground and formed a light yellow pond that gave off steam as it spread out.

"Listen, Chopin, it's best you give the whole thing up," reasoned my father sympathetically as he tapped in a staccato on the belly of the box with a hand that he had stuck out through the hole. "You had better stop this useless struggling. A man who's got a mania for indecent exposure is not suited to marriage . . . it's common sense . . . to young girls today."

"But I don't have any mania for indecent exposure!"

"It probably seems so to her. You were seen, you know."

"But we're going to be married anyway, so what difference . . ."

"Out of consideration for your father who has gone as far as to take the place of a horse, couldn't you bow out like a man? I beg of you. Fortunately there were no other eyewitnesses. No matter how many hundreds of volumes of Chopin's biography may be written, I won't want anyone to know of this scandal. A fate governed by urinating is not at all suitable for a biography. Really not at all. Of course, I don't say you're at fault. Responsibility should be placed on the prejudice about indecent exposure and on the municipal administration that neglects the construction of public toilets. Well, let's get going. You don't have any attachment to this town. Let's go to a big city where there are a lot of public johns. If only we could find a public toilet, we could urinate and defecate to our heart's content."

The wound to my heart would not be cured by going to a city. But why did my father refer to me as Chopin? Thinking that I was not the only one who was hurt, I decided not to persist. Hold on . . . I quite agreed with Father when he said that this town was no longer any place to stay. My defenselessness as I stood urinating made me feel keenly uneasy.

We abandoned the carriage. But my father flatly refused to take off the box. As the responsibility for the present situation was half his, he insisted that it was his duty as my father to go on playing the role of the horse for the time being. Thereupon I got astride my father's box and turned my back on the town I had lived in for so long.

When we arrived in the city we at once took a garret room with a piano and decided to put our time to good use. I had the impression that we had simply turned and entered her house from the back, but that point was not clear. Handwork is best for diverting attention from grief. Father got hold of some art paper and pens somewhere or other. Using the piano as my desk, I devoted myself to drawing her from memory. Needless to say, as I became more practiced, the portraits turned into those of a nude woman.

"Chopin, your talent's not bad. I admit that, and I think you realize it, but then our financial situation is not so terribly brilliant. So how about it? Try to go easy on the paper and paint smaller pictures."

Father was right. But whether the paper was large or small was not the point. It was easier to draw smaller pen sketches. I continued working, gradually decreasing the size of the paper. Since I was proportionately more rapid finishing a drawing when I reduced the dimensions, I used more and more paper. At length, using a magnifying glass and attaching pieces of paper the size of the flat of my thumb with pins to my board, I accustomed myself to drawing lines so fine that they were indistinguishable to the naked eye. Only during the time I concentrated on this work could I be with her.

At one point I noticed something strange. The garret room, which should have been perfectly quiet, was filled with people. Why had I not noticed until now? From the door to the front of the piano a queue had formed and apparently stretched out into the corridor. The person at the head put money into the box (my father, of course) beside the piano and received with great deference the picture I had just finished painting. I was not all that taken aback. I also sensed that this situation had been going on for quite some time. That is, the food had got much better lately, and the old piano that served as a desk had at one point transformed into a new grand. Father's box as well had made great progress; from cardboard it had turned into one of genuine red leather with buckles. All unbeknownst to me we were apparently beginning to be widely accepted by the world. No sooner did I make a picture than it was sold, and no matter how many I went on sketching, the line of buyers showed absolutely no signs of slackening.

But at this point such a state of affairs was without importance. Apparently with the money we earned we had bought a real horse, but that had nothing to do with me. Actually, since the breakup of the marriage I had never seen my father once leave the box, and so I was in fact suspicious whether he was my real father or not. My dejection came from the fact that although the girl in my pictures was always the same, the real girl had grown older with the passage of time, and I should never be able to get her back. Every time I thought about it, the pain of our parting was vividly re-

vived, and from my slackened tear ducts tears began to overflow for no reason at all. Instantly, my father stretched his
hand from the box, shook out a new silk handkerchief, and
applied it to my eyes. Anyway since the picture I was drawing
was small, it would smudge at once with a single teardrop and
be useless.

Since I have been painting these pictures there is no
person who does not know my name now. You won't see an
encyclopedia that doesn't have an article on Chopin as the
producer as well as the inventor of the first stamp in the
world. But mail operations have progressed, and along with
their gradual nationalization my name has become known
as that of a counterfeiter of stamps. This is apparently
the most convincing reason why my portrait cannot be ex-
hibited in any post office. Only the red of the red box that
my father regularly used at the end of his life is even now,
in part, used on postboxes.

Five Minutes
to Curtain Time

—A sultry wind is blowing between you and me now. A
sensual, burning wind is blowing around us. I do not know
precisely when it began. In the force of the wind and in the
heat I seem to have lost my sense of time.

But in any case I realize too that the direction of the
wind will probably change. Suddenly it will turn into a cool
westerly wind. And then this hot wind will be stripped away
from my skin like a mirage, and I shall not even be able to

recollect it. Yes, the hot wind is too violent. Within itself is concealed the premonition of its end.

Why, I wonder? If I search for the explanation it will not be impossible to find. Yet the important thing is whether or not you intend to listen to it. Anyway I realize that I'm putting on a one-man show, but I don't want to bore you. What about it . . . shall I go on, or . . . ?

—Yes, yes, if you make it short. . . .

—Short? About five minutes . . . ?

—Five minutes will be just about right, I think.

—Of course, we're in love, you know. It's a different love from one that gradually grows, turning into a soaring tower of mist, solidifying, and reaching completion. It's a paradoxical love, beginning at the end . . . a love that commences from the realization that it is lost. A poet said it well. It is beautiful to love, but ugly to be loved. In love that begins with lost love, therefore, there are no shadows at all. I do not know whether it is beautiful or not, but in any case there is no grief in the pain of this kind of love.

—Why is that?

—Why is what?

—What's the purpose of going on talking about what's over and done?

—It's not over. Our affair begins with love lost. Actually the fiery wind is blowing harder.

—It's because it's summer that it's hot.

—Apparently you're incapable of understanding. This is a tale, of course. This story is in the act of taking place. Since you hear it you have the obligation of being one of the cast of characters. Now you're told someone's in love with you. What a quandary I'll be in if you don't play the part you're assigned, no matter how uncomfortable or ridiculous.

—Why, I wonder?

—The important thing is not the end. The thing to consider is the reality of your feeling the fiery wind on your skin. The denouement is not the problem. Now the fiery wind itself is important. In this fiery wind words and sensations that have been asleep give out a blue light as if they possess high-voltage electricity. This is a rare time when a man can see with his eyes the soul as substance.

—Amazing. If you woo one like that you'll manage never to be hurt. But your intentions are too obvious.

—I suppose . . . about half is true. But if you can't accept the other half at all, we might as well stop.

—You do want to go on don't you?

—Of course.

—You have the right to two minutes more.

—You're forcing yourself.

—You had better not waste any time.

—All right, I'll be careful of the time. I don't expect to get time back. Compared to the you in my heart, the I in yours is insignificant. But when I try to escape from that pain time melts slowly away. If I seriously command the techniques of wooing, then there is hope of coming into possession of a little peace and happiness. So I want to cherish that fiery wind that is so difficult to come by, that begins with love lost. Marvelous forests of words and seas of desire . . . time stops just by touching your skin lightly with my fingers, and eternity draws near. In the pain of this fiery wind a physical transformation that will not disappear until I die is effected on me.

Whereupon the Play Came to an End Without Even the Bell Ringing for the Curtain

Now I can speak out clearly with confidence. I was not wrong. Perhaps I failed, but I was not wrong. My failure is no cause for regret. Because I have not particularly gone on living for the conclusion.

I hear the sound of the front door shutting.

She has gone. At this point I am neither angry nor bitter. The sound of the door closing was filled with deep sympathy and compassion. There was no enmity or strife between us. I imagine that even she, if it were possible, would have wished to disappear without using the front door. Thus she was hesitant about slamming it. After waiting ten minutes I shall nail up the door. I don't really expect her back. I shall simply wait until she gets far enough away so that she will not hear the sound of hammering.

When I finish with the entrance, there only remains the lock on the door of the emergency stairs on the second floor. As the windows and vents are securely blocked with plywood or cardboard, there is no place for the sunlight to enter during the day. This is all the more true now on this overcast evening. The whole building is entirely cut off from the outside world, and there are neither entrances nor exits. After seeing to this, I leave. It is an escape of which only a box man is capable. As for where I escape to and by what means, I intend to write about that last of all in these notes.

A ten-minute lapse.

Now I have just nailed up the entrance. My aim was off, and I grazed the base of the nail of my left thumb. A little blood seeped out, but the pain went away at once.

When I think about it, we did not after all exchange a single word from the time I returned from outside to when she left. I had some regret. But I imagined that the regret would not vanish just by having talked with her. The stage where words were useful had already passed. By just exchanging glances we already understood each other. This too-complete communication was a phenomenon that appeared in the process of our disintegrating love.

Her expression was a little tense. Or perhaps it just looked that way because of the light makeup. Anyway the change of expression was of little importance to me, being merely a small part of the change in her. The important thing was that she was dressed. What the clothing was was scarcely the question at this juncture. For close to two months she had been living naked. I, too, in my box, was naked. At home we were naked together. And except for us there was nobody there. We had taken off the name plate and the sign from the door and turned out the red lamp at the gate, and even callers who stopped in by mistake completely ceased coming. There was no need even to put out the sign canceling examinations.

Once a day I would put on the box and go out into the town. Wandering about the streets like a transparent person, I would go around collecting miscellaneous items for daily use, principally foodstuffs. If I did not go into a given store more than once a month, I had no worry about being chal-

lenged. We could not live high on the hog, but we also
didn't lack any comforts. I was confident that if there were
just the two of us, we could go on living like this for any
number of years.

When I would come up the back emergency stairs and
take off my boots and box in the corridor on the second floor,
she would be waiting for me and come running up from below. This was the most exciting moment in the whole day.
I would always get an erection, though for a short while.
Swaying, we would hug each other so closely there was not
a sliver of space between us. However, our vocabulary was
comically poor. Her head came just to my nose, and when
I would murmur how fragrant her hair smelled, she would
follow up with how smooth and round my buttocks were,
giving them a succession of little pats. But I hardly think
that's the point. The efficacy of words extends up to a line
eight feet away, at which point one can distinguish the other
person clearly as different. Nor could I imagine that the
morgue by the stairway would cast its shadow between the
two of us. We had decided to ignore it completely, and when
we did the room was in fact nonexistent.

After some minutes, at about the time my erection was
going down, we at length broke our embrace and turned
toward the kitchen at the end of the corridor. Even though
we had separated, we always kept our bodies in contact. For
example, while she was peeling potatoes or chopping leeks
at the sink, I would sit at her feet and slowly keep passing
my hand over her legs. Mold was growing faintly on the
kitchen floor. The real kitchen was downstairs, and this one
was neglected, almost unused; it had been set up previously
for the inpatients of the hospital. That was the only reason
why we began using this one. There was an empty room
across the corridor where it was convenient to pile up the

kitchen wastes. Old vegetables, fish heads, and similar things were temporarily kept in plastic bags, but the mice broke into them for food, and the contents lay scattered everywhere on the floor. After a half day they began to rot, and a clinging stench spilled out every time the door was opened and closed. We took no notice of that. For one thing, when you're touching skin with someone else it seems that your sense of smell undergoes a transformation. And then too perhaps we sensed without realizing it that it provided a good opportunity to forget the existence of the morgue. We talked only about our optimistic estimate that it would take at least half a year to fill up the room with garbage.

But was it in fact optimistic? I think we had simply abandoned hope from the beginning. Passion is the urge to burn oneself out. Perhaps we were only too much in a hurry to burn ourselves out. We were afraid of our love stopping before burning out, but we were not sure we wanted to go on the way people usually do. We could not imagine things as far as a half year in the future, when the room would be full of garbage. We continued touching one part or another of each other's bodies the whole day long. We rarely went out of a circle eight feet in diameter. At that distance the other person could almost not be seen, but we didn't consider that particularly inconvenient. If in our imaginations we connected the various parts of ourselves together, we had the feeling of actually seeing each other, and more than that our sense of liberation at not being seen by the other one was great. I dissolved into parts in front of her. Other than her comments on the feel of my buttocks, she gave absolutely no voice to any opinion touching my whole personality . . . whether she liked it or whether she abhorred it. That didn't particularly bother me. Words themselves had already begun to lose their meaning. Time had stopped.

Three days, three weeks, were all the same. No matter how long our love goes on burning, when it is burnt out it is over in an instant.

Thus when I noticed that instead of a naked girl running up, the one today was dressed and looking up at me in silence, I was not particularly nonplused and was able to manage merely experiencing a little disappointment, as if returning to the starting point. But my own nakedness seemed terribly piteous. As if sent away, I returned to my box, and there was nothing to do but to wait motionlessly for her to leave. She frowned and looked around, but pretended not to take notice of me. She seemed only to be trying to identify the source of the stench. She slowly looked over her shoulder and then withdrew to her own room. Muffling my steps, I too returned to the former examination room. If this was the starting point, would we be successful commencing all over again from the beginning? Of course, it should be possible to start over again any number of times. Straining my ears, I listened for her out in the corridor. There was no sign of her moving. Could she be waiting for me to suggest starting over again? But no matter how many times we began again, the same time, the same place would simply repeat.

The dial of the clock wears out unevenly;
Most worn
Is the area round eight.
As it is stared at with abrasive glances
unfailingly twice a day,
It is weathered away.
On the other side

The area at two
Is only half as worn,
For closed eyes at night
Pass without stopping.
If there is one who possesses a flat watch evenly
      worn,
It is he who, failing at the start, is running
      one lap behind.

Thus the world is always
A lap fast—
The world he thinks he sees
Has not yet begun.
Illusory time,
When the hands stand vertically on the dial;
Without the bell announcing the raising of the
      curtain,
The play has come to an end.

.   .   .

And now my last confession. I actually heard the noise of
the door to her room. I could not have heard the front door.
That has been nailed up from the first. It had been the most
trouble and was firmly closed off. She cannot get out that
way. The emergency stairs are locked; she has to be confined
within the building now. Only that confounded blouse and
skirt are separating her from me. But if I cut off the electricity the effect of her clothes too will end. If she cannot be
seen, that will be the same as her being naked. I can't stand
being seen by her when she is wearing clothes. In the dark-

ness it's the same as being with a blind man. She will again become gentle. I am completely liberated from the need to wrack my brains for some uninviting plan to gouge out her eyes or anything like that.

Instead of leaving the box, I shall enclose the world within it. Now the world must have closed its eyes. Things will definitely go the way I wish. In the building articles such as matches, candles, lighters, to say nothing of my flashlight, anything that creates shadows or form has been disposed of.

After a time, I cut the power. I looked in at her room, not purposely making myself conspicuous, but not especially stealthily either. Of course, I have taken off the box and am naked. I expected only faint signs of her in the depths of the darkness and was astounded at the unexpected change in the room. There was much too much discrepancy with what I had expected. I was more greatly perplexed than surprised. The space that was supposed to be a room had changed into an alleyway, like one behind shops, adjoining some station. Across the alley from the shops stood a building with a real estate office combined with a privately run baggage room. It was a narrow alley barely large enough to let a person by, and even without any special knowledge of the place one could at once assume from the topography and the direction that it was a dead-end alley cut off by the precincts of some station. Except to urinate, no one would be entering.

The passage was blocked by bundles of rubber hose, an incinerator made from a metal drum, cardboard boxes piled up, and a line of about five bowls of bonsai that had begun to dry out, mixed in with old bicycles. For what purpose, I wondered, had she lost herself in such a place? Even supposing her objective was to find cardboard, did she intend to steal out of here and go somewhere?

When I went ahead, treading my way through the trash, I came to a narrow little stairway in concrete just where it seemed to be a dead end. It was not very steep and was about five steps high. When I reached the bottom, it was hard to believe, but a sturdy concrete balcony jutted out. One could at once infer that the plans for an overpass had altered during the course of construction and that it had been abandoned in its present state.

I went down to the balcony. Suddenly the wind strengthened, and the sounds of night construction on the railroad sighed in the distance. The sky was tinged a reddish purple, doubtless the reflection against the clouds of the neon lights in the streets. I took another step, and suddenly right before me there was nothing, and I could see the roadbed twenty or twenty-five feet below. I had the feeling of being in a construction elevator suspended in the skeleton of an unfinished building and between two concrete walls that were shedding tears like bird droppings.

I must find her. But there is no place further to advance from here. This is a part of closed space after all. Nevertheless, where could she have vanished to? Gingerly I looked down, but it was dark and I could see nothing. If I tried taking another step further, what would happen? I was curious. But I supposed I would be no closer to finding her. Anyway the whole thing was simply taking place in the same building.

Oh, yes, before I forget, one more important addition. In processing the box the most important thing in all events is to ensure leaving plenty of blank space for scribbling. No, there'll always be plenty of blank space. No matter how assiduous one is in scribbling, one can never cover all the blank space. It always surprises me, but scribbling of a certain type is blank itself. At least there'll always remain enough space to write one's name in. But if you don't wish to believe even that, it doesn't make the slightest difference.

Actually a box, in appearance, is purely and simply a right-angled parallelepiped, but when you look at it from within it's a labyrinth of a hundred interconnecting puzzle rings. The more you struggle the more the box, like an extra outer skin growing from the body, creates new twists for the labyrinth, making the inner disposition increasingly more complex.

One thing alone is certain and that is that even she, who has at present vanished, is hiding somewhere in this labyrinth. She's not necessarily running away, she just can't find where I am. At this point I can speak out clearly with assurance. I have no regret. The clues are numerous, and it is reasonable that the truth should exist in proportion to their number.

I hear the siren of an approaching ambulance.

A Note About the Author

Kobo Abé was born in Tokyo in 1924 but grew up in Muk-
den, Manchuria, where his father, a doctor, was on the staff
of the medical school. As a young man Mr. Abé was interested
in mathematics and insect collecting, as well as the works of
Poe, Dostoevsky, Nietzsche, Heidegger, Jaspers, and Kafka. He
received a medical degree from Tokyo University in 1948, but
he has never practiced medicine. In that same year he published
his first book, *The Road Sign at the End of the Street*. In 1951
he was awarded the most important Japanese literary prize, the
Akutagawa, for his novella *The Crime of Mr. S. Karuma*. In
1960 his novel *The Woman in the Dunes* won the Yomiuri
Prize for Literature. It was made into a film by Hiroshi Teshigahara in 1963 and won the Jury Prize at the Cannes Film
Festival, and was the first of Mr. Abé's novels to be published in
translation in the United States (1964). *The Face of Another*
(1966)was also made into a film by Mr. Teshigahara. Most recently published here were his novels *The Ruined Map* (1969)
and *Inter Ice Age 4* (1970). Mr. Abé lives with his wife, Machi,
an artist, on the outskirts of Tokyo.

A Note About the Translator

E. Dale Saunders, translator of Kobo Abé's *The Woman in the Dunes* (1964), *The Face of Another* (1966), *The Ruined Map* (1969), and *Inter Ice Age 4* (1970), received his A.B. from Western Reserve University (1941), his M.A. from Harvard (1948), and his Ph.D. from the University of Paris (1952). He is Professor of Japanese at the University of Pennsylvania and has also taught at International Christian University, Tokyo, and at Harvard University. Among his publications are *Mudrā: A Study of Symbolic Gestures in Japanese Buddhist Sculpture* (1960) and *Buddhism in Japan* (1964).

'It is one of those purely sad, sadly pure novels that deserves
to be rediscovered'
Julian Barnes, *Guardian*

'I have read few novels as deep̶ ̶ ̶ ̶ ̶ ̶lear as John
Williams' *Stoner*. It deserves t̶ ̶ ̶ ̶ ̶ ̶d̶ ̶a̶ ̶quiet classic of
Ameri̶ ̶
Chad Harbach̶ ̶ ̶ ̶ *e Art of Fielding*

'A beautiful a̶ ̶ ̶ing ̶ ̶ovel, as sweeping, intimate and
̶ ̶erious as life itself'
Geoff Dyer

'A great American novel . . . the masterly prose is hypnotic
. . . a very powerful reading experience'
Bret Easton Ellis

'A wonderful novel. Simple and direct, executed in a calm
and faultless prose, it is also subtle and incredibly moving.
A biography of Stoner, a diligent Midwestern academic and
a seemingly unexceptional man, the novel amounts to one
of fiction's most profound and unforgettable portraits.'
Adam Foulds

'A stunning novel . . . more timeless, more important, more
real, than most novels can ever hope to be. *Stoner* is something rare and precious that should never be forgotten'
Eowyn Ivey, author of the international bestseller
The Snow Child

EX LIBRIS

VINTAGE CLASSICS

STONER

John Williams was born on 29 August 1922 in Clarksville, Texas. He served in the United States Army Air Force from 1942 to 1945 in China, Burma and India. The Swallow Press published his first novel, *Nothing But the Night*, in 1948, as well as his first book of poems, *The Broken Landscape*, in 1949. Macmillan published Williams' second novel, *Butcher's Crossing*, in 1960. After receiving his B.A. and M.A. from the University of Denver, and his Ph.D from the University of Missouri, Williams returned in 1954 to the University of Denver where he taught literature and the craft of writing for thirty years. In 1963 Williams received a fellowship to study at Oxford University where he received a Rockefeller grant that enabled him to travel and research in Italy for his last novel, *Augustus*, published in 1972. John Williams died in Fayetteville, Arkansas on March 4, 1994.

OTHER WORKS BY JOHN WILLIAMS

Nothing But the Night
Butcher's Crossing
Augustus

JOHN WILLIAMS

Stoner

WITH AN INTRODUCTION BY
John McGahern

VINTAGE BOOKS
London

Published by Vintage 2012

30

Copyright © John Williams 1965
Introduction © John McGahern 2003

First published in Great Britain by Longman in 1973
First published by Vintage in 2003

Vintage
Random House, 20 Vauxhall Bridge Road,
London SW1V 2SA

www.vintage-classics.info

Addresses for companies within The Random House Group Limited can be
found at: www.randomhouse.co.uk/offices.htm

The Random House Group Limited Reg. No. 954009

A CIP catalogue record for this book
is available from the British Library

ISBN 9780099561545

The Random House Group Limited supports The Forest Stewardship
Council® (FSC®), the leading international forest-certification organisation.
Our books carrying the FSC label are printed on FSC®-certified paper. FSC is
the only forest-certification scheme supported by the leading environmental
organisations, including Greenpeace. Our paper procurement policy can be
found at www.randomhouse.co.uk/environment

Typeset in Bembo by Palimpsest Book Production Limited,
Falkirk, Stirlingshire
Printed and bound by
CPI Group (UK) Ltd, Croydon, CR0 4YY

Introduction

On the opening page of this classic novel of university life, and the life of the heart and the mind, John Williams states bluntly the mark Stoner left behind: 'Stoner's colleagues, who held him in no particular esteem when he was alive, speak of him rarely now; to the older ones his name is a reminder of the end that awaits them all, and to the younger ones it is merely a sound that evokes no sense of the past and no identity with which they can associate themselves or their careers.' In plain prose, which seems able to reflect effortlessly every shade of thought and feeling, Williams proceeds to subvert that familiar worldly judgement by bringing Stoner, and everything linked to him – the time, the place, the people – vividly to life, the passion of the writing masked by a coolness and clarity of intelligence.

Stoner's origins were as humble as the earth his parents worked. In the beginning they are shown as hardly more animate than their own clay, but in vivid scenes, such as their attendance at Stoner's wedding to a banker's daughter, their innate dignity and gentleness contradict that easy judgement, and towards the novel's end Stoner himself seems to acquire their mute, patient strength.

Stoner was an only child, and though good at school had no other expectation than to one day take over the fields he was already helping to work. One evening after the day's toil his father said, 'Country agent came by last week . . . Says they have a new school at the University of Columbia. They call it a college of agriculture. Says he thinks you ought to go.'

At the university he earns his bed and board by working on a nearby farm owned by a first cousin of his mother. This is bare board and hard, brutal work, but he gets through it stoically, in much the same way as he gets through the science courses at the university. 'The course in soil chemistry caught his interest in a general way . . . But the required survey of English literature troubled and disquieted him in a way nothing had ever done before.'

The instructor Archer Sloane changes his life. He abandons science to study literature. At the prompting of his mentor, he stays on at the university, labouring on the cousin's farm while obtaining his Master of Arts. At his graduation he tries to tell his parents that he will not be returning to their farm when they come to attend the degree ceremony. 'If you think you ought to stay here and study your books, then that's what you ought to do,' his father concludes towards the end of that moving scene.

The novel then details the outwardly undistinguished career of an assistant professor of English within the walls of the university: his teaching, his reading and his writing, his friendships, his falling in love with an idealised woman, his slow and bitter discovery of that person once they marry, and how their gentle, pliable daughter becomes the wife's chosen battleground. Outside the marriage, Stoner's affair with a young teacher becomes entwined in bitter, vindictive university politics.

This love affair between two intelligent people is brought to life with a rare delicacy. A healthy sensuality is set against their vulnerability as they discover the glory of the first day of the world. 'The life they had together was one that neither of them had really imagined. They grew from passion to lust to a deep sensuality that renewed itself from moment to moment.' They study, they converse, they play. 'They learned to be together without speaking and they got the habit of repose.' Not only did they find pleasure in one another but meaning, which is drawn with playful, affectionate irony. 'Like all lovers, they spoke much of themselves, as if they might thereby understand the world which made them possible.'

Integral as it is to the plot, the love affair serves more importantly in the overall vision as a source of light in the darkness of Stoner's marriage, a powerful suggestion of the happiness that might have been.

Stoner's wife is a type that can be glimpsed in much American writing, through such different sensibilities as O'Neill, Tennessee Williams, Faulkner, Scott Fitzgerald – beautiful, unstable, educated to observe the surfaces of a privileged and protected society – but never can that type of wife have been revealed as remorselessly as here:

She was educated upon the premise that she would be protected from the gross events that life might thrust in her way, and upon the premise that she had no other duty than to be a graceful and accomplished accessory to that protection, since she belonged to a social and economic class to which protection was an almost sacred obligation . . . Her moral training, both at the schools she attended and at home, was negative in nature, prohibitive in intent, and almost entirely sexual. The sexuality, however, was indirect and unacknow-ledged; therefore it suffused every other part of her education, which received most of its energy from that recessive and unspoken moral force. She learned that she would have duties towards her husband and family and that she must fulfill them . . . Her needlepoint was delicate and useless, she painted misty landscapes of thin water-color washes, and she played the piano with a forceless but precise hand; yet she was ignorant of her own bodily functions, she had never been alone to care for her own self one day of her life, nor could it ever have occurred to her that she might become responsible for the well-being of another . . . Upon that inner privacy William Stoner now intruded.

They marry without knowledge of one another and with nothing in common but desire. Their sexual incompatibility is described with the same chasteness as the deep sensuality of the lovers:

> When he returned, Edith was in bed with the covers pulled to her chin, her face turned upward, her eyes closed, a thin frown creasing her forehead. Silently, as if she were asleep, Stoner undressed and got into bed beside her. For several moments he lay with his desire, which had become an impersonal thing, belonging to himself alone. He spoke to Edith, as if to find a haven for what he felt; she did not answer. He put his hand upon her and felt beneath the thin cloth of her nightgown the flesh he had longed for. He moved his hand upon her; she did not stir; her frown deepened. Again he spoke, saying her name to silence; then he moved his body upon her, gentle in his clumsiness. When he touched the softness of her thighs she turned her head sharply away and lifted her arm to cover her eyes. She made no sound.

Her sexuality then changes violently when she decides she wants a child and ceases completely as soon as she is pregnant. Soon after their daughter is born, the child becomes the focus of the mother's inner turmoil, her unresolved hatred of Stoner. If the portrait has a flaw, it is in its remorselessness, yet such is the clarity of the understanding that we come to accept it simply as the way things are, in the same way as the love affair becomes the way things ought to have been.

In the many minor portraits the touch is equally sure and psychologically astute: 'Like many men who consider their success incomplete, he was extraordinarily vain and consumed with a sense of his own importance. Every ten or fifteen minutes he removed a large gold watch from his vest pocket, looked at it, and nodded to himself.' There are Stoner's friends, the brilliant David Masters, who gives voice to some of John Williams's own views on the nature of a university, goes to the war and is killed in France; the worldly Gordon Finch who returns from the war with military honours to the university, where he rises to be dean of the faculty. Finch remains Stoner's loyal if sometimes exasperated ally and protector within the university, and his uncomplicated friendship is there for the whole of Stoner's life. We witness, too, the slow decline of Stoner's mentor, Archer Sloane, and the rise of his replacement, Hollis Lomax, who becomes Stoner's implacable enemy. In a novel of brilliant portraits, that of Hollis Lomax is the most complex. Some of the scenes of conflict are almost unbearable in their intensity.

Stoner is also a novel about work, the hard unyielding work of the farms; the work of living within a destructive marriage and bringing up a daughter with patient mutability in a poisoned household; the work of teaching literature to mostly unresponsive students. How Williams manages to dramatise this almost impossible material is itself a small miracle.

In a rare interview given late in life, John Williams says of Stoner:

> I think he's a *real* hero. A lot of people who have read the novel think that Stoner had such a sad and bad life. I think he had a very good life. He had a better life than most people do, certainly. He was doing what he wanted to do, he had some feeling for what he was doing, he had some sense of the importance of the job he was doing. He was a witness to values that are important . . . The important thing in the novel to me is Stoner's sense of a *job*. Teaching to him is a job—a job in the good and honourable sense of the word. His job gave him a particular kind of identity and made him what he was . . . It's the love of the thing that's essential. And if you love something, you're going to understand it. And if you understand it, you're going to learn a lot. The lack of that love defines a bad teacher . . . You never know all the results of what you do. I think it all boils down to what I was trying to get at in *Stoner*. You've got to keep the faith. The important thing is to keep the tradition going, because the tradition is civilisation.

John Williams is best known for his novels, *Nothing But the Night, Stoner, Butcher's Crossing*, and *Augustus*, for which he won the National Book Award in 1973. He also published two volumes of verse and edited a classic anthology of English Renaissance poetry. The novels are not only remarkable for their style but also for the diversity of their settings. No two novels are alike except for the clarity of the prose; they could easily pass for the work of four different writers. In the course of the long and fascinating interview that Williams gave to Brian Wooley from which I have quoted his remarks about Stoner, it grows clear that of the four novels *Stoner* is the most personal, in that it is closely linked to John Williams's own life and career, without in any way being autobiographical. The interview was given in 1985, the year Williams retired as Professor of English from the University of Denver where he had taught for thirty years. Pressed towards the end of the interview he complains about the change away from pure study within the universities, the results of which cannot be predicted, towards a purely utilitarian, problem-solving way of doing things more efficiently, both in the arts and sciences, all of which can be predicated and measured. Then, more specifically, Williams complains about the changes in the teaching of literature and the attitude to the text 'as if a novel or poem is something to be *studied* and *understood* rather than *experienced*.' Wooley then suggests playfully, 'It's to be exegeted, in other words.' 'Yes. As if it were a kind of puzzle.' 'And literature is written to be entertaining?' Wooley suggests again. 'Absolutely. My God, to read without joy is stupid.'

There is entertainment of a very high order to be found in *Stoner*, what Williams himself describes as 'an escape into reality' as well as pain and joy. The clarity of the prose is in itself an unadulterated joy. Set a generation back from Williams's own, the novel is distanced not only by this clarity and intelligence but by the way the often unpromising material is so coolly dramatised. The small world of the university opens out to war and politics, to the years of the Depression and the millions who 'once walked erect in their own identities', and then to the whole of life.

If the novel can be said to have one central idea, it is surely that of love, the many forms love takes and all the

forces that oppose it. 'It [love] was a passion neither of
the mind nor of the heart, it was a force that comprehended
them both, as if they were but the matter of love, its specific
substance.'

JOHN MCGAHERN
2002

1

William Stoner entered the University of Missouri as a freshman in the year 1910, at the age of nineteen. Eight years later, during the height of World War I, he received his Doctor of Philosophy degree and accepted an instructorship at the same University, where he taught until his death in 1956. He did not rise above the rank of assistant professor, and few students remembered him with any sharpness after they had taken his courses. When he died his colleagues made a memorial contribution of a medieval manuscript to the University library. This manuscript may still be found in the Rare Books Collection, bearing the inscription: 'Presented to the Library of the University of Missouri, in memory of William Stoner, Department of English. By his colleagues.'

An occasional student who comes upon the name may wonder idly who William Stoner was, but he seldom pursues his curiosity beyond a casual question. Stoner's colleagues, who held him in no particular esteem when he was alive, speak of him rarely now; to the older ones, his name is a reminder of the end that awaits them all, and to the younger ones it is merely a sound which evokes no sense of the past and no identity with which they can associate themselves or their careers.

★

He was born in 1891 on a small farm in central Missouri near the village of Booneville, some forty miles from Columbia, the home of the University. Though his parents were young at the time of his birth—his father twenty-five, his mother barely twenty—Stoner thought of them, even when he was a boy, as old. At thirty his father looked fifty; stooped by labor, he gazed without hope at the arid patch of land that sustained the family from one year to the next. His mother regarded her life patiently, as if it were a long moment that she had to endure. Her eyes were pale and blurred, and the tiny wrinkles around them were enhanced by thin graying hair worn straight over her head and caught in a bun at the back.

From the earliest time he could remember, William Stoner had his duties. At the age of six he milked the bony cows, slopped the pigs in the sty a few yards from the house, and gathered small eggs from a flock of spindly chickens. And even when he started attending the rural school eight miles from the farm, his day, from before dawn until after dark, was filled with work of one sort or another. At seventeen his shoulders were already beginning to stoop beneath the weight of his occupation.

It was a lonely household, of which he was an only child, and it was bound together by the necessity of its toil. In the evenings the three of them sat in the small kitchen lighted by a single kerosene lamp, staring into the yellow flame; often during the hour or so between supper and bed, the only sound that could be heard was the weary movement of a body in a straight chair and the soft creak of a timber giving a little beneath the age of the house.

The house was built in a crude square, and the unpainted timbers sagged around the porch and doors. It had with the years taken on the colors of the dry land—gray and brown, streaked with white. On one side of the house was a long parlor, sparsely furnished with straight chairs and a few hewn tables, and a kitchen, where the family spent most of its little time together. On the other side were two bedrooms, each furnished with an iron bedstead enameled white, a single straight chair, and a table, with a lamp and a wash basin on it. The floors were of unpainted plank, unevenly spaced and cracking with age, up through which dust steadily seeped and was swept back each day by Stoner's mother.

At school he did his lessons as if they were chores only somewhat less exhausting than those around the farm. When he finished high school in the spring of 1910, he expected to take over more of the work in the fields; it seemed to him that his father grew slower and more weary with the passing months.

But one evening in late spring, after the two men had spent a full day hoeing corn, his father spoke to him in the kitchen, after the supper dishes had been cleared away.

'County agent come by last week.'

William looked up from the red-and-white-checked oilcloth spread smoothly over the round kitchen table. He did not speak.

'Says they have a new school at the University in Columbia. They call it a College of Agriculture. Says he thinks you ought to go. It takes four years.'

'Four years,' William said. 'Does it cost money?'

'You could work your room and board,' his father said. 'Your ma has a first cousin owns a place just outside Columbia. There would be books and things. I could send you two or three dollars a month.'

William spread his hands on the tablecloth, which gleamed dully under the lamplight. He had never been farther from home than Booneville, fifteen miles away. He swallowed to steady his voice.

'Think you could manage the place all by yourself?' he asked.

'Your ma and me could manage. I'd plant the upper twenty in wheat; that would cut down the hand work.'

William looked at his mother. 'Ma?' he asked.

She said tonelessly, 'You do what your pa says.'

'You really want me to go?' he asked, as if he half hoped for a denial. 'You really want me to?'

His father shifted his weight on the chair. He looked at his thick, callused fingers, into the cracks of which soil had penetrated so deeply that it could not be washed away. He laced his fingers together and held them up from the table, almost in an attitude of prayer.

'I never had no schooling to speak of,' he said, looking at his hands. 'I started working a farm when I finished sixth grade. Never held with schooling when I was a young 'un. But now I don't know. Seems like the land gets drier and harder to work every year; it ain't rich like it was when I was a boy. County agent says they got new ideas, ways of doing things they teach you at the University. Maybe he's right. Sometimes when I'm working the field I get to thinking.' He paused. His fingers tightened upon themselves, and his clasped hands dropped to the table. 'I get to thinking—' He scowled at his hands and shook his head. 'You go on to the University come fall. Your ma and me will manage.'

It was the longest speech he had ever heard his father make. That fall he went to Columbia and enrolled in the University as a freshman in the College of Agriculture.

He came to Columbia with a new black broadcloth suit ordered from the catalogue of Sears & Roebuck and paid

4

for with his mother's egg money, a worn greatcoat that had belonged to his father, a pair of blue serge trousers that once a month he had worn to the Methodist church in Booneville, two white shirts, two changes of work clothing, and twenty-five dollars in cash, which his father had borrowed from a neighbor against the fall wheat. He started walking from Booneville, where in the early morning his father and mother brought him on the farm's flat-bed, mule-drawn wagon.

It was a hot fall day, and the road from Booneville to Columbia was dusty; he had been walking for nearly an hour before a goods wagon came up beside him and the driver asked him if he wanted a ride. He nodded and got up on the wagon seat. His serge trousers were red with dust to his knees, and his sun- and wind-browned face was caked with dirt, where the road dust had mingled with his sweat. During the long ride he kept brushing at his trousers with awkward hands and running his fingers through his straight sandy hair, which would not lie flat on his head.

They got to Columbia in the late afternoon. The driver let Stoner off at the outskirts of town and pointed to a group of buildings shaded by tall elms. 'That's your University,' he said. 'That's where you'll be going to school.'

For several minutes after the man had driven off, Stoner stood unmoving, staring at the complex of buildings. He had never before seen anything so imposing. The red brick buildings stretched upward from a broad field of green that was broken by stone walks and small patches of garden. Beneath his awe, he had a sudden sense of security and serenity he had never felt before. Though it was late, he walked for many minutes about the edges of the campus, only looking, as if he had no right to enter.

It was nearly dark when he asked a passer-by directions

to Ashland Gravel, the road that would lead him to the farm owned by Jim Foote, the first cousin of his mother for whom he was to work; and it was after dark when he got to the white two-storied frame house where he was to live. He had not seen the Footes before, and he felt strange going to them so late.

They greeted him with a nod, inspecting him closely. After a moment, during which Stoner stood awkwardly in the door-way, Jim Foote motioned him into a small dim parlor crowded with overstuffed furniture and bric-a-brac on dully gleaming tables. He did not sit.

'Et supper?' Foote asked.

'No, sir,' Stoner answered.

Mrs Foote crooked an index finger at him and padded away. Stoner followed her through several rooms into a kitchen, where she motioned him to sit at a table. She put a pitcher of milk and several squares of cold cornbread before him. He sipped the milk, but his mouth, dry from excitement, would not take the bread.

Foote came into the room and stood beside his wife. He was a small man, not more than five feet three inches, with a lean face and a sharp nose. His wife was four inches taller, and heavy; rimless spectacles hid her eyes, and her thin lips were tight. The two of them watched hungrily as he sipped his milk.

'Feed and water the livestock, slop the pigs in the morning,' Foote said rapidly.

Stoner looked at him blankly. 'What?'

'That's what you do in the morning,' Foote said, 'before you leave for your school. Then in the evening you feed and slop again, gather the eggs, milk the cows. Chop firewood when you find time. Weekends, you help me with whatever I'm doing.'

6

'Yes, sir,' Stoner said.

Foote studied him for a moment. 'College,' he said and shook his head.

So for nine months' room and board he fed and watered the livestock, slopped pigs, gathered eggs, milked cows, and chopped firewood. He also plowed and harrowed fields, dug stumps (in the winter breaking through three inches of frozen soil), and churned butter for Mrs Foote, who watched him with her head bobbing in grim approval as the wooden churner splashed up and down through the milk.

He was quartered on an upper floor that had once been a storeroom; his only furniture was a black iron bedstead with sagging frames that supported a thin feather mattress, a broken table that held a kerosene lamp, a straight chair that sat unevenly on the floor, and a large box that he used as a desk. In the winter the only heat he got seeped up through the floor from the rooms below; he wrapped himself in the tattered quilts and blankets allowed him and blew on his hands so that they could turn the pages of his books without tearing them.

He did his work at the University as he did his work on the farm—thoroughly, conscientiously, with neither pleasure nor distress. At the end of his first year his grade average was slightly below a B; he was pleased that it was no lower and not concerned that it was no higher. He was aware that he had learned things that he had not known before, but this meant to him only that he might do as well in his second year as he had done in his first.

The summer after his first year of college he returned to his father's farm and helped with the crops. Once his father asked him how he liked school, and he replied that he liked it fine. His father nodded and did not mention the matter again.

It was not until he returned for his second year that William Stoner learned why he had come to college.

By his second year he was a familiar figure on the campus. In every season he wore the same black broadcloth suit, white shirt, and string tie; his wrists protruded from the sleeves of the jacket, and the trousers rode awkwardly about his legs, as if it were a uniform that had once belonged to someone else.

His hours of work increased with his employers' growing indolence, and he spent the long evenings in his room methodically doing his class assignments; he had begun the sequence that would lead him to a Bachelor of Science degree in the College of Agriculture, and during this first semester of his second year he had two basic sciences, a course from the school of Agriculture in soil chemistry, and a course that was rather perfunctorily required of all University students—a semester survey of English literature.

After the first few weeks he had little difficulty with the science courses; there was so much work to be done, so many things to be remembered. The course in soil chemistry caught his interest in a general way; it had not occurred to him that the brownish clods with which he had worked for most of his life were anything other than what they appeared to be, and he began vaguely to see that his growing knowledge of them might be useful when he returned to his father's farm. But the required survey of English literature troubled and disquieted him in a way nothing had ever done before.

The instructor was a man of middle age, in his early fifties; his name was Archer Sloane, and he came to his task of teaching with a seeming disdain and contempt, as if he perceived between his knowledge and what he could say a

8

gulf so profound that he would make no effort to close it. He was feared and disliked by most of his students, and he responded with a detached, ironic amusement. He was a man of middle height, with a long, deeply lined face, cleanly shaven; he had an impatient gesture of running his fingers through the shock of his gray curling hair. His voice was flat and dry, and it came through barely moving lips without expression or intonation; but his long thin fingers moved with grace and persuasion, as if giving to the words a shape that his voice could not.

Away from the classroom, doing his chores about the farm or blinking against the dim lamplight as he studied in his windowless attic room, Stoner was often aware that the image of this man had risen up before the eye of his mind. He had difficulty summoning up the face of any other of his instructors or remembering anything very specific about any other of his classes; but always on the threshold of his awareness waited the figure of Archer Sloane, and his dry voice, and his contemptuously offhand words about some passage from *Beowulf*, or some couplet of Chaucer's.

He found that he could not handle the survey as he did his other courses. Though he remembered the authors and their works and their dates and their influences, he nearly failed his first examination; and he did little better on his second. He read and reread his literature assignments so frequently that his work in other courses began to suffer; and still the words he read were words on pages, and he could not see the use of what he did.

And he pondered the words that Archer Sloane spoke in class, as if beneath their flat, dry meaning he might discover a clue that would lead him where he was intended to go; he hunched forward over the desk-top of a chair too small to hold him comfortably, grasping the edges of the desk-top so tightly that his knuckles showed white against his brown hard skin; he frowned intently and gnawed at his underlip. But as Stoner's and his classmates' attention grew more desperate, Archer Sloane's contempt grew more compelling. And once that contempt erupted into anger and was directed at William Stoner alone.

The class had read two plays by Shakespeare and was ending the week with a study of the sonnets. The students were edgy and puzzled, half frightened at the tension growing between themselves and the slouching figure that regarded them from behind the lectern. Sloane had read aloud to them the seventy-third sonnet; his eyes roved about the room and his lips tightened in a humorless smile.

'What does the sonnet mean?' he asked abruptly, and paused, his eyes searching the room with a grim and almost pleased hopelessness. 'Mr Wilbur?' There was no answer. 'Mr Schmidt?' Someone coughed. Sloane turned his dark bright eyes upon Stoner. 'Mr Stoner, what does the sonnet mean?'

Stoner swallowed and tried to open his mouth.

'It is a sonnet, Mr Stoner,' Sloane said dryly, 'a poetical composition of fourteen lines, with a certain pattern I am sure you have memorized. It is written in the English language, which I believe you have been speaking for some years. Its author is William Shakespeare, a poet who is dead, but who nevertheless occupies a position of some importance in the minds of a few.' He looked at Stoner for a moment more, and then his eyes went blank as they fixed unseeingly beyond the class. Without looking at his book he spoke the poem again; and his voice deepened and softened, as if the words and sounds and rhythms had for a moment become himself:

'That time of year thou mayst in me behold
When yellow leaves, or none, or few, do hang
Upon those boughs which shake against the cold,
Bare ruin'd choirs where late the sweet birds sang.
In me thou see'st the twilight of such day
As after sunset fadeth in the west;
Which by and by black night doth take away,
Death's second self, that seals up all in rest.
In me thou see'st the glowing of such fire,
That on the ashes of his youth doth lie,
As the death-bed whereon it must expire,
Consumed with that which it was nourisht by.
    This thou perceivest, which makes thy love
      more strong,
    To love that well which thou must leave ere long.'

In a moment of silence, someone cleared his throat. Sloane repeated the lines, his voice becoming flat, his own again.

'This thou perceivest, which makes thy love more
    strong,
To love that well which thou must leave ere long.'

Sloane's eyes came back to William Stoner, and he said dryly, 'Mr Shakespeare speaks to you across three hundred years, Mr Stoner; do you hear him?'

William Stoner realized that for several moments he had been holding his breath. He expelled it gently, minutely aware of his clothing moving upon his body as his breath went out of his lungs. He looked away from Sloane about the room. Light slanted from the windows and settled upon the faces of his fellow students, so that the illumination seemed to come from within them and go out against a dimness; a student blinked, and a thin shadow fell upon a cheek whose down had caught the sunlight. Stoner became aware that his fingers were unclenching their hard grip on his desk-top. He turned his hands about under his gaze, marveling at their brownness, at the intricate way the nails fit into his blunt finger-ends; he thought he could feel the blood flowing invisibly through the tiny veins and arteries, throbbing delicately and precariously from his fingertips through his body.

Sloane was speaking again. 'What does he say to you, Mr Stoner? What does his sonnet mean?'

Stoner's eyes lifted slowly and reluctantly. 'It means,' he said, and with a small movement raised his hands up toward the air; he felt his eyes glaze over as they sought the figure of Archer Sloane. 'It means,' he said again, and could not finish what he had begun to say.

Sloane looked at him curiously. Then he nodded abruptly and said, 'Class is dismissed.' Without looking at anyone he turned and walked out of the room.

William Stoner was hardly aware of the students about him who rose grumbling and muttering from their seats and shuffled out of the room. For several minutes after they left he sat unmoving, staring out before him at the narrow planked flooring that had been worn bare of varnish by the restless feet of students he would never see or know. He slid his own feet across the floor, hearing the dry rasp of wood on his soles, and feeling the rough-ness through the leather. Then he too got up and went slowly out of the room.

The thin chill of the late fall day cut through his clothing. He looked around him, at the bare gnarled branches of the trees that curled and twisted against the pale sky. Students, hurrying across the campus to their classes, brushed against him; he heard the mutter of their voices and the click of their heels upon the stone paths, and saw their faces, flushed by the cold, bent downward against a slight breeze. He looked at them curiously, as if he had not seen them before, and felt very distant from them and very close to them. He held the feeling to him as he hurried to his next class, and held it through the lecture by his professor in soil chemistry, against the droning voice that recited things to be written in notebooks and remembered by a process of drudgery that even now was becoming unfamiliar to him.

In the second semester of that school year William Stoner dropped his basic science courses and interrupted his Ag School sequence; he took introductory courses in philosophy and ancient history and two courses in English literature. In the summer he returned again to his parents' farm and helped his father with the crops and did not mention his work at the University.

When he was much older, he was to look back upon his last two undergraduate years as if they were an unreal time that belonged to someone else, a time that passed, not in the regular flow to which he was used, but in fits and starts. One moment was juxtaposed against another, yet isolated from it, and he had the feeling that he was removed from time, watching as it passed before him like a great unevenly turned diorama.

He became conscious of himself in a way that he had not done before. Sometimes he looked at himself in a mirror, at the long face with its thatch of dry brown hair, and touched his sharp cheekbones; he saw the thin wrists that protruded inches out of his coat sleeves; and he wondered if he appeared as ludicrous to others as he did to himself.

He had no plans for the future, and he spoke to no one

of his uncertainty. He continued to work at the Footes' for his room and board, but he no longer worked the long hours of his first two years at the University. For three hours every afternoon and for half a day on the weekends he allowed himself to be used as Jim and Serena Foote desired; the rest of the time he claimed as his own.

Some of this time he spent in his little attic room atop the Foote house; but as often as he could, after his classes were over and his work at the Footes' done, he returned to the University. Sometimes, in the evenings, he wandered in the long open quadrangle, among couples who strolled together and murmured softly; though he did not know any of them, and though he did not speak to them, he felt a kinship with them. Sometimes he stood in the center of the quad, looking at the five huge columns in front of Jesse Hall that thrust upward into the night out of the cool grass; he had learned that these columns were the remains of the original main building of the University, destroyed many years ago by fire. Grayish silver in the moonlight, bare and pure, they seemed to him to represent the way of life he had embraced, as a temple represents a god.

In the University library he wandered through the stacks, among the thousands of books, inhaling the musty odor of leather, cloth, and drying page as if it were an exotic incense. Sometimes he would pause, remove a volume from the shelves, and hold it for a moment in his large hands, which tingled at the still unfamiliar feel of spine and board and unresisting page. Then he would leaf through the book, reading a paragraph here and there, his stiff fingers careful as they turned the pages, as if in their clumsiness they might tear and destroy what they took such pains to uncover.

He had no friends, and for the first time in his life he became aware of loneliness. Sometimes, in his attic room at night, he would look up from a book he was reading and gaze in the dark corners of his room, where the lamplight flickered against the shadows. If he stared long and intently, the darkness gathered into a light, which took the insubstantial shape of what he had been reading. And he would feel that he was out of time, as he had felt that day in class when Archer Sloane had spoken to him. The past gathered out of the darkness where it stayed, and the dead raised themselves to live before him; and the past and the dead flowed into the present among the alive, so that he had for an intense instant a vision of denseness into which he was compacted and from which he could not escape, and had no wish to escape. Tristan, Iseult the fair, walked before him; Paolo and Francesca whirled in the glowing dark; Helen and bright Paris, their faces bitter with consequence, rose from the gloom. And he was with them in a way that he could never be with his fellows who went from class to class, who found a local habitation in a large university in Columbia, Missouri, and who walked unheeding in a midwestern air.

In a year he learned Greek and Latin well enough to read simple texts; often his eyes were red and burning from strain and lack of sleep. Sometimes he thought of himself as he had been a few years before and was astonished by the memory of that strange figure, brown and passive as the earth from which it had emerged. He thought of his parents, and they were nearly as strange as the child they had borne; he felt a mixed pity for them and a distant love.

Near the middle of his fourth year at the University, Archer Sloane stopped him one day after class and asked him to drop by his office for a chat.

It was winter, and a low damp midwestern mist floated over the campus. Even at midmorning the thin branches of the dogwood trees glistened with hoarfrost, and the black vines that trailed up the great columns before Jesse Hall were rimmed with iridescent crystals that winked against the grayness. Stoner's greatcoat was so shabby and worn that he had decided not to wear it to see Sloane even though the weather was freezing. He was shivering as he hurried up the walk and up the wide stone steps that led into Jesse Hall.

After the cold, the heat inside the building was intense. The grayness outside trickled through the windows and glassed doors on either side of the hall, so that the yellow tiled floors glowed brighter than the gray light upon them, and the great oaken columns and the rubbed walls gleamed from their dark. Shuffling footsteps hissed upon the floors, and a murmur of voices was muted by the great expanse of the hall; dim figures moved slowly, mingling and parting; and the oppressive air gathered the smell of the oiled walls and the wet odor of woolen clothing. Stoner went up the smooth marble stairs to Archer Sloane's second-floor office. He knocked on the closed door, heard a voice, and went in.

The office was long and narrow, lighted by a single window at the far end. Shelves crowded with books rose to the high ceiling. Near the window a desk was wedged, and before this desk, half turned and outlined darkly against the light, sat Archer Sloane.

'Mr Stoner,' Sloane said dryly, half rising and indicating a leather-covered chair facing him. Stoner sat down.

'I have been looking through your records.' Sloane paused and lifted a folder from his desk, regarding it with detached irony. 'I hope you do not mind my inquisitiveness.'

Stoner wet his lips and shifted on the chair. He tried to fold his large hands together so that they would be invisible. 'No, sir,' he said in a husky voice.

Sloane nodded. 'Good. I note that you began your course of studies here as an agriculture student and that sometime during your sophomore year you switched your program to literature. Is that correct?'

'Yes, sir,' Stoner said.

Sloane leaned back in his chair and gazed up at the square of light that came in from the high small window. He tapped his fingertips together and turned back to the young man who sat stiffly in front of him.

'The official purpose of this conference is to inform you that you will have to make a formal change of study program, declaring your intention to abandon your initial course of study and declare your final one. It's a matter of five minutes or so at the registrar's office. You will take care of that, won't you?'

'Yes, sir,' Stoner said.

'But as you may have guessed, that is not the reason I asked you to drop by. Do you mind if I inquire a little about your future plans?'

'No, sir,' Stoner said. He looked at his hands, which were twisted tightly together.

Sloane touched the folder of papers that he had dropped on his desk. 'I gather that you were a bit older than the ordinary student when you first entered the University. Nearly twenty, I believe?'

'Yes, sir,' Stoner said.

'And at that time your plans were to undertake the sequence offered by the school of Agriculture?'

'Yes, sir.'

Sloane leaned back in his chair and regarded the high dim ceiling. He asked abruptly, 'And what are your plans now?'

Stoner was silent. This was something he had not thought

17

about, had not wanted to think about. He said at last, with a touch of resentment, 'I don't know. I haven't given it much thought.'

Sloane said, 'Are you looking forward to the day when you emerge from these cloistered walls into what some call the world?'

Stoner grinned through his embarrassment. 'No, sir.'

Sloane tapped the folder of papers on his desk. 'I am informed by these records that you come from a farming community. I take it that your parents are farm people?'

Stoner nodded.

'And do you intend to return to the farm after you receive your degree here?'

'No, sir,' Stoner said, and the decisiveness of his voice surprised him. He thought with some wonder of the decision he had suddenly made.

Sloane nodded. 'I should imagine a serious student of literature *might* find his skills not precisely suited to the persuasion of the soil.'

'I won't go back,' Stoner said as if Sloane had not spoken. 'I don't know what I'll do exactly.' He looked at his hands and said to them, 'I can't quite realize that I'll be through so soon, that I'll be leaving the University at the end of the year.'

Sloane said casually, 'There is, of course, no absolute need for you to leave. I take it that you have no independent means?'

Stoner shook his head.

'You have an excellent undergraduate record. Except for your'—he lifted his eyebrows and smiled—'except for your sophomore survey of English literature, you have all A's in your English courses; nothing below a B elsewhere. If you could maintain yourself for a year or so beyond graduation,

18

you could, I'm sure, successfully complete the work for your Master of Arts; after which you would probably be able to teach while you worked toward your doctorate. If that sort of thing would interest you at all.'

Stoner drew back. 'What do you mean?' he asked and heard something like fear in his voice.

Sloane leaned forward until his face was close; Stoner saw the lines on the long thin face soften, and he heard the dry mocking voice become gentle and unprotected.

'But don't you know, Mr Stoner?' Sloane asked. 'Don't you understand about yourself yet? You're going to be a teacher.'

Suddenly Sloane seemed very distant, and the walls of the office receded. Stoner felt himself suspended in the wide air, and he heard his voice ask, 'Are you sure?'

'I'm sure,' Sloane said softly.

'How can you tell? How can you be sure?'

'It's love, Mr Stoner,' Sloane said cheerfully. 'You are in love. It's as simple as that.'

It was as simple as that. He was aware that he nodded to Sloane and said something inconsequential. Then he was walking out of the office. His lips were tingling and his fingertips were numb; he walked as if he were asleep, yet he was intensely aware of his surroundings. He brushed against the polished wooden walls in the corridor, and he thought he could feel the warmth and age of the wood; he went slowly down the stairs and wondered at the veined cold marble that seemed to slip a little beneath his feet. In the halls the voices of the students became distinct and individual out of the hushed murmur, and their faces were close and strange and familiar. He went out of Jesse Hall into the morning, and the grayness no longer seemed to oppress the campus; it led his eyes outward and upward into the sky, where he looked as if toward a possibility for which he had no name.

In the first week of June, in the year 1914, William Stoner, with sixty other young men and a few young ladies, received his Bachelor of Arts degree from the University of Missouri.

To attend the ceremony, his parents—in a borrowed buggy drawn by their old dun mare—had started the day before, driving overnight the forty-odd miles from the farm, so that they arrived at the Footes' shortly after dawn, stiff from their sleepless journey. Stoner went down into the yard to meet them. They stood side by side in the crisp morning light and awaited his approach.

Stoner and his father shook hands with a single quick pumping action, not looking at each other.

'How do,' his father said.

His mother nodded. 'Your pa and me come down to see you graduate.'

For a moment he did not speak. Then he said, 'You'd better come in and get some breakfast.'

They were alone in the kitchen; since Stoner had come to the farm the Footes had got in the habit of sleeping late. But neither then nor after his parents had finished breakfast could he bring himself to tell them of his change of plans, of his decision not to return to the farm. Once or twice he started to speak; then he looked at the brown faces that rose nakedly out of their new clothing, and thought of the long journey they had made and of the years they had awaited his return. He sat stiffly with them until they finished the last of their coffee, and until the Footes roused themselves and came into the kitchen. Then he told them that he had to go early to the University and that he would see them there later in the day, at the exercises.

He wandered about the campus, carrying the black robe

and cap that he had hired; they were heavy and troublesome, but he could find no place to leave them. He thought of what he would have to tell his parents, and for the first time realized the finality of his decision, and almost wished that he could recall it. He felt his inadequacy to the goal he had so recklessly chosen and felt the attraction of the world he had abandoned. He grieved for his own loss and for that of his parents, and even in his grief felt himself drawing away from them.

He carried this feeling of loss with him throughout the graduation exercises; when his name was spoken and he walked across the platform to receive a scroll from a man faceless behind a soft gray beard, he could not believe his own presence, and the roll of parchment in his hand had no meaning. He could only think of his mother and father sitting stiffly and uneasily in the great crowd.

When the ceremonies were over he drove with them back to the Footes', where they were to stay overnight and start the journey home the following dawn.

They sat late in the Footes' parlor. Jim and Serena Foote stayed up with them for a while. Every now and then Jim and Stoner's mother would exchange the name of a relative and lapse into silence. His father sat on a straight chair, his legs spread apart, leaning a little forward, his broad hands clasping his kneecaps. Finally the Footes looked at each other and yawned and announced that it was late. They went to their bedroom, and the three were left alone.

There was another silence. His parents, who looked straight ahead in the shadows cast by their own bodies, every now and then glanced sideways at their son, as if they did not wish to disturb him in his new estate.

After several minutes William Stoner leaned forward and spoke, his voice louder and more forceful than he had intended. 'I ought to have told you sooner. I ought to have told you last summer, or this morning.'

His parents' faces were dull and expressionless in the lamplight.

'What I'm trying to say is, I'm not coming back with you to the farm.'

No one moved. His father said, 'You got some things to finish up here, we can go back in the morning and you can come on home in a few days.'

Stoner rubbed his face with his open palm. 'That's—not what I meant. I'm trying to tell you I won't be coming back to the farm at all.'

His father's hands tightened on his kneecaps and he drew back in the chair. He said, 'You get yourself in some kind of trouble?'

Stoner smiled. 'It's nothing like that. I'm going on to school for another year, maybe two or three.'

His father shook his head. 'I seen you get through this evening. And the county agent said the farm school took four years.'

Stoner tried to explain to his father what he intended to do, tried to evoke in him his own sense of significance and purpose. He listened to his words fall as if from the mouth of another, and watched his father's face, which received those words as a stone receives the repeated blows of a fist. When he had finished he sat with his hands clasped between his knees and his head bowed. He listened to the silence of the room.

Finally his father moved in his chair. Stoner looked up. His parents' faces confronted him; he almost cried out to them.

'I don't know,' his father said. His voice was husky and tired. 'I didn't figure it would turn out like this. I thought

22

I was doing the best for you I could, sending you here. Your ma and me has always done the best we could for you.'

'I know,' Stoner said. He could not look at them longer. 'Will you be all right? I could come back for a while this summer and help. I could—'

'If you think you ought to stay here and study your books, then that's what you ought to do. Your ma and me can manage.'

His mother was facing him, but she did not see him. Her eyes were squeezed shut; she was breathing heavily, her face twisted as if in pain, and her closed fists were pressed against her cheeks. With wonder Stoner realized that she was crying, deeply and silently, with the shame and awkwardness of one who seldom weeps. He watched her for a moment more; then he got heavily to his feet and walked out of the parlor. He found his way up the narrow stairs that led to his attic room; for a long time he lay on his bed and stared with open eyes into the darkness above him.

2

Two weeks after Stoner received his Bachelor of Arts degree, Archduke Francis Ferdinand was assassinated at Sarajevo by a Serbian nationalist; and before autumn war was general all over Europe. It was a topic of continuing interest among the older students; they wondered about the part America would eventually play, and they were pleasantly unsure of their own futures.

But before William Stoner the future lay bright and certain and unchanging. He saw it, not as a flux of event and change and potentiality, but as a territory ahead that awaited his exploration. He saw it as the great University library, to which new wings might be built, to which new books might be added and from which old ones might be withdrawn, while its true nature remained essentially unchanged. He saw the future in the institution to which he had committed himself and which he so imperfectly understood; he conceived himself changing in that future, but he saw the future itself as the instrument of change rather than its object.

Near the end of that summer, just before the beginning of the autumn semester, he visited his parents. He had intended to help with the summer crop; but he found that his father had hired a Negro field hand who worked with a quiet, fierce intensity, accomplishing by himself in a day nearly as much as William and his father together had once done in the same time. His parents were happy to see him, and they seemed not to resent his decision. But he found that he had nothing to say to them; already, he realized, he and his parents were becoming strangers; and he felt his love increased by its loss. He returned to Columbia a week earlier than he had intended.

He began to resent the time he had to spend at work on the Foote farm. Having come to his studies late, he felt the urgency of study. Sometimes, immersed in his books, there would come to him the awareness of all that he did not know, of all that he had not read; and the serenity for which he labored was shattered as he realized the little time he had in life to read so much, to learn what he had to know.

He finished his course work for the Master of Arts degree in the spring of 1915 and spent the summer completing his thesis, a prosodic study of one of Chaucer's *Canterbury Tales*. Before the summer was out the Footes told him that they would not need him any longer on the farm.

He had expected his dismissal and in some ways he welcomed it; but for a moment after it happened he had a twinge of panic. It was as if the last tie between himself and the old life had been cut. He spent the last weeks of the summer at his father's farm, putting the finishing touches on his thesis. By that time Archer Sloane had arranged for him to teach two classes of beginning English to incoming freshmen, while he started to work toward his Ph.D. For this he received four hundred dollars a year. He removed his belongings from the Footes' tiny attic room, which he had occupied for five years, and took an even smaller room near the University.

Though he was to teach only the fundamentals of grammar and composition to a group of unselected freshmen, he looked forward to his task with enthusiasm and with a strong sense of its significance. He planned the course during the week before the opening of the autumn semester, and saw the kinds of possibility that one sees as one struggles with the materials and subjects of an endeavor; he felt the logic of grammar, and he thought he perceived how it spread out from itself, permeating the language and supporting human thought. In the simple compositional exercises he made for his students he saw the potentialities of prose and its beauties, and he looked forward to animating his students with the sense of what he perceived.

But in the first classes he met, after the opening routines of rolls and study plans, when he began to address himself to his subject and his students, he found that his sense of wonder remained hidden within him. Sometimes, as he spoke to his students, it was as if he stood outside himself and observed a stranger speaking to a group assembled unwillingly; he heard his own flat voice reciting the materials he had prepared, and nothing of his own excitement came through that recitation.

He found his release and fulfillment in the classes in which he himself was a student. There he was able to recapture the sense of discovery he had felt on that first day, when Archer Sloane had spoken to him in class and he had, in an instant, become someone other than who he had been. As his mind engaged itself with its subject, as it grappled with the power of the literature he studied and tried to understand its nature, he was aware of a constant change within himself; and as he was aware of that, he moved outward from himself into the world which contained him, so that he knew that the poem of Milton's that he read or the essay of Bacon's or the drama of Ben Jonson's changed the world which was its subject, and changed it because of its dependence upon it. He seldom spoke in class, and his papers rarely satisfied him. Like his lectures to his young students, they did not betray what he most profoundly knew.

He began to be on familiar terms with a few of his fellow students who were also acting instructors in the department. Among those were two with whom he became friendly, David Masters and Gordon Finch.

Masters was a slight dark youth with a sharp tongue and gentle eyes. Like Stoner, he was just beginning his doctoral program, though he was a year or so younger than Stoner. Among the faculty and the graduate students he had a reputation for arrogance and impertinence, and it was generally conceded that he would have some difficulty in finally obtaining his degree. Stoner thought him the most brilliant man he had ever known and deferred to him without envy or resentment.

Gordon Finch was large and blond, and already, at the age of twenty-three, beginning to run to fat. He had taken an undergraduate degree from a commercial college in St Louis, and at the University had made various stabs at advanced degrees in the departments of economics, history, and engineering. He had begun work on his degree in literature largely because he had been able, at the last minute, to get a small instructing job in the English Department. He quickly showed himself to be the most nearly indifferent student in the department. But he was popular with the freshmen, and he got along well with the older faculty members and with the officers of the administration.

The three of them—Stoner, Masters, and Finch—got in the habit of meeting on Friday afternoons at a small saloon in downtown Columbia, drinking large schooners of beer and talking late into the night. Though he found the only social pleasure he knew in these evenings, Stoner often wondered at their relationship. Though they got along well enough together, they had not become close friends; they had no confidences and seldom saw each other outside their weekly gatherings.

None of them ever raised the question of that relationship. Stoner knew that it had not occurred to Gordon Finch, but he suspected that it had to David Masters. Once, late in the evening, as they sat at a rear table in the dimness of the saloon, Stoner and Masters talked of their teaching and study with the awkward facetiousness of the very serious. Masters, holding aloft a hard-boiled egg from the free lunch as if it were a crystal ball, said, 'Have you gentlemen ever considered the question of the true nature of the University? Mr Stoner? Mr Finch?'

Smiling, they shook their heads.

'I'll bet you haven't. Stoner, here, I imagine, sees it as a great repository, like a library or a whorehouse, where men come of their free will and select that which will complete them, where all work together like little bees in a common hive. The True, the Good, the Beautiful. They're just around the corner, in the next corridor; they're in the next book, the one you haven't read, or in the next stack, the one you haven't got to. But you'll get to it someday. And when you do—when you do—' He looked at the egg for a moment more, then took a large bite of it and turned to Stoner, his jaws working and his dark eyes bright.

Stoner smiled uncomfortably, and Finch laughed aloud and slapped the table. 'He's got you, Bill. He's got you good.'

Masters chewed for a moment more, swallowed, and turned his gaze to Finch. 'And you, Finch. What's your idea?' He held up his hand. 'You'll protest you haven't thought of it. But you have. Beneath that bluff and hearty exterior there works a simple mind. To you, the institution is an instrument of good—to the world at large, of course, and just incidentally to yourself. You see it as a kind of spiritual sulphur-and-molasses that you administer every fall to get the little bastards through another winter; and you're the kindly old doctor who benignly pats their heads and pockets their fees.'

Finch laughed again and shook his head. 'I swear, Dave, when you get going—'

Masters put the rest of the egg in his mouth, chewed contentedly for a moment, and took a long swallow of beer. 'But you're both wrong,' he said. 'It is an asylum or—what do they call them now?—a rest home, for the infirm, the aged, the discontent, and the otherwise incompetent. Look at the three of us—*we* are the University. The stranger would not know that we have so much in common, but *we* know, don't we? We know well.'

Finch was laughing. 'What's that, Dave?'

Interested now in what he was saying, Masters leaned intently across the table. 'Let's take you first, Finch. Being as kind as I can, I would say that you are the incompetent. As you yourself know, you're not really very bright—though that doesn't have everything to do with it.'

'Here, now,' Finch said, still laughing.

'But you're bright enough—and *just* bright enough—to realize what would happen to you in the world. You're cut out for failure, and you know it. Though you're capable of being a son-of-a-bitch, you're not quite ruthless enough to be so consistently. Though you're not precisely the most honest man I've ever known, neither are you heroically dishonest. On the one hand, you're capable of work, but you're just lazy enough so that you can't work as hard as the world would want you to. On the other hand, you're not quite so lazy that you can impress upon the world a sense of your importance. And you're not lucky—not really. No aura rises from you, and you wear a puzzled expression. In the world you would always be on the fringe of success, and you would be destroyed by your failure. So you are chosen, elected; providence, whose sense of humor has always amused me, has snatched you from the jaws of the world and placed you safely here, among your brothers.'

Still smiling and ironically malevolent, he turned to Stoner. 'Nor do you escape, my friend. No indeed. Who are you? A simple son of the soil, as you pretend to yourself? Oh, no. You, too, are among the infirm—you are the dreamer, the madman in a madder world, our own midwestern Don Quixote without his Sancho, gamboling under the blue sky. You're bright enough—brighter anyhow than our mutual friend. But you have the taint, the old infirmity. You think there's something *here*, something to find. Well, in the world you'd learn soon enough. You, too, are cut out for failure; not that you'd fight the world. You'd let it chew you up and spit you out, and you'd lie there wondering what was wrong. Because you'd always expect the world to be something it wasn't, something it had no wish to be. The weevil in the cotton, the worm in the beanstalk, the borer in the corn. You couldn't face them, and you couldn't fight them; because you're too weak, and you're too strong. And you have no place to go in the world.'

'What about you?' Finch asked. 'What about yourself?'

'Oh,' Masters said, leaning back, 'I'm one of you. Worse, in fact. I'm too bright for the world, and I won't keep my mouth shut about it; it's a disease for which there is no cure. So I must be locked up, where I can be safely irresponsible, where I can do no harm.' He leaned forward again and smiled at them. 'We're all poor Toms, and we're a-cold.'

'King Lear,' Stoner said seriously.

'Act Three, Scene Four,' said Masters. 'And so providence, or society, or fate, or whatever name you want to give it, has created this hovel for us, so that we can go in out of the storm. It's for us that the University exists, for the dispossessed of the world; not for the students, not for the selfless pursuit of knowledge, not for any of the reasons that you hear. We give out the reasons, and we let a few of the ordinary ones in, those that would do in the world; but that's just protective coloration. Like the church in the Middle Ages, which didn't give a damn about the laity or even about God, we have our pretenses in order to survive. And we shall survive—because we have to.'

Finch shook his head admiringly. 'You sure make us sound bad, Dave.'

'Maybe I do,' Masters said. 'But bad as we are, we're better than those on the outside, in the muck, the poor bastards of the world. We do no harm, we say what we want, and we get paid for it; and that's a triumph of natural virtue, or pretty damn close to it.'

Masters leaned back from the table, indifferent, no longer concerned with what he had said.

Gordon Finch cleared his throat. 'Well, now,' he said earnestly. 'You may have something in what you say, Dave. But I think you go too far. I really do.'

Stoner and Masters smiled at each other, and they spoke no more of the question that evening. But for years afterward, at odd moments, Stoner remembered what Masters had said; and though it brought him no vision of the University to which he had committed himself, it did reveal to him something about his relationship to the two men, and it gave him a glimpse of the corrosive and unspoiled bitterness of youth.

★

On May 7, 1915, a German submarine sank the British liner *Lusitania*, with a hundred and fourteen American passengers on board; by the end of 1916 submarine warfare by the Germans was unrestricted, and relations between the United States and Germany steadily worsened. In February 1917 President Wilson broke off diplomatic relations. On April 6 a state of war was declared by Congress to exist between Germany and the United States.

With that declaration, thousands of young men across the nation, as if relieved that the tension of uncertainty had finally been broken, besieged the recruiting stations that had been hastily set up some weeks before. Indeed, hundreds of young men had not been able to wait for America's intervention and had as early as 1915 signed up for duty with the Royal Canadian forces or as ambulance drivers for one of the European allied armies. A few of the older students at the University had done so; and although William Stoner had not known any of these, he heard their legendary names with increasing frequency as the months and weeks drew on to the moment that they all knew must eventually come.

War was declared on a Friday, and although classes remained scheduled the following week, few students or professors made a pretense of meeting them. They milled about in the halls and gathered in small groups, murmuring in hushed voices. Occasionally the tense quietness erupted into near violence; twice there were general anti-German demonstrations, in which students shouted incoherently and waved American flags. Once there was a brief-lived demonstration against one of the professors, an old and bearded teacher of Germanic languages, who had been born in Munich and who as a youth had attended the University of Berlin. But when the professor met the angry and flushed little group of students, blinked in bewilderment, and held

32

out his thin, shaking hands to them, they disbanded in sullen confusion.

During those first days after the declaration of war Stoner also suffered a confusion, but it was profoundly different from that which gripped most of the others on the campus. Though he had talked about the war in Europe with the older students and instructors, he had never quite believed in it; and now that it was upon him, upon them all, he discovered within himself a vast reserve of indifference. He resented the disruption which the war forced upon the University; but he could find in himself no very strong feelings of patriotism, and he could not bring himself to hate the Germans.

But the Germans were there to be hated. Once Stoner came upon Gordon Finch talking to a group of older faculty members; Finch's face was twisted, and he was speaking of the 'Huns' as if he were spitting on the floor. Later, when he approached Stoner in the large office which half a dozen of the younger instructors shared, Finch's mood had shifted; feverishly jovial, he clapped Stoner on the shoulder.

'Can't let them get away with it, Bill,' he said rapidly. A film of sweat like oil glistened on his round face, and his thin blond hair lay in lank strands over his skull. 'No, sir. I'm going to join up. I've already talked to old Sloane about it, and he said to go ahead. I'm going down to St Louis tomorrow and sign up.' For an instant he managed to compose his features into a semblance of gravity. 'We've all got to do our part.' Then he grinned and clapped Stoner's shoulder again. 'You better come along with me.'

'Me?' Stoner said, and said again, incredulously, 'Me?'

Finch laughed. 'Sure. Everybody's signing up. I just talked to Dave—he's coming with me.'

Stoner shook his head as if dazed. 'Dave Masters?'

'Sure. Old Dave talks kind of funny sometimes, but when the chips are down he's no different from anybody else; he'll do his part. Just like you'll do yours, Bill.' Finch punched him on the arm. 'Just like you'll do yours.'

Stoner was silent for a moment. 'I hadn't thought about it,' he said. 'It all seems to have happened so quickly. I'll have to talk to Sloane. I'll let you know.'

'Sure,' Finch said. 'You'll do your part.' His voice thickened with feeling. 'We're all in this together now, Bill; we're all in it together.'

Stoner left Finch then, but he did not go to see Archer Sloane. Instead he looked about the campus and inquired after David Masters. He found him in one of the library carrels, alone, puffing on a pipe and staring at a shelf of books.

Stoner sat across from him at the carrel desk. When he questioned him about his decision to join the Army, Masters said, 'Sure. Why not?'

And when Stoner asked him why, Masters said, 'You know me pretty well, Bill. I don't give a damn about the Germans. When it comes down to it, I don't really give a damn about the Americans either, I guess.' He knocked his pipe ashes out on the floor and swept them around with his foot. 'I suppose I'm doing it because it doesn't matter whether I do it or not. And it might be amusing to pass through the world once more before I return to the cloistered and slow extinction that awaits us all.'

Though he did not understand, Stoner nodded, accepting what Masters told him. He said, 'Gordon wants me to enlist with you.'

Masters smiled. 'Gordon feels the first strength of virtue he's ever been allowed to feel; and he naturally wants to include the rest of the world in it, so that he can keep on believing. Sure. Why not? Join up with us. It might do you good to see what the world's like.' He paused and looked intently at Stoner. 'But if you do, for Christ's sake don't do it for God, country, and the dear old U. of M. Do it for yourself.'

Stoner waited several moments. Then he said, 'I'll talk to Sloane and let you know.'

He did not know what he expected Archer Sloane's response to be; nevertheless he was surprised when he confronted him in his narrow book-lined office and told him of what was not quite yet his decision.

Sloane, who had always maintained toward him an attitude of detached and courtly irony, lost his temper. His long thin face went red, and the lines on either side of his mouth deepened in anger; he half rose from his chair toward Stoner, his fists clenched. Then he settled back and deliberately loosened his fists and spread his hands upon his desk; the fingers were trembling, but his voice was steady and harsh.

'I ask you to forgive my sudden display. But in the last few days I have lost nearly a third of the members of the department, and I see no hope of replacing them. It is not you at whom I am angry, but—' He turned away from Stoner and looked up at the high window at the far end of his office. The light struck his face sharply, accentuating the lines and deepening the shadows under his eyes, so that for a moment he seemed old and sick. 'I was born in 1860, just before the War of the Rebellion. I don't remember it, of course; I was too young. I don't remember my father either; he was killed in the first year of the war, at the Battle of Shiloh.' He looked quickly at Stoner. 'But I can see what has ensued. A war doesn't merely kill off a few thousand or a few hundred thousand young men. It kills off something in a people that can never be brought back. And if a people goes through enough wars, pretty soon all that's left is the brute, the creature that we—you and I and others like us—have brought up from the slime.' He paused for a long moment; then he smiled slightly. 'The scholar should not be asked to destroy what he has aimed his life to build.'

Stoner cleared his throat and said diffidently, 'Everything seems to have happened so quickly. Somehow it had never occurred to me, until I talked to Finch and Masters. It still doesn't seem quite real.'

'It's not, of course,' Sloane said. Then he moved restlessly, turning away from Stoner. 'I'm not going to tell you what to do. I'll simply say this: it's your choice to make. There'll be a conscription; but you can be excepted, if you want to be. You're not afraid to go, are you?'

'No, sir,' Stoner said. 'I don't believe so.'

'Then you do have a choice, and you'll have to make it for yourself. It goes without saying that if you decide to join you will upon your return be reinstated in your present position. If you decide not to join you can stay on here, but of course you will have no particular advantage; it is possible that you will have a disadvantage, either now or in the future.'

'I understand,' Stoner said.

There was a long silence, and Stoner decided at last that Sloane had finished with him. But just as he got up to leave the office Sloane spoke again.

He said slowly, 'You must remember what you are and what you have chosen to become, and the significance of what you are doing. There are wars and defeats and victories of the human race that are not military and that are not recorded in the annals of history. Remember that while you're trying to decide what to do.'

For two days Stoner did not meet his classes and did not speak to anyone he knew. He stayed in his small room, struggling with his decision. His books and the quiet of his room surrounded him; only rarely was he aware of the world outside his room, of the far murmur of shouting students, of the swift clatter of a buggy on the brick streets, and the flat chug of one of the dozen or so automobiles in town. He had never got in the habit of introspection, and he found the task of searching his motives a difficult and slightly distasteful one; he felt that he had little to offer to himself and that there was little within him which he could find.

When at last he came to his decision, it seemed to him that he had known all along what it would be. He met Masters and Finch on Friday and told them that he would not join them to fight the Germans.

Gordon Finch, sustained still by his accession to virtue, stiffened and allowed an expression of reproachful sorrow to settle on his features. 'You're letting us down, Bill,' he said thickly. 'You're letting us all down.'

'Be quiet,' Masters said. He looked keenly at Stoner. 'I thought you might decide not to. You've always had that lean, dedicated look about you. It doesn't matter, of course; but what made you finally decide?'

Stoner did not speak for a moment. He thought of the last two days, of the silent struggle that seemed toward no end and no meaning; he thought of his life at the University for the past seven years; he thought of the years before, the distant years with his parents on the farm, and of the deadness from which he had been miraculously revived.

'I don't know,' he said at last. 'Everything, I guess. I can't say.'

'It's going to be hard,' Masters said, 'staying here.'

'I know,' Stoner said.

'But it's worth it, you think?'

Stoner nodded.

Masters grinned and said with his old irony, 'You have the lean and hungry look, sure enough. You're doomed.'

Finch's sorrowful reproach had turned into a kind of tentative contempt. 'You'll live to regret this, Bill,' he said hoarsely, and his voice hesitated between threat and pity.

Stoner nodded. 'It may be,' he said.

He told them good-by then, and turned away. They were to go to St Louis the next day to enlist, and Stoner had classes to prepare for the following week.

He felt no guilt for his decision, and when conscription became general he applied for his deferment with no particular feeling of remorse; but he was aware of the looks that he received from his older colleagues and of the thin edge of disrespect that showed through his students' conventional behavior toward him. He even suspected that Archer Sloane, who had at one time expressed a warm approval of his decision to continue at the University, grew colder and more distant as the months of the war wore on.

He finished the requirements for his doctorate in the spring of 1918 and took his degree in June of that year. A month before he received his degree he got a letter from Gordon Finch, who had gone through Officer's Training School and had been assigned to a training camp just outside New York City. The letter informed him that Finch had been allowed, in his spare time, to attend Columbia University, where he, too, had managed to fulfill the requirements necessary for a doctorate, which he would take in the summer from Teachers College there.

It also told him that Dave Masters had been sent to France and that almost exactly a year after his enlistment, with the first American troops to see action, he had been killed at Château-Thierry.

3

A week before commencement, at which Stoner was to receive his doctorate, Archer Sloane offered him a full-time instructorship at the University. Sloane explained that it was not the policy of the University to employ its own graduates, but because of the wartime shortage of trained and experienced college teachers he had been able to persuade the administration to make an exception.

Somewhat reluctantly Stoner had written a few letters of application to universities and colleges in the general area, abruptly setting forth his qualifications; when nothing came from any of them, he felt curiously relieved. He half understood his relief; he had known at the University at Columbia the kind of security and warmth that he should have been able to feel as a child in his home, and had not been able to, and he was unsure of his ability to find those elsewhere. He accepted Sloane's offer with gratitude.

And as he did so it occurred to him that Sloane had aged greatly during the year of the war. In his late fifties, he looked ten years older; his hair, which had once curled in an unruly iron-gray shock, now was white and lay flat and lifeless about his bony skull. His black eyes had gone dull, as if filmed over with layers of moisture; his long, lined face, which had once been tough as thin leather, now had the fragility of ancient, drying paper; and his flat, ironical voice had begun to develop a tremor. Looking at him, Stoner thought: He is going to die—in a year, or two years, or ten, he will die. A premature sense of loss gripped him, and he turned away.

His thoughts were much upon death that summer of 1918. The death of Masters had shocked him more than he wished to admit; and the first American casualty lists from Europe were beginning to be released. When he had thought of death before, he had thought of it either as a literary event or as the slow, quiet attrition of time against imperfect flesh. He had not thought of it as the explosion of violence upon a battlefield, as the gush of blood from the ruptured throat. He wondered at the difference between the two kinds of dying, and what the difference meant; and he found growing in him some of that bitterness he had glimpsed once in the living heart of his friend David Masters.

His dissertation topic had been 'The Influence of the Classical Tradition upon the Medieval Lyric.' He spent much of the summer rereading the classical and medieval Latin poets, and especially their poems upon death. He wondered again at the easy, graceful manner in which the Roman lyricists accepted the fact of death, as if the nothingness they faced were a tribute to the richness of the years they had enjoyed; and he marveled at the bitterness, the terror, the barely concealed hatred he found in some of the later Christian poets of the Latin tradition when they looked to that death which promised, however vaguely, a rich and ecstatic eternity of life, as if that death and promise were a mockery that soured the days of their living. When he thought of Masters, he thought of him as a Catullus or a more gentle and lyrical Juvenal, an exile in his own country, and thought of his death as another exile, more strange and lasting than he had known before.

When the semester opened in the autumn of 1918 it was clear to everyone that the war in Europe could not go on much longer. The last, desperate German counter-offensive had been stopped short of Paris, and Marshal Foch had ordered a general allied counterattack that quickly pushed the Germans back to their original line. The British advanced to the north and the Americans went through the Argonne, at a cost that was widely ignored in the general elation. The newspapers were predicting a collapse of the Germans before Christmas.

So the semester began in an atmosphere of tense geniality and well-being. The students and instructors found themselves smiling at each other and nodding vigorously in the halls; out-bursts of exuberance and small violence among the students were ignored by the faculty and administration; and an unidentified student, who immediately became a kind of local folk hero, shinnied up one of the huge columns in front of Jesse Hall and hung from its top a straw-stuffed effigy of the Kaiser.

The only person in the University who seemed untouched by the general excitement was Archer Sloane. Since the day of America's entrance into the war he had begun to withdraw into himself, and the withdrawal became more pronounced as the war neared its end. He did not speak to his colleagues unless departmental business forced him to do so, and it was whispered that his teaching had become so eccentric that his students attended his classes in dread; he read dully and mechanically from his notes, never meeting his students' eyes; frequently his voice trailed off as he stared at his notes, and there would be one, two, and sometimes as many as five minutes of silence, during which he neither moved nor responded to embarrassed questions from the class.

William Stoner saw the last vestige of the bright, ironic man he had known as a student when Archer Sloane gave him his teaching assignment for the academic year. Sloane gave Stoner two sections of freshman composition and an upper division survey of Middle English literature; and then he said, with a flash of his old irony, 'You, as well as many of our colleagues and not a few of our students, will be pleased to know that I am giving up a number of my classes. Among these is one that has been my rather unfashionable favorite, the sophomore survey of English literature. You may recall the course?'

Stoner nodded, smiling.

'Yes,' Sloane continued, 'I rather thought you would. I am asking you to take it over for me. Not that it's a great gift; but I thought it might amuse you to begin your formal career as a teacher where you started as a student.' Sloane looked at him for a moment, his eyes bright and intent as they had been before the war. Then the film of indifference settled over them, and he turned away from Stoner and shuffled some papers on his desk.

So Stoner began where he had started, a tall, thin, stooped man in the same room in which he had sat as a tall, thin, stooped boy listening to the words that had led him to where he had come. He never went into that room that he did not glance at the seat he had once occupied, and he was always slightly surprised to discover that he was not there.

On November 11 of that year, two months after the semester began, the Armistice was signed. The news came on a class day, and immediately the classes broke up; students ran aimlessly about the campus and started small parades that gathered, dispersed, and gathered again, winding through halls, classrooms, and offices. Half against his will, Stoner

42

was caught up in one of these which went into Jesse Hall, through corridors, up stairs, and through corridors again. Swept along in a small mass of students and teachers, he passed the open door of Archer Sloane's office; and he had a glimpse of Sloane sitting in his chair before his desk, his face uncovered and twisted, weeping bitterly, the tears streaming down the deep lines of the flesh.

For a moment more, as if in shock, Stoner allowed himself to be carried along by the crowd. Then he broke away and went to his room near the campus. He sat in the dimness of his room and heard outside the shouts of joy and release, and thought of Archer Sloane who wept at a defeat that only he saw, or thought he saw; and he knew that Sloane was a broken man and would never again be what he had been.

Late in November many of those who had gone away to war began to return to Columbia, and the campus at the University was dotted with the olive drab of army uniforms. Among those who returned on extended leaves was Gordon Finch. He had put on weight during his year and a half away from the University, and the broad, open face that had been amiably acquiescent now held an expression of friendly but portentous gravity; he wore the bars of a captain and spoke often with a paternal fondness of 'my men.' He was distantly friendly to William Stoner, and he took exaggerated care to behave with deference toward the older members of the department. It was too late in the fall semester to assign him any classes, so for the rest of the academic year he was given what was understood to be a temporary sinecure as administrative assistant to the dean of Arts and Sciences. He was sensitive enough to be aware of the ambiguity of his new position and shrewd enough to see its possibilities; his relations with his colleagues were tentative and courteously noncommittal.

The dean of Arts and Sciences, Josiah Claremont, was a small bearded man of advanced age, several years beyond the point of compulsory retirement; he had been with the University ever since its transition, in the early seventies of the preceding century, from a normal college to a full University, and his father had been one of its early presidents. He was so firmly entrenched and so much a part of the history of the University that no one quite had the courage to insist upon his retirement, despite the increasing incompetence with which he managed his office. His memory was nearly gone; sometimes he became lost in the corridors of Jesse Hall, where his office was located, and had to be led like a child to his desk.

So vague had he become about University affairs that when an announcement came from his office that a reception in honor of the returning veterans on the faculty and administrative staff would be held at his home, most of those who received invitations felt that an elaborate joke was being played or that a mistake had been made. But it was not a joke, and it was not a mistake. Gordon Finch confirmed the invitations; and it was widely hinted that it was he who had instigated the reception and who had carried through the plans.

Josiah Claremont, widowed many years before, lived alone, with three colored servants nearly as old as himself, in one of the large pre-Civil War homes that had once been common around Columbia but were fast disappearing before the coming of the small, independent farmer and the real-estate developer. The architecture of the place was pleasant but unidentifiable; though 'Southern' in its general shape and expansiveness, it had none of the neo-classic rigidity of

44

the Virginia home. Its boards were painted white, and green trim framed the windows and the balustrades of the small balconies that projected here and there from the upper story. The grounds extended into a wood that surrounded the place, and tall poplars, leafless in the December afternoon, lined the drive and the walks. It was the grandest house that William Stoner had ever been near; and on that Friday afternoon he walked with some dread up the driveway and joined a group of faculty whom he did not know, who were waiting at the front door to be admitted.

Gordon Finch, still wearing his army uniform, opened the door to let them in; the group stepped into a small square foyer, at the end of which a steep staircase with polished oaken banisters led upward to the second story. A small French tapestry, its blues and golds so faded that the pattern was hardly visible in the dim yellow light given by the small bulbs, hung on the staircase wall directly in front of the men who had entered. Stoner stood gazing up at it while those who had come in with him milled about the small foyer.

'Give me your coat, Bill.' The voice, close to his ear, startled him. He turned. Finch was smiling and holding his hand out to receive the coat which Stoner had not removed.

'You haven't been here before, have you?' Finch asked almost in a whisper. Stoner shook his head.

Finch turned to the other men and without raising his voice managed to call out to them. 'You gentlemen go on into the main living room.' He pointed to a door at the right of the foyer. 'Everybody's in there.'

He returned his attention to Stoner. 'It's a fine old house,' he said, hanging Stoner's coat in a large closet beneath the staircase. 'It's one of the real showplaces around here.'

'Yes,' Stoner said. 'I've heard people talk about it.'

'And Dean Claremont's a fine old man. He asked me to kind of look out for things for him this evening.'

Stoner nodded.

Finch took his arm and guided him toward the door to which he had pointed earlier. 'We'll have to get together for a talk later on this evening. You go on in now. I'll be there in a minute. There are some people I want you to meet.'

Stoner started to speak, but Finch had turned away to greet another group that had come in the front door. Stoner took a deep breath and opened the door to the main living room.

When he came into the room from the cold foyer the warmth pushed against him, as if to force him back; the slow murmur of the people inside, released by his opening the door, swelled for a moment before his ears accustomed themselves to it.

Perhaps two dozen people milled about the room, and for an instant he recognized none of them; he saw the sober black and gray and brown of men's suits, the olive drab of army uniforms, and here and there the delicate pink or blue of a woman's dress. The people moved sluggishly through the warmth, and he moved with them, conscious of his height among the seated figures, nodding to the faces he now recognized.

At the far end another door led into a sitting parlor, which was adjacent to the long, narrow dining hall. The double doors of the hall were open, revealing a massive walnut dining table covered with yellow damask and laden with white dishes and bowls of gleaming silver. Several people were gathered around the table, at the head of which a young woman, tall and slender and fair, dressed in a gown of blue watered silk, stood pouring tea into gold-rimmed china cups. Stoner paused in the doorway, caught by his vision of the young woman. Her long, delicately featured face smiled at those around her, and her slender, almost fragile fingers deftly manipulated urn and cup; looking at her, Stoner was assailed by a consciousness of his own heavy clumsiness.

For several moments he did not move from the doorway; he heard the girl's soft, thin voice rise above the murmur of the assembled guests she served. She raised her head, and suddenly he met her eyes; they were pale and large and seemed to shine with a light within themselves. In some confusion he backed from the doorway and turned into the sitting room; he found an empty chair in a space by the wall, and he sat there looking at the carpet beneath his feet. He did not look in the direction of the dining room, but every now and then he thought he felt the gaze of the young woman brush warmly across his face.

The guests moved around him, exchanged seats, altered their inflections as they found new partners for conversation. Stoner saw them through a haze, as if he were an audience. After a while Gordon Finch came into the room, and Stoner got up from his chair and walked across the room to him. Almost rudely he interrupted Finch's conversation with an older man. Drawing him aside but not lowering his voice, he asked to be introduced to the young woman pouring tea.

Finch looked at him for a moment, the annoyed frown that had begun to pucker his forehead smoothing as his eyes widened. 'You what?' Finch said. Though he was shorter than Stoner, he seemed to be looking down on him.

'I want you to introduce me,' Stoner said. He felt his face warm. 'Do you know her?'

'Sure,' Finch said. The start of a grin began to tug at his

mouth. 'She's some kind of cousin of the dean's, down from St Louis, visiting an aunt.' The grin widened. 'Old Bill. What do you know. Sure, I'll introduce you. Come on.'

Her name was Edith Elaine Bostwick, and she lived with her parents in St Louis, where the previous spring she had finished a two-year course of study at a private seminary for young ladies; she was visiting her mother's older sister in Columbia for a few weeks, and in the spring they were to make the Grand Tour of Europe—an event once again possible, now that the war was over. Her father, the president of one of the smaller St Louis banks, was a transplanted New Englander; he had come west in the seventies and married the oldest daughter of a well-to-do central Missouri family. Edith had lived all her life in St Louis; a few years before she had gone east with her parents to Boston for the season; she had been to the opera in New York and had visited the museums. She was twenty years of age, she played the piano, and had artistic leanings which her mother encouraged.

Later, William Stoner could not remember how he learned these things, that first afternoon and early evening at Josiah Claremont's house; for the time of his meeting was blurred and formal, like the figured tapestry on the stair wall off the foyer. He remembered that he spoke to her that she might look at him, remain near him, and give him the pleasure of hearing her soft, thin voice answering his questions and making perfunctory questions in return.

The guests began to leave. Voices called good-bys, doors slammed, and the rooms emptied. Stoner remained behind after most of the other guests had departed; and when Edith's carriage came he followed her into the foyer and helped her with her coat. Just before she started outside he asked her if he might call on her the following evening.

As if she had not heard him she opened the door and stood

for several moments without moving: the cold air swept through the doorway and touched Stoner's hot face. She turned and looked at him and blinked several times; her pale eyes were speculative, almost bold. At last she nodded and said, 'Yes. You may call.' She did not smile.

And so he called, walking across town to her aunt's house on an intensely cold midwestern winter night. No cloud was overhead; the half-moon shone upon a light snow that had fallen earlier in the afternoon. The streets were deserted, and the muffled silence was broken by the dry snow crunching underfoot as he walked. He stood for a long while outside the large house to which he had come, listening to the silence. The cold numbed his feet, but he did not move. From the curtained windows a dim light fell upon the blue-white snow like a yellow smudge; he thought he saw movement inside, but he could not be sure. Deliberately, as if committing himself to something, he stepped forward and walked down the path to the porch and knocked on the front door.

Edith's aunt (her name, Stoner had learned earlier, was Emma Darley, and she had been widowed for a number of years) met him at the door and asked him to come in. She was a short, plump woman with fine white hair that floated about her face; her dark eyes twinkled moistly, and she spoke softly and breathlessly as if she were telling secrets. Stoner followed her into the parlor and sat, facing her, on a long walnut sofa, the seat and back of which were covered with thick blue velvet. Snow had clung to his shoes; he watched it melt and form damp patches on the thick floral rug under his feet.

'Edith tells me you teach at the University, Mr Stoner,' Mrs Darley said.

'Yes, ma'am,' he said and cleared his throat.

'It's so *nice* to be able to talk to one of the young professors there again,' Mrs Darley said brightly. 'My late husband, Mr Darley, was on the board of trustees at the University for a number of years—but I guess you know that.'

'No, ma'am,' Stoner said.

'Oh,' Mrs Darley said. 'Well, we used to have some of the younger professors over for tea in the afternoons. But that was quite a few years ago, before the war. You were in the war, Professor Stoner?'

'No, ma'am,' Stoner said. 'I was at the University.'

'Yes,' Mrs Darley said. She nodded brightly. 'And you teach—?'

'English,' Stoner said. 'And I'm not a professor. I'm just an instructor.' He knew his voice was harsh; he could not control it. He tried to smile.

'Ah, yes,' she said. 'Shakespeare . . . Browning . . .'

A silence came between them. Stoner twisted his hands together and looked at the floor.

Mrs Darley said, 'I'll see if Edith is ready. If you'll excuse me?'

Stoner nodded and got to his feet as she went out. He heard fierce whispers in a back room. He stood for several minutes more.

Suddenly Edith was standing in the wide doorway, pale and unsmiling. They looked at each other without recognition. Edith took a backward step and then came forward, her lips thin and tense. They shook hands gravely and sat together on the sofa. They had not spoken.

She was even taller than he remembered, and more fragile. Her face was long and slender, and she kept her lips closed over rather strong teeth. Her skin had the kind of transparency that shows a hint of color and warmth upon any provocation. Her hair was a light reddish-brown, and she wore it piled in thick tresses upon her head. But it was her eyes that caught and held him, as they had done the day before. They were very large and of the palest blue that he could imagine. When he looked at them he seemed drawn out of himself, into a mystery that he could not apprehend. He thought her the most beautiful woman he had ever seen, and he said impulsively, 'I—I want to know about you.' She drew back from him a little. He said hastily, 'I mean—yesterday, at the reception, we didn't really have a chance to talk. I wanted to talk to you, but there were so many people. People sometimes get in your way.'

'It was a very nice reception,' Edith said faintly. 'I thought everyone was very nice.'

'Oh, yes, of course,' Stoner said. 'I meant . . .' He did not go on. Edith was silent.

He said, 'I understand you and your aunt will be going to Europe in a little while.'

'Yes,' she said.

'Europe . . .' He shook his head. 'You must be very excited.'

She nodded reluctantly.

'Where will you go? I mean—what places?'

'England,' she said. 'France. Italy.'

'And you'll be going—in the spring?'

'April,' she said.

'Five months,' he said. 'It isn't very long. I hope that in that time we can—'

'I'm only here for three more weeks,' she said quickly. 'Then I go back to St Louis. For Christmas.'

'That *is* a short time.' He smiled and said awkwardly, 'Then I'll have to see you as often as I can, so that we can get to know each other.'

She looked at him almost with horror. 'I didn't mean that,' she said. 'Please . . .'

Stoner was silent for a moment. 'I'm sorry, I— But I do want to call on you again, as often as you'll let me. May I?'

'Oh,' she said. 'Well.' Her thin fingers were laced together in her lap, and her knuckles were white where the skin was stretched. She had very pale freckles on the backs of her hands.

Stoner said, 'This is going badly, isn't it? You must forgive me. I haven't known anyone like you before, and I say clumsy things. You must forgive me if I've embarrassed you.'

'Oh, no,' she said. She turned to him and pulled her lips in what he knew must be a smile. 'Not at all. I'm having a lovely time. Really.'

He did not know what to say. He mentioned the weather outside and apologized for having tracked snow upon the rug; she murmured something. He spoke of the classes he had to teach at the University, and she nodded, puzzled. At last they sat in silence. Stoner got to his feet; he moved slowly and heavily, as if he were tired. Edith looked up at him expressionlessly.

'Well,' he said and cleared his throat. 'It's getting late, and I— Look. I'm sorry. May I call on you again in a few days? Perhaps . . .'

It was as if he had not spoken to her. He nodded, said, 'Good night,' and turned to go.

Edith Bostwick said in a high shrill voice without inflection, 'When I was a little girl about six years old I could play the piano and I liked to paint and I was very shy so my mother sent me to Miss Thorndyke's School for Girls in St Louis. I was the youngest one there, but that was all right because Daddy was a member of the board and he arranged it. I didn't like it at first but finally I just loved it.

They were all very nice girls and well-to-do and I made some lifelong friends there, and—'

Stoner had turned back when she began to speak, and he looked at her with an amazement that did not show on his face. Her eyes were fixed straight before her, her face was blank, and her lips moved as if, without understanding, she read from an invisible book. He walked slowly across the room and sat down beside her. She did not seem to notice him; her eyes remained fixed straight ahead, and she continued to tell him about herself, as he had asked her to do. He wanted to tell her to stop, to comfort her, to touch her. He did not move or speak.

She continued to talk, and after a while he began to hear what she was saying. Years later it was to occur to him that in that hour and a half on that December evening of their first extended time together, she told him more about herself than she ever told him again. And when it was over, he felt that they were strangers in a way that he had not thought they would be, and he knew that he was in love.

Edith Elaine Bostwick was probably not aware of what she said to William Stoner that evening, and if she had been she could not have realized its significance. But Stoner knew what she said, and he never forgot it; what he heard was a kind of confession, and what he thought he understood was a plea for help.

As he got to know her better, he learned more of her childhood; and he came to realize that it was typical of that of most girls of her time and circumstance. She was educated upon the premise that she would be protected from the gross events that life might thrust in her way, and upon the premise that she had no other duty than to be a graceful and accomplished accessory to that protection, since she belonged to a social and economic class to which protection was an almost sacred obligation. She attended private schools for girls where she learned to read, to write, and to do simple arithmetic; in her leisure she was encouraged to do needlepoint, to play the piano, to paint water colors, and to discuss some of the more gentle works of literature. She was also instructed in matters of dress, carriage, ladylike diction, and morality.

Her moral training, both at the schools she attended and at home, was negative in nature, prohibitive in intent, and almost entirely sexual. The sexuality, however, was indirect and unacknowledged; therefore it suffused every other part of her education, which received most of its energy from that recessive and unspoken moral force. She learned that she would have duties toward her husband and family and that she must fulfill them.

Her childhood was an exceedingly formal one, even in the most ordinary moments of family life. Her parents behaved toward each other with a distant courtesy; Edith never saw pass between them the spontaneous warmth of either anger or love. Anger was days of courteous silence, and love was a word of courteous endearment. She was an only child, and loneliness was one of the earliest conditions of her life.

So she grew up with a frail talent in the more genteel arts, and no knowledge of the necessity of living from day to day. Her needlepoint was delicate and useless, she painted misty landscapes of thin water-color washes, and she played the piano with a forceless but precise hand; yet she was ignorant of her own bodily functions, she had never been alone to care for her own self one day of her life, nor could it ever have occurred to her that she might become responsible for the well-being of another. Her life was invariable, like a low hum; and it was watched over by her mother, who, when Edith was a child, would sit for hours watching her paint her pictures or play her piano, as if no other occupation were possible for either of them.

At the age of thirteen Edith went through the usual sexual transformation; she also went through a physical transformation that was more uncommon. In the space of a few months she grew almost a foot, so that her height was near that of a grown man. And the association between the ungainliness of her body and her awkward new sexual estate was one from which she never fully recovered. These changes intensified a natural shyness—she was distant from her classmates at school, she had no one at home to whom she could talk, and she turned more and more inward upon herself.

Upon that inner privacy William Stoner now intruded. And something unsuspected within her, some instinct, made her call him back when he started to go out the door, made her speak quickly and desperately, as she had never spoken before, and as she would never speak again.

During the next two weeks he saw her nearly every evening. They went to a concert sponsored by the new music department at the University; on evenings when it was not too cold they took slow, solemn walks through the streets of Columbia; but more often they sat in Mrs Darley's parlor. Sometimes they talked, and Edith played for him, while he listened and watched her hands move lifelessly over the keys. After that first evening together their conversation was curiously impersonal; he was unable to draw her out of her reserve, and when he saw that his efforts to do so embarrassed her, he stopped trying. Yet there was a kind of ease between them, and he imagined that they had an understanding. Less than a week before she was to return to St Louis he declared his love to her and proposed marriage.

Though he did not know exactly how she would take the declaration and proposal, he was surprised at her equanimity. After he spoke she gave him a long look that was deliberative and curiously bold; and he was reminded of the first afternoon, after he had asked permission to call on her, when she had looked at him from the doorway where a cold wind was blowing upon them. Then she dropped her glance; and the surprise that came upon her face seemed to him unreal. She said she had never thought of him that way, that she had never imagined, that she did not know.

'You must have known I loved you,' he said. 'I don't see how I could have hidden it.'

She said with some hint of animation, 'I didn't. I don't know anything about that.'

'Then I must tell you again,' he said gently. 'And you must get used to it. I love you, and I cannot imagine living without you.'

She shook her head, as if confused. 'My trip to Europe,' she said faintly. 'Aunt Emma . . .'

He felt a laugh come up in his throat, and he said in happy confidence, 'Ah, Europe. I'll take you to Europe. We'll see it together someday.'

She pulled away from him and put her fingertips upon her forehead. 'You must give me time to think. And I would have to talk to Mother and Daddy before I could even consider . . .'

And she would not commit herself further than that. She was not to see him again before she left for St Louis in a few days, and she would write him from there after she talked to her parents and had things settled in her mind.

When he left that evening he stooped to kiss her; she turned her head, and his lips brushed her cheek. She gave his hand a little squeeze and let him out the front door without looking at him again.

Ten days later he got his letter from her. It was a curiously formal note, and it mentioned nothing that had passed between them; it said that she would like him to meet her parents and that they were all looking forward to seeing him when he came to St Louis, the following weekend if that was possible.

Edith's parents met him with the cool formality he had expected, and they tried at once to destroy any sense of ease he might have had. Mrs Bostwick would ask him a question, and upon his answer would say, 'Y-e-es,' in a most doubtful manner, and look at him curiously, as if his face were smudged or his nose were bleeding. She was tall and thin like Edith, and at first Stoner was startled by a resemblance he had not anticipated; but Mrs Bostwick's face was heavy and lethargic, without any strength or delicacy, and it bore the deep marks of what must have been a habitual dissatisfaction.

Horace Bostwick was also tall, but he was curiously and unsubstantially heavy, almost corpulent; a fringe of gray hair curled about an otherwise bald skull, and folds of skin hung loosely around his jaws. When he spoke to Stoner he looked directly above his head as if he saw something behind him, and when Stoner answered he drummed his thick fingers upon the center piping of his vest.

Edith greeted Stoner as if he were a casual visitor and then drifted away unconcernedly, busying herself with inconsequential tasks. His eyes followed her, but he could not make her look at him.

It was the largest and most elegant house that Stoner had

ever been in. The rooms were very high and dark, and they were crowded with vases of all sizes and shapes, dully gleaming silverwork upon marble-topped tables and commodes and chests, and richly tapestried furniture with most delicate lines. They drifted through several rooms to a large parlor, where, Mrs Bostwick murmured, she and her husband were in the habit of sitting and chatting informally with friends. Stoner sat in a chair so fragile that he was afraid to move upon it; he felt it shift beneath his weight.

Edith had disappeared; Stoner looked around for her almost frantically. But she did not come back down to the parlor for nearly two hours, until after Stoner and her parents had had their 'talk.'

The 'talk' was indirect and allusive and slow, interrupted by long silences. Horace Bostwick talked about himself in brief speeches directed several inches over Stoner's head. Stoner learned that Bostwick was a Bostonian whose father, late in his life, had ruined his banking career and his son's future in New England by a series of unwise investments that had closed his bank. ('Betrayed,' Bostwick announced to the ceiling, 'by false friends.') Thus the son had come to Missouri shortly after the Civil War, intending to move west; but he had never got farther than Kansas City, where he went occasionally on business trips. Remembering his father's failure, or betrayal, he stayed with his first job in a small St Louis bank; and in his late thirties, secure in a minor vice-presidency, he married a local girl of good family. From the marriage had come only one child; he had wanted a son and had got a girl, and that was another disappointment he hardly bothered to conceal. Like many men who consider their success incomplete, he was extraordinarily vain and consumed with a sense of his own importance. Every ten or fifteen minutes he removed a large gold watch from his vest pocket, looked at it, and nodded to himself.

Mrs Bostwick spoke less frequently and less directly of herself, but Stoner quickly had an understanding of her. She was a Southern lady of a certain type. Of an old and discreetly impoverished family, she had grown up with the presumption that the circumstances of need under which the family existed were inappropriate to its quality. She had been taught to look forward to some betterment of that condition, but the betterment had never been very precisely specified. She had gone into her marriage to Horace Bostwick with that dissatisfaction so habitual within her that it was a part of her person; and as the years went on, the dissatisfaction and bitterness increased, so general and pervasive that no specific remedy might assuage them. Her voice was thin and high, and it held a note of hopelessness that gave a special value to every word she said.

It was late in the afternoon before either of them mentioned the matter that had brought them together.

They told him how dear Edith was to them, how concerned they were for her future happiness, of the advantages she had had. Stoner sat in an agony of embarrassment and tried to make responses he hoped were appropriate.

'An extraordinary girl,' Mrs Bostwick said. 'So sensitive.' The lines in her face deepened, and she said with old bitterness, 'No man—no one can fully understand the delicacy of—of—'

'Yes,' Horace Bostwick said shortly. And he began to inquire into what he called Stoner's 'prospects.' Stoner answered as best he could; he had never thought of his 'prospects' before, and he was surprised at how meager they sounded.

Bostwick said, 'And you have no—means—beyond your profession?'

'No, sir,' Stoner said.

Mr Bostwick shook his head unhappily. 'Edith has had—advantages—you know. A fine home, servants, the best schools. I'm wondering—I find myself afraid, with the reduced standard which would be inevitable with your—ah, condition—that . . .' His voice trailed away.

Stoner felt a sickness rise within him, and an anger. He waited a few moments before he replied, and he made his voice as flat and expressionless as he could.

'I must tell you, sir, that I had not considered these material matters before. Edith's happiness is, of course, my— If you believe that Edith would be unhappy, then I must . . .' He paused, searching for words. He wanted to tell Edith's father of his love for his daughter, of his certainty of their happiness together, of the kind of life they could have. But he did not go on. He caught on Horace Bostwick's face such an expression of concern, dismay, and something like fear that he was surprised into silence.

'No,' Horace Bostwick said hastily, and his expression cleared. 'You misunderstand me. I was merely attempting to lay before you certain—difficulties—that might arise in the future. I'm sure you young people have talked these things over, and I'm sure you know your own minds. I respect your judgment and . . .'

And it was settled. A few more words were said, and Mrs Bostwick wondered aloud where Edith could have been keeping herself all this time. She called out the name in her high, thin voice, and in a few moments Edith came into the room where they all waited. She did not look at Stoner.

Horace Bostwick told her that he and her 'young man' had had a nice talk and that they had his blessing. Edith nodded.

'Well,' her mother said, 'we must make plans. A spring wedding. June, perhaps.'

'No,' Edith said.

'What, my dear?' her mother asked pleasantly.

'If it's to be done,' Edith said, 'I want it done quickly.'

'The impatience of youth,' Mr Bostwick said and cleared his throat. 'But perhaps your mother is right, my dear. There are plans to be made; time is required.'

'No,' Edith said again, and there was a firmness in her voice that made them all look at her. 'It must be soon.'

There was a silence. Then her father said in a surprisingly mild voice, 'Very well, my dear. As you say. You young people make your plans.'

Edith nodded, murmured something about a task she had to do, and slipped out of the room. Stoner did not see her again until dinner that night, which was presided over in regal silence by Horace Bostwick. After dinner Edith played the piano for them, but she played stiffly and badly, with many mistakes. She announced that she was feeling unwell and went to her room.

In the guest room that night, William Stoner could not sleep. He stared up into the dark and wondered at the strangeness that had come over his life, and for the first time questioned the wisdom of what he was about to do. He thought of Edith and felt some reassurance. He supposed that all men were as uncertain as he suddenly had become, and had the same doubts.

He had to catch an early train back to Columbia the next morning, so that he had little time after breakfast. He wanted to take a trolley to the station, but Mr Bostwick insisted that one of the servants drive him in the landau. Edith was to write him in a few days about the wedding plans. He thanked the Bostwicks and bade them good-by; they walked with him and Edith to the front door. He had almost reached the front gate when he heard footsteps running behind him. He turned. It was Edith. She stood very stiff and tall, her face was pale, and she was looking straight at him.

'I'll try to be a good wife to you, William,' she said. 'I'll try.'

He realized that it was the first time anyone had spoken his name since he had come there.

4

For reasons she would not explain, Edith did not want to be married in St Louis, so the wedding was held in Columbia, in the large drawing room of Emma Darley, where they had spent their first hours together. It was the first week in February, just after classes were dismissed for the semester break. The Bostwicks took the train from St Louis, and William's parents, who had not met Edith, drove down from the farm, arriving on Saturday afternoon, the day before the wedding.

Stoner wanted to put them up at a hotel, but they preferred to stay with the Footes, even though the Footes had grown cold and distant since William had left their employ.

'Wouldn't know how to do in a hotel,' his father said seriously. 'And the Footes can put up with us for one night.'

That evening William rented a gig and drove his parents into town to Emma Darley's house so that they could meet Edith.

They were met at the door by Mrs Darley, who gave William's parents a brief, embarrassed glance and asked them into the parlor. His mother and father sat carefully, as if afraid to move in their stiff new clothes.

'I don't know what can be keeping Edith,' Mrs Darley murmured after a while. 'If you'll excuse me.' She went out of the room to get her niece.

After a long time Edith came down; she entered the parlor slowly, reluctantly, with a kind of frightened defiance.

They rose to their feet, and for several moments the four of them stood awkwardly, not knowing what to say. Then Edith came forward stiffly and gave her hand first to William's mother and then to his father.

'How do,' his father said formally and released her hand, as if afraid it would break.

Edith glanced at him, tried to smile, and backed away. 'Sit down,' she said. 'Please sit down.'

They sat. William said something. His voice sounded strained to him.

In a silence, quietly and wonderingly, as if she spoke her thoughts aloud, his mother said, 'My, she's a pretty thing, isn't she?'

William laughed a little and said gently, 'Yes, ma'am, she is.'

They were able to speak more easily then, though they darted glances at each other and then looked away into the distances of the room. Edith murmured that she was glad to meet them, that she was sorry they hadn't met before.

'And when we get settled—' She paused, and William wondered if she was going to continue. 'When we get settled you must come to visit us.'

'Thank you kindly,' his mother said.

The talk went on, but it was interrupted by long silences. Edith's nervousness increased, became more apparent, and once or twice she did not respond to a question someone asked her. William got to his feet, and his mother, with a nervous look around her, stood also. But his father did not move. He looked directly at Edith and kept his eyes on her for a long time.

Finally he said, 'William was always a good boy. I'm

glad he's getting himself a fine woman. A man needs himself a woman, to do for him and give him comfort. Now you be good to William. He ought to have someone who can be good to him.'

Edith's head came back in a kind of reflex of shock; her eyes were wide, and for a moment William thought she was angry. But she was not. His father and Edith looked at each other for a long time, and their eyes did not waver.

'I'll try, Mr Stoner,' Edith said. 'I'll try.'

Then his father got to his feet and bowed clumsily and said, 'It's getting late. We'd best be getting along.' And he walked with his wife, shapeless and dark and small beside him, to the door, leaving Edith and his son together.

Edith did not speak to him. But when he turned to bid her good night William saw that tears were swimming in her eyes. He bent to kiss her, and he felt the frail strength of her slender fingers on his arms.

The cold clear sunlight of the February afternoon slanted through the front windows of the Darley house and was broken by the figures that moved about in the large parlor. His parents stood curiously alone in a corner of the room; the Bostwicks, who had come in only an hour before on the morning train, stood near them, not looking at them; Gordon Finch walked heavily and anxiously around, as if he were in charge of something; there were a few people, friends of Edith or her parents, whom he did not know. He heard himself speaking to those about him, felt his lips smiling, and heard voices come to him as if muffled by layers of thick cloth.

Gordon Finch was beside him; his face was sweaty, and it glowed above his dark suit. He grinned nervously. 'You about ready, Bill?'

Stoner felt his head nod.

Finch said, 'Does the doomed man have any last requests?'
Stoner smiled and shook his head.

Finch clapped him on the shoulder. 'You just stick by me; do what I tell you; everything's under control. Edith will be down in a few minutes.'

He wondered if he would remember this after it was over; everything seemed a blur, as if he saw through a haze. He heard himself ask Finch, 'The minister—I haven't seen him. Is he here?'

Finch laughed and shook his head and said something. Then a murmur came over the room. Edith was walking down the stairs.

In her white dress she was like a cold light coming into the room. Stoner started involuntarily toward her and felt Finch's hand on his arm, restraining him. Edith was pale, but she gave him a small smile. Then she was beside him, and they were walking together. A stranger with a round collar stood before them; he was short and fat and he had a vague face. He was mumbling words and looking at a white book in his hands. William heard himself responding to silences. He felt Edith trembling beside him.

Then there was a long silence, and another murmur, and the sound of laughter. Someone said, 'Kiss the bride!' He felt himself turned; Finch was grinning at him. He smiled down at Edith, whose face swam before him, and kissed her; her lips were as dry as his own.

He felt his hand being pumped; people were clapping him on the back and laughing; the room was milling. New people came in the door. A large cut-glass bowl of punch seemed to have appeared on a long table at one end of the parlor. There was a cake. Someone held his and Edith's hands together; there was a knife; he understood that he was supposed to guide her hand as she cut the cake.

Then he was separated from Edith and couldn't see her in the throng of people. He was talking and laughing, nodding, and looking around the room to see if he could find Edith. He saw his mother and father standing in the same corner of the room, from which they had not moved. His mother was smiling, and his father had his hand awkwardly on her shoulder. He started to go to them, but he could not break away from whoever was talking to him.

Then he saw Edith. She was with her father and mother and her aunt; her father, with a slight frown on his face, was surveying the room as if impatient with it; and her mother was weeping, her eyes red and puffed above her heavy cheekbones and her mouth pursed downward like a child's. Mrs Darley and Edith had their arms about her; Mrs Darley was talking to her, rapidly, as if trying to explain something. But even across the room William could see that Edith was silent; her face was like a mask, expressionless and white. After a moment they led Mrs Bostwick from the room, and William did not see Edith again until the reception was over, until Gordon Finch whispered something in his ear, led him to a side door that opened onto a little garden, and pushed him outside. Edith was waiting there, bundled against the cold, her collar turned up about her face so that he could not see it. Gordon Finch, laughing and saying words that William could not understand, hustled them down a path to the street, where a covered buggy was waiting to carry them to the station. It was not until they were on the train, which would take them to St Louis for their week's honeymoon, that William Stoner realized that it was all over and that he had a wife.

★

They went into marriage innocent, but innocent in profoundly different ways. They were both virginal, and they were conscious of their inexperience; but whereas William, having been raised on a farm, took as unremarkable the natural processes of life, they were to Edith profoundly mysterious and unexpected. She knew nothing of them, and there was something within her which did not wish to know of them.

And so, like many others, their honeymoon was a failure; yet they would not admit this to themselves, and they did not realize the significance of the failure until long afterward.

They arrived in St Louis late Sunday night. On the train, surrounded by strangers who looked curiously and approvingly at them, Edith had been animated and almost gay. They laughed and held hands and spoke of the days to come. Once in the city, and by the time William had found a carriage to take them to their hotel, Edith's gaiety had become faintly hysterical.

He half carried her, laughing, through the entrance of the Ambassador Hotel, a massive structure of brown cut stone. The lobby was nearly deserted, dark and heavy like a cavern; when they got inside, Edith abruptly quieted and swayed uncertainly beside him as they walked across the immense floor to the desk. By the time they got to their room she was nearly physically ill; she trembled as if in a fever, and her lips were blue against her chalk-like skin. William wanted to find her a doctor, but she insisted that she was only tired, that she needed rest. They spoke gravely of the strain of the day, and Edith hinted at some delicacy that troubled her from time to time. She murmured, but without looking at him and without intonation in her voice, that she wanted their first hours together to be perfect.

And William said, 'They are—they will be. You must rest. Our marriage will begin tomorrow.'

And like other new husbands of whom he had heard and at whose expense he had at one time or another made jokes, he spent his wedding night apart from his wife, his long body curled stiffly and sleeplessly on a small sofa, his eyes open to the passing night.

He awoke early. Their suite, arranged and paid for by Edith's parents, as a wedding gift, was on the tenth floor, and it commanded a view of the city. He called softly to Edith, and in a few minutes she came out of the bedroom, tying the sash of her dressing gown, yawning sleepily, smiling a little. William felt his love for her grip his throat; he took her by the hand, and they stood before the window in their sitting room, looking down. Automobiles, pedestrians, and carriages crept on the narrow streets below them; they seemed to themselves far removed from the run of humanity and its pursuits. In the distance, visible beyond the square buildings of red brick and stone, the Mississippi River wound its bluish-brown length in the morning sun; the riverboats and tugs that crawled up and down its stiff bends were like toys, though their stacks gave off great quantities of gray smoke to the winter air. A sense of calm came over him; he put his arm around his wife and held her lightly, and they both gazed down upon a world that seemed full of promise and quiet adventure.

They breakfasted early. Edith seemed refreshed, fully recovered from her indisposition of the night before; she was almost gay again, and she looked at William with an intimacy and warmth that he thought were from gratitude and love. They did not speak of the night before; every now and then Edith looked at her new ring and adjusted it on her finger.

★

They wrapped themselves against the cold and walked the St Louis streets, which were just beginning to crowd with people; they looked at goods in windows, they spoke of the future and gravely thought of how they would fill it. William began to regain the ease and fluency he had discovered during his early courtship of this woman who had become his wife; Edith clung to his arm and seemed to attend to what he said as she had never done before. They had midmorning coffee in a small warm shop and watched the passers-by scurry through the cold. They found a carriage and drove to the Art Museum. Arm in arm they walked through the high rooms, through the rich glow of light reflected from the paintings. In the quietness, in the warmth, in the air that took on a timelessness from the old paintings and statuary, William Stoner felt an outrush of affection for the tall, delicate girl who walked beside him, and he felt a quiet passion rise within him, warm and formally sensuous, like the colors that came out from the walls around him.

When they left there late in the afternoon the sky had clouded and a thin drizzle had started; but William Stoner carried within him the warmth he had gathered in the museum. They got back to the hotel shortly after sunset; Edith went into the bedroom to rest, and William called downstairs to have a light dinner sent to their rooms; and on a sudden inspiration, he went downstairs himself into the saloon and asked for a bottle of champagne to be iced and sent up within the hour. The bartender nodded glumly and told him that it would not be a good champagne. By the first of July, Prohibition would be national; already it was illegal to brew or distill liquors; and there were no more than fifty bottles of champagne of any sort in the cellars of the hotel. And he would have to charge more than the champagne was worth. Stoner smiled and told him that would be all right.

Although on special occasions of celebration in her parents' home Edith had taken a little wine, she had never before tasted champagne. As they ate their dinner, set up on a small square table in their sitting room, she glanced nervously at the strange bottle in its bucket of ice. Two white candles in dull brass holders glowed unevenly against the darkness; William had turned out the other lights. The candles flickered between them as they talked, and the light caught the curves of the smooth dark bottle and glittered upon the ice that surrounded it. They were nervous and cautiously gay.

Inexpertly he withdrew the cork from the champagne; Edith jumped at the loud report; white froth spurted from the bottle neck and drenched his hand. They laughed at his clumsiness. They drank a glass of the wine, and Edith pretended tipsiness. They drank another glass. William thought he saw a languor come over her, a quietness fall upon her face, a pensiveness darken her eyes. He rose and went behind her, where she sat at the little table; he put his hands upon her shoulders, marveling at the thickness and heaviness of his fingers upon the delicacy of her flesh and bone. She stiffened beneath his touch, and he made his hands go gently to the sides of her thin neck and let them brush into the fine reddish hair; her neck was rigid, the cords vibrant in their tensity. He put his hands on her arms and lifted gently, so that she rose from the chair; he turned her to face him. Her eyes, wide and pale and nearly transparent in the candlelight, looked upon him blankly. He felt a distant closeness to her, and a pity for her helplessness; desire thickened in his throat so that he could not speak. He pulled her a little toward the bedroom, feeling a quick hard resistance in her body, and feeling at the same moment a willed putting away of the resistance.

He left the door to the unlighted bedroom open; the candle-light glowed feebly in the darkness. He murmured as if to comfort and assure her, but his words were smothered and he could not hear what he said. He put his hands upon her body and fumbled for the buttons that would open her to him. She pushed him away impersonally; in the dimness her eyes were closed and her lips tight. She turned away from him and with a quick movement loosened her dress so that it fell crumpled about her feet. Her arms and shoulders were bare; she shuddered as if from cold and said in a flat voice, 'Go in the other room. I'll be ready in a minute.' He touched her arms and put his lips to her shoulder, but she would not turn to him.

In the sitting room he stared at the candles that flickered over the remains of their dinner, in the midst of which rested the bottle of champagne, still more than half full. He poured a little of the wine into a glass and tasted it; it had grown warm and sweetish.

When he returned, Edith was in bed with the covers pulled to her chin, her face turned upward, her eyes closed, a thin frown creasing her forehead. Silently, as if she were asleep, Stoner undressed and got into bed beside her. For several moments he lay with his desire, which had become an impersonal thing, belonging to himself alone. He spoke to Edith, as if to find a haven for what he felt; she did not answer. He put his hand upon her and felt beneath the thin cloth of her night-gown the flesh he had longed for. He moved his hand upon her; she did not stir; her frown deepened. Again he spoke, saying her name to silence; then he moved his body upon her, gentle in his clumsiness. When he touched the softness of her thighs she turned her head sharply away and lifted her arm to cover her eyes. She made no sound.

Afterward he lay beside her and spoke to her in the quietness of his love. Her eyes were open then, and they stared at him out of the shadow; there was no expression on her face. Suddenly she flung the covers from her and crossed swiftly to the bathroom. He saw the light go on and heard her retch loudly and agonizingly. He called to her and went across the room; the door to the bathroom was locked. He called to her again; she did not answer. He went back to the bed and waited for her. After several minutes of silence the light in the bathroom went off and the door opened. Edith came out and walked stiffly to the bed.

'It was the champagne,' she said. 'I shouldn't have had the second glass.'

She pulled the covers over her and turned away from him; in a few moments her breathing was regular and heavy in sleep.

5

They returned to Columbia two days earlier than they had planned; restless and strained by their isolation, it was as if they walked together in a prison. Edith said that they really ought to get back to Columbia so that William could prepare for his classes and so that she could begin to get them settled in their new apartment. Stoner agreed at once—and told himself that things would be better once they were in a place of their own, among people they knew and in surroundings that were familiar. They packed their belongings that afternoon and were on the train to Columbia the same evening.

In the hurried, vague days before their marriage Stoner had found a vacant second-floor apartment in an old barn-like house five blocks from the University. It was dark and bare, with a small bedroom, a tiny kitchen, and a huge living room with high windows; it had at one time been occupied by an artist, a teacher at the University, who had been none too tidy; the dark, wide-planked floors were splotched with brilliant yellows and blues and reds, and the walls were smudged with paint and dirt. Stoner thought the place romantic and commodious, and he judged it to be a good place to start a new life.

Edith moved into the apartment as if it were an enemy to be conquered. Though unused to physical labor, she scraped

74

away most of the paint from the floors and walls and scrubbed at the dirt she imagined secreted everywhere; her hands blistered and her face became strained, with dark hollows beneath the eyes. When Stoner tried to help her she became stubborn, her lips tightened, and she shook her head; he needed the time for his studies, she said; this was *her* job. When he forced his help upon her, she became almost sullen, thinking herself to be humiliated. Puzzled and helpless, he withdrew his aid and watched as, grimly, Edith continued awkwardly to scrub the gleaming floors and walls, to sew curtains and hang them unevenly from the high windows, to repair and paint and repaint the used furniture they had begun to accumulate. Though inept, she worked with a silent and intense ferocity, so that by the time William got home from the University in the afternoon she was exhausted. She would drag herself to prepare the evening meal, eat a few bites, and then with a murmur vanish into the bedroom to sleep like one drugged until after William had left for his classes the next morning.

Within a month he knew that his marriage was a failure; within a year he stopped hoping that it would improve. He learned silence and did not insist upon his love. If he spoke to her or touched her in tenderness, she turned away from him within herself and became wordless, enduring, and for days afterward drove herself to new limits of exhaustion. Out of an unspoken stubbornness they both had, they shared the same bed; sometimes at night, in her sleep, she unknow-ingly moved against him. And sometimes, then, his resolve and knowledge crumbled before his love, and he moved upon her. If she was sufficiently roused from her sleep she tensed and stiffened, turning her head sideways in a familiar gesture and burying it in her pillow, enduring violation; at such times Stoner performed his love as quickly as he could, hating himself for his haste and regretting his passion. Less frequently she remained half numbed by sleep; then she was passive, and she murmured drowsily, whether in protest or surprise he did not know. He came to look forward to these rare and unpredictable moments, for in that sleep-drugged acquiescence he could pretend to himself that he found a kind of response.

And he could not speak to her of what he took to be her unhappiness. When he attempted to do so, she accepted what he said as a reflection upon her adequacy and her self, and she became as morosely withdrawn from him as she did when he made love to her. He blamed his clumsiness for her withdrawal and took upon himself the responsibility for what she felt.

With a quiet ruthlessness that came from his desperation, he experimented with small ways of pleasing her. He brought her gifts, which she accepted indifferently, sometimes commenting mildly upon their expense; he took her on walks and picnics in the wooded countryside around Columbia, but she tired easily and sometimes became ill; he talked to her of his work, as he had done in their courtship, but her interest had become perfunctory and indulgent.

At last, though he knew her to be shy, he insisted as gently as he could that they begin to entertain. They had an informal tea to which a few of the younger instructors and assistant professors in the department were invited, and they gave several small dinner parties. In no way did Edith show whether she was pleased or displeased; but her preparations for the events were so frenzied and obsessive that by the time the guests arrived she was half hysterical from strain and weariness, though no one except William was really aware of this.

She was a good hostess. She talked to her guests with an animation and ease that made her seem a stranger to William, and she spoke to him in their presence with an intimacy and fondness that always surprised him. She called him Willy, which touched him oddly, and sometimes she laid a soft hand upon his shoulder.

But when the guests left, the façade fell upon itself and revealed her collapse. She spoke bitterly of the departed guests, imagining obscure insults and slights; she quietly and desperately recounted what she thought to be unforgivable failures of her own; she sat still and brooding in the litter the guests had left and would not be roused by William and would answer him briefly and distraughtly in a flat, monotonous voice.

Only once had the façade cracked when guests were present.

Several months after Stoner's and Edith's marriage, Gordon Finch had become engaged to a girl whom he had met casually while he was stationed in New York and whose parents lived in Columbia. Finch had been given a permanent post as assistant dean, and it was tacitly understood that when Josiah Claremont died Finch would be among the first to be considered for the deanship of the College. Somewhat belatedly, in celebration of both Finch's new position and the announcement of his engagement, Stoner asked him and his fiancée to dinner.

They came just before dusk on a warm evening in late May, in a shining black new touring car which gave off a series of explosions as Finch expertly brought it to a halt on the brick road in front of Stoner's house. He honked the horn and waved gaily until William and Edith came downstairs. A small dark girl with a round, smiling face sat beside him.

He introduced her as Caroline Wingate, and the four of them talked for a moment while Finch helped her descend from the car.

'Well, how do you like it?' Finch asked, thumping the front fender of the car with his closed fist. 'A beauty, isn't it? Belongs to Caroline's father. I'm thinking of getting one just like it, so . . .' His voice trailed away and his eyes narrowed; he regarded the automobile speculatively and coolly, as if it were the future.

Then he became lively and jocular again. With mock secrecy he put his forefinger to his lips, looked furtively around, and took a large brown paper bag from the front seat of the car. 'Hooch,' he whispered. 'Just off the boat. Cover me, pal; maybe we can make it to the house.'

The dinner went well. Finch was more affable than Stoner had seen him in years; Stoner thought of himself and Finch and Dave Masters sitting together on those distant Friday afternoons after class, drinking beer and talking. The fiancée, Caroline, said little; she smiled happily as Finch joked and winked. It came to Stoner as an almost envious shock to realize that Finch was genuinely fond of this dark pretty girl, and that her silence came from a rapt affection for him.

Even Edith lost some of her strain and tenseness; she smiled easily, and her laughter was spontaneous. Finch was playful and familiar with Edith in a way, Stoner realized, that he, her own husband, could never be; and Edith seemed happier than she had been in months.

After dinner Finch removed the brown paper bag from the icebox, where he had placed it earlier to cool, and took from it a number of dark brown bottles. It was a home brew that he made with great secrecy and ceremony in the closet of his bachelor apartment.

'No room for my clothes,' he said, 'but a man's got to keep his sense of values.'

Carefully, with his eyes squinted, with the light glistening upon his fair skin and thinning blond hair, like a chemist measuring a rare substance, he poured the beer from the bottles into glasses.

'Got to be careful with this stuff,' he said. 'You get a lot of sediment at the bottom, and if you pour it off too quick, you get it in the glass.'

They each drank a glass of the beer, complimenting Finch upon its taste. It was, indeed, surprisingly good, dry and light and of a good color. Even Edith finished her glass and took another.

They became a little drunk; they laughed vaguely and sentimentally; they saw each other anew.

Holding his glass up to the light, Stoner said, 'I wonder how Dave would have liked this beer.'

'Dave?' Finch asked.

'Dave Masters. Remember how he used to love beer?'

'Dave Masters,' Finch said. 'Good old Dave. It's a damned shame.'

'Masters,' Edith said. She was smiling fuzzily. 'Wasn't he that friend of yours that was killed in the war?'

'Yes,' Stoner said. 'That's the one.' The old sadness came over him, but he smiled at Edith.

'Good old Dave,' Finch said. 'Edie, your husband and I and Dave used to really lap it up—long before he knew of you, of course. Good old Dave . . .'

They smiled at the memory of David Masters.

'He was a good friend of yours?' Edith asked.

Stoner nodded. 'He was a good friend.'

'Château-Thierry.' Finch drained his glass. 'War's a hell of a thing.' He shook his head. 'But old Dave. He's probably somewhere laughing at us right now. He wouldn't be feeling sorry for himself. I wonder if he ever really got to see any of France?'

'I don't know,' Stoner said. 'He was killed so soon after he got over.'

'Be a shame if he didn't. I always thought that was one of the main reasons he joined up. To see some of Europe.'

'Europe,' Edith said distinctly.

'Yeah,' Finch said. 'Old Dave didn't want too many things, but he did want to see Europe before he died.'

'I was going to Europe once,' Edith said. She was smiling, and her eyes glittered helplessly. 'Do you remember, Willy? I was going with my Aunt Emma just before we got married. Do you remember?'

'I remember,' Stoner said.

Edith laughed gratingly and shook her head as if she were puzzled. 'It seems like a long time ago, but it wasn't. How long has it been, Willy?'

'Edith—' Stoner said.

'Let's see, we were going in April. And then a year. And now it's May. I would have been . . .' Suddenly her eyes filled with tears, though she was still smiling with a fixed brightness. 'I'll never get there now, I guess. Aunt Emma is going to die pretty soon, and I'll never have a chance to . . .'

Then, with the smile still tightening her lips and her eyes streaming with tears, she began to sob. Stoner and Finch rose from their chairs.

'Edith,' Stoner said helplessly.

'Oh, leave me alone!' With a curious twisting motion she stood erect before them, her eyes shut tight and her hands clenched at her sides. 'All of you! Just leave me alone!' And she turned and stumbled into the bedroom, slamming the door behind her.

For a moment no one spoke; they listened to the muffled sound of Edith's sobbing. Then Stoner said, 'You'll have to excuse her. She has been tired and not too well. The strain—'

'Sure, I know how it is, Bill.' Finch laughed hollowly. 'Women and all. Guess I'll be getting used to it pretty soon myself.' He looked at Caroline, laughed again, and lowered his voice. 'Well, we won't disturb Edie right now. You just thank her for us, tell her it was a fine meal, and you folks'll have to come over to our place after we get settled in.'

'Thanks, Gordon,' Stoner said. 'I'll tell her.'

'And don't *worry*,' Finch said. He punched Stoner on the arm. 'These things happen.'

After Gordon and Caroline had left, after he heard the new car roar and sputter away into the night, William Stoner stood in the middle of the living room and listened to Edith's dry and regular sobbing. It was a sound curiously flat and without emotion, and it went on as if it would never stop. He wanted to comfort her; he wanted to soothe her; but he did not know what to say. So he stood and listened; and after a while he realized that he had never before heard Edith cry.

After the disastrous party with Gordon Finch and Caroline Wingate, Edith seemed almost contented, calmer than she had been at any time during their marriage. But she did not want to have anyone in, and she showed a reluctance to go outside the apartment. Stoner did most of their shopping from lists that Edith made for him in a curiously laborious and childlike handwriting on little sheets of blue notepaper. She seemed happiest when she was alone; she would sit for hours working needlepoint or embroidering tablecloths and napkins, with a tiny indrawn smile on her lips. Her aunt Emma Darley began more and more frequently to visit her; when William came from the University in the afternoon he often found the two of them together, drinking tea and conversing in tones so low that they might have been whispers. They always greeted him politely, but William knew that they saw him with regret; Mrs Darley seldom stayed for more than a few minutes after he arrived. He learned to maintain an unobtrusive and delicate regard for the world in which Edith had begun to live.

In the summer of 1920 he spent a week with his parents while Edith visited her relatives in St Louis; he had not seen his mother and father since the wedding.

He worked in the fields for a day or two, helping his father and the Negro hired hand; but the give of the warm moist clods beneath his feet and the smell of the new-turned earth in his nostrils evoked in him no feeling of return or familiarity. He came back to Columbia and spent the rest of the summer preparing for a new class that he was to teach the following academic year. He spent most of each day in the library, sometimes returning to Edith and the apartment late in the evening, through the heavy sweet scent of honeysuckle that moved in the warm air and among the delicate leaves of dogwood trees that rustled and turned, ghost-like in the darkness. His eyes burned from their concentration upon dim texts, his mind was heavy with what it observed, and his fingers tingled numbly from the retained feel of old leather and board and paper; but he was open to the world through which for a moment he walked, and he found some joy in it.

A few new faces appeared at departmental meetings; some familiar ones were not there; and Archer Sloane continued the slow decline which Stoner had begun to notice during the war. His hands shook, and he was unable to keep his attention upon what he said. The department went on with the momentum it had gathered through its tradition and the mere fact of its being.

Stoner went about his teaching with an intensity and ferocity that awed some of the newer members of the department and that caused a small concern among the colleagues who had known him for a longer time. His face grew haggard, he lost weight, and the stoop of his shoulders increased. In the second semester of that year he had a chance to take a teaching overload for extra pay, and he took it; also for extra pay, he taught in the new summer school that year. He had a vague notion of saving enough money to go abroad, so that he could show Edith the Europe she had given up for his sake.

In the summer of 1921, searching for a reference to a Latin poem that he had forgotten, he glanced at his dissertation for the first time since he had submitted it for approval three years earlier; he read it through and judged it to be sound. A little frightened at his presumption, he considered reworking it into a book. Though he was again teaching the full summer session, he reread most of the texts he had used and began to extend his research. Late in January he decided that a book was possible; by early spring he was far enough along to be able to write the first tentative pages.

It was in the spring of the same year that, calmly and almost indifferently, Edith told him that she had decided she wanted a child.

The decision came suddenly and without apparent source, so that when she made the announcement one morning at breakfast, only a few minutes before William had to leave for his first class, she spoke almost with surprise, as if she had made a discovery.

'What?' William said. 'What did you say?'

'I want a baby,' Edith said. 'I think I want to have a baby.'

She was nibbling a piece of toast. She wiped her lips with the corner of a napkin and smiled fixedly.

'Don't you think we ought to have one?' she asked. 'We've been married for nearly three years.'

'Of course,' William said. He set his cup down in its saucer with great care. He did not look at her. 'Are you sure? We've never talked about it. I wouldn't want you to—'

'Oh, yes,' she said. 'I'm quite sure. I think we ought to have a child.'

William looked at his watch. 'I'm late. I wish we had more time to talk. I want you to be sure.'

A small frown came between her eyes. 'I told you I was sure. Don't *you* want one? Why do you keep asking me? I don't want to talk about it any more.'

'All right,' William said. He sat looking at her for a moment. 'I've got to go.' But he did not move. Then awkwardly he put his hand over her long fingers that rested on the tablecloth and kept it there until she moved her hand away. He got up from the table and edged around her, almost shyly, and gathered his books and papers. As she always did, Edith came into the living room to wait for him to leave. He kissed her on the cheek—something he had not done for a long while.

At the door he turned and said, 'I'm—I'm glad you want a child, Edith. I know that in some ways our marriage has been a disappointment to you. I hope this will make a difference between us.'

'Yes,' Edith said. 'You'll be late for your class. You'd better hurry.'

After he had gone Edith remained for some minutes in the center of the room, staring at the closed door, as if trying to remember something. Then she moved restlessly across

84

the floor, walking from one place to another, moving within her clothing as if she could not endure its rustling and shifting upon her flesh. She unbuttoned her stiff gray taffeta morning robe and let it drop to the floor. She crossed her arms over her breasts and hugged herself, kneading the flesh of her upper arms through her thin flannel nightgown. Again she paused in her moving and walked purposefully into the tiny bedroom and opened a closet door, upon the inside of which hung a full-length mirror. She adjusted the mirror to the light and stood back from it, inspecting the long thin figure in the straight blue nightgown that it reflected. Without removing her eyes from the mirror she unbuttoned the top of her gown and pulled it up from her body and over her head, so that she stood naked in the morning light. She wadded the nightgown and threw it in the closet. Then she turned about before the mirror, inspecting the body as if it belonged to someone else. She passed her hands over her small drooping breasts and let her hands go lightly down her long waist and over her flat belly.

She moved away from the mirror and went to the bed, which was still unmade. She pulled the covers off, folded them carelessly, and put them in the closet. She smoothed the sheet on the bed and lay there on her back, her legs straight and her arms at her side. Unblinking and motion-less, she stared up at the ceiling and waited through the morning and the long afternoon.

When William Stoner got home that evening it was nearly dark, but no light came from the second-floor windows. Vaguely apprehensive, he went up the stairs and flipped the living-room light on. The room was empty. He called, 'Edith?'

There was no reply. He called again.

He looked in the kitchen; the dishes from breakfast were

still on the tiny table. He went swiftly across the living room and opened the door to the bedroom.

Edith lay naked on the bare bed. When the door opened and the light from the living room fell upon her, she turned her head to him; but she did not get up. Her eyes were wide and staring, and little sounds came from her parted mouth.

'Edith!' he said and went to where she lay, kneeling beside her. 'Are you all right? What's the matter?'

She did not answer, but the sounds she had been making became louder and her body moved beside him. Suddenly her hands came out at him like claws, and he almost jerked away; but they went to his clothing, clutching and tearing at it, pulling him upon the bed beside her. Her mouth came up to him, gaping and hot; her hands were going over him, pulling at his clothes, seeking him; and all the time her eyes were wide and staring and untroubled, as if they belonged to somebody else and saw nothing.

It was a new knowledge he had of Edith, this desire that was like a hunger so intense that it seemed to have nothing to do with her self; and no sooner was it sated than it began at once to grow again within her, so that they both lived in the tense expectation of its presence.

Although the next two months were the only time of passion William and Edith Stoner ever had together, their relationship did not really change. Very soon Stoner realized that the force which drew their bodies together had little to do with love; they coupled with a fierce yet detached determination, drew apart, and coupled again, without the strength to surfeit their need.

Sometimes during the day, while William was at the University, the need came so strongly upon Edith that she could not remain still; she would leave the apartment and walk swiftly up and down the streets, going aimlessly from one place to another. And then she would return, draw closed the curtains of the windows, undress herself, and wait, crouched in the semidarkness, for William to get home. And when he opened the door she was upon him, her hands wild and demanding, as if they had a life of their own, pulling him toward the bedroom, upon the bed which was still rumpled from their use of it the night or the morning before.

Edith became pregnant in June and immediately fell into an illness from which she did not wholly recover during the full time of her waiting. Nearly at the moment she became pregnant, even before the fact was confirmed by her calendar and her physician, the hunger for William that had raged within her for the better part of two months ceased. She made it clear to her husband that she could not endure the touch of his hand upon her, and it began to seem to him that even his looking at her was a kind of violation. The hunger of their passion became a memory, and at last Stoner looked upon it as if it were a dream that had nothing to do with either of them.

So the bed that had been the arena of their passion became the support of her illness. She kept to it most of the day, rising only to relieve her nausea in the morning and to walk unsteadily about the living room for a few minutes in the afternoon. In the afternoon and evening, after he had hurried from his work at the University, William cleaned the rooms, washed the dishes, and made the evening meal; he carried Edith's dinner to her on a tray. Though she did not want him to eat with her, she did seem to enjoy sharing a cup of weak tea with him after dinner. For a few moments in the evening, then, they talked quietly and casually, as if they were old friends or exhausted enemies. Edith would fall asleep soon afterward; and William would return to the kitchen, complete the housework, and then set up a table before the living-room sofa, where he would grade papers or prepare lectures. Then, past midnight, he would cover himself with a blanket he kept neatly folded behind the couch; and with his length curled up on the couch he would sleep fitfully until morning.

The child, a girl, was born after a three-day period of labor in the middle of March in the year 1923. They named her Grace, after one of Edith's aunts who had died many years before.

Even at birth Grace was a beautiful child, with distinct features and a light down of golden hair. Within a few days the first redness of her skin turned into a glowing golden pink. She seldom cried, and she seemed almost aware of her surroundings. William fell instantly in love with her; the affection he could not show to Edith he could show to his daughter, and he found a pleasure in caring for her that he had not anticipated.

For nearly a year after the birth of Grace, Edith remained partly bedridden; there was some fear that she might become a permanent invalid, though the doctor could find no specific trouble. William hired a woman to come in during the morning to care for Edith, and he arranged his classes so that he would be at home early in the afternoon.

Thus for more than a year William kept the house and cared for two helpless people. He was up before dawn, grading papers and preparing lectures; before going to the University he fed Grace, prepared breakfast for himself and Edith, and fixed a lunch for himself, which he took to school in his briefcase. After his classes he came back to the apartment, which he swept, dusted, and cleaned.

88

And he was more nearly a mother than a father to his daughter. He changed her diapers and washed them; he chose her clothing and mended it when it was torn; he fed her and bathed her and rocked her in his arms when she was distressed. Every now and then Edith would call querulously for her baby; William would bring Grace to her, and Edith, propped up in bed, would hold her for a few moments, silently and uncomfortably, as if the child belonged to someone else who was a stranger. Then she would tire and with a sigh hand the baby back to William. Moved by some obscure emotion, she would weep a little, dab at her eyes, and turn away from him.

So for the first year of her life, Grace Stoner knew only her father's touch, and his voice, and his love.

6

Early in the summer of 1924, on a Friday afternoon, Archer Sloane was seen by several students going into his office. He was discovered shortly after dawn the following Monday by a janitor who made the rounds of the offices in Jesse Hall to empty the wastebaskets. Sloane was sitting rigidly slumped in his chair before his desk, his head at an odd angle, his eyes open and fixed in a terrible stare. The janitor spoke to him and then ran shouting through the empty halls. There was some delay in the removal of the body from the office, and a few early students were milling in the corridors when the curiously humped and sheeted figure was carried on a stretcher down the steps to the waiting ambulance. It was later determined that Sloane had died sometime late Friday night or early Saturday morning, of causes that were obviously natural but never precisely determined, and had remained the whole weekend at the desk staring endlessly before him. The coroner announced heart failure as the cause of death, but William Stoner always felt that in a moment of anger and despair Sloane had willed his heart to cease, as if in a last mute gesture of love and contempt for a world that had betrayed him so profoundly that he could not endure in it.

Stoner was one of the pallbearers at the funeral. At the services he could not keep his mind on the words the minister said, but he knew that they were empty. He remembered Sloane as he had first seen him in the classroom; he remembered their first talks together; and he thought of the slow decline of this man who had been his distant friend. Later, after the services were over, when he lifted his handle of the gray casket and helped to carry it out to the hearse, what he carried seemed so light that he could not believe there was anything inside the narrow box.

Sloane had no family; only his colleagues and a few people from town gathered around the narrow pit and listened in awe, embarrassment, and respect as the minister said his words. And because he had no family or loved ones to mourn his passing, it was Stoner who wept when the casket was lowered, as if that weeping might reduce the loneliness of the last descent. Whether he wept for himself, for the part of his history and youth that went down to the earth, or whether for the poor thin figure that once kept the man he had loved, he did not know.

Gordon Finch drove him back to town, and for most of the ride they did not speak. Then, when they neared town, Gordon asked about Edith; William said something and inquired after Caroline. Gordon replied, and there was a long silence. Just before they drove up to William's apartment Gordon Finch spoke again.

'I don't know. All during the service I kept thinking about Dave Masters. About Dave dying in France, and about old Sloane sitting there at his desk, dead two days; like they were the same kinds of dying. I never knew Sloane very well, but I guess he was a good man; at least I hear he used to be. And now we'll have to bring somebody else in and find a new chairman for the department. It's like it all just goes around and around and keeps on going. It makes you wonder.'

'Yes,' William said and did not speak further. But he was for a moment very fond of Gordon Finch; and when he got out of the car and watched Gordon drive away, he felt the keen knowledge that another part of himself, of his past, was drawing slowly, almost imperceptibly away from him, into the darkness.

In addition to his duties as assistant dean, Gordon Finch was given the interim chairmanship of the English Department; and it became his immediate duty to find a replacement for Archer Sloane.

It was July before the matter was settled. Then Finch called those members of the department who had remained in Columbia over the summer and announced the replacement. It was, Finch told the little group, a nineteenth-century specialist, Hollis N. Lomax, who had recently received his Ph.D. from Harvard University but who had nevertheless taught for several years at a small downstate New York liberal-arts college. He came with high recommendations, he had already started publishing, and he was being hired at the assistant professor level. There were, Finch emphasized, no present plans about the departmental chairmanship; Finch was to remain interim chairman for at least one more year.

For the rest of the summer Lomax remained a figure of mystery and the object of speculation by the permanent members of the faculty. The essays that he had published in the journals were dug out, read, and passed around with judicious nods. Lomax did not make his appearance during New Student Week, nor was he present at the general faculty meeting on the Friday before Monday student registration. And at registration the members of the department, sitting in a line behind the long desks, wearily helping students choose their classes and assisting them in the deadly routine of filling out forms, looked surreptitiously around for a new face. Still Lomax did not make an appearance.

He was not seen until the departmental meeting late Tuesday afternoon, after registration had been completed. By that time, numbed by the monotony of the last two days and yet tense with the excitement that begins a new school year, the English faculty had nearly forgotten about Lomax. They sprawled in desk-top chairs in a large lecture room in the east wing of Jesse Hall and looked up with contemptuous yet eager expectancy at the podium where Gordon Finch stood surveying them with massive benevolence. A low hum of voices filled the room; chairs scraped on the floor; now and then someone laughed deliberately, raucously. Gordon Finch raised his right hand and held it palm outward to his audience; the hum quieted a little.

It quieted enough for everyone in the room to hear the door at the rear of the hall creak open and to hear a distinctive, slow shuffle of feet on the bare wood floor. They turned; and the hum of their conversation died. Someone whispered, 'It's Lomax,' and the sound was sharp and audible through the room.

He had come through the door, closed it, and had advanced a few steps beyond the threshold, where he now stood. He was a man barely over five feet in height, and his body was grotesquely misshapen. A small hump raised his left shoulder to his neck, and his left arm hung laxly at his side. His upper body was heavy and curved, so that he appeared to be always struggling for balance; his legs were thin, and he walked with a hitch in his stiff right leg. For several moments he stood with his blond head bent downward, as if he were inspecting his highly polished black shoes and the sharp crease of his black trousers. Then he lifted his head and shot his right arm out, exposing a stiff white length of cuff with gold links; there was a cigarette in his long pale fingers. He took a deep drag, inhaled, and expelled the smoke in a thin stream. And then they could see his face.

It was the face of a matinee idol. Long and thin and mobile, it was nevertheless strongly featured; his forehead was high and narrow, with heavy veins, and his thick waving hair, the color of ripe wheat, swept back from it in a somewhat theatrical pompadour. He dropped his cigarette on the floor, ground it beneath his sole, and spoke.

'I am Lomax.' He paused; his voice, rich and deep, articulated his words precisely, with a dramatic resonance. 'I hope I have not disrupted your meeting.'

The meeting went on, but no one paid much attention to what Gordon Finch said. Lomax sat alone in the back of the room, smoking and looking at the high ceiling, apparently oblivious of the heads that turned now and then to look at him. After the meeting was over he remained in his chair and let his colleagues come up to him, introduce themselves, and say what they had to say. He greeted each of them briefly, with a courtesy that was oddly mocking.

During the next few weeks it became evident that Lomax did not intend to fit himself into the social, cultural, and academic routine of Columbia, Missouri. Though he was ironically pleasant to his colleagues, he neither accepted nor extended any social invitations; he did not even attend the annual open house at Dean Claremont's, though the event was so traditional that attendance was almost obligatory; he was seen at none of the University concerts or lectures; it was said that his classes were lively and that his classroom behavior was eccentric. He was a popular teacher; students clustered around his desk during his off-hours, and they followed him in the halls. It was known that he occasionally invited groups of students to his rooms, where he entertained them with conversation and recordings of string quartets.

William Stoner wished to know him better, but he did not know how to do so. He spoke to him when he had something to say, and he invited him to dinner. When Lomax answered him as he did everyone else—ironically polite and impersonal—and when he refused the invitation to dinner, Stoner could think of nothing else to do.

It was some time before Stoner recognized the source of his attraction to Hollis Lomax. In Lomax's arrogance, his fluency, and his cheerful bitterness, Stoner saw, distorted but recognizable, an image of his friend David Masters. He wished to talk to him as he had talked to Dave; but he could not, even after he admitted his wish to himself. The awkwardness of his youth had not left him, but the eagerness and straightforwardness that might have made the friendship possible had. He knew what he wished was impossible, and the knowledge saddened him.

In the evenings, after he had cleaned the apartment, washed the dinner dishes, and put Grace to bed in a crib set in a corner of the living room, he worked on the revision of his book. By the end of the year it was finished; and though he was not altogether pleased with it he sent it to a publisher. To his surprise the study was accepted and scheduled for publication in the fall of 1925. On the strength of the unpublished book he was promoted to assistant professor and granted permanent tenure.

The assurance of his promotion came a few weeks after his book was accepted; upon that assurance, Edith announced that she and the baby would spend a week in St Louis visiting her parents.

She returned to Columbia in less than a week, harried

and tired but quietly triumphant. She had cut her visit short because the strain of caring for an infant had been too much for her mother, and the trip had so tired her that she was unable to care for Grace herself. But she had accomplished something. She drew from her bag a sheaf of papers and handed a small slip to William.

It was a check for six thousand dollars, made out to Mr and Mrs William Stoner and signed with the bold, nearly illegible scrawl of Horace Bostwick. 'What's this?' Stoner asked.

She handed him the other papers. 'It's a loan,' she said. 'All you have to do is sign these. I already have.'

'But six thousand dollars! What's it for?'

'A house,' Edith said. 'A *real* house of our own.'

William Stoner looked again at the papers, shuffled through them quickly, and said, 'Edith, we can't. I'm sorry, but—look, I'll only be making sixteen hundred next year. The payments on this will be more than sixty dollars a month—that's almost half my salary. And there will be taxes and insurance and—I just don't see how we can do it. I wish you had talked to me.'

Her face became sorrowful; she turned away from him. 'I wanted to surprise you. I'm able to do so little. And I *could* do this.'

He protested that he was grateful, but Edith would not be consoled.

'I was thinking of you and the baby,' she said. 'You could have a study, and Grace could have a yard to play in.'

'I know,' William said. 'Maybe in a few years.'

'In a few years,' Edith repeated. There was a silence. Then she said dully, 'I can't live like this. Not any longer. In an apartment. No matter where I go I can hear you, and hear the baby, and—the smell. I—can't—stand—the—smell! Day after day, the smell of diapers, and—I can't stand it, and I can't get away from it. Don't you know? Don't you *know*?'

In the end they accepted the money. Stoner decided that he could give up to teaching the summers he had promised himself for study and writing, at least for a few years.

Edith took it upon herself to look for the house. Throughout the late spring and early summer she was tireless in her search, which seemed to work an immediate cure of her illness. As soon as William came home from his classes she went out and often did not return until dusk. Sometimes she walked and sometimes she drove around with Caroline Finch, with whom she had become casually friendly. Late in June she discovered the house she wanted; she signed an option to buy and agreed to take possession by the middle of August.

It was an old two-storied house only a few blocks from the campus; its previous owners had allowed it to run down, the dark green paint was peeling from the boards, and the lawn was brown and infested with weeds. But the yard was large and the house was roomy; it had a bedraggled grandeur that Edith could imagine renewed.

She borrowed another five hundred dollars from her father for furniture, and in the time between the summer session and the beginning of the fall semester William repainted the house; Edith wanted it white, and he had to put three coats on so that the dark green would not show through. Suddenly, in the first week of September, Edith decided that she wanted a party—a housewarming, she called it. She made the announcement with some resolution, as if it were a new beginning.

They invited all those members of the department who had returned from their summer vacations as well as a few town acquaintances of Edith; Hollis Lomax surprised everyone by accepting the invitation, the first he had accepted since his arrival in Columbia a year earlier. Stoner found a bootlegger and bought several bottles of gin; Gordon Finch promised to bring some beer; and Edith's Aunt Emma contributed two bottles of old sherry for those who would not drink hard liquor. Edith was reluctant to serve liquor at all; it was technically illegal to do so. But Caroline Finch intimated that no one at the University would think it really improper, and so she was persuaded.

Fall came early that year. A light snow fell on the tenth of September, the day before registration; during the night a hard freeze gripped the land. By the end of the week, the time of the party, the cold weather had lifted, so that there was only a chill in the air; but the trees were leafless, the grass was beginning to brown, and there was a general bareness that presaged a hard winter. By the chill weather outside, by the stripped poplars and elms that stood starkly in their yard, and by the warmth and the ranked implements of the impending party inside, William Stoner was reminded of another day. For some time he could not decide what he was trying to remember—then he realized that it was on such a day, almost seven years before, that he had gone to Josiah Claremont's house and had seen Edith for the first time. It seemed far away to him, and long ago; he could not reckon the changes that these few years had wrought.

For nearly the whole week before the party Edith lost herself in a frenzy of preparation; she hired a Negro girl for a week to help with the preparations and to serve, and the two of them scrubbed the floors and the walls, waxed the wood, dusted and cleaned the furniture, arranged it and rearranged it—so that on the night of the party Edith was in a state of near exhaustion. There were dark hollows under her eyes, and her voice was on the quiet edge of hysteria.

At six o'clock—the guests were supposed to arrive at seven—she counted the glasses once again and discovered that she did not have enough for the guests expected. She broke into tears, rushed upstairs, sobbing that she didn't care what happened, she wasn't coming back down. Stoner tried to reassure her, but she would not answer him. He told her not to worry, that he would get the glasses. He told the maid that he would return soon and hurried out of the house. For nearly an hour he searched for a store still open where he could purchase glasses; by the time he found one, selected the glasses, and returned to the house it was well after seven, and the first guests had arrived. Edith was among them in the living room, smiling and chatting as if she had no care or apprehension; she greeted William casually and told him to take the package into the kitchen.

The party was like many another. Conversation began desultorily, gathered a swift but feeble energy, and trailed irrelevantly into other conversations; laughter was quick and nervous, and it burst like tiny explosives in a continuous but unrelated barrage all over the room; and the members of the party flowed casually from one place to another, as if quietly occupying shifting positions of strategy. A few of them, like spies, wandered through the house, led by either Edith or William, and commented upon the superiority of such older houses as this over the new, flimsier structures going up here and there on the outskirts of town.

By ten o'clock most of the guests had taken plates piled with sliced cold ham and turkey, pickled apricots, and the varied garniture of tiny tomatoes, celery stalks, olives, pickles, crisp radishes, and little raw cauliflower ears; a few were drunk and would not eat. By eleven most of the guests had gone; among those who remained were Gordon and Caroline Finch, a few members of the department whom

Stoner had known for several years, and Hollis Lomax. Lomax was quite drunk, though not ostentatiously so; he walked carefully, as if he carried a burden over uneven terrain, and his thin pale face shone through a film of sweat. The liquor loosened his tongue; and though he spoke precisely, his voice lost its edge of irony, and he appeared without defenses.

He spoke of the loneliness of his childhood in Ohio, where his father had been a fairly successful small businessman; he told, as if of another person, of the isolation that his deformity had forced upon him, of the early shame which had no source that he could understand and no defense that he could muster. And when he told of the long days and evenings he had spent alone in his room, reading to escape the limitations that his twisted body imposed upon him and finding gradually a sense of freedom that grew more intense as he came to understand the nature of that freedom—when he told of this, William Stoner felt a kinship that he had not suspected; he knew that Lomax had gone through a kind of conversion, an epiphany of knowing something through words that could not be put in words, as Stoner himself had once done, in the class taught by Archer Sloane. Lomax had come to it early, and alone, so that the knowledge was more nearly a part of himself than it was a part of Stoner; but in the way that was finally most important, the two men were alike, though neither of them might wish to admit it to the other, or even to himself.

They talked till nearly four in the morning; and though they drank more, their talk grew quieter and quieter, until at last no one spoke at all. They sat close together amid the debris of the party, as if on an island, huddling together for warmth and assurance. After a while Gordon and Caroline Finch got up and offered to drive Lomax to his rooms.

Lomax shook Stoner's hand, asked him about his book, and wished him success with it; he walked over to Edith, who was sitting erect on a straight chair, and took her hand; he thanked her for the party. Then, as if on a quiet impulse, he bent a little and touched his lips to hers; Edith's hand came up lightly to his hair, and they remained so for several moments while the others looked on. It was the chastest kiss Stoner had ever seen, and it seemed perfectly natural.

Stoner saw his guests out the front door and lingered a few moments, watching them descend the steps and walk out of the light from the porch. The cold air settled around him and clung; he breathed deeply, and the sharp coldness invigorated him. He closed the door reluctantly and turned; the living room was empty; Edith had already gone upstairs. He turned the lights off and made his way across the cluttered room to the stairs. Already the house was becoming familiar to him; he grasped a balustrade he could not see and let himself be guided upward. When he got to the top of the stairs he could see his way, for the hall was illumined by the light from the half-opened door of the bedroom. The boards creaked as he walked down the hall and went into the bedroom.

Edith's clothes were flung in disarray on the floor beside the bed, the covers of which had been thrown back carelessly; she lay naked and glistening under the light on the white unwrinkled sheet. Her body was lax and wanton in its naked sprawl, and it shone like pale gold. William came nearer the bed. She was fast asleep, but in a trick of the light her slightly opened mouth seemed to shape the soundless words of passion and love. He stood looking at her for a long time. He felt a distant pity and reluctant friendship and familiar respect; and he felt also a weary sadness, for he knew that no longer could the sight of her bring upon him the agony of desire that he had once known, and knew that he would never again be moved as he had once been moved by her presence. The sadness lessened, and he covered her gently, turned out the light, and got in bed beside her.

The next morning Edith was ill and tired, and she spent the day in her room. William cleaned the house and attended to his daughter. On Monday he saw Lomax and spoke to him with a warmth that trailed from the night of the party; Lomax answered him with an irony that was like cold anger, and did not speak of the party that day or thereafter. It was as if he had discovered an enmity to hold him apart from Stoner, and he would not let it go.

As William had feared, the house soon proved to be an almost destructive financial burden. Though he allocated his salary with some care, the end of the month found him always without funds, and each month he reduced the steadily dwindling reserve made by his summer teaching. The first year they owned the house he missed two payments to Edith's father, and he received a frosty and principled letter of advice upon sound financial planning.

Nevertheless he began to feel a joy in property and to know a comfort that he had not anticipated. His study was on the first floor off the living room, with a high north window; in the daytime the room was softly illumined, and the wood paneling glowed with the richness of age. He found in the cellar a quantity of boards which, beneath the ravages of dirt and mold, matched the paneling of the room. He refinished these boards and constructed bookcases, so that he might be surrounded by his books; at a used furniture store he found some dilapidated chairs, a couch, and an ancient desk for which he paid a few dollars and which he spent many weeks repairing.

As he worked on the room, and as it began slowly to take a shape, he realized that for many years, unknown to himself, he had had an image locked somewhere within him like a shamed secret, an image that was ostensibly of a place but which was actually of himself. So it was himself that he was attempting to define as he worked on his study. As he sanded the old boards for his bookcases, and saw the surface roughnesses disappear, the gray weathering flake away to the essential wood and finally to a rich purity of grain and texture—as he repaired his furniture and arranged it in the room, it was himself that he was slowly shaping, it was himself that he was putting into a kind of order, it was himself that he was making possible.

Thus, despite the regularly recurring pressures of debt and need, the next few years were happy, and he lived much as he had dreamed that he might live when he was a young student in graduate school and when he had first married. Edith did not partake of so large a part of his life as he had once hoped; indeed, it seemed that they had entered into a long truce that was like a stalemate. They spent most of their lives apart; Edith kept the house, which seldom had visitors, in spotless condition. When she was not sweeping or dusting or washing or polishing, she stayed in her room and seemed content to do so. She never entered William's study; it was as if it did not exist to her.

William still had most of the care of their daughter. In the afternoons when he came home from the University, he took Grace from the upstairs bedroom that he had converted into a nursery and let her play in the study while he worked. She played quietly and contentedly on the floor, satisfied to be alone. Every now and then William spoke to her, and she paused to look at him in solemn and slow delight.

Sometimes he asked students to drop by for conferences and chats. He brewed tea for them on a little hotplate that he kept beside his desk, and felt an awkward fondness for them as they sat self-consciously on the chairs, remarked upon his library, and complimented him on the beauty of his daughter. He apologized for the absence of his wife and explained her illness, until at last he realized that his repetitions of apology were stressing her absence rather than accounting for it; he said no more and hoped that his silence was less compromising than were his explanations.

Except for Edith's absence from it, his life was nearly what he wanted it to be. He studied and wrote when he was not preparing for class, or grading papers, or reading theses. He hoped in time to make a reputation for himself as both a scholar and a teacher. His expectations for his first book had been both cautious and modest, and they had been appropriate; one reviewer had called it 'pedestrian' and another had called it 'a competent survey.' At first he had been very proud of the book; he had held it in his hands and caressed its plain wrapper and turned its pages. It seemed delicate and alive, like a child. He had reread it in print, mildly surprised that it was neither better nor worse than he had thought it would be. After a while he tired of seeing it; but he never thought of it, and his authorship, without a sense of wonder and disbelief at his own temerity and at the responsibility he had assumed.

7

One evening in the spring of 1927 William Stoner came home late. The scent of budding flowers mingled and hung in the moist warm air; crickets hummed in the shadows; in the distance a lone automobile raised dust and sent into the stillness a loud, defiant clatter. He walked slowly, caught in the somnolence of a new season, bemused by the tiny green buds that glowed out of the shade of bush and tree.

When he went into the house Edith was at the far end of the living room, holding the telephone receiver to her ear and looking at him.

'You're late,' she said.

'Yes,' he said pleasantly. 'We had doctor's orals.'

She handed him the receiver. 'It's for you, long distance. Someone's been trying to get you all afternoon. I told them you were at the University, but they've been calling back here every hour.'

William took the receiver and spoke into the mouthpiece. No one answered. 'Hello,' he said again.

The thin strange voice of a man answered him.

'This Bill Stoner?'

'Yes, who is this?'

'You don't know me. I was passing by, and your ma asked me to call. I been trying all afternoon.'

'Yes,' Stoner said. His hand holding the mouthpiece was shaking. 'What's wrong?'

'It's your pa,' the voice said. 'I don't rightly know how to start.'

The dry, laconic, frightened voice went on, and William Stoner listened to it dully, as if it had no existence beyond the receiver that he held to his ear. What he heard concerned his father. He had been (the voice said) feeling poorly for nearly a week; and because his field hand by himself had not been able to keep up with the furrowing and planting, and even though he had a high fever, he had started out early in the morning to get some planting done. His field hand had found him at midmorning, lying face down on the broken field, unconscious. He had carried him to the house, put him in bed, and gone to fetch a doctor; but by noon he was dead.

'Thank you for calling,' Stoner said mechanically. 'Tell my mother that I'll be there tomorrow.'

He put the receiver back on its hook and stared for a long time at the bell-shaped mouthpiece attached to the narrow black cylinder. He turned around and looked at the room. Edith was regarding him expectantly.

'Well? What is it?' she asked.

'It's my father,' Stoner said. 'He's dead.'

'Oh, Willy!' Edith said. Then she nodded. 'You'll probably be gone for the rest of the week then.'

'Yes,' Stoner said.

'Then I'll get Aunt Emma to come over and help with Grace.'

'Yes,' Stoner said mechanically. 'Yes.'

He got someone to take his classes for the rest of the week and early the next morning caught the bus for Booneville. The highway from Columbia to Kansas City, which cut through Booneville, was the one that he had

106

traveled seventeen years before, when he had first come to the University; now it was wide and paved, and neat straight fences enclosed fields of wheat and corn that flashed by him outside the bus window.

Booneville had changed little during the years he had not seen it. A few new buildings had gone up, a few old ones had been torn down; but the town retained its bareness and flimsiness, and looked still as if it were only a temporary arrangement that could be dispensed with at any moment. Though most of the streets had been paved in the last few years, a thin haze of dust hung about the town, and a few horse-drawn, steel-tired wagons were still around, the wheels sometimes giving off sparks as they scraped against the concrete paving of street and curb.

Nor had the house changed substantially. It was perhaps drier and grayer than it had been; not even a fleck of paint remained on the clapboards, and the unpainted timber of the porch sagged a bit nearer to the bare earth.

There were some people in the house—neighbors—whom Stoner did not remember; a tall gaunt man in a black suit, white shirt, and string tie was bending over his mother, who sat in a straight chair beside the narrow wooden box that held the body of his father. Stoner started across the room. The tall man saw him and walked to meet him; the man's eyes were gray and flat like pieces of glazed crockery. A deep and unctuous baritone voice, hushed and thick, uttered some words; the man called Stoner 'brother' and spoke of 'bereavement,' and 'God, who hath taken away,' and wanted to know if Stoner wished to pray with him. Stoner brushed past the man and stood in front of his mother; her face swam before him. Through a blur he saw her nod to him and get up from the chair. She took his arm and said, 'You'll want to see your pa.'

With a touch that was so frail that he could hardly feel it, she led him beside the open coffin. He looked down. He looked until his eyes cleared, and then he started back in shock. The body that he saw seemed that of a stranger; it was shrunken and tiny, and its face was like a thin brown-paper mask, with black deep depressions where the eyes should have been. The dark blue suit which enfolded the body was grotesquely large, and the hands that folded out of the sleeves over the chest were like the dried claws of an animal. Stoner turned to his mother, and he knew that the horror he felt was in his eyes.

'Your pa lost a lot of weight the last week or two,' she said. 'I asked him not to go out in the field, but he got up before I was awake and was gone. He was out of his head. He was just so sick he was out of his head and didn't know what he was doing. The doctor said he must have been, or he couldn't have managed it.'

As she spoke Stoner saw her clearly; it was as if she too were dead as she spoke, a part of her gone irretrievably into that box with her husband, not to emerge again. He saw her now; her face was thin and shrunken; even in repose it was so drawn that the tips of her teeth were disclosed beneath her thin lips. She walked as if she had no weight or strength. He muttered a word and left the parlor; he went to the room in which he had grown up and stood in its bareness. His eyes were hot and dry, and he could not weep.

He made the arrangements that had to be made for the funeral and signed the papers that needed to be signed. Like all country folk, his parents had burial policies, toward which for most of their lives they had set aside a few pennies each week, even during the times of most desperate need. There was something pitiful about the policies that his mother got from an old trunk in her bedroom; the gilt from the elaborate printing was beginning to fleck away, and the cheap paper was brittle with age. He talked to his mother about the future; he wanted her to return with him to Columbia. There was plenty of room, he said, and (he twinged at the lie) Edith would welcome her company.

But his mother would not return with him. 'I wouldn't feel right,' she said. 'Your pa and I—I've lived here nearly all my life. I just don't think I could settle anywhere else and feel right about it. And besides, Tobe'—Stoner remembered that Tobe was the Negro field hand his father had hired many years ago—'Tobe has said he'd stay on here as long as I need him. He's got him a nice room fixed up in the cellar. We'll be all right.'

Stoner argued with her, but she would not be moved. At last he realized that she wished only to die, and wished to do so where she had lived; and he knew that she deserved the little dignity she could find in doing as she wanted to do.

They buried his father in a small plot on the outskirts of Booneville, and William returned to the farm with his mother. That night he could not sleep. He dressed and walked into the field that his father had worked year after year, to the end that he now had found. He tried to remember his father, but the face that he had known in his youth would not come to him. He knelt in the field and took a dry clod of earth in his hand. He broke it and watched the grains, dark in the moonlight, crumble and flow through his fingers. He brushed his hand on his trouser leg and got up and went back to the house. He did not sleep; he lay on the bed and looked out the single window until the dawn came, until there were no shadows upon the land, until it stretched gray and barren and infinite before him.

After the death of his father Stoner made weekend trips

to the farm as often as he could; and each time he saw his mother, he saw her grown thinner and paler and stiller, until at last it seemed that only her sunken, bright eyes were alive. During her last days she did not speak to him at all; her eyes flickered faintly as she stared up from her bed, and occasionally a small sigh came from her lips.

He buried her beside her husband. After the services were over and the few mourners had gone, he stood alone in a cold November wind and looked at the two graves, one open to its burden and the other mounded and covered by a thin fuzz of grass. He turned on the bare, treeless little plot that held others like his mother and father and looked across the flat land in the direction of the farm where he had been born, where his mother and father had spent their years. He thought of the cost exacted, year after year, by the soil; and it remained as it had been—a little more barren, perhaps, a little more frugal of increase. Nothing had changed. Their lives had been expended in cheerless labor, their wills broken, their intelligences numbed. Now they were in the earth to which they had given their lives; and slowly, year by year, the earth would take them. Slowly the damp and rot would infest the pine boxes which held their bodies, and slowly it would touch their flesh, and finally it would consume the last vestiges of their substances. And they would become a meaningless part of that stubborn earth to which they had long ago given themselves.

He let Tobe stay on at the farm through the winter; in the spring of 1928 he put the farm up for sale. The understanding was that Tobe was to remain on the farm until it was sold, and whatever he raised would belong to him. Tobe fixed the place up as best he could, repairing the house and repainting the small barn. Even so, it was not until early in the spring of 1929 that Stoner found a suitable buyer. He accepted the first offer he received, of a little over two thousand dollars; he gave Tobe a few hundred dollars, and in late August sent the rest of it to his father-in-law, to reduce the amount owed on the house in Columbia.

In October of that year the stock market failed, and local newspapers carried stories about Wall Street, about fortunes ruined and great lives altered. Few people in Columbia were touched; it was a conservative community, and almost none of the townspeople had money in stocks or bonds. But news began to come in of bank failures across the country, and the beginnings of uncertainty touched some of the towns-people; a few farmers withdrew their savings, and a few more (urged by the local bankers) increased their deposits. But no one was really apprehensive until word came of the failure of a small private bank, the Merchant's Trust, in St Louis.

Stoner was at lunch in the University cafeteria when the news came, and he immediately went home to tell Edith. The Merchant's Trust was the bank that held the mortgage on their home, and the bank of which Edith's father was president. Edith called St Louis that afternoon and talked to her mother; her mother was cheerful, and she told Edith that Mr Bostwick had assured her that there was nothing to worry about, that everything would be all right in a few weeks.

Three days after that Horace Bostwick was dead, a suicide. He went to his office at the bank one morning in an unusually cheerful mood; he greeted several of the bank employees who still worked behind the closed doors of the bank, went into his office after telling his secretary that he would receive no calls, and locked his door. At about ten o'clock in the morning he shot himself in the head with a revolver he had purchased the day before and brought with him in his briefcase. He left no note behind him; but the papers neatly arranged on his desk told all that he had to tell. And what he had to tell was simply financial ruin. Like his Bostonian father, he had invested unwisely, not only his own money but also the bank's; and his ruin was so complete that he could imagine no relief. As it turned out, the ruin was not so nearly total as he thought at the moment of his suicide. After the estate was settled, the family house remained intact, and some minor real estate on the outskirts of St Louis was sufficient to furnish his wife with a small income for the rest of her life.

But this was not known immediately. William Stoner received the telephone call that informed him of Horace Bostwick's ruin and suicide, and he broke the news to Edith as gently as his estrangement from her would allow him.

Edith took the news calmly, almost as if she had been expecting it. She looked at Stoner for several moments without speaking; then she shook her head and said absently, 'Poor mother. What will she do? There has always been someone to take care of her. How will she live?'

Stoner said, 'Tell her'—he paused awkwardly—'tell her that, if she wants to, she can come live with us. She will be welcome.'

Edith smiled at him with a curious mixture of fondness and contempt. 'Oh, Willy. She'd rather die herself. Don't you know that?'

Stoner nodded. 'I suppose I do,' he said.

So on the evening of the day that Stoner received the call, Edith left Columbia to go to St Louis for the funeral and to stay there as long as she was needed. When she had been gone a week Stoner received a brief note informing him that she would remain with her mother for another two weeks, perhaps longer. She was gone for nearly two months, and William was alone in the big house with his daughter.

For the first few days the emptiness of the house was strangely and unexpectedly disquieting. But he got used to the emptiness and began to enjoy it; within a week he knew himself to be as happy as he had been in years, and when he thought of Edith's inevitable return, it was with a quiet regret that he no longer needed to hide from himself.

Grace had had her sixth birthday in the spring of that year, and she started her first year of school that fall. Every morning Stoner got her ready for school, and he was back from the University in the afternoon in time to greet her when she came home.

At the age of six Grace was a tall, slender child with hair that was more blond than red; her skin was perfectly fair, and her eyes were dark blue, almost violet. She was quiet and cheerful, and she had a delight in things that gave her father a feeling that was like nostalgic reverence.

Sometimes Grace played with neighbor children, but more often she sat with her father in his large study and watched him as he graded papers, or read, or wrote. She spoke to him, and they conversed—so quietly and seriously that William Stoner was moved by a tenderness that he never foresaw. Grace drew awkward and charming pictures on sheets of yellow paper and presented them solemnly to her father, or she read aloud to him from her first-grade reader. At night, when Stoner put her to bed and returned to his study, he was aware of her absence from his room and was comforted by the knowledge that she slept securely above him. In ways of which he was barely conscious he started her education, and he watched with amazement and love as she grew before him and as her face began to show the intelligence that worked within her.

Edith did not return to Columbia until after the first of the year, so William Stoner and his daughter spent Christmas by themselves. On Christmas morning they exchanged gifts; for her father, who did not smoke, Grace had modeled, at the cautiously progressive school attached to the University, a crude ashtray. William gave her a new dress that he had selected himself at a downtown store, several books, and a coloring set. They sat most of the day before the small tree, talked, and watched the lights twinkle on the ornaments and the tinsel wink from the dark green fir like buried fire.

During the Christmas holiday, that curious, suspended pause in the rushing semester, William Stoner began to realize two things: he began to know how centrally import- ant Grace had become to his existence, and he began to understand that it might be possible for him to become a good teacher.

He was ready to admit to himself that he had not been a good teacher. Always, from the time he had fumbled through his first classes of freshman English, he had been aware of the gulf that lay between what he felt for his subject and what he delivered in the classroom. He had hoped that time and experience would repair the gulf; but they had not done so. Those things that he held most deeply were most profoundly betrayed when he spoke of them to his classes; what was most alive withered in his words; and what moved him most became cold in its utterance. And the consciousness of his inadequacy distressed him so greatly that the sense of it grew habitual, as much a part of him as the stoop of his shoulders.

But during the weeks that Edith was in St Louis, when he lectured, he now and then found himself so lost in his subject that he became forgetful of his inadequacy, of himself, and even of the students before him. Now and then he became so caught by his enthusiasm that he stuttered, gesticulated, and ignored the lecture notes that usually guided his talks. At first he was disturbed by his outbursts, as if he presumed too familiarly upon his subject, and he apologized to his students; but when they began coming up to him after class, and when in their papers they began to show hints of imagination and the revelation of a tentative love, he was encouraged to do what he had never been taught to do. The love of literature, of language, of the mystery of the mind and heart showing themselves in the minute, strange, and unexpected combinations of letters and words, in the blackest and coldest print—the love which he had hidden as if it were illicit and dangerous, he began to display, tentatively at first, and then boldly, and then proudly.

He was both saddened and heartened by his discovery of what he might do; beyond his intention, he felt he had cheated both his students and himself. The students who had been able theretofore to plod through his courses by the repetition of mechanical steps began to look at him with puzzlement and resentment; those who had not taken courses from him began to sit in on his lectures and nod to him in the halls. He spoke more confidently and felt a warm hard severity gather within him. He suspected that he was beginning, ten years late, to discover who he was; and the figure he saw was both more and less than he had once imagined it to be. He felt himself at last beginning to be a teacher, which was simply a man to whom his book is true, to whom is given a dignity of art that has little to do with his foolishness or weakness or inadequacy as a man. It was a knowledge of which he could not speak, but one which changed him, once he had it, so that no one could mistake its presence.

Thus, when Edith came back from St Louis, she found him changed in a way that she could not understand but of which she was instantly aware. She returned without warning on an afternoon train and walked through the living room into the study where her husband and her daughter quietly sat. She had meant to shock them both by her sudden presence and by her changed appearance; but when William looked up at her, and she saw the surprise in his eyes, she knew at once that the real change had come over him, and that it was so deep that the effect of her appearance was lost; and she thought to herself, a little distantly and yet with some surprise, I know him better than I ever realized.

William was surprised at her presence and her altered appearance, but neither could move him now as they might once have done. He looked at her for several moments and then got up from his desk, went across the room, and greeted her gravely.

Edith had bobbed her hair and wore over it one of those hats that hugged her head so tightly that the cropped hair lay close to her face like an irregular frame; her lips were painted a bright orange-red, and two small spots of rouge sharpened her cheekbones. She wore one of those short dresses that had become fashionable among the younger women during the past few years; it hung straight down from her shoulders and ended just above her knees. She smiled self-consciously at her husband and walked across the room to her daughter, who sat on the floor and looked up at her quietly and studiously. She knelt awkwardly, her new dress tight around her legs.

'Gracie, honey,' she said in a voice that seemed to William

to be strained and brittle, 'did you miss your mommy? Did you think she was never coming back?'

Grace kissed her mother on the cheek and looked at her solemnly. 'You look different,' she said.

Edith laughed and got up from the floor; she whirled around, holding her hands above her head. 'I have a new dress and new shoes and a new hair-do. Do you like them?'

Grace nodded dubiously. 'You look different,' she said again.

Edith's smile widened; there was a pale smear of lipstick on one of her teeth. She turned to William and asked, 'Do I look different?'

'Yes,' William said. 'Very charming. Very pretty.'

She laughed at him and shook her head. 'Poor Willy,' she said. Then she turned again to her daughter. 'I am different, I believe,' she said to her. 'I really believe I am.'

But William Stoner knew that she was speaking to him. And at that moment, somehow, he also knew that beyond her intention or understanding, unknown to herself, Edith was trying to announce to him a new declaration of war.

8

The declaration was a part of the change that Edith had started bringing about during the weeks she had spent at 'home' in St Louis after her father's death. And it was intensified, and finally given point and savagery, by that other change that came and slowly grew upon William Stoner after he discovered that he might become a good teacher.

Edith had been curiously unmoved at her father's funeral. During the elaborate ceremonies she sat erect and hard-faced, and her expression did not alter when she had to go past her father's body, resplendent and plump, in the ornate coffin. But at the cemetery, when the coffin was lowered into the narrow hole masked by mats of artificial grass, she lowered her expressionless face into her hands and did not raise it until someone touched her shoulder.

After the funeral she spent several days in her old room, the room in which she had grown up; she saw her mother only at breakfast and at dinner. It was thought by callers that she was secluded in her grief. 'They were very close,' Edith's mother said mysteriously. 'Much closer than they seemed.'

But in that room Edith walked about as if for the first time, freely, touching the walls and windows, testing their solidity. She had a trunk full of her childhood belongings brought down from the attic; she went through her bureau drawers, which had remained undisturbed for more than a decade. With a bemused air of leisure, as if she had all the time in the world, she went through her things, fondling them, turning them this way and that, examining them with an almost ritualistic care. When she came upon a letter she had received as a child, she read it through from beginning to end as if for the first time; when she came upon a forgotten doll, she smiled at it and caressed the painted bisque of its cheek as if she were a child again who had received a gift.

Finally she arranged all of her childhood belongings neatly in two piles. One of these consisted of toys and trinkets she had acquired for herself, of secret photographs and letters from school friends, of gifts she had at one time received from distant relatives; the other pile consisted of those things that her father had given her and of things with which he had been directly or indirectly connected. It was to this pile that she gave her attention. Methodically, expressionlessly, with neither anger nor joy, she took the objects there, one by one, and destroyed them. The letters and clothes, the stuffing from the dolls, the pincushions and pictures, she burned in the fireplace; the clay and porcelain heads, the hands and arms and feet of the dolls she pounded to a fine powder on the hearth; and what remained after the burning and pounding she swept into a small pile and flushed down the toilet in the bathroom that adjoined her room.

When the job was done—the room cleared of smoke, the hearth swept, the few remaining belongings returned to the chest of drawers—Edith Bostwick Stoner sat at her small dressing table and looked at herself in the mirror, the silver backing of which was thinning and flecking away, so that here and there her image was imperfectly reflected, or not reflected at all, giving her face a curiously incomplete look. She was thirty years old. The youthful gloss was beginning to fall from her hair, tiny lines were starting out from around her eyes, and the skin of her face was beginning to tighten around her sharp cheekbones. She nodded to the image in the mirror, got up abruptly, and went downstairs, where for the first time in days she talked cheerfully and almost intimately to her mother.

She wanted (she said) a change in herself. She had too long been what she was; she spoke of her childhood, of her marriage. And from sources that she could speak of but vaguely and uncertainly, she fixed an image that she wished to fulfill; and for nearly the whole of the two months that she stayed in St Louis with her mother, she devoted herself to that fulfillment.

She asked to borrow a sum of money from her mother, who made her an impetuous gift of it. She bought a new wardrobe, burning all the clothes she had brought with her from Columbia; she had her hair cut short and fashioned in the mode of the day; she bought cosmetics and perfumes, the use of which she practiced daily in her room. She learned to smoke, and she cultivated a new way of speaking which was brittle, vaguely English, and a little shrill. She returned to Columbia with this outward change well under control, and with another change secret and potential within her.

During the first few months after her return to Columbia, she was furious with activity; no longer did it seem necessary to pretend to herself that she was ill or weak. She joined a little theater group and devoted herself to the work that was given her; she designed and painted sets, raised money for the group, and even had a few small parts in the productions. When Stoner came home in the afternoons he found the living room filled with her friends, strangers who looked at him as if he were an intruder, to whom he nodded politely and retreated to his study, where he could hear their voices, muted and declamatory, beyond his walls.

Edith purchased a used upright piano and had it put in the living room, against the wall which separated that room from William's study; she had given up the practice of music shortly before her marriage, and she now started almost anew, practicing scales, laboring through exercises that were too difficult for her, playing sometimes two or three hours a day, often in the evening, after Grace had been put to bed.

The groups of students whom Stoner invited to his study for conversation grew larger and the meetings more frequent; and no longer was Edith content to remain upstairs, away from the gatherings. She insisted upon serving them tea or coffee; and when she did she seated herself in the room. She talked loudly and gaily, managing to turn the conversation toward her work in the little theater, or her music, or her painting and sculpture, which (she announced) she was planning to take up again, as soon as she found time. The students, mystified and embarrassed, gradually stopped coming, and Stoner began meeting them for coffee in the University cafeteria or in one of the small cafés scattered around the campus.

He did not speak to Edith about her new behavior; her activities caused him only minor annoyance, and she seemed happy, though perhaps a bit desperately so. It was, finally, himself that he held responsible for the new direction her life had taken; he had been unable to discover for her any meaning in their life together, in their marriage. Thus it was right for her to take what meaning she could find in areas that had nothing to do with him and go ways he could not follow.

Emboldened by his new success as a teacher and by his growing popularity among the better graduate students, he started a new book in the summer of 1930. He now spent nearly all of his free time in his study. He and Edith kept up between themselves the pretense of sharing the same bedroom, but he seldom entered that room, and never at night. He slept on his studio couch and even kept his clothes in a small closet he constructed in one corner of the room.

He was able to be with Grace. As had become her habit during her mother's first long absence, she spent much of her time with her father in his study; Stoner even found a small desk and chair for her, so that she had a place to read and do her homework. They had their meals more often than not alone; Edith was away from the house a great deal, and when she was not away she frequently entertained her theater friends at little parties which did not admit the presence of a child.

Then, abruptly, Edith began staying home. The three of them started taking their meals together again, and Edith even made a few movements toward caring for the house. The house was quiet; even the piano was unused, so that dust gathered on the keyboard.

They had come to that point in their life together when they seldom spoke of themselves or each other, lest the delicate balance that made their living together possible be broken. So it was only after long hesitation and deliberation about consequences that Stoner finally asked her if anything was wrong.

They were at the dinner table; Grace had been excused and had taken a book into Stoner's study.

'What do you mean?' Edith asked.

'Your friends,' William said. 'They haven't been around for some time, and you don't seem to be so involved with your theater work any more. I was just wondering if there was anything wrong.'

With an almost masculine gesture, Edith shook a cigarette from the package beside her plate, stuck it between her lips, and lighted it with the stub of another that she had half finished. She inhaled deeply without taking the cigarette from her lips and tilted her head back, so that when she looked at William her eyes were narrowed and quizzical and calculating.

'Nothing's wrong,' she said. 'I just got bored with them and the work. Does there always have to be something wrong?'

'No,' William said. 'I just thought maybe you weren't feeling well or something.'

He thought no more about the conversation and shortly thereafter he left the table and went into the study, where Grace was sitting at her desk, immersed in her book. The desk light gleamed in her hair and threw her small, serious face into sharp outline. She has grown during the past year, William thought; and a small, not unpleasant sadness caught briefly at his throat. He smiled and went quietly to his desk.

Within a few moments he was immersed in his work. The evening before, he had caught up with the routine of his class-work; papers had been graded and lectures prepared for the whole week that was to follow. He saw the evening before him, and several evenings more, in which he would be free to work on his book. What he wanted to do in this new book was not yet precisely clear to him; in general, he wished to extend himself beyond his first study, in both time and scope. He wanted to work in the period of the English Renaissance and to extend his study of classical and medieval Latin influences into that area. He was in the stage of planning his study, and it was that stage which gave him the most pleasure—the selection among alternative approaches, the rejection of certain strategies, the mysteries and uncertainties that lay in unexplored possibilities, the consequences of choice . . . The possibilities he could see so exhilarated him that he could not keep still. He got up from his desk, paced a little, and in a kind of frustrated joy spoke to his daughter, who looked up from her book and answered him.

She caught his mood, and something he said caused her to laugh. Then the two of them were laughing together, senselessly, as if they both were children. Suddenly the door to the study came open, and the hard light from the living room streamed into the shadowed recesses of the study. Edith stood outlined in that light.

'Grace,' she said distinctly and slowly, 'your father is trying to work. You mustn't disturb him.'

For several moments William and his daughter were so stunned by this sudden intrusion that neither of them moved or spoke. Then William managed to say, 'It's all right, Edith. She doesn't bother me.'

As if he had not spoken, Edith said, 'Grace, did you hear me? Come out of there this instant.'

Bewildered, Grace got down from her chair and walked across the room. In the center she paused, looking first at her father and then at her mother. Edith started to speak again, but William managed to cut her off.

'It's all right, Grace,' he said as gently as he could. 'It's all right. Go with your mother.'

As Grace went through the study door to the living room, Edith said to her husband, 'The child has had entirely too much freedom. It isn't natural for her to be so quiet, so withdrawn. She's been too much alone. She should be more active, play with children her own age. Don't you realize how unhappy she has been?'

And she shut the door before he could answer.

He did not move for a long while. He looked at his desk, littered with notes and open books; he walked slowly across the room and aimlessly rearranged the sheets of paper, the books. He stood there, frowning, for several minutes more, as if he were trying to remember something. Then he turned again and walked to Grace's small desk; he stood there for some time, as he had stood at his own desk. He turned off the lamp there, so that the desk top was gray and lifeless, and went across to the couch, where he lay with his eyes open, staring at the ceiling.

The enormity came upon him gradually, so that it was several weeks before he could admit to himself what Edith was doing; and when he was able at last to make that admission, he made it almost without surprise. Edith's was a campaign waged with such cleverness and skill that he could find no rational grounds for complaint. After her abrupt and almost brutal entrance into his study that night, an entrance which in retrospect seemed to him a surprise attack, Edith's strategy became more indirect, more quiet and contained. It was a strategy that disguised itself as love and concern, and thus one against which he was helpless.

Edith was at home nearly all the time now. During the morning and early afternoon, while Grace was at school, she occupied herself with redecorating Grace's bedroom. She removed the small desk from Stoner's study, refinished and repainted it a pale pink, attaching around the top a broad ribbon of matching ruffled satin, so that it bore no resemblance to the desk Grace had grown used to; one afternoon, with Grace standing mutely beside her, she went through all the clothing William had bought for her, discarded most of it, and promised Grace that they would, this weekend, go downtown and replace the discarded items with things more fitting, something 'girlish.' And they did. Late in the afternoon, weary but triumphant, Edith returned with a load of packages and an exhausted daughter desperately uncomfortable in a new dress stiff with starch and a myriad of ruffles, from beneath the ballooning hem of which her thin legs stuck out like pathetic sticks.

Edith bought her daughter dolls and toys and hovered about her while she played with them, as if it were a duty; she started her on piano lessons and sat beside her on the bench as she practiced; upon the slightest occasion she gave little parties for her, which neighborhood children attended, vindictive and sullen in their stiff, formal clothing; and she strictly supervised her daughter's reading and homework, not allowing her to work beyond the time she had allotted.

Now Edith's visitors were neighborhood mothers. They came in the mornings and drank coffee and talked while their children were in school; in the afternoons they brought their children with them and watched them playing games in the large living room and talked aimlessly above the noise of games and running.

On these afternoons Stoner was usually in his study and could hear what the mothers said as they spoke loudly across the room, above their children's voices.

Once, when there was a lull in the noise, he heard Edith say, 'Poor Grace. She's so fond of her father, but he has so little time to devote to her. His work, you know; and he has started a new book . . .'

Curiously, almost detachedly, he watched his hands, which had been holding a book, begin to shake. They shook for several moments before he brought them under control by jamming them deep in his pockets, clenching them, and holding them there.

He saw his daughter seldom now. The three of them took their meals together, but on these occasions he hardly dared to speak to her, for when he did, and when Grace answered him, Edith soon found something wanting in Grace's table manners, or in the way she sat in her chair, and she spoke so sharply that her daughter remained silent and downcast through the rest of the meal.

Grace's already slender body was becoming thinner; Edith laughed gently about her 'growing up but not out.' Her eyes were becoming watchful, almost wary; the expression that had once been quietly serene was now either faintly sullen at one extreme or gleeful and animated on the thin edge of hysteria at the other; she seldom smiled any more, although she laughed a great deal. And when she did smile, it was as if a ghost flitted across her face. Once, while Edith was upstairs, William and his daughter passed each other in the living room. Grace smiled shyly at him, and involuntarily he knelt on the floor and embraced her. He felt her body stiffen, and he saw her face go bewildered and afraid. He raised himself gently away from her, said something inconsequential, and retreated to his study.

The morning after this he stayed at the breakfast table until Grace left for school, even though he knew he would be late for his nine o'clock class. After seeing Grace out the front door, Edith did not return to the dining room, and he knew that she was avoiding him. He went into the living room, where his wife sat at one end of the sofa with a cup of coffee and a cigarette.

Without preliminaries he said, 'Edith, I don't like what's happening to Grace.'

127

Instantly, as if she were picking up a cue, she said, 'What do you mean?'

He let himself down on the other end of the sofa, away from Edith. A feeling of helplessness came over him. 'You know what I mean,' he said wearily. 'Let up on her. Don't drive her so hard.'

Edith ground her cigarette out in her saucer. 'Grace has never been happier. She has friends now, things to occupy her. I know you're too busy to notice these things, but—surely you must realize how much more outgoing she's been recently. And she laughs. She never used to laugh. Almost never.'

William looked at her in quiet amazement. 'You believe that, don't you?'

'Of course I do,' Edith said. 'I'm her mother.'

And she did believe it, Stoner realized. He shook his head.

'I've never wanted to admit it to myself,' he said with something like tranquillity, 'but you really do hate me, don't you, Edith?'

'What?' The amazement in her voice was genuine. 'Oh, Willy!' She laughed clearly and unrestrainedly. 'Don't be foolish. Of course not. You're my husband.'

'Don't use the child.' He could not keep his voice from trembling. 'You don't have to any longer; you know that. Anything else. But if you keep on using Grace, I'll—' He did not finish.

After a moment Edith said, 'You'll what?' She spoke quietly and without challenge. 'All you could do is leave me, and you'd never do that. We both know it.'

He nodded. 'I suppose you're right.' He got up blindly and went into his study. He got his coat from the closet and picked up his briefcase from beside his desk. As he crossed the living room Edith spoke to him again.

'Willy, I wouldn't hurt Grace. You ought to know that. I love her. She's my very own daughter.'

And he knew that it was true; she did love her. The truth of the knowledge almost made him cry out. He shook his head and went out into the weather.

When he got home that evening he found that during the day Edith had, with the help of a local handyman, moved all of his belongings out of his study. Jammed together in one corner of the living room were his desk and couch, and surrounding them in a careless jumble were his clothes, his papers, and all of his books.

Since she would be home more now, she had (she told him) decided to take up her painting and her sculpting again; and his study, with its north light, would give her the only really decent illumination the house had. She knew he wouldn't mind a move; he could use the glassed-in sun porch at the back of the house; it was farther away from the living room than his study had been, and he would have more quiet in which to do his work.

But the sun porch was so small that he could not keep his books in any order, and there was no room for either the desk or the couch that he had had in the study, so he stored both of them in the cellar. It was difficult to warm the sun porch in the winter, and in the summer, he knew, the sun would beat through the glass panes that enclosed the porch, so that it would be nearly uninhabitable. Yet he worked there for several months. He got a small table and used it as a desk, and he purchased a portable radiant heater to mitigate a little the cold that in the evenings seeped through the thin clap-board sidings. At night he slept wrapped in a blanket on the sofa in the living room.

After a few months of relative though uncomfortable

peace, he began finding, when he returned in the afternoon from the University, odds and ends of discarded household goods—broken lamps, scatter rugs, small chests, and boxes of bric-a-brac—left carelessly in the room that now served as his study.

'It's so damp in the cellar,' Edith said, 'they'd be ruined. You don't mind if I keep them in here for a while, do you?'

One spring afternoon he returned home during a driving rainstorm and discovered that somehow one of the panes had got broken and that the rain had damaged several of his books and had rendered many of his notes illegible; a few weeks later he came in to find that Grace and a few of her friends had been allowed to play in the room and that more of his notes and the first pages of the manuscript of his new book had been torn and mutilated. 'I only let them go in there a few minutes,' Edith said. 'They have to have someplace to play. But I had no idea. You ought to speak to Grace. I've told her how important your work is to you.'

He gave up then. He moved as many of his books as he could to his office at the University, which he shared with three younger instructors; thereafter he spent much of the time that he had formerly spent at home at the University, coming home early only when his loneliness for a brief glimpse of his daughter, or a word with her, made it impossible for him to stay away.

But he had room in his office for only a few of his books, and his work on his manuscript was often interrupted because he did not have the necessary texts; moreover one of his office mates, an earnest young man, had the habit of scheduling student conferences in the evenings, and the sibilant, labored conversations carried on across the room distracted him, so that he found it difficult to concentrate.

He lost interest in his book; his work slowed and came to a halt. Finally he realized that it had become a refuge, a haven, an excuse to come to the office at night. He read and studied, and at last came to find some comfort, some pleasure, and even a ghost of the old joy in that which he did, a learning toward no particular end.

And Edith had relaxed her pursuit and obsessive concern for Grace, so that the child was beginning occasionally to smile and even to speak to him with some ease. Thus he found it possible to live, and even to be happy, now and then.

9

The interim chairmanship of the English Department, which Gordon Finch had assumed after the death of Archer Sloane, was renewed year after year, until all the members of the department grew used to a casual anarchy in which somehow classes got scheduled and taught, in which new appointments to the staff were made, in which the trivial departmental details somehow got taken care of, and in which year somehow succeeded year. It was generally understood that a permanent chairman would be appointed as soon as it became possible to make Finch the dean of Arts and Sciences, a position that he held in fact if not in office; Josiah Claremont threatened never to die, though he was seldom seen any longer wandering through the halls.

The members of the department went their ways, taught the classes they had taught the year before, and visited one another's offices in the hours between classes. They met together formally only at the beginning of each semester when Gordon Finch called a perfunctory departmental meeting, and on those occasions when the dean of the Graduate College sent them memos requesting that they give oral and thesis examinations to graduate students who were nearing completion of their work.

Such examinations took up an increasing amount of Stoner's time. To his surprise he began to enjoy a modest popularity as a teacher; he had to turn away students who wanted to get into his graduate seminar on the Latin Tradition and Renaissance Literature, and his undergraduate survey classes were always filled. Several graduate students asked him to direct their theses, and several more asked him to be on their thesis committees.

In the fall of 1931 the seminar was nearly filled even before registration; many students had made arrangements with Stoner at the end of the preceding year or during the summer. A week after the semester started, and after the seminar had held one meeting, a student came to Stoner's office and asked to be let in the class.

Stoner was at his desk with a list of the seminar students before him; he was attempting to decide upon seminar tasks for them, and it was particularly difficult since many were new to him. It was a September afternoon, and he had the window next to his desk open; the front of the great building lay in shadow, so that the green lawn before it showed the precise shape of the building, with its semicircular dome and irregular roofline darkening the green and creeping imperceptibly outward over the campus and beyond. A cool breeze flowed through the window, bringing the crisp redolence of fall.

A knock came; he turned to his opened doorway and said, 'Come in.'

A figure shuffled out of the darkness of the hall into the light of the room. Stoner blinked sleepily against the dimness, recognizing a student whom he had noticed in the halls but did not know. The young man's left arm hung stiffly at his side, and his left foot dragged as he walked. His face was pale and round, his horn-rimmed eyeglasses were round, and his black thin hair was parted precisely on the side and lay close to the round skull.

'Dr Stoner?' he asked; his voice was reedy and clipped, and he spoke distinctly.

'Yes,' Stoner said. 'Won't you have a chair?'

The young man lowered himself into the straight wooden chair beside Stoner's desk; his leg was extended in a straight line, and his left hand, which was permanently twisted into a half-closed fist, rested upon it. He smiled, bobbed his head, and said with a curious air of self-depreciation, 'You may not know me, sir; I'm Charles Walker. I'm a second-year Ph.D. candidate; I assist Dr Lomax.'

'Yes, Mr Walker,' Stoner said. 'What can I do for you?'

'Well, I'm here to ask a favor, sir.' Walker smiled again. 'I know your seminar is filled, but I want very much to get in it.' He paused and said pointedly, 'Dr Lomax suggested that I talk to you.'

'I see,' Stoner said. 'What's your specialty, Mr Walker?'

'The Romantic poets,' Walker said. 'Dr Lomax will be the director of my dissertation.'

Stoner nodded. 'How far along are you in your course work?'

'I hope to finish within two years,' Walker said.

'Well, that makes it easier,' Stoner said. 'I offer the seminar every year. It's really so full now that it's hardly a seminar any longer, and one more person would just about finish the job. Why can't you wait until next year if you really want the course?'

Walker's eyes shifted away from him. 'Well, frankly,' he said and flashed his smile again, 'I'm the victim of a misunderstanding. All my own fault, of course. I didn't realize that each Ph.D. student has to have at least four graduate seminars to get his degree, and I didn't take any at all last year. And as you know, they don't allow you to take more than one each semester. So if I'm to graduate in two years, I have to have one this semester.'

Stoner sighed. 'I see. So you don't really have a very special interest in the influence of the Latin tradition?'

'Oh, indeed I do, sir. Indeed I do. It will be most helpful in my dissertation.'

'Mr Walker, you should know this is a rather specialized class, and I don't encourage people to enter it unless they have a particular interest.'

'Yes, sir,' Walker said. 'I assure you that I *do* have a particular interest.'

Stoner nodded. 'How is your Latin?'

Walker bobbed his head. 'Oh, it's fine, sir. I haven't taken my Latin exam yet, but I read it very well.'

'Do you have French or German?'

'Oh, yes, sir. Again, I haven't taken the exams yet; I thought I'd get them all out of the way at the same time, at the end of this year. But I read them both very well.' Walker paused, then added, 'Dr Lomax said he thought I would surely be able to do the work in the seminar.'

Stoner sighed. 'Very well,' he said. 'Much of the reading will be in Latin, a little in French and German, though you might be able to get by without those. I'll give you a reading list, and we'll talk about your seminar topic next Wednesday afternoon.'

Walker thanked him effusively and arose from his chair with some difficulty. 'I'll get right on to the reading,' he said. 'I'm sure you won't regret letting me in your class, sir.'

Stoner looked at him with faint surprise. 'The question had not occurred to me, Mr Walker,' he said dryly. 'I'll see you on Wednesday.'

The seminar was held in a small basement room in the

south wing of Jesse Hall. A dank but not unpleasant odor seeped from the cement walls, and feet shuffled in hollow whispers upon the bare cement floor. A single light hung from the ceiling in the center of the room and shone downward, so that those seated at desk-top chairs in the center of the room rested in a splash of brightness; but the walls were a dim gray and the corners were almost black, as if the smooth unpainted cement sucked in the light that streamed from the ceiling.

On that second Wednesday of the seminar William Stoner came into the room a few minutes late; he spoke to the students and began to arrange his books and papers on the small stained-oak desk that stood squatly before the center of a blackboard wall. He glanced at the small group scattered about the room. Some of them he knew; two of the men were Ph.D. candidates whose work he was directing; four others were M.A. students in the department who had done undergraduate work with him; of the remaining students, three were candidates for advanced degrees in modern language, one was a philosophy student doing his dissertation on the Scholastics, one was a woman of advanced middle age, a high-school teacher trying to get an M.A. during her sabbatical, and the last was a dark-haired young woman, a new instructor in the department, who had taken a job for two years while she completed a dissertation she had begun after finishing her course work at an eastern university. She had asked Stoner if she might audit the seminar, and he had agreed that she might. Charles Walker was not among the group. Stoner waited a few moments more, shuffling his papers; then he cleared his throat and began the class.

'During our first meeting we discussed the scope of this seminar, and we decided that we should limit our study of the medieval Latin tradition to the first three of the seven liberal arts—that is, to grammar, rhetoric, and dialectic.' He paused and watched the faces—tentative, curious, and mask-like—focus upon him and what he said.

'Such a limiting may seem foolishly rigorous to some of you; but I have no doubt that we shall find enough to keep us occupied even if we trace only superficially the course of the trivium upward into the sixteenth century. It is important that we realize that these arts of rhetoric, grammar, and dialectic meant something to a late medieval and early Renaissance man that we, today, can only dimly sense without an exercise of the historical imagination. To such a scholar, the art of grammar, for example, was not merely a mechanical disposition of the parts of speech. From late Hellenistic times through the Middle Ages, the study and practice of grammar included not only the "skill of letters" mentioned by Plato and Aristotle; it included also, and this became very important, a study of poetry in its technical felicities, an exegesis of poetry both in form and substance, and nicety of style, insofar as that can be distinguished from rhetoric.'

He felt himself warming to his subject, and he was aware that several of the students had leaned forward and had stopped taking notes. He continued: 'Moreover, if we in the twentieth century are asked which of these three arts is the most important, we might choose dialectic, or rhetoric—but we would be most unlikely to choose grammar. Yet the Roman and medieval scholar—and poet—would almost certainly consider grammar the most significant. We must remember—'

A loud noise interrupted him. The door had opened and Charles Walker entered the room; as he closed the door the books he carried under his crippled arm slipped and crashed to the floor. He bent awkwardly, his bad leg extended behind him, and slowly gathered his books and papers. Then he drew himself erect and shuffled across the room, the scrape of his foot across the bare cement raising a loud and grating hiss that sounded sibilantly hollow in the room. He found a chair in the front row and sat down.

After Walker had settled himself and got his papers and books in order around his desk chair, Stoner continued: 'We must remember that the medieval conception of grammar was even more general than the late Hellenistic or Roman. Not only did it include the science of correct speech and the art of exegesis, it included as well the modern conceptions of analogy, etymology, methods of presentation, construction, the condition of poetic license and the exceptions to that condition—and even metaphorical language or figures of speech.'

As he continued, elaborating upon the categories of grammar he had named, Stoner's eyes flitted over the class; he realized that he had lost them during Walker's entrance and knew that it would be some time before he could once more persuade them out of themselves. Again and again his glance fell curiously upon Walker, who, after having taken notes furiously for a few moments, gradually let his pencil rest on his notebook, while he gazed at Stoner with a puzzled frown. Finally Walker's hand shot up; Stoner finished the sentence he had begun and nodded to him.

'Sir,' Walker said, 'pardon me, but I don't understand. What can'—he paused and let his mouth curl around the word—'*grammar* have to do with poetry? Fundamentally I mean. *Real* poetry.'

Stoner said gently, 'As I was explaining before you came in, Mr Walker, the term "grammar" to both the Roman and medieval rhetoricians was a great deal more comprehensive than it is today. To them, it meant—' He paused, realizing that he was about to repeat the early part of his lecture; he sensed the students stirring restlessly. 'I think this relationship will become clearer to you as we go on, as we see the extent to which the poets and dramatists even of the middle and late Renaissance were indebted to the Latin rhetoricians.'

'All of them, sir?' Walker smiled and leaned back in his chair. 'Wasn't it Samuel Johnson who said of Shakespeare himself that he had little Latin and less Greek?'

As the repressed laughter stirred in the room Stoner felt a kind of pity come over him. 'You mean Ben Jonson, of course.'

Walker took off his glasses and polished them, blinking helplessly. 'Of course,' he said. 'A slip of the tongue.'

Though Walker interrupted him several times, Stoner managed to get through his lecture without serious difficulty, and he was able to make assignments for the first reports. He let the seminar out nearly half an hour early, and hurried away from the classroom when he saw Walker shuffling toward him with a fixed grin on his face. He clattered up the wooden stairs from the basement and took two at a time the smooth marble stairs that led to the second floor; he had the curious feeling that Walker was doggedly shuffling behind him, trying to overtake him in his flight. A hasty wash of shame and guilt came over him.

On the third floor he went directly to Lomax's office. Lomax was in conference with a student. Stoner stuck his head in the door and said, 'Holly, can I see you for a minute after you're through?'

Lomax waved genially. 'Come on in. We're just breaking up.'

Stoner came in and pretended to examine the rows of books in their cases as Lomax and the student said their last words. When the student left, Stoner sat in the chair that he had vacated. Lomax looked at him inquiringly.

'It's about a student,' Stoner said. 'Charles Walker. He said you sent him around to me.'

Lomax placed the tips of his fingers together and contemplated them as he nodded. 'Yes. I believe I did suggest that he might profit from your seminar—what is it?—in the Latin tradition.'

'Can you tell me something about him?'

Lomax looked up from his hands and gazed at the ceiling, his lower lip thrust out judiciously. 'A good student. A superior student, I might say. He is doing his dissertation on Shelley and the Hellenistic Ideal. It promises to be brilliant, really brilliant. It will not be what some would call'—he hesitated delicately over the word—'*sound*, but it is most imaginative. Did you have a particular reason for asking?'

'Yes,' Stoner said. 'He behaved rather foolishly in the seminar today. I was just wondering if I should attach any special significance to it.'

Lomax's early geniality had disappeared, and the more familiar mask of irony had slipped over him. 'Ah, yes,' he said with a frosty smile. 'The gaucherie and foolishness of the young. Walker is, for reasons you may understand, rather awkwardly shy and therefore at times defensive and rather too assertive. As do we all, he has his problems; but his scholarly and critical abilities are not, I hope, to be judged in the light of his rather understandable psychic disturbances.' He looked directly at Stoner and said with cheerful malevolence, 'As you may have noticed, he is a cripple.'

'It may be that,' Stoner said thoughtfully. He sighed and got up from the chair. 'I suppose it's really too soon for me to be concerned. I just wanted to check with you.'

Suddenly Lomax's voice was tight and near trembling

with suppressed anger. 'You will find him to be a superior student. I assure you, you will find him to be an *excellent* student.'

Stoner looked at him for a moment, frowning perplexedly. Then he nodded and went out of the room.

The seminar met weekly. For the first several meetings Walker interrupted the class with questions and comments that were so bewilderingly far off the mark that Stoner was at a loss as to how to meet them. Soon Walker's questions and statements were greeted with laughter or pointedly disregarded by the students themselves; and after a few weeks he spoke not at all but sat with a stony indignation and an air of outraged integrity as the seminar surged around him. It would, Stoner thought, have been amusing had there not been something so naked in Walker's outrage and resentment.

But despite Walker it was a successful seminar, one of the best classes Stoner had ever taught. Almost from the first, the implications of the subject caught the students, and they all had that sense of discovery that comes when one feels that the subject at hand lies at the center of a much larger subject, and when one feels intensely that a pursuit of the subject is likely to lead—where, one does not know. The seminar organized itself, and the students so involved themselves that Stoner himself became simply one of them, searching as diligently as they. Even the auditor—the young instructor who was stopping over at Columbia while finishing her dissertation—asked if she might report on a seminar topic; she thought that she had come upon something that might be of value to the others. Her name was Katherine Driscoll, and she was in her late twenties. Stoner had never really noticed her until she talked to him after class about the report and asked him if he would be willing to read her dissertation when she got it finished. He told her that he welcomed the report and that he would be glad to read her dissertation.

The seminar reports were scheduled for the second half of the semester, after the Christmas vacation. Walker's report on 'Hellenism and the Medieval Latin Tradition' was due early in the term, but he kept delaying it, explaining to Stoner his difficulty in obtaining books he needed, which were not available in the University library.

It had been understood that Miss Driscoll, being an auditor, would give her report after the credit students had given theirs; but on the last day Stoner had allowed for the seminar reports, two weeks before the end of the semester, Walker again begged that he be allowed one more week; he had been ill, his eyes had been troubling him, and a crucial book had not arrived from inter-library loan. So Miss Driscoll gave her paper on the day vacated by Walker's defection.

Her paper was entitled 'Donatus and Renaissance Tragedy.' Her concentration was upon Shakespeare's use of the Donatan tradition, a tradition that had persisted in the grammars and handbooks of the Middle Ages. A few moments after she began, Stoner knew that the paper would be good, and he listened with an excitement that he had not felt for a long time. After she had finished the paper, and the class had discussed it, he detained her for a few moments while the other students went out of the room.

'Miss Driscoll, I just want to say—' He paused, and for an instant a wave of awkwardness and self-consciousness came over him. She was looking at him inquiringly with large dark eyes; her face was very white against the severe black frame of her hair, drawn tight and caught in a small bun at the back. He continued, 'I just want to say that your paper was the best discussion I know of the subject, and I'm grateful that you volunteered to give it.'

She did not reply. Her expression did not change, but Stoner thought for a moment that she was angry; something fierce glinted behind her eyes. Then she blushed furiously and ducked her head, whether in anger or acknowledgment Stoner did not know, and hurried away from him. Stoner walked slowly out of the room, disquieted and puzzled, fearful that in his clumsiness he might somehow have offended her.

He had warned Walker as gently as he could that it would be necessary for him to deliver his paper the next Wednesday if he was to receive credit for the course; as he half expected, Walker became coldly and respectfully angry at the warning, repeated the various conditions and difficulties that had delayed him, and assured Stoner that there was no need to worry, that his paper was nearly completed.

On that last Wednesday, Stoner was delayed several minutes in his office by a desperate undergraduate who wished to be assured that he would receive a C in the sophomore survey course, so that he would not be kicked out of his fraternity. Stoner hurried downstairs and entered the basement seminar room a little out of breath; he found Charles Walker seated at his desk, looking imperiously and somberly at the small group of students. It was apparent that he was engaged in some private fantasy. He turned to Stoner and gazed at him haughtily, as if he were a professor putting down a rowdy freshman. Then Walker's expression broke and he said, 'We were just about to start without you'—he paused at the last minute, let a smile through his lips, bobbed his head, and added, so that Stoner would know a joke was being made—'sir.'

Stoner looked at him for a moment and then turned to

the class. 'I'm sorry I'm late. As you know, Mr Walker is to deliver his seminar paper today upon the topic of "Hellenism and the Medieval Latin Tradition."' And he found a seat in the first row, next to Katherine Driscoll.

Charles Walker fiddled for a moment with the sheaf of papers on the desk before him and allowed the remoteness to creep back into his face. He tapped the forefinger of his right hand on his manuscript and looked toward the corner of the room away from where Stoner and Katherine Driscoll sat, as if he were waiting for something. Then, glancing every now and then at the sheaf of papers on the desk, he began.

'Confronted as we are by the mystery of literature, and by its inenarrable power, we are behooved to discover the source of the power and mystery. And yet, finally, what can avail? The work of literature throws before us a profound veil which we cannot plumb. And we are but votaries before it, helpless in its sway. Who would have the temerity to lift that veil aside, to discover the undiscoverable, to reach the unreachable? The strongest of us are but the puniest weaklings, are but tinkling cymbals and sounding brass, before the eternal mystery.'

His voice rose and fell, his right hand went out with its fingers curled supplicatingly upward, and his body swayed to the rhythm of his words; his eyes rolled slightly upward, as if he were making an invocation. There was something grotesquely familiar in what he said and did. And suddenly Stoner knew what it was. This was Hollis Lomax—or, rather, a broad caricature of him, which came unsuspected from the caricaturer, a gesture not of contempt or dislike, but of respect and love.

Walker's voice dropped to a conversational level, and he addressed the back wall of the room in a tone that was calm and equable with reason. 'Recently we have heard a paper that, to the mind of academe, must be accounted most excellent. These remarks that follow are remarks that are not personal. I wish to exemplify a point. We have heard, in this paper, an account that purports to be an explanation of the mystery and soaring lyricism of Shakespeare's art. Well, I say to you'—and he thrust a forefinger at his audience as if he would impale them—'I say to you, it is not true.' He leaned back in his chair and consulted the papers on the desk. 'We are asked to believe that one Donatus—an obscure Roman *grammarian* of the fourth century A.D.—we are asked to believe that such a man, a pedant, had sufficient power to determine the work of one of the greatest geniuses in all of the history of art. May we not suspect, on the face of it, such a theory? *Must* we not suspect it?'

Anger, simple and dull, rose within Stoner, overwhelming the complexity of feeling he had had at the beginning of the paper. His immediate impulse was to rise, to cut short the farce that was developing; he knew that if he did not stop Walker at once he would have to let him go on for as long as he wanted to talk. His head turned slightly so that he could see Katherine Driscoll's face; it was serene and without any expression, save one of polite and detached interest; the dark eyes regarded Walker with an unconcern that was like boredom. Covertly, Stoner looked at her for several moments; he found himself wondering what she was feeling and what she wished him to do. When he finally shifted his gaze away from her he had to realize that his decision was made. He had waited too long to interrupt, and Walker was rushing impetuously through what he had to say.

'. . . the monumental edifice that is Renaissance literature, that edifice which is the cornerstone of the great poetry of the nineteenth century. The question of proof, endemic to the dull course of scholarship as distinguished from criticism, is also sadly at lack. What *proof* is offered that Shakespeare even read this obscure Roman grammarian? We must remember it was Ben Jonson'—he hesitated for a brief moment—'it was Ben Jonson himself, Shakespeare's friend and contemporary, who said he had little Latin and less Greek. And certainly Jonson, who idolized Shakespeare this side of idolatry, did not impute to his great friend any lack. On the contrary, he wished to suggest, as do I, that the soaring lyricism of Shakespeare was not attributable to the burning of the midnight oil, but to a genius natural and supreme to rule and mundane law. Unlike lesser poets, Shakespeare was not born to blush unseen and waste his sweetness on the desert air; partaking of that mysterious source to whence all poets go for their sustenance, what need had the immortal bard of such stultifying rules as are to be found in a mere grammar? What would Donatus be to him, even if he had read him? Genius, unique and a law unto itself, needs not the support of such a "tradition" as has been described to us, whether it be generically Latin or Donatan or whatever. Genius, soaring and free, must . . .'

After he became used to his anger Stoner found a reluctant and perverse admiration stealing over him. However florid and imprecise, the man's powers of rhetoric and invention were dismayingly impressive; and however grotesque, his presence was real. There was something cold and calculating and watchful in his eyes, something needlessly reckless and yet desperately cautious. Stoner became aware that he was in the presence of a bluff so colossal and bold that he had no ready means of dealing with it.

For it was clear even to the most inattentive students in the class that Walker was engaged in a performance that was entirely impromptu. Stoner doubted that he had had any very clear idea of what he was going to say until he had sat at the desk before the class and looked at the students in his cold, imperious way. It became clear that the sheaf of papers on the desk before him was only a sheaf of papers; as he became heated, he did not even glance at them in pretense, and toward the end of his talk, in his excitement and urgency he shoved them away from him.

He talked for nearly an hour. Toward the end the other students in the seminar were glancing worriedly at one another, almost as if they were in some danger, as if they were contemplating escape; they carefully avoided looking at either Stoner or the young woman who sat impassively beside him. Abruptly, as if sensing the unrest, Walker brought his talk to a close, leaned back in the chair behind the desk, and smiled triumphantly.

The moment Walker stopped talking Stoner got to his feet and dismissed the class; though he did not realize it at the time, he did so out of a vague consideration for Walker, so that none of them might have the chance to discuss what he had said. Then Stoner went to the desk where Walker remained and asked him if he would stay for a few moments. As if his mind were somewhere else, Walker nodded distantly. Stoner then turned and followed a few straggling students out of the room into the hall. He saw Katherine Driscoll starting away, walking alone down the hall. He called her name, and when she stopped he walked up and stood in front of her. And as he spoke to her he felt again the awkwardness that had come over him when, last week, he had complimented her on her paper.

'Miss Driscoll, I—I'm sorry. It was really most unfair. I feel that somehow I am responsible. Perhaps I should have stopped it.'

Still she did not reply, nor did any expression come on

147

her face; she looked up at him as she had looked across the room at Walker.

'Anyhow,' he continued, still more awkwardly, 'I'm sorry he attacked you.'

And then she smiled. It was a slow smile that started in her eyes and pulled at her lips until her face was wreathed in radiant, secret, and intimate delight. Stoner almost pulled back from the sudden and involuntary warmth.

'Oh, it wasn't me,' she said, a tiny tremor of suppressed laughter giving timbre to her low voice. 'It wasn't me at all. It was *you* he was attacking. I was hardly even involved.'

Stoner felt lifted from him a burden of regret and worry that he had not known he carried; the relief was almost physical, and he felt light on his feet and a little giddy. He laughed.

'Of course,' he said. 'Of course that's true.'

The smile eased itself off her face, and she looked at him gravely for a moment more. Then she bobbed her head, turned away from him, and walked swiftly down the hall. Her body was slim and straight, and she carried herself unobtrusively. Stoner stood looking down the hall for several moments after she disappeared. Then he sighed and went back into the room where Walker waited.

Walker had not moved from the desk. He gazed at Stoner and smiled, upon his face an odd mixture of obsequiousness and arrogance. Stoner sat in the chair he had vacated a few minutes before and looked curiously at Walker.

'Yes, sir?' Walker said.

'Do you have an explanation?' Stoner asked quietly.

A look of hurt surprise came upon Walker's round face. 'What do you mean, sir?'

'Mr Walker, please,' Stoner said wearily. 'It has been a long day, and we're both tired. Do you have an explanation for your performance this afternoon?'

'I'm sure, sir, I intended no offense.' He removed his glasses and polished them rapidly; again Stoner was struck by the naked vulnerability of his face. 'I said my remarks were not intended personally. If feelings have been hurt, I shall be most happy to explain to the young lady—'

'Mr Walker,' Stoner said. 'You know that isn't the point.'

'Has the young lady been complaining to you?' Walker asked. His fingers were trembling as he put his glasses back on. With them on, his face managed a frown of anger. 'Really, sir, the complaints of a student whose feelings have been hurt should not—'

'Mr Walker!' Stoner heard his voice go a little out of control. He took a deep breath. 'This has nothing to do with the young lady, or with myself, or with anything except your performance. And I still await any explanation you have to offer.'

'Then I'm afraid I don't understand at all, sir. Unless . . .'

'Unless what, Mr Walker?'

'Unless it is simply a matter of disagreement,' Walker said. 'I realize that my ideas do not coincide with yours, but I have always thought that disagreement was healthy. I assumed that you were big enough to—'

'I will not allow you to evade the issue,' Stoner said. His voice was cold and level. 'Now. What was the seminar topic assigned to you?'

'You're angry,' Walker said.

'Yes, I am angry. What was the seminar topic assigned to you?'

Walker became stiffly formal and polite. 'My topic was "Hellenism and the Medieval Latin Tradition," sir.'

'And when did you complete that paper, Mr Walker?'

'Two days ago. As I told you, it was nearly complete a couple of weeks ago, but a book I had to get through inter-library loan didn't come in until—'

'Mr Walker, if your paper was *nearly* finished two weeks ago, how could you have based it, in its entirety, upon Miss Driscoll's report, which was given only last week?'

'I made a number of changes, sir, at the last minute.' His voice became heavy with irony. 'I assumed that that was permissible. And I did depart from the text now and then. I noticed that other students did the same, and I thought the privilege would be allowed me also.'

Stoner fought down a near-hysterical impulse to laugh. 'Mr Walker, will you explain to me what your attack on Miss Driscoll's paper has to do with the survival of Hellenism in the medieval Latin tradition?'

'I approached my subject indirectly, sir,' Walker said. 'I thought we were allowed a certain latitude in developing our concepts.'

Stoner was silent for a moment. Then he said wearily, 'Mr Walker, I dislike having to flunk a graduate student. Especially I dislike having to flunk one who simply has got in over his head.'

'Sir!' Walker said indignantly.

'But you're making it very difficult for me not to. Now, it seems to me that there are only a few alternatives. I can give you an incomplete in the course, with the understanding that you will do a satisfactory paper on the assigned topic within the next three weeks.'

'But, sir,' Walker said. 'I have already done my paper. If I agree to do another one I will be admitting—I will admit—'

'All right,' Stoner said. 'Then if you will give me the manuscript from which you—deviated this afternoon, I shall see if something can be salvaged.'

'Sir,' Walker cried. 'I would hesitate to let it out of my possession just now. The draft is *very* rough.'

With a grim and restless shame, Stoner continued, 'That's all right. I shall be able to find out what I want to know.'

Walker looked at him craftily. 'Tell me, sir, have you asked anyone else to hand his manuscript in to you?'

'I have not,' Stoner said.

'Then,' Walker said triumphantly, almost happily, 'I must refuse also to hand *my* manuscript in to you on principle. Unless you require everyone else to hand theirs in.'

Stoner looked at him steadily for a moment. 'Very well, Mr Walker. You have made your decision. That will be all.'

Walker said, 'What am I to understand then, sir? What may I expect from this course?'

Stoner laughed shortly. 'Mr Walker, you amaze me. You will, of course, receive an F.'

Walker tried to make his round face long. With the patient bitterness of a martyr he said, 'I see. Very well, sir. One must be prepared to suffer for one's beliefs.'

'And for one's laziness and dishonesty and ignorance,' Stoner said. 'Mr Walker, it seems almost superfluous to say this, but I would most strongly advise you to re-examine your position here. I seriously question whether you have a place in a graduate program.'

For the first time Walker's emotion appeared genuine; his anger gave him something that was close to dignity. 'Mr Stoner, you're going too far! You can't mean that.'

'I most certainly mean it,' Stoner said.

For a moment Walker was quiet; he looked thoughtfully at Stoner. Then he said, 'I was willing to accept the grade you gave me. But you must realize that I cannot accept this. You are questioning my competence!'

'Yes, Mr Walker,' Stoner said wearily. He raised himself

from the chair. 'Now, if you will excuse me . . .' He started for the door.

But the sound of his shouted name halted him. He turned. Walker's face was a deep red; the skin was puffed so that the eyes behind their thick glasses were like tiny dots. 'Mr Stoner!' he shouted again. 'You have not heard the last of this. Believe me, you have not heard the last of this!'

Stoner looked at him dully, incuriously. He nodded distractedly, turned, and went out into the hall. His feet were heavy, and they dragged on the bare cement floor. He was drained of feeling, and he felt very old and tired.

10

And he had not heard the last of it.

He turned his grades in on the Monday following the Friday closing of the semester. It was the part of teaching he most disliked, and he always got it out of the way as soon as he could. He gave Walker his F and thought no more about the matter. He spent most of the week between semesters reading the first drafts of two theses due for final presentation in the spring. They were awkwardly done, and they needed much of his attention. The Walker incident was crowded from his mind.

But two weeks after the second semester started he was again reminded of it. He found one morning in his mailbox a note from Gordon Finch asking him to drop by the office at his convenience for a chat.

The friendship between Gordon Finch and William Stoner had reached a point that all such relationships, carried on long enough, come to; it was casual, deep, and so guardedly intimate that it was almost impersonal. They seldom saw each other socially, although occasionally Caroline Finch made a perfunctory call on Edith. While they talked they remembered the years of their youth, and each thought of the other as he had been at another time.

In his early middle age Finch had the erect soft bearing of one who tries vigorously to keep his weight under control;

his face was heavy and as yet unlined, though his jowls were beginning to sag and the flesh was gathering in rolls on the back of his neck. His hair was very thin, and he had begun to comb it so that the baldness would not be readily apparent.

On the afternoon that Stoner stopped by his office, they spoke for a few moments casually about their families; Finch maintained the easy convention of pretending that Stoner's marriage was a normal one, and Stoner professed his conventional disbelief that Gordon and Caroline could be the parents of two children, the younger of which was already in kindergarten.

After they had made their automatic gestures toward their casual intimacy, Finch looked out his window distractedly and said, 'Now, what was it I wanted to talk to you about? Oh, yes. The dean of the Graduate College—he thought, since we were friends, I ought to mention it to you. Nothing of any importance.' He looked at a note on his memo book. 'Just an irate graduate student who thinks he got screwed in one of your classes last semester.'

'Walker,' Stoner said. 'Charles Walker.'

Finch nodded. 'That's the one. What's the story on him?'

Stoner shrugged. 'As far as I could tell, he didn't do any of the reading assigned—it was my seminar in the Latin Tradition. He tried to fake his seminar report, and when I gave him the chance either to do another one or produce a copy of his paper, he refused. I had no alternative but to flunk him.'

Finch nodded again. 'I figured it was something like that. God knows, I wish they wouldn't waste my time with stuff like this; but it has to be checked out, as much for your protection as anything else.'

Stoner asked, 'Is there some—special difficulty here?'

'No, no,' Finch said. 'Not at all. Just a complaint. You

know how these things go. As a matter of fact, Walker received a C in the first course he took here as a graduate student; he could be kicked out of the program right now if we wanted to do it. But I think we've about decided to let him take his preliminary orals next month, and let that tell the story. I'm sorry I even had to bother you about it.'

They talked for a few moments about other things. Then, just as Stoner was about to leave, Finch detained him casually.

'Oh, there was something else I wanted to mention to you. The president and the board have finally decided that something's going to have to be done about Claremont. So I guess, beginning next year, I'll be dean of Arts and Sciences—officially.'

'I'm glad, Gordon,' Stoner said. 'It's about time.'

'So that means we're going to have to get a new chairman of the department. Do you have any thoughts on it?'

'No,' Stoner said, 'I really haven't thought of it at all.'

'We can either go outside the department and bring in somebody new, or we can make one of the present men chairman. What I'm trying to find out is, if we *did* choose someone from the department— Well, do *you* have your eyes on the job?'

Stoner thought for a moment. 'I hadn't thought about it, but—no. No, I don't think I'd want it.'

Finch's relief was so obvious that Stoner smiled. 'Good. I didn't think you would. It means a lot of horse-shit. Entertaining and socializing and—' He looked away from Stoner. 'I know you don't go in for that sort of thing. But since old Sloane died, and since Huggins and what's-his-name, Cooper, retired last year, you're the senior member of the department. But if you haven't been casting covetous eyes, then—'

'No,' Stoner said definitely. 'I'd probably be a rotten chairman. I neither expect nor want the appointment.'

'Good,' Finch said. 'Good. That simplifies things a great deal.'

They said their good-bys, and Stoner did not think of the conversation again for some time.

Charles Walker's preliminary oral comprehensives were scheduled for the middle of March; somewhat to Stoner's surprise, he received a note from Finch informing him that he would be a member of the three-man committee who would examine him. He reminded Finch that he had flunked Walker, that Walker had taken the flunk personally, and he asked to be relieved of this particular duty.

'Regulations,' Finch answered with a sigh. 'You know how it is. The committee is made up of the candidate's adviser, one professor who has had him in a graduate seminar, and one outside his field of specialization. Lomax is the adviser, you're the only one he's had a graduate seminar from, and I've picked the new man, Jim Holland, for the one outside his specialty. Dean Rutherford of the Graduate College and I will be sitting in ex-officio. I'll try to make it as painless as possible.'

But it was an ordeal that could not be made painless. Though Stoner wished to ask as few questions as possible, the rules that governed the preliminary oral were inflexible; each professor was allowed forty-five minutes to ask the candidate any questions that he wished, though other professors habitually joined in.

On the afternoon set for the examination Stoner came deliberately late to the seminar room on the third floor of Jesse Hall. Walker was seated at the end of a long, highly polished table; the four examiners already present—Finch,

Lomax, the new man, Holland, and Henry Rutherford—were ranged down the table from him. Stoner slipped in the door and took a chair at the end of the table opposite Walker. Finch and Holland nodded to him; Lomax, slumped in his chair, stared straight ahead, tapping his long white fingers on the mirrorlike surface of the table. Walker stared down the length of the table, his head held stiff and high in cold disdain.

Rutherford cleared his throat. 'Ah, Mr'—he consulted a sheet of paper in front of him—'Mr Stoner.' Rutherford was a slight thin gray man with round shoulders; his eyes and brows dropped at the outer corners, so that his expression was always one of gentle hopelessness. Though he had known Stoner for many years, he never remembered his name. He cleared his throat again. 'We were just about to begin.'

Stoner nodded, rested his forearms on the table, clasped his fingers, and contemplated them as Rutherford's voice droned through the formal preliminaries of the oral examination.

Mr Walker was being examined (Rutherford's voice dropped to a steady, uninflected hum) to determine his ability to continue in the doctoral program in the Department of English at the University of Missouri. This was an examination which all doctoral candidates underwent, and it was designed not only to judge the candidate's general fitness, but also to determine strengths and weaknesses, so that his future course of study could be profitably guided. Three results were possible: a pass, a conditional pass, and a failure. Rutherford described the terms of these eventualities, and without looking up performed the ritualistic introduction of the examiners and the candidate. Then he pushed the sheet of paper away from him and looked hopelessly at those around him.

'The custom is,' he said softly, 'for the candidate's thesis adviser to begin the questioning. Mr'—he glanced at the paper—'Mr Lomax is, I believe, Mr Walker's adviser. So . . .'

Lomax's head jerked back as if he had been suddenly awakened from a doze. He glanced around the table, blinking, a little smile on his lips; but his eyes were shrewd and alert.

'Mr Walker, you are planning a dissertation on Shelley and the Hellenistic Ideal. It is unlikely that you have thought through your subject yet, but would you begin by giving us some of the background, your reason for choosing it, and so forth.'

Walker nodded and began swiftly to speak. 'I intend to trace Shelley's first rejection of Godwinian necessitarianism for a more or less Platonic ideal, in the "Hymn to Intellectual Beauty," through the mature use of that ideal, in *Prometheus Unbound*, as a comprehensive synthesis of his earlier atheism, radicalism, Christianity, and scientific necessitarianism, and ultimately to account for the decay of the ideal in such a late work as *Hellas*. It is to my mind an important topic for three reasons: First, it shows the quality of Shelley's mind, and hence leads us into a better understanding of his poetry. Second, it demonstrates the leading philosophical and literary conflicts of the early nineteenth century, and hence enlarges our understanding and appreciation of Romantic poetry. And third, it is a subject that might have a peculiar relevance to our own time, a time in which we face many of the same conflicts that confronted Shelley and his contemporaries.'

Stoner listened, and as he listened his astonishment grew. He could not believe that this was the same man who had taken his seminar, whom he thought he knew. Walker's presentation was lucid, forthright, and intelligent; at times it was almost brilliant. Lomax was right; if the dissertation fulfilled its promise, it would be brilliant. Hope, warm and exhilarating, rushed upon him, and he leaned forward attentively.

Walker talked upon the subject of his dissertation for perhaps ten minutes and then abruptly stopped. Quickly Lomax asked another question, and Walker responded at once. Gordon Finch caught Stoner's eye and gave him a look of mild inquiry; Stoner smiled slightly, self-deprecatingly, and gave a small shrug of his shoulders.

When Walker stopped again, Jim Holland spoke immediately. He was a thin young man, intense and pale, with slightly protuberant blue eyes; he spoke with a deliberate slowness, with a voice that seemed always to tremble before a forced restraint. 'Mr Walker, you mentioned a bit earlier Godwin's necessitarianism. I wonder if you could make a connection between that and the phenomenalism of John Locke?' Stoner remembered that Holland was an eighteenth-century man.

There was a moment of silence. Walker turned to Holland, removed the round glasses, and polished them; his eyes blinked and stared, at random. He put them back on and blinked again. 'Would you repeat the question, please.'

Holland started to speak, but Lomax interrupted. 'Jim,' he said affably, 'do you mind if I extend the question a bit?' He turned quickly to Walker before Holland could answer. 'Mr Walker, proceeding from the implications of Professor Holland's question—namely, that Godwin accepted Locke's theory of the sensational nature of knowledge—the *tabula rasa*, and all that—and that Godwin believed with Locke that judgment and knowledge falsified by the accidents of passion and the inevitability of ignorance could be rectified by education—given these implications, would you comment on Shelley's principle of knowledge—specifically, the principle of beauty—enunciated in the final stanzas of "Adonais"?'

Holland leaned back in his chair, a puzzled frown on his face. Walker nodded and said rapidly, 'Though the opening stanzas of "Adonais," Shelley's tribute to his friend and peer, John Keats, are conventionally classical, what with their allusions to the Mother, the Hours, to Urania and so forth, and with their repetitive invocations—the really classical moment does not appear until the final stanzas, which are, in effect, a sublime hymn to the eternal Principle of Beauty. If, for a moment, we may focus our attention upon these famous lines:

> Life, like a dome of many-colored glass,
> Stains the white radiance of eternity,
> Until Death tramples it to fragments.

"The symbolism implicit in these lines is not clear until we take the lines in their context. "The One remains," Shelley writes a few lines earlier, "the many change and pass." And we are reminded of Keats' equally famous lines,

> "Beauty is truth, truth Beauty,"—that is all
> Ye know on earth, and all ye need to know.

The principle, then, is Beauty; but beauty is also knowledge. And it is a conception that has its roots . . .'

Walker's voice continued, fluent and sure of itself, the words emerging from his rapidly moving mouth almost as if—Stoner started, and the hope that had begun in him died as abruptly as it had been born. For a moment he felt almost physically ill. He looked down at the table and saw between his arms the image of his face reflected in the high polish of the walnut top. The image was dark, and he could not make out its features; it was as if he saw a ghost glimmering unsubstantially out of a hardness, coming to meet him.

Lomax finished his questioning, and Holland began. It was, Stoner admitted, a masterful performance; unobtrusively, with great charm and good humor, Lomax managed it all. Sometimes, when Holland asked a question, Lomax pretended a good-natured puzzlement and asked for a clarification. At other times, apologizing for his own enthusiasm, he followed up one of Holland's questions with a speculation of his own, drawing Walker into the discussion, so that it seemed that he was an actual participant. He rephrased questions (always apologetically), changing them so that the original intent was lost in the elucidation. He engaged Walker in what seemed to be elaborately theoretical arguments, although he did most of the talking. And finally, still apologizing, he cut into Holland's questions with questions of his own that led Walker where he wanted him to go.

During this time Stoner did not speak. He listened to the talk that swirled around him; he gazed at Finch's face, which had become a heavy mask; he looked at Rutherford, who sat with his eyes closed, his head nodding; and he looked at Holland's bewilderment, at Walker's courteous disdain, and at Lomax's feverish animation. He was waiting to do what he knew he had to do, and he was waiting with a dread and an anger and a sorrow that grew more intense with every minute that passed. He was glad that none of their eyes met his own as he gazed at them.

Finally Holland's period of questioning was over. As if he somehow participated in the dread that Stoner felt, Finch glanced at his watch and nodded. He did not speak.

Stoner took a deep breath. Still looking at the ghost of his face in the mirrorlike finish of the tabletop, he said expressionlessly, 'Mr Walker, I'm going to ask you a few questions about English literature. They will be simple questions, and they will not require elaborate answers. I shall start early and I shall proceed chronologically, so far as time will allow me. Will you begin by describing to me the principles of Anglo-Saxon versification?'

'Yes, sir,' Walker said. His face was frozen. 'To begin with, the Anglo-Saxon poets, existing as they did in the Dark Ages, did not have the advantages of sensibility as did later poets in the English tradition. Indeed, I should say that their poetry was characterized by primitivism. Nevertheless, within this primitivism there is potential, though perhaps hidden to some eyes, there is potential that subtlety of feeling that is to characterize—'

'Mr Walker,' Stoner said, 'I asked for the principles of versification. Can you give them to me?'

'Well, sir,' Walker said, 'it is very rough and irregular. The versification, I mean.'

'Is that all you can tell me about it?'

'Mr Walker,' Lomax said quickly—a little wildly, Stoner thought—'this roughness you speak of—could you account for this, give the—'

'No,' Stoner said firmly, looking at no one. 'I want my question answered. Is that all you can tell me about Anglo-Saxon versification?'

'Well, sir,' Walker said; he smiled, and the smile became a nervous giggle. 'Frankly, I haven't had my required course in Anglo-Saxon yet, and I hesitate to discuss such matters without that authority.'

'Very well,' Stoner said. 'Let's skip Anglo-Saxon literature. Can you name for me a medieval drama that had any influence in the development of Renaissance drama?'

Walker nodded. 'Of course, all medieval dramas, in their

own way, led into the high accomplishment of the Renaissance. It is difficult to realize that out of the barren soil of the Middle Ages the drama of Shakespeare was, only a few years later, to flower and—'

'Mr Walker, I am asking simple questions. I must insist upon simple answers. I shall make the question even simpler. Name three medieval dramas.'

'Early or late, sir?' He had taken his glasses off and was polishing them furiously.

'*Any* three, Mr Walker.'

'There are so many,' Walker said. 'It's difficult to— There's *Everyman* . . .'

'Can you name any more?'

'No, sir,' Walker said. 'I must confess to a weakness in the areas that you—'

'Can you name any other titles—just the titles—of any of the literary works of the Middle Ages?'

Walker's hands were trembling. 'As I have said, sir, I must confess to a weakness in—'

'Then we shall go on to the Renaissance. What genre do you feel most confident of in this period, Mr Walker?'

'The'—Walker hesitated and despite himself looked supplicatingly at Lomax—'the poem, sir. Or—the drama. The drama, perhaps.'

'The drama then. What is the first blank verse tragedy in English, Mr Walker?'

'The first?' Walker licked his lips. 'Scholarship is divided on the question, sir. I should hesitate to—'

'Can you name any drama of significance before Shakespeare?'

'Certainly, sir,' Walker said. 'There's Marlowe—the mighty line—'

'Name some plays of Marlowe.'

With an effort Walker pulled himself together. 'There is, of course, the justly famous *Dr Faust*. And—and the—*The Jew of Malfi*.'

'*Faustus* and *The Jew of Malta*. Can you name any more?'

'Frankly, sir, those are the only two plays that I have had a chance to reread in the last year or so. So I would prefer not to—'

'All right. Tell me something about *The Jew of Malta*.'

'Mr Walker,' Lomax cried out. 'If I may broaden the question a bit. If you will—'

'No!' Stoner said grimly, not looking at Lomax. 'I want answers to my questions. Mr Walker?'

Walker said desperately, 'Marlowe's mighty line—'

'Let's forget about the "mighty line,"' Stoner said wearily. 'What happens in the play?'

'Well,' Walker said a little wildly, 'Marlowe is attacking the problem of anti-Semitism as it manifested itself in the early sixteenth century. The sympathy, I might even say, the profound sympathy—'

'Never mind, Mr Walker. Let's go on to—'

Lomax shouted, 'Let the candidate answer the question! Give him time to answer at least.'

'Very well,' Stoner said mildly. 'Do you wish to continue with your answer, Mr Walker?'

Walker hesitated for a moment. 'No, sir,' he said.

Relentlessly Stoner continued his questioning. What had been an anger and outrage that included both Walker and Lomax became a kind of pity and sick regret that included them too. After a while it seemed to Stoner that he had gone outside himself, and it was as if he heard a voice going on and on, impersonal and deadly.

At last he heard the voice say, 'All right, Mr Walker. Your period of specialization is the nineteenth century. You seem to know little about the literature of earlier centuries; perhaps you will feel more at ease among the Romantic poets.'

He tried not to look at Walker's face, but he could not prevent his eyes from rising now and then to see the round, staring mask that faced him with a cold, pale malevolence. Walker nodded curtly.

'You are familiar with Lord Byron's more important poems, are you not?'

'Of course,' Walker said.

'Then would you care to comment upon "English Bards and Scottish Reviewers"?'

Walker looked at him suspiciously for a moment. Then he smiled triumphantly. 'Ah, sir,' he said and nodded his head vigorously. 'I see. *Now* I see. You're trying to trick me. Of course. "English Bards and Scottish Reviewers" is not by Byron at all. It is John Keats's famous reply to the journalists who attempted to smirch his reputation as a poet, after the publication of his first poems. Very good, sir. Very—'

'All right, Mr Walker,' Stoner said wearily. 'I have no more questions.'

For several moments silence lay upon the group. Then Rutherford cleared his throat, shuffled the papers on the table before him, and said, 'Thank you, Mr Walker. If you will step outside for a few moments and wait, the committee will discuss your examination and let you know its decision.'

In the few moments that it took Rutherford to say what he had to say, Walker recomposed himself. He rose and rested his crippled hand upon the tabletop. He smiled at the group almost condescendingly. 'Thank you, gentlemen,' he said. 'It has been a most rewarding experience.' He limped out of the room and shut the door behind him.

Rutherford sighed. 'Well, gentlemen, is there any discussion?'

Another silence came over the room.

Lomax said, 'I thought he did *quite* well on my part of the examination. And he did rather well on Holland's portion. I must confess that I was somewhat disappointed by the way the latter part of the exam went, but I imagine he was rather tired by that time. He *is* a good student, but he doesn't show up as well as he might under pressure.' He flashed an empty, pained smile at Stoner. 'And you did press him a bit, Bill. You must admit that. I vote pass.'

Rutherford said, 'Mr—Holland?'

Holland looked from Lomax to Stoner; he was frowning in puzzlement, and his eyes blinked. 'But—well, he seemed awfully weak to me. I don't know exactly how to figure it.' He swallowed uncomfortably. 'This is the first orals I've sat in on here. I really don't know what the standards are, but—well, he seemed awfully weak. Let me think about it for a minute.'

Rutherford nodded. 'Mr—Stoner?'

'Fail,' Stoner said. 'It's a clear failure.'

'Oh, come now, Bill,' Lomax cried. 'You're being a bit hard on the boy, aren't you?'

'No,' Stoner said levelly, his eyes straight before him. 'You know I'm not, Holly.'

'What do you mean by that?' Lomax asked; it was as if he were trying to generate feeling in his voice by raising it. 'Just what do you mean?'

'Come off it, Holly,' Stoner said tiredly. 'The man's incompetent. There can be no question of that. The questions I asked him were those that should have been asked a fair undergraduate; and he was unable to answer a single one of them satisfactorily. And he's both lazy and dishonest. In my seminar last semester—'

'Your seminar!' Lomax laughed curtly. 'Well, I've heard

about that. And besides, that's another matter. The question is, how he did today. And it's clear'—his eyes narrowed—'it's clear that he did quite well today until you started in on him.'

'I asked him questions,' Stoner said. 'The simplest questions I could imagine. I was prepared to give him every chance.' He paused and said carefully, 'You are his thesis adviser, and it is natural that you two should have talked over his thesis subject. So when you questioned him on his thesis he did very well. But when we got beyond that—'

'What do you mean!' Lomax shouted. 'Are you suggesting that I—that there was any—'

'I am suggesting nothing, except that in my opinion the candidate did not do an adequate job. I cannot consent to his passing.'

'Look,' Lomax said. His voice had quieted, and he tried to smile. 'I can see how I would have a higher opinion of his work than you would. He has been in several of my classes, and—no matter. I'm willing to compromise. Though I think it's too severe, I'm willing to offer him a conditional pass. That would mean he could review for a couple of semesters, and then he—'

'Well,' Holland said with some relief, 'that would seem to be better than giving him a clear pass. I don't know the man, but it's obvious that he isn't ready to—'

'Good,' Lomax said, smiling vigorously at Holland. 'Then that's settled. We'll—'

'No,' Stoner said. 'I must vote for failure.'

'God *damn* it,' Lomax shouted. 'Do you realize what you're doing, Stoner? Do you realize what you're doing to the boy?'

'Yes,' Stoner said quietly, 'and I'm sorry for him. I am preventing him from getting his degree, and I'm preventing him from teaching in a college or university. Which is precisely what I want to do. For him to be a teacher would be a—disaster.'

Lomax was very still. 'That is your final word?' he asked icily.

'Yes,' Stoner said.

Lomax nodded. 'Well, let me warn you, Professor Stoner, I do not intend to let the matter drop here. You have made—you have implied certain accusations here today—you have shown a prejudice that—that—'

'Gentlemen, please,' Rutherford said. He looked as if he were going to weep. 'Let us keep our perspective. As you know, for the candidate to pass, there must be unanimous consent. Is there no way that we can resolve this difference?'

No one spoke.

Rutherford sighed. 'Very well, then, I have no alternative but to declare that—'

'Just a minute.' It was Gordon Finch; during the entire examination he had been so still that the others had nearly forgotten his presence. Now he raised himself a little in his chair and addressed the top of the table in a tired but determined voice. 'As acting chairman of the department I am going to make a recommendation. I trust it will be followed. I recommend that we defer the decision until the day after tomorrow. That will give us time to cool off and talk it over.'

'There's nothing to talk over,' Lomax said hotly. 'If Stoner wants to—'

'I have made my recommendation,' Finch said softly, 'and it will be followed. Dean Rutherford, I suggest that we inform the candidate of our resolution of this matter.'

They found Walker sitting in perfect ease in the corridor outside the conference room. He held a cigarette negligently in his right hand, and he was looking boredly at the ceiling.

'Mr Walker,' Lomax called and limped toward him.

Walker stood up; he was several inches taller than Lomax, so that he had to look down at him.

'Mr Walker, I have been directed to inform you that the committee has been unable to reach agreement concerning your examination; you will be informed the day after tomorrow. But I assure you'—his voice rose—'I assure you that you have nothing to worry about. Nothing at all.'

Walker stood for a moment looking coolly from one of them to another. 'I thank you again, gentlemen, for your consideration.' He caught Stoner's eye, and the flicker of a smile went across his lips.

Gordon Finch hurried away without speaking to any of them; Stoner, Rutherford, and Holland wandered down the hall together; Lomax remained behind, talking earnestly to Walker.

'Well,' Rutherford said, walking between Stoner and Holland, 'it's an unpleasant business. No matter how you look at it, it's an unpleasant business.'

'Yes, it is,' Stoner said and turned away from them. He walked down the marble steps, his steps becoming more rapid as he neared the first floor, and went outside. He breathed deeply the smoky fragrance of the afternoon air, and breathed again, as if he were a swimmer emerging from water. Then he walked slowly toward his house.

Early the next afternoon, before he had a chance to get lunch, he received a call from Gordon Finch's secretary, asking him to come down to the office at once.

Finch was waiting impatiently when Stoner came into the room. He rose and motioned for Stoner to sit in the chair he had drawn beside his desk.

'Is this about the Walker business?' Stoner asked.

'In a way,' Finch replied. 'Lomax has asked me for a meeting to try to settle this thing. It's likely to be unpleasant. I wanted to talk to you for a few minutes alone, before Lomax gets here.' He sat again and for several minutes rocked back and forth in the swivel chair, looking contemplatively at Stoner. He said abruptly, 'Lomax is a good man.'

'I know he is,' Stoner said. 'In some ways he's probably the best man in the department.'

As if Stoner had not spoken Finch went on, 'He has his problems, but they don't crop up very often; and when they do he's usually able to handle them. It's unfortunate that this business should have come up just now; the timing is awkward as hell. A split in the department right now—' Finch shook his head.

'Gordon,' Stoner said uncomfortably, 'I hope you're not—'

Finch held up his hand. 'Wait,' he said. 'I wish I had told you this before. But then it wasn't supposed to be let out, and it wasn't really official. It's still supposed to be confidential, but—do you remember a few weeks back our talking about the chairmanship?'

Stoner nodded.

'Well, it's Lomax. He's the new head. It's finished, settled. The suggestion came from upstairs, but I ought to tell you that I went along with it.' He laughed shortly. 'Not that I was in a position to do anything else. But even if I had been I would have gone along with it—then. Now I'm not so sure.'

'I see,' Stoner said thoughtfully. After a few moments he continued, 'I'm glad you didn't tell me. I don't think it would have made any difference, but at least it wasn't there to cloud the issue.'

'God damn it, Bill,' Finch said. 'You've got to understand. I don't give a damn about Walker, or Lomax, or—but you're an old friend. Look. I think you're right in this. Damn it, I know you're right. But let's be practical. Lomax is taking this very seriously, and he's not going to let it drop. And if it comes to a fight it's going to be awkward as hell. Lomax can be vindictive; you know that as well as I do. He can't fire you, but he can do damn near everything else. And to a certain extent I'll have to go along with him.' He laughed again, bitterly. 'Hell, to a *large* extent I'll have to go along with him. If a dean starts reversing the decisions of a department head he has to fire him from his chairmanship. Now, if Lomax got out of line, I could remove him from the chairmanship; or at least I could try. I might even get away with it, or I might not. But even if I did, there would be a fight that would split the department, maybe even the college, wide open. And, God damn it—' Finch was suddenly embarrassed; he mumbled, 'God damn it, I've got to think of the college.' He looked directly at Stoner. 'Do you see what I'm trying to say?'

A warmth of feeling, of love and fond respect for his old friend, came over Stoner. He said, 'Of course I do, Gordon. Did you think I wouldn't understand?'

'All right,' Finch said. 'And there's one more thing. Somehow Lomax has got his finger in the president's nose, and he leads him around like a cut bull. So it may be even rougher than you think. Look, all you'd have to do is say you'd reconsidered. You could even blame it on me—say I made you do it.'

'It isn't a matter of my saving face, Gordon.'

'I know that,' Finch said. 'I said it wrong. Look at it this way. What does it matter about Walker? Sure, I know; it's the principle of the thing; but there's another principle you ought to think of.'

'It's not the principle,' Stoner said. 'It's Walker. It would be a disaster to let him loose in a classroom.'

'Hell,' Finch said wearily. 'If he doesn't make it here, he can go somewhere else and get his degree; and despite everything he might even make it here. You could lose this, you know, no matter what you do. We can't keep the Walkers out.'

'Maybe not,' Stoner said. 'But we can try.'

Finch was silent for several moments. He sighed. 'All right. There's no use keeping Lomax waiting any longer. We might as well get it over with.' He got up from his desk and started for the door that led to the small anteroom. But as he passed Stoner, Stoner put his hand on his arm, delaying him for a moment.

'Gordon, do you remember something Dave Masters said once?'

Finch raised his brows in puzzlement. 'Why do you bring Dave Masters up?'

Stoner looked across the room, out of the window, trying to remember. 'The three of us were together, and he said—something about the University being an asylum, a refuge from the world, for the dispossessed, the crippled. But he didn't mean Walker. Dave would have thought of Walker as—as the world. And we can't let him in. For if we do, we become like the world, just as unreal, just as . . . The only hope we have is to keep him out.'

Finch looked at him for several moments. Then he grinned. 'You son-of-a-bitch,' he said cheerfully. 'We'd better see Lomax now.' He opened the door, beckoned, and Lomax came into the room.

He came into the room so stiffly and formally that the slight hitch in his right leg was barely noticeable; his thin handsome face was set and cold, and he held his head high, so that his rather long and wavy hair nearly touched the hump that disfigured his back beneath his left shoulder. He did not look at either of the two men in the room with him; he took a chair opposite Finch's desk and sat as erect as he could, staring at the space between Finch and Stoner. He turned his head slightly toward Finch.

'I asked for the three of us to meet for a simple purpose. I wish to know whether Professor Stoner has reconsidered his ill-advised vote yesterday.'

'Mr Stoner and I have been discussing the matter,' Finch said. 'I'm afraid that we've been unable to resolve it.'

Lomax turned to Stoner and stared at him; his light blue eyes were dull, as if a translucent film had dropped over them. 'Then I'm afraid I'm going to have to bring some rather serious charges out in the open.'

'Charges?' Finch's voice was surprised, a little angry. 'You never mentioned anything about—'

'I'm sorry,' Lomax said. 'But this is necessary.' He said to Stoner, 'The first time you spoke to Charles Walker was when he asked you for admittance to your graduate seminar. Is that right?'

'That's right,' Stoner said.

'You were reluctant to admit him, were you not?'

'Yes,' Stoner said. 'The class already had twelve students.'

Lomax glanced at some notes he held in his right hand. 'And when the student told you he *had* to get in, you reluctantly admitted him, at the same time saying that his admission would virtually ruin the seminar. Is that right?'

'Not exactly,' Stoner said. 'As I remember, I said one *more* in the class would—'

Lomax waved his hand. 'It doesn't matter. I'm just trying to establish a context. Now, during this first conversation, did you not question his competence to do the work in the seminar?'

Gordon Finch said tiredly, 'Holly, where's all this getting us? What good do you—'

'Please,' Lomax said. 'I have said that I have charges to bring. You must allow me to develop them. Now. Did you not question his competence?'

Stoner said calmly, 'I asked him a few questions, yes, to see whether he was capable of doing the work.'

'And did you satisfy yourself that he was?'

'I was unsure, I believe,' Stoner said. 'It's difficult to remember.'

Lomax turned to Finch. 'We have established, then, first that Professor Stoner was reluctant to admit Walker to his seminar; second, that his reluctance was so intense that he threatened Walker with the fact that his admission would ruin the seminar; third, that he was at least doubtful that Walker was competent to do the work; and fourth, that despite this doubt and these strong feelings of resentment, he allowed him in the class anyway.'

Finch shook his head hopelessly. 'Holly, this is all pointless.'

'Wait,' Lomax said. He glanced hastily at his notes and then looked up shrewdly at Finch. 'I have a number of other points to make. I could develop them by "cross examination"'—he gave the words an ironic inflection—'but I am no attorney. But I assure you I am prepared to specify these charges, if it becomes necessary.' He paused, as if gathering his strength. 'I am prepared to demonstrate, first, that Professor Stoner allowed Mr Walker into his seminar while holding incipiently prejudiced feelings against him; I am prepared to demonstrate that this prejudicial feeling was intensified by the fact that certain conflicts of temperament and feeling came out during the course of this seminar, that the conflict was aided and intensified by Mr Stoner himself, who allowed, and indeed at times encouraged, other members of the class to ridicule and laugh at Mr Walker. I am prepared to demonstrate that on more than one occasion this prejudice was manifested by statements by Professor Stoner, to students and others; that he accused Mr Walker of "attacking" a member of the class, when Mr Walker was merely expressing a contrary opinion, that he admitted anger about this so-called "attack" and that he moreover indulged in loose talk about Mr Walker's "behaving foolishly." I am prepared to demonstrate, too, that without provocation Professor Stoner, out of this prejudice, accused Mr Walker of laziness, of ignorance, and of dishonesty. And, finally, that of all the thirteen members of the class, Mr Walker was the only one—the *only* one—that Professor Stoner singled out for suspicion, asking him *alone* to hand in the text of his seminar report. Now I call upon Professor Stoner to deny these charges, either singly or categorically.'

Stoner shook his head, almost in admiration. 'My God,' he said. 'How you make it sound! Sure, everything you say is a fact, but none of it is true. Not the way you say it.'

Lomax nodded, as if he had expected the answer. 'I am prepared to demonstrate the truth of everything I have said. It would be a simple matter, if necessary, to call the members of that seminar, individually, and question them.'

'No!' Stoner said sharply. 'That is in some ways the most outrageous thing you've said all afternoon. I will not have the students dragged into this mess.'

'You may have no choice, Stoner,' Lomax said softly. 'You may have no choice at all.'

Gordon Finch looked at Lomax and said quietly, 'What are you getting at?'

Lomax ignored him. He said to Stoner, 'Mr Walker has told me that, although he is against doing so in principle, he is now willing to deliver over to you the seminar paper that you cast so many ugly doubts about; he is willing to abide by any decision that you and any other two qualified members of the department may make. If it receives a passing grade from a majority of the three, he will receive a passing grade in the seminar, and he will be allowed to remain in graduate school.'

Stoner shook his head; he was ashamed to look at Lomax. 'You know I can't do that.'

'Very well. I dislike doing this, but—if you do not change your vote of yesterday I shall be compelled to bring formal charges against you.'

Gordon Finch's voice rose. 'You'll be compelled to do *what*?'

Lomax said coolly, 'The constitution of the University of Missouri allows any faculty member with tenure to bring charges against any other faculty member with tenure, if there is compelling reason to believe that the charged faculty member is incompetent, unethical, or not performing his duties in accord with the ethical standards laid out in Article Six, Section Three of the Constitution. These charges, and the evidence to support them, will be heard by the entire faculty, and at the end of the trial the faculty will either uphold the charges by a two-thirds vote or dismiss them with a lesser vote.'

Gordon Finch sat back in his chair, his mouth open; he shook his head unbelievingly. He said, 'Now, look. This thing is getting out of hand. You can't be serious, Holly.'

'I assure you that I am,' Lomax said. 'This is a serious matter. It's a matter of principle; and—and my integrity has been questioned. It is my right to bring charges if I see fit.'

Finch said, 'You could never make them stick.'

'It is my right, nevertheless, to bring charges.'

For a moment Finch gazed at Lomax. Then he said quietly, almost affably, 'There will be no charges. I don't know how this thing is going to resolve itself, and I don't particularly care. But there will be no charges. We're all going to walk out of here in a few minutes, and we're going to try to forget most of what has been said this afternoon. Or at least we're going to pretend to. I'm not going to have the department or the college dragged into a mess. There will be no charges. Because,' he added pleasantly, 'if there are, I promise you that I will do my damnedest to see that you are ruined. I will stop at nothing. I will use every ounce of influence I have; I will lie if necessary; I will frame you if I have to. I am now going to report to Dean Rutherford that the vote on Mr Walker stands. If you still want to carry through on this, you can take it up with him, with the president, or with God. But this office is through with the matter. I want to hear no more about it.'

During Finch's speech, Lomax's expression had gone thoughtful and cool. When Finch finished, Lomax nodded almost casually and got up from his chair. He looked once at Stoner, and then he limped across the room and went out. For several moments Finch and Stoner sat in silence. Finally Finch said, 'I wonder what it is between him and Walker.'

Stoner shook his head. 'It isn't what you're thinking,' he said. 'I don't know what it is. I don't believe I want to know.'

Ten days later Hollis Lomax's appointment as chairman of the Department of English was announced; and two weeks after that the schedule of classes for the following year was distributed among the members of the department. Without surprise Stoner discovered that for each of the two semesters that made up the academic year he had been assigned three classes of freshman composition and one sophomore survey course; his upper-class Readings in Medieval Literature and his graduate seminar had been dropped from the program. It was, Stoner realized, the kind of schedule that a beginning instructor might expect. It was worse in some ways; for the schedule was so arranged that he taught at odd, widely separated hours, six days a week. He made no protest about his schedule and resolved to teach the following year as if nothing were amiss.

But for the first time since he had started teaching it began to seem to him that it was possible that he might leave the University, that he might teach elsewhere. He spoke to Edith of the possibility, and she looked at him as if he had struck her.

'I couldn't,' she said. 'Oh, I couldn't.' And then, aware that she had betrayed herself by showing her fear, she became angry. 'What are you thinking of?' she asked. 'Our home—our lovely home. And our friends. And Grace's school. It isn't good for a child to be shifted around from school to school.'

'It may be necessary,' he said. He had not told her about the incident of Charles Walker and of Lomax's involvement; but it became quickly evident that she knew all about it.

'Thoughtless,' she said. 'Absolutely thoughtless.' But her anger was oddly distracted, almost perfunctory; her pale blue eyes wandered from their regard of him and rested casually upon odd objects in the living room, as if she were reassuring herself of their continued presence; her thin, lightly freckled fingers moved restlessly. 'Oh, I know all about your trouble. I've never interfered with your work, but—really, you're very stubborn. I mean, *Grace* and I are involved in this. And certainly we can't be expected to pick up and move just because you've put yourself in an awkward position.'

'But it's for you and Grace, partly, at least, that I'm thinking about it. It isn't likely that I'll—go much farther in the department if I stay here.'

'Oh,' Edith said distantly, summoning bitterness to her voice. 'That isn't important. We've been poor so far; there's no reason we can't go on like this. You should have thought of this before, of what it might lead to. A cripple.' Suddenly her voice changed, and she laughed indulgently, almost fondly. 'Honestly, things are so important to you. What *difference* could it make?'

And she would not consider leaving Columbia. If it came to that, she said, she and Grace could always move in with Aunt Emma; she was getting very feeble and would welcome the company.

So he dropped the possibility almost as soon as he broached it. He was to teach that summer, and two of his classes were ones in which he had a particular interest; they had been scheduled before Lomax became chairman. He resolved to give them all of his attention, for he knew that it might be some time before he had a chance to teach them again.

11

A few weeks after the fall semester of 1932 began, it was clear to William Stoner that he had been unsuccessful in his battle to keep Charles Walker out of the graduate English program. After the summer holidays Walker returned to the campus as if triumphantly entering an arena; and when he saw Stoner in the corridors of Jesse Hall he inclined his head in an ironic bow and grinned at him maliciously. Stoner learned from Jim Holland that Dean Rutherford had delayed making the vote of last year official and that finally it had been decided that Walker would be allowed to take his oral preliminaries again, his examiners to be selected by the chairman of the department.

The battle was over then, and Stoner was willing to concede his defeat; but the fighting did not end. When Stoner met Lomax in the corridors or at a department meeting, or at a college function, he spoke to him as he had spoken before, as if nothing had happened between them. But Lomax would not respond to his greeting; he stared coldly and turned his eyes away, as if to say that he would not be appeased.

One day in late fall Stoner walked casually into Lomax's office and stood beside his desk for several minutes until, reluctantly, Lomax looked up at him, his lips tight and his eyes hard.

When he realized that Lomax was not going to speak Stoner said awkwardly, 'Look, Holly, it's over and done with. Can't we just drop it?'

Lomax looked at him steadily.

Stoner continued, 'We've had a disagreement, but that isn't unusual. We've been friends before, and I see no reason—'

'We have never been friends,' Lomax said distinctly.

'All right,' Stoner said. 'But we've got along at least. We can keep whatever differences we have, but for God's sake, there's no need to display them. Even the students are beginning to notice.'

'And well the students might,' Lomax said bitterly, 'since one of their own number nearly had his career ruined. A brilliant student, whose only crimes were his imagination, an enthusiasm and integrity that forced him into conflict with you—and, yes, I might as well say it—an unfortunate physical affliction that would have called forth sympathy in a normal human being.' With his good right hand Lomax held a pencil, and it trembled before him; almost with horror Stoner realized that Lomax was dreadfully and irrevocably sincere. 'No,' Lomax went on passionately, 'for that I cannot forgive you.'

Stoner tried to keep his voice from becoming stiff. 'It isn't a question of forgiving. It's simply a question of our behaving toward each other so that not too much discomfort is made for the students and the other members of the department.'

'I'm going to be very frank with you, Stoner,' Lomax said. His anger had quieted, and his voice was calm, matter of fact. 'I don't think you're fit to be a teacher; no man is, whose prejudices override his talents and his learning. I should probably fire you if I had the power; but I don't have the power, as we both know. We are—you are protected by the tenure system. I must accept that. But I don't have to play the hypocrite. I want to have nothing to do with you. Nothing at all. And I will not pretend otherwise.'

Stoner looked at him steadily for several moments. Then he shook his head. 'All right, Holly,' he said tiredly. He started to go.

'Just a minute,' Lomax called.

Stoner turned. Lomax was gazing intently at some papers on his desk; his face was red, and he seemed to be struggling with himself. Stoner realized that what he saw was not anger but shame.

Lomax said, 'Hereafter, if you want to see me—on department business—you will make an appointment with the secretary.' And although Stoner stood looking at him for several moments more, Lomax did not raise his head. A brief writhing went across his face; then it was still. Stoner went out of the room.

And for more than twenty years neither man was to speak again directly to the other.

It was, Stoner realized later, inevitable that the students be affected; even if he had been successful in persuading Lomax to put on an appearance, he could not in the long run have protected them from a consciousness of the battle.

Former students of his, even students he had known rather well, began nodding and speaking to him self-consciously, even furtively. A few were ostentatiously friendly, going out of their way to speak to him or to be seen walking with him in the halls. But he no longer had the rapport with them that he once had had; he was a special figure, and one was seen with him, or not seen with him, for special reasons.

He came to feel that his presence was an embarrassment both to his friends and his enemies, and so he kept more and more to himself.

A kind of lethargy descended upon him. He taught his classes as well as he could, though the steady routine of required freshman and sophomore classes drained him of enthusiasm and left him at the end of the day exhausted and numb. As well as he could, he filled the hours between his widely separated classes with student conferences, painstakingly going over the students' work, keeping them until they became restless and impatient.

Time dragged slowly around him. He tried to spend more of that time at home with his wife and child; but because of his odd schedule the hours he could spend there were unusual and not accounted for by Edith's tight disposition of each day; he discovered (not to his surprise) that his regular presence was so upsetting to his wife that she became nervous and silent and sometimes physically ill. And he was able to see Grace infrequently in all the time he spent at home. Edith had scheduled her daughter's days carefully; her only 'free' time was in the evening, and Stoner was scheduled to teach a late class four evenings a week. By the time the class was over Grace was usually in bed.

So he continued to see Grace only briefly in the mornings, at breakfast; and he was alone with her for only the few minutes it took Edith to clear the breakfast dishes from the table and put them to soak in the kitchen sink. He watched her body lengthen, an awkward grace come into her limbs, and an intelligence grow in her quiet eyes and watchful face. And at times he felt that some closeness remained between them, a closeness which neither of them could afford to admit.

At last he went back to his old habit of spending most

of his time at his office in Jesse Hall. He told himself that he should be grateful for the chance of reading on his own, free from the pressures of preparing for particular classes, free from the predetermined directions of his learning. He tried to read at random, for his own pleasure and indulgence, many of the things that he had been waiting for years to read. But his mind would not be led where he wished it to go; his attention wandered from the pages he held before him, and more and more often he found himself staring dully in front of him, at nothing; it was as if from moment to moment his mind were emptied of all it knew and as if his will were drained of its strength. He felt at times that he was a kind of vegetable, and he longed for something—even pain—to pierce him, to bring him alive.

He had come to that moment in his age when there occurred to him, with increasing intensity, a question of such overwhelming simplicity that he had no means to face it. He found himself wondering if his life were worth the living; if it had ever been. It was a question, he suspected, that came to all men at one time or another; he wondered if it came to them with such impersonal force as it came to him. The question brought with it a sadness, but it was a general sadness which (he thought) had little to do with himself or with his particular fate; he was not even sure that the question sprang from the most immediate and obvious causes, from what his own life had become. It came, he believed, from the accretion of his years, from the density of accident and circumstance, and from what he had come to understand of them. He took a grim and ironic pleasure from the possibility that what little learning he had managed to acquire had led him to this knowledge: that in the long run all things, even the learning that let him know this, were futile and empty, and at last diminished into a noth-ingness they did not alter.

Once, late, after his evening class, he returned to his office and sat at his desk, trying to read. It was winter, and a snow had fallen during the day, so that the out-of-doors was covered with a white softness. The office was overheated; he opened a window beside the desk so that the cool air might come into the close room. He breathed deeply, and let his eyes wander over the white floor of the campus. On an impulse he switched out the light on his desk and sat in the hot darkness of his office; the cold air filled his lungs, and he leaned toward the open window. He heard the silence of the winter night, and it seemed to him that he somehow felt the sounds that were absorbed by the delicate and intricately cellular being of the snow. Nothing moved upon the white-ness; it was a dead scene, which seemed to pull at him, to suck at his consciousness just as it pulled the sound from the air and buried it within a cold white softness. He felt himself pulled outward toward the whiteness, which spread as far as he could see, and which was a part of the darkness from which it glowed, of the clear and cloudless sky without height or depth. For an instant he felt himself go out of the body that sat motionless before the window; and as he felt himself slip away, everything—the flat whiteness, the trees, the tall columns, the night, the far stars—seemed incredibly tiny and far away, as if they were dwindling to a nothingness. Then, behind him, a radiator clanked. He moved, and the scene became itself. With a curiously reluctant relief he again snapped on his desk lamp. He gathered a book and a few papers, went out of the office, walked through the darkened corridors, and let himself out of the wide double doors at the back of Jesse Hall. He walked slowly home, aware of each footstep crunching with muffled loudness in the dry snow.

12

During that year, and especially in the winter months, he found himself returning more and more frequently to such a state of unreality; at will, he seemed able to remove his consciousness from the body that contained it, and he observed himself as if he were an oddly familiar stranger doing the oddly familiar things that he had to do. It was a dissociation that he had never felt before; he knew that he ought to be troubled by it, but he was numb, and he could not convince himself that it mattered. He was forty-two years old, and he could see nothing before him that he wished to enjoy and little behind him that he cared to remember.

In its forty-third year William Stoner's body was nearly as lean as it had been when he was a youth, when he had first walked in dazed awe upon the campus that had never wholly lost its effect upon him. Year by year the stoop of his shoulders had increased, and he had learned to slow his movements so that his farmer's clumsiness of hand and foot seemed a deliberation rather than an awkwardness bred in the bone. His long face had softened with time; and although the flesh was still like tanned leather, it no longer stretched so tautly over the sharp cheekbones; it was loosened by thin lines around his eyes and mouth. Still sharp and clear, his gray eyes were sunk more deeply in his face, the shrewd watchfulness there half hidden; his hair, once light brown, had darkened, although a few touches of gray were beginning around his temples. He did not think often of the years, or regret their passing; but when he saw his face in a mirror, or when he approached his reflection in one of the glass doors that led into Jesse Hall, he recognized the changes that had come over him with a mild shock.

Late one afternoon in the early spring he sat alone in his office. A pile of freshman themes lay on his desk; he held one of the papers in his hand, but he was not looking at it. As he had been doing frequently of late, he gazed out the window upon that part of the campus he could see from his office. The day was bright, and the shadow cast by Jesse Hall had crept, while he watched, nearly up to the base of the five columns that stood in powerful, isolate grace in the center of the rectangular quad. The portion of the quad in shadow was a deep brownish-gray; beyond the edge of the shadow the winter grass was a light tan, overlaid with a shimmering film of the palest green. Against the spidery black tracings of vine stems that curled around them, the marble columns were brilliantly white; soon the shadow would creep upon them, Stoner thought, and the bases would darken, and the darkness would creep up, slowly and then more rapidly, until . . . He became aware that someone was standing behind him.

He turned in his chair and looked up. It was Katherine Driscoll, the young instructor who last year had sat in on his seminar. Since that time, though they sometimes met in the corridors and nodded, they had not really spoken to each other. Stoner was aware that he was dimly annoyed by this confrontation; he did not wish to be reminded of the seminar and of what had ensued from it. He pushed his chair back and got awkwardly to his feet.

'Miss Driscoll,' he said soberly and motioned to the chair beside his desk. She gazed at him for a moment; her eyes were large and dark, and he thought that her face was extraordinarily pale. With a slight ducking motion of the head she moved away from him and took the chair to which he vaguely motioned.

Stoner seated himself again and stared at her for a moment without really seeing her. Then, aware that his regard of her might be taken as rudeness, he tried to smile, and he murmured an inane, automatic question about her classes.

She spoke abruptly. 'You—you said once that you would be willing to look over my dissertation whenever I had a good start on it.'

'Yes,' Stoner said and nodded. 'I believe I did. Of course.' Then, for the first time, he noticed that she clutched a folder of papers in her lap.

'Of course, if you're busy,' she said tentatively.

'Not at all,' Stoner said, trying to put some enthusiasm in his voice. 'I'm sorry. I didn't intend to sound distracted.'

She hesitantly lifted the folder toward him. He took it, hefted it, and smiled at her. 'I thought you would be further along than this,' he said.

'I was,' she said. 'But I started over. I'm taking a new tack, and—and I'll be grateful if you'll tell me what you think.'

He smiled at her again and nodded; he did not know what to say. They sat in awkward silence for a moment.

Finally he said, 'When do you need this back?'

She shook her head. 'Any time. Whenever you can get around to it.'

'I don't want to hold you up,' he said. 'How about this coming Friday? That should give me plenty of time. About three o'clock?'

She rose as abruptly as she had sat down. 'Thank you,'

she said. 'I don't want to be a bother. Thank you.' And she turned and walked, slim and erect, out of his office.

He held the folder in his hands for a few moments, staring at it. Then he put it on his desk and got back to his freshman themes.

That was on a Tuesday, and for the next two days the manuscript lay untouched on his desk. For reasons that he did not fully understand, he could not bring himself to open the folder, to begin the reading which a few months before would have been a duty of pleasure. He watched it warily, as if it were an enemy that was trying to entice him again into a war that he had renounced.

And then it was Friday, and he still had not read it. He saw it lying accusingly on his desk in the morning when he gathered his books and papers for his eight o'clock class; when he returned at a little after nine he nearly decided to leave a note in Miss Driscoll's mailbox in the main office, begging off for another week; but he resolved to look at it hurriedly before his eleven o'clock class and say a few perfunctory words to her when she came by that afternoon. But he could not make himself get to it; and just before he had to leave for the class, his last of the day, he grabbed the folder from his desk, stuck it among his other papers, and hurried across campus to his classroom.

After the class was over at noon he was delayed by several students who needed to talk to him, so that it was after one o'clock when he was able to break away. He headed, with a kind of grim determination, toward the library; he intended to find an empty carrel and give the manuscript a hasty hour's reading before his three o'clock appointment with Miss Driscoll.

But even in the dim, familiar quiet of the library, in an empty carrel that he found hidden in the lower depths of the stacks, he had a hard time making himself look at the pages he carried with him. He opened other books and read paragraphs at random; he sat still, inhaling the musty odor that came from the old books. Finally he sighed; unable to put it off longer, he opened the folder and glanced hastily at the first pages.

At first only a nervous edge of his mind touched what he read; but gradually the words forced themselves upon him. He frowned and read more carefully. And then he was caught; he turned back to where he had begun, and his attention flowed upon the page. Yes, he said to himself, of course. Much of the material that she had given in her seminar report was contained here, but rearranged, reorganized, pointing in directions that he himself had only dimly glimpsed. My God, he said to himself in a kind of wonder; and his fingers trembled with excitement as he turned the pages.

When he came to the last sheet of typescript he leaned back in happy exhaustion and stared at the gray cement wall before him. Although it seemed only a few minutes had elapsed since he started reading, he glanced at his watch. It was nearly four-thirty. He scrambled to his feet, gathered the manuscript hastily, and hurried out of the library; and though he knew it was too late for it to make any difference, he half ran across the campus to Jesse Hall.

As he passed the open door of the main office on his way to his own, he heard his name called. He halted and stuck his head in the doorway. The secretary—a new girl that Lomax had recently hired—said to him accusingly, almost insolently, 'Miss Driscoll was here to see you at three o'clock. She waited nearly an hour.'

He nodded, thanked her, and proceeded more slowly to his office. He told himself that it didn't matter, that he could return the manuscript to her on Monday and make his apologies then. But the excitement he had felt when he finished the manuscript would not subside, and he paced restlessly around his office; every now and then he paused and nodded to himself. Finally he went to his bookcase, searched for a moment, and withdrew a slender pamphlet with smeared black lettering on the cover: *Faculty and Staff Directory, University of Missouri.* He found Katherine Driscoll's name; she did not have a telephone. He noted her address, gathered her manuscript from his desk, and went out of his office.

About three blocks from the campus, toward town, a cluster of large old houses had, some years before, been converted into apartments; these were filled by older students, younger faculty, staff members of the University, and a scattering of townspeople. The house in which Katherine Driscoll lived stood in the midst of these. It was a huge three-storied building of gray stone, with a bewildering variety of entrances and exits, with turrets and bay windows and balconies projecting outward and upward on all sides. Stoner finally found Katherine Driscoll's name on a mailbox at the side of the building, where a short flight of cement steps led down to a basement door. He hesitated for a moment, then knocked.

When Katherine Driscoll opened the door for him William Stoner almost did not recognize her; she had swept her hair up and caught it carelessly high in the back, so that her small pink-white ears were bare; she wore dark-rimmed glasses, behind which her dark eyes were wide and startled; she had on a mannish shirt, open at the neck; and she was wearing dark slacks that made her appear slimmer and more graceful than he remembered her.

'I'm—I'm sorry I missed our appointment,' Stoner said

awkwardly. He thrust the folder toward her. 'I thought you might need this over the weekend.'

For several moments she did not speak. She looked at him expressionlessly and bit her lower lip. She moved back from the door. 'Won't you come in?'

He followed her through a very short, narrow hall into a tiny room, low-ceilinged and dim, with a low three-quarter bed that served as a couch, a long, low table before it, a single upholstered chair, a small desk and chair, and a book-case filled with books on one wall. Several books were lying open on the floor and on the couch, and papers were scattered on the desk.

'It's very small,' Katherine Driscoll said, stooping to pick up one of the books on the floor, 'but I don't need much room.'

He sat in the upholstered chair across from the couch. She asked him if he would like some coffee, and he said he would. She went into the little kitchen off the living room, and he relaxed and gazed around him, listening to the quiet sounds of her moving around in the kitchen.

She brought the coffee, in delicate white china cups, on a black lacquered tray, which she set on the table before the couch. They sipped the coffee and talked strainedly for a few moments. Then Stoner spoke of the part of the manuscript he had read, and the excitement he had felt earlier, in the library, came over him; he leaned forward, speaking intensely.

For many minutes the two of them were able to talk together unselfconsciously, hiding themselves under the cover of their discourse. Katherine Driscoll sat on the edge of the couch, her eyes flashing, her slender fingers clasping and unclasping above the coffee table. William Stoner hitched his chair forward and leaned intently toward her;

they were so close that he could have extended his hand and touched her.

They spoke of the problems raised by the early chapters of her work, of where the inquiry might lead, of the importance of the subject.

'You mustn't give it up,' he said, and his voice took on an urgency that he could not understand. 'No matter how hard it will seem sometimes, you mustn't give it up. It's too good for you to give it up. Oh, it's good, there's no doubt of it.'

She was silent, and for a moment the animation left her face. She leaned back, looked away from him, and said, as if absently, 'The seminar—some of the things you said—it was very helpful.'

He smiled and shook his head. 'You didn't need the seminar. But I am glad you were able to sit in on it. It was a good one, I think.'

'Oh, it's shameful!' she burst out. 'It's shameful. The seminar—you were—I *had* to start it over, after the seminar. It's shameful that they should—' She paused in bitter, furious confusion, got up from the couch, and walked restlessly to the desk.

Stoner, taken aback by her outburst, for a moment did not speak. Then he said, 'You shouldn't concern yourself. These things happen. It will all work out in time. It really isn't important.'

And suddenly, after he said the words, it was not important. For an instant he felt the truth of what he said, and for the first time in months he felt lift away from him the weight of a despair whose heaviness he had not fully realized. Nearly giddy, almost laughing, he said again, 'It *really* isn't important.'

But an awkwardness had come between them, and they

could not speak as freely as they had a few moments before. Soon Stoner got up, thanked her for the coffee, and took his leave. She walked with him to the door and seemed almost curt when she told him good night.

It was dark outside, and a spring chill was in the evening air. He breathed deeply and felt his body tingle in the coolness. Beyond the jagged outline of the apartment houses the town lights glowed upon a thin mist that hung in the air. At the corner a street light pushed feebly against the darkness that closed around it; from the darkness beyond it the sound of laughter broke abruptly into the silence, lingered and died. The smell of smoke from trash burning in back yards was held by the mist; and as he walked slowly through the evening, breathing the fragrance and tasting upon his tongue the sharp night-time air, it seemed to him that the moment he walked in was enough and that he might not need a great deal more.

And so he had his love affair.

The knowledge of his feeling for Katherine Driscoll came upon him slowly. He found himself discovering pretexts for going to her apartment in the afternoons; the title of a book or article would occur to him, he would note it, and deliberately avoid seeing her in the corridors of Jesse Hall so that he might drop by her place in the afternoon to give her the title, have a cup of coffee, and talk. Once he spent half a day in the library pursuing a reference that might reinforce a point that he thought dubious in her second chapter; another time he laboriously transcribed a portion of a little-known Latin manuscript of which the library owned a photostat, and was thus able to spend several afternoons helping her with the translation.

During the afternoons they spent together Katherine

Driscoll was courteous, friendly, and reserved; she was quietly grateful for the time and interest he expended upon her work, and she hoped she was not keeping him from more important things. It did not occur to him that she might think of him other than as an interested professor whom she admired and whose aid, though friendly, was little beyond the call of his duty. He thought of himself as a faintly ludicrous figure, one in whom no one could take an interest other than impersonal; and after he admitted to himself his feeling for Katherine Driscoll, he was desperately careful that he not show this feeling in any way that could be easily discerned.

For more than a month he dropped by her apartment two or three times a week, staying no more than two hours at any one time; he was fearful that she would become annoyed at his continued reappearances, so he was careful to come only when he was sure that he could be genuinely helpful to her work. With a kind of grim amusement he realized that he was preparing for his visits to her with the same diligence that he prepared for lectures; and he told himself that this would be enough, that he would be contented only to see her and talk to her for as long as she might endure his presence.

But despite his care and effort the afternoons they spent together became more and more strained. For long moments they found themselves with nothing to say; they sipped their coffee and looked away from each other, they said, 'Well . . . ,' in tentative and guarded voices, and they found reasons for moving restlessly around the room, away from each other. With a sadness the intensity of which he had not expected, Stoner told himself that his visits were becoming a burden to her and that her courtesy forbade her to let him be aware of that. As he had known he would have to do, he came to his decision; he would withdraw from her, gradually, so that she would not realize he had noticed her restlessness, as if he had given her all the help that he could.

He dropped by her apartment only once the next week, and the following week he did not visit her at all. He had not anticipated the struggle that he would have with himself; in the afternoons, as he sat in his office, he had almost physically to restrain himself from rising from his desk, hurrying outside, and walking to her apartment. Once or twice he saw her at a distance, in the halls, as she was hurrying to or from class; he turned away and walked in another direction, so that they would not have to meet.

After a while a kind of numbness came upon him, and he told himself that it would be all right, that in a few days he would be able to see her in the halls, nod to her and smile, perhaps even detain her for a moment and ask her how her work was going.

Then, one afternoon in the main office, as he was removing some mail from his box, he overheard a young instructor mention to another that Katherine Driscoll was ill, that she hadn't met her classes for the past two days. And the numbness left him; he felt a sharp pain in his chest, and his resolve and the strength of his will went out of him. He walked jerkily to his own office and looked with a kind of desperation at his bookcase, selected a book, and went out. By the time he got to Katherine Driscoll's apartment he was out of breath, so that he had to wait several moments in front of her door. He put a smile on his face that he hoped was casual, fixed it there, and knocked at her door.

She was even paler than usual, and there were dark smudges around her eyes; she wore a plain dark blue dressing gown, and her hair was drawn back severely from her face.

Stoner was aware that he spoke nervously and foolishly,

yet he was unable to stop the flow of his words. 'Hello,' he said brightly, 'I heard you were ill, I thought I would drop over to see how you were, I have a book that might be helpful to you, are you all right? I don't want to—' He listened to the sounds tumble from his stiff smile and could not keep his eyes from searching her face.

When at last he was silent she moved back from the door and said quietly, 'Come in.'

Once inside the little sitting-bedroom, his nervous inanity dropped away. He sat in the chair opposite the bed and felt the beginnings of a familiar ease come over him when Katherine Driscoll sat across from him. For several moments neither of them spoke.

Finally she asked, 'Do you want some coffee?'

'You mustn't bother,' Stoner said.

'It's no bother.' Her voice was brusque and had that under-tone of anger that he had heard before. 'I'll just heat it up.'

She went into the kitchen. Stoner, alone in the little room, stared glumly at the coffee table and told himself that he should not have come. He wondered at the foolishness that drove men to do the things they did.

Katherine Driscoll came back with the coffee pot and two cups; she poured their coffee, and they sat watching the steam rise from the black liquid. She took a cigarette from a crumpled package, lit it, and puffed nervously for a moment. Stoner became aware of the book he had carried with him and that he still clutched in his hands. He put it on the coffee table between them.

'Perhaps you aren't feeling up to it,' he said, 'but I ran across something that might be helpful to you, and I thought—'

'I haven't seen you in nearly two weeks,' she said and stubbed her cigarette out, twisting it fiercely in the ashtray.

He was taken aback; he said distractedly, 'I've been rather busy—so many things—'

'It doesn't matter,' she said. 'Really, it doesn't. I shouldn't have . . .' She rubbed the palm of her hand across her forehead.

He looked at her with concern; he thought she must be feverish. 'I'm sorry you're ill. If there's anything I can—'

'I am not ill,' she said. And she added in a voice that was calm, speculative, and almost uninterested, 'I am desperately, desperately unhappy.'

And still he did not understand. The bare sharp utterance went into him like a blade; he turned a little away from her; he said confusedly, 'I'm sorry. Could you tell me about it? If there's anything I can do . . .'

She lifted her head. Her features were stiff, but her eyes were brilliant in pools of tears. 'I didn't intend to embarrass you. I'm sorry. You must think me very foolish.'

'No,' he said. He looked at her for a moment more, at the pale face that seemed held expressionless by an effort of will. Then he gazed at his large bony hands that were clasped together on one knee; the fingers were blunt and heavy, and the knuckles were like white knobs upon the brown flesh.

He said at last, heavily and slowly, 'In many ways I am an ignorant man; it is I who am foolish, not you. I have not come to see you because I thought—I felt that I was becoming a nuisance. Maybe that was not true.'

'No,' she said. 'No, it wasn't true.'

Still not looking at her, he continued, 'And I didn't want to cause you the discomfort of having to deal with—with my feelings for you, which, I knew, sooner or later, would become obvious if I kept seeing you.'

She did not move; two tears welled over her lashes and ran down her cheeks; she did not brush them away.

'I was perhaps selfish. I felt that nothing could come of this except awkwardness for you and unhappiness for me. You know my—circumstances. It seemed to me impossible that you could—that you could feel for me anything but—'

'Shut up,' she said softly, fiercely. 'Oh, my dear, shut up and come over here.'

He found himself trembling; as awkwardly as a boy he went around the coffee table and sat beside her. Tentatively, clumsily, their hands went out to each other; they clasped each other in an awkward, strained embrace; and for a long time they sat together without moving, as if any movement might let escape from them the strange and terrible thing that they held between them in a single grasp.

Her eyes, that he had thought to be a dark brown or black, were a deep violet. Sometimes they caught the dim light of a lamp in the room and glittered moistly; he could turn his head one way and another, and the eyes beneath his gaze would change color as he moved, so that it seemed, even in repose, they were never still. Her flesh, that had at a distance seemed so cool and pale, had beneath it a warm ruddy undertone like light flowing beneath a milky trans-lucence. And like the translucent flesh, the calm and poise and reserve which he had thought were herself, masked a warmth and playfulness and humor whose intensity was made possible by the appearance that disguised them.

In his forty-third year William Stoner learned what others, much younger, had learned before him: that the person one loves at first is not the person one loves at last, and that love is not an end but a process through which one person attempts to know another.

They were both very shy, and they knew each other slowly, tentatively; they came close and drew apart, they touched and withdrew, neither wishing to impose upon the other more than might be welcomed. Day by day the layers of reserve that protected them dropped away, so that at last they were like many who are extraordinarily shy, each open to the other, unprotected, perfectly and unselfconsciously at ease.

Nearly every afternoon, when his classes were over, he came to her apartment. They made love, and talked, and made love again, like children who did not think of tiring at their play. The spring days lengthened, and they looked forward to the summer.

13

In his extreme youth Stoner had thought of love as an absolute state of being to which, if one were lucky, one might find access; in his maturity he had decided it was the heaven of a false religion, toward which one ought to gaze with an amused disbelief, a gently familiar contempt, and an embarrassed nostalgia. Now in his middle age he began to know that it was neither a state of grace nor an illusion; he saw it as a human act of becoming, a condition that was invented and modified moment by moment and day by day, by the will and the intelligence and the heart.

The hours that he once had spent in his office gazing out of the window upon a landscape that shimmered and emptied before his blank regard, he now spent with Katherine. Every morning, early, he went to his office and sat restlessly for ten or fifteen minutes; then, unable to achieve repose, he wandered out of Jesse Hall and across campus to the library, where he browsed in the stacks for ten or fifteen minutes more. And at last, as if it were a game he played with himself, he delivered himself from his self-imposed suspense, slipped out a side door of the library, and made his way to the house where Katherine lived.

She often worked late into the night, and some mornings when he came to her apartment he found her just awakened, warm and sensual with sleep, naked beneath the dark blue robe she had thrown on to come to the door. On such mornings they often made love almost before they spoke, going to the narrow bed that was still rumpled and hot from Katherine's sleeping.

Her body was long and delicate and softly fierce; and when he touched it his awkward hand seemed to come alive above that flesh. Sometimes he looked at her body as if it were a sturdy treasure put in his keeping; he let his blunt fingers play upon the moist, faintly pink skin of thigh and belly and marveled at the intricately simple delicacy of her small firm breasts. It occurred to him that he had never before known the body of another; and it occurred to him further that that was the reason he had always somehow separated the self of another from the body that carried that self around. And it occurred to him at last, with the finality of knowledge, that he had never known another human being with any intimacy or trust or with the human warmth of commitment.

Like all lovers, they spoke much of themselves, as if they might thereby understand the world which made them possible.

'My God, how I used to lust after you,' Katherine said once. 'I used to see you standing there in front of the class, so big and lovely and awkward, and I used to lust after you something fierce. You never knew, did you?'

'No,' William said. 'I thought you were a very proper young lady.'

She laughed delightedly. 'Proper, indeed!' She sobered a little and smiled reminiscently. 'I suppose I thought I was too. Oh, how proper we seem to ourselves when we have no reason to be improper! It takes being in love to know something about yourself. Sometimes, with you, I feel like the slut of the world, the eager, faithful slut of the world. Does that seem proper to you?'

'No,' William said, smiling, and reached out for her. 'Come here.'

She had had one lover, William learned; it had been during her senior year in college, and it had ended badly, with tears and recriminations and betrayals.

'Most affairs end badly,' she said, and for a moment both were somber.

William was shocked to discover his surprise when he learned that she had had a lover before him; he realized that he had started to think of themselves as never really having existed before they came together.

'He was such a shy boy,' she said. 'Like you, I suppose, in some ways; only he was bitter and afraid, and I could never learn what about. He used to wait for me at the end of the dorm walk, under a big tree, because he was too shy to come up where there were so many people. We used to walk miles, out in the country, where there wasn't a chance of our seeing anybody. But we were never really—together. Even when we made love.'

Stoner could almost see this shadowy figure who had no face and no name; his shock turned to sadness, and he felt a generous pity for an unknown boy who, out of an obscure lost bitterness, had thrust away from him what Stoner now possessed.

Sometimes, in the sleepy laziness that followed their love-making, he lay in what seemed to him a slow and gentle flux of sensation and unhurried thought; and in that flux he hardly knew whether he spoke aloud or whether he merely recognized the words that sensation and thought finally came to.

He dreamed of perfections, of worlds in which they could always be together, and half believed in the possibility of what he dreamed. 'What,' he said, 'would it be like if,' and went on to construct a possibility hardly more attractive than the one in which they existed. It was an unspoken knowledge they both had, that the possibilities they imagined and elaborated were gestures of love and a celebration of the life they had together now.

The life they had together was one that neither of them had really imagined. They grew from passion to lust to a deep sensuality that renewed itself from moment to moment.

'Lust and learning,' Katherine once said. 'That's really all there is, isn't it?'

And it seemed to Stoner that that was exactly true, that that was one of the things he had learned.

For their life together that summer was not all love-making and talk. They learned to be together without speaking, and they got the habit of repose; Stoner brought books to Katherine's apartment and left them, until finally they had to install an extra bookcase for them. In the days they spent together Stoner found himself returning to the studies he had all but abandoned; and Katherine continued to work on the book that was to be her dissertation. For hours at a time she would sit at the tiny desk against the wall, her head bent down in intense concentration over books and papers, her slender pale neck curving and flowing out of the dark blue robe she habitually wore; Stoner sprawled in the chair or lay on the bed in like concentration.

Sometimes they would lift their eyes from their studies, smile at each other, and return to their reading; sometimes Stoner would look up from his book and let his gaze rest upon the graceful curve of Katherine's back and upon the slender neck where a tendril of hair always fell. Then a slow, easy desire would come over him like a calm, and he would rise and stand behind her and let his arms rest lightly on her shoulders. She would straighten and let her head go back against his chest, and his hands would go forward into the loose robe and gently touch her breasts. Then they would make love, and lie quietly for a while, and return to their studies, as if their love and learning were one process.

That was one of the oddities of what they called 'given opinion' that they learned that summer. They had been brought up in a tradition that told them in one way or another that the life of the mind and the life of the senses were separate and, indeed, inimical; they had believed, without ever having really thought about it, that one had to be chosen at some expense of the other. That the one could intensify the other had never occurred to them; and since the embodiment came before the recognition of the truth, it seemed a discovery that belonged to them alone. They began to collect these oddities of 'given opinion,' and they hoarded them as if they were treasures; it helped to isolate them from the world that would give them these opinions, and it helped draw them together in a small but moving way.

But there was another oddity of which Stoner became aware and of which he did not speak to Katherine. That was one that had to do with his relationship with his wife and daughter.

It was a relationship that, according to 'given opinion,' ought to have worsened steadily as what given opinion would describe as his 'affair' went on. But it did no such thing. On the contrary, it seemed steadily to improve. His lengthening absences away from what he still had to call his 'home' seemed to bring him closer to both Edith and Grace than he had been in years. He began to have for Edith a curious friendliness that was close to affection, and they even talked together, now and then, of nothing in particular. During that summer she even cleaned the glassed-in sun porch, had repaired the damage done by the weather, and put a day bed there, so that he no longer had to sleep on the living-room couch.

And sometimes on weekends she made calls upon neighbors and left Grace alone with her father. Occasionally Edith was away long enough for him to take walks in the country with his daughter. Away from the house Grace's hard, watchful reserve dropped away, and at times she smiled with a quietness and charm that Stoner had almost forgotten. She had grown rapidly in the last year and was very thin.

Only by an effort of the will could he remind himself that he was deceiving Edith. The two parts of his life were as separate as the two parts of a life can be; and though he knew that his powers of introspection were weak and that he was capable of self-deception, he could not make himself believe that he was doing harm to anyone for whom he felt responsibility.

He had no talent for dissimulation, nor did it occur to him to dissemble his affair with Katherine Driscoll; neither did it occur to him to display it for anyone to see. It did not seem possible to him that anyone on the outside might be aware of their affair, or even be interested in it.

It was, therefore, a deep yet impersonal shock when he discovered, at the end of the summer, that Edith knew something of the affair and that she had known of it almost from the beginning.

She spoke of it casually one morning while he lingered over his breakfast coffee, chatting with Grace. Edith spoke a little sharply, told Grace to stop dawdling over her breakfast, that she had an hour of piano practice before she could waste any time. William watched the thin, erect figure of his daughter walk out of the dining room and waited absently until he heard the first resonant tones coming from the old piano.

'Well,' Edith said with some of the sharpness still in her voice, 'you're a little late this morning, aren't you?'

William turned to her questioningly; the absent expression remained on his face.

Edith said, 'Won't your little co-ed be angry if you keep her waiting?'

He felt a numbness come to his lips. 'What?' he asked. 'What's that?'

'Oh, Willy,' Edith said and laughed indulgently. 'Did you think I didn't know about your—little flirtation? Why, I've known it all along. What's her name? I heard it, but I've forgotten what it is.'

In its shock and confusion his mind grasped but one word; and when he spoke his voice sounded to him petulantly annoyed. 'You don't understand,' he said. 'There's no—flirtation, as you call it. It's—'

'Oh, Willy,' she said and laughed again. 'You look so flustered. Oh, I know all about these things. A man your age and all. It's natural, I suppose. At least they say it is.'

For a moment he was silent. Then reluctantly he said, 'Edith, if you want to talk about this—'

'No!' she said; there was an edge of fear in her voice. 'There's nothing to talk about. Nothing at all.'

And they did not then or thereafter talk about it. Most of the time Edith maintained the convention that it was his work that kept him away from home; but occasionally, and almost absently, she spoke the knowledge that was always somewhere within her. Sometimes she spoke playfully, with something like a teasing affection; sometimes she spoke with no feeling at all, as if it were the most casual topic of conversation she could imagine; sometimes she spoke petulantly, as if some triviality had annoyed her.

She said, 'Oh, I know. Once a man gets in his forties.

But really, Willy, you're old enough to be her father, aren't you?'

It had not occurred to him how he must appear to an outsider, to the world. For a moment he saw himself as he must thus appear; and what Edith said was part of what he saw. He had a glimpse of a figure that flitted through smoking-room anecdotes, and through the pages of cheap fiction—a pitiable fellow going into his middle age, misunderstood by his wife, seeking to renew his youth, taking up with a girl years younger than himself, awkwardly and apishly reaching for the youth he could not have, a fatuous, garishly got-up clown at whom the world laughed out of discomfort, pity, and contempt. He looked at this figure as closely as he could; but the longer he looked, the less familiar it became. It was not himself that he saw, and he knew suddenly that it was no one.

But he knew that the world was creeping up on him, up on Katherine, and up on the little niche of it that they had thought was their own; and he watched the approach with a sadness of which he could not speak, even to Katherine.

The fall semester began that September in an intensely colorful Indian summer that came after an early frost. Stoner returned to his classes with an eagerness that he had not felt for a long time; even the prospect of facing a hundred freshman faces did not dim the renewal of his energy.

His life with Katherine continued much as it had been before, except that with the return of the students and many of the faculty he began to find it necessary to practice circumspection. During the summer the old house where Katherine lived had been almost deserted; they had been able thus to be together in almost complete isolation, with no fear that they might be noticed. Now William had to exercise caution when he came to her place in the afternoon; he found himself looking up and down the street before he approached the house, and going furtively down the stairs to the little well that opened into her apartment.

They thought of gestures and talked of rebellion; they told each other that they were tempted to do something outrageous, to make a display. But they did not, and they had no real desire to do so. They wanted only to be left alone, to be themselves; and, wanting this, they knew they would not be left alone and they suspected that they could not be themselves. They imagined themselves to be discreet, and it hardly occurred to them that their affair would be suspected. They made a point of not encountering each other at the University, and when they could not avoid meeting publicly, they greeted each other with a formality whose irony they did not believe to be evident.

But the affair was known, and known very quickly after the fall semester began. It was likely that the discovery came out of the peculiar clairvoyance that people have about such matters; for neither of them had given an outward sign of their private lives. Or perhaps someone had made an idle speculation that had a ring of truth to someone else, which caused a closer regard of them both, which in turn . . . Their speculations were, they knew, to no end; but they continued to make them.

There were signs by which both knew that they were discovered. Once, walking behind two male graduate students, Stoner heard one say, half in admiration and half in contempt, 'Old Stoner. By God, who would have believed it?'—and saw them shake their heads in mockery and puzzlement over the human condition. Acquaintances of Katherine made oblique references to Stoner and offered her confidences about their own love-lives that she had not invited.

What surprised them both was that it did not seem to matter. No one refused to speak to them; no one gave them black looks; they were not made to suffer by the world they had feared. They began to believe that they could live in the place they had thought to be inimical to their love, and live there with some dignity and ease.

Over the Christmas holiday Edith decided to take Grace for a visit with her mother in St Louis; and for the only time during their life together William and Katherine were able to be with each other for an extended period.

Separately and casually, both let it be known that they would be away from the University during the Christmas holiday; Katherine was to visit relatives in the East, and William was to work at the bibliographical center and museum in Kansas City. At different hours they took separate buses, and met at Lake Ozark, a resort village in the outlying mountains of the great Ozark range.

They were the only guests of the only lodge in the village that remained open the year around; and they had ten days together.

There had been a heavy snow three days before their arrival, and during their stay it snowed again, so that the gently rolling hills remained white all the time they were there.

They had a cabin with a bedroom, a sitting room, and a small kitchen; it was somewhat removed from the other cabins, and it overlooked a lake that remained frozen during the winter months. In the morning they awoke to find themselves twined together, their bodies warm and luxuriant beneath the heavy blankets. They poked their heads out of the blankets and watched their breath condense in great clouds in the cold air; they laughed like children and pulled the covers back over their heads and pressed themselves more closely together. Sometimes they made love and stayed in bed all morning and talked, until the sun came through an east window; sometimes Stoner sprang out of bed as soon as they were awake and pulled the covers from Katherine's naked body and laughed at her screams as he kindled a fire in the great fireplace. Then they huddled together before the fireplace, with only a blanket around them, and waited to be warmed by the growing fire and the natural warmth of their own bodies.

Despite the cold, they walked nearly every day in the woods. The great pines, greenish-black against the snow, reared up massively toward the pale-blue cloudless sky; the occasional slither and plop of a mass of snow from one of the branches intensified the silence around them, as the occasional chatter of a lone bird intensified the isolation in which they walked. Once they saw a deer that had come down from the higher mountains in search of food. It was a doe, brilliantly yellow-tan against the starkness of dark pine and white snow. Now fifty yards away it faced them, one forepaw lifted delicately above the snow, the small ears pitched forward, the brown eyes perfectly round and incredibly soft. No one moved. The doe's delicate face tilted, as if regarding them with polite inquiry; then, unhurriedly, it turned and walked away from them, lifting its feet daintily out of the snow and placing them precisely, with a tiny sound of crunching.

In the afternoon they went to the main office of the lodge, which also served as the village's general store and restaurant. They had coffee there and talked to whoever had dropped in and perhaps picked up a few things for their evening meal, which they always took in their cabin.

In the evening they sometimes lighted the oil lamp and read; but more often they sat on folded blankets in front of the fireplace and talked and were silent and watched the flames play intricately upon the logs and watched the play of firelight upon each other's faces.

One evening, near the end of the time they had together, Katherine said quietly, almost absently, 'Bill, if we never have anything else, we will have had this week. Does that sound like a girlish thing to say?'

'It doesn't matter what it sounds like,' Stoner said. He nodded. 'It's true.'

'Then I'll say it,' Katherine said. 'We will have had this week.'

On their last morning Katherine straightened the furniture and cleaned the place with slow care. She took off the wedding band she had worn and wedged it in a crevice between the wall and the fireplace. She smiled self-consciously. 'I wanted,' she said, 'to leave something of our own here; something I knew would stay here, as long as this place stays. Maybe it's silly.'

Stoner could not answer her. He took her arm and they walked out of the cabin and trudged through the snow to the lodge office, where the bus would pick them up and take them back to Columbia.

On an afternoon late in February, a few days after the second semester had begun, Stoner received a call from Gordon Finch's secretary; she told him that the dean would like to talk with him and asked if he would drop by that afternoon or the next morning. Stoner told her that he would—and sat for several minutes with one hand on the phone after having hung up. Then he sighed and nodded to himself and went downstairs to Finch's office.

Gordon Finch was in his shirt sleeves, his tie was loosened, and he was leaning back in his swivel chair with his hands clasped behind his head. When Stoner came into the room he nodded genially and waved toward the leather-covered easy chair set at an angle beside his desk.

'Take a load off, Bill. How have you been?'

Stoner nodded. 'All right.'

'Classes keeping you busy?'

Stoner said dryly, 'Reasonably so. I have a full schedule.'

'I know,' Finch said and shook his head. 'I can't interfere there, you know. But it's a damned shame.'

'It's all right,' Stoner said a bit impatiently.

'Well.' Finch straightened in his chair and clasped his hands on the desk in front of him. 'There's nothing official about this visit, Bill. I just wanted to chat with you for a while.'

There was a long silence. Stoner said gently, 'What is it, Gordon?'

Finch sighed, and then said abruptly, 'Okay. I'm talking to you right now as a friend. There's been talk. It isn't anything that, as a dean, I have to pay any attention to yet, but—well, sometime I might have to pay attention to it, and I thought I ought to speak to you—as a friend, mind you—before anything serious develops.'

Stoner nodded. 'What kind of talk?'

'Oh, hell, Bill. You and the Driscoll girl. You know.'

'Yes,' Stoner said. 'I know. I just wanted to know how far it has gone.'

'Not far yet. Innuendos, remarks, things like that.'

'I see,' Stoner said. 'I don't know what I can do about it.'

Finch creased a sheet of paper carefully. 'Is it serious, Bill?'

Stoner nodded and looked out the window. 'It's serious, I'm afraid.'

'What are you going to do?'

'I don't know.'

With sudden violence Finch crumpled the paper that he had so carefully folded and threw it at a wastebasket. He said, 'In theory, your life is your own to lead. In theory, you ought to be able to screw anybody you want to, do anything you want to, and it shouldn't matter so long as it doesn't interfere with your teaching. But damn it, your life *isn't* your own to lead. It's—oh, hell. You know what I mean.'

Stoner smiled. 'I'm afraid I do.'

'It's a bad business. What about Edith?'

'Apparently,' Stoner said, 'she takes the whole thing a good deal less seriously than anyone else. And it's a funny thing, Gordon; I don't believe we've ever got along any better than we have the last year.'

Finch laughed shortly. 'You never can tell, can you? But what I meant was, will there be a divorce? Anything like that?'

'I don't know. Possibly. But Edith would fight it. It would be a mess.'

'What about Grace?'

A sudden pain caught at Stoner's throat, and he knew that his expression showed what he felt. 'That's—something else. I don't know, Gordon.'

Finch said impersonally, as if they were discussing someone else, 'You might survive a divorce—if it weren't too messy. It would be rough, but you'd probably survive it. And if this—thing with the Driscoll girl weren't serious, if you were just screwing around, well, that could be handled too. But you're sticking your neck out, Bill; you're asking for it.'

'I suppose I am,' Stoner said.

There was a pause. 'This is a hell of a job I have,' Finch said heavily. 'Sometimes I think I'm not the man for it at all.'

Stoner smiled. 'Dave Masters once said you weren't a big enough son-of-a-bitch to be really successful.'

'Maybe he was right,' Finch said. 'But I feel like one often enough.'

'Don't worry about it, Gordon,' Stoner said. 'I understand your position. And if I could make it easier for you I—' He paused and shook his head sharply. 'But I can't do anything right now. It will have to wait. Somehow . . .'

Finch nodded and did not look at Stoner; he stared at his desk top as if it were a doom that approached him with slow inevitability. Stoner waited for a few moments, and when Finch did not speak he got up quietly and went out of the office.

Because of his conversation with Gordon Finch, Stoner was late that afternoon getting to Katherine's apartment. Without bothering to look up or down the street he went down the walk and let himself in. Katherine was waiting for him; she had not changed clothes, and she waited almost formally, sitting erect and alert upon the couch.

'You're late,' she said flatly.

'Sorry,' he said. 'I got held up.'

Katherine lit a cigarette; her hand was trembling slightly. She surveyed the match for a moment, and blew it out with a puff of smoke. She said, 'One of my fellow instructors made rather a point of telling me that Dean Finch called you in this afternoon.'

'Yes,' Stoner said. 'That's what held me up.'

'Was it about us?'

Stoner nodded. 'He had heard a few things.'

'I imagined that was it,' Katherine said. 'My instructor friend seemed to know something that she didn't want to tell. Oh, Christ, Bill!'

'It's not like that at all,' Stoner said. 'Gordon is an old friend. I actually believe he wants to protect us. I believe he will if he can.'

Katherine did not speak for several moments. She kicked off her shoes and lay back on the couch, staring at the ceiling. She said calmly, 'Now it begins. I suppose it was too much, hoping that they would leave us alone. I suppose we never really seriously thought they would.'

'If it gets too bad,' Stoner said, 'we can go away. We can do something.'

'Oh, Bill!' Katherine was laughing a little, throatily and softly. She sat up on the couch. 'You are the dearest love, the dearest, dearest anyone could imagine. And I will not let them bother us. I will not!'

And for the next several weeks they lived much as they had before. With a strategy that they would not have been able to manage a year earlier, with a strength they would not have known they had, they practiced evasions and withdrawals, deploying their powers like skillful generals who must survive with meager forces. They became genuinely circumspect and cautious, and got a grim pleasure from their maneuverings. Stoner came to her apartment only after dark, when no one could see him enter; in the daytime, between classes, Katherine allowed herself to be seen at coffee shops with younger male instructors; and the hours they spent together were intensified by their common determination. They told themselves and each other that they were closer than they ever had been; and to their surprise, they realized that it was true, that the words they spoke to comfort themselves were more than consolatory. They made a closeness possible and a commitment inevitable.

It was a world of half-light in which they lived and to which they brought the better parts of themselves—so that, after a while, the outer world where people walked and spoke, where there was change and continual movement, seemed to them false and unreal. Their lives were sharply divided between the two worlds, and it seemed to them natural that they should live so divided.

During the late winter and early spring months they found together a quietness they had not had before. As the outer world closed upon them they became less aware of its presence; and their happiness was such that they had no need to speak of it to each other, or even to think of it. In Katherine's small, dim apartment, hidden like a cave beneath the massive old house, they seemed to themselves to move outside of time, in a timeless universe of their own discovery.

Then, one day in late April, Gordon Finch again called Stoner into his office; and Stoner went down with a numbness that came from a knowledge he would not admit.

What had happened was classically simple, something that Stoner should have foreseen yet had not.

'It's Lomax,' Finch said. 'Somehow the son-of-a-bitch has got hold of it and he's not about to let go.'

Stoner nodded. 'I should have thought of that. I should have expected it. Do you think it would do any good if I talked to him?'

Finch shook his head, walked across his office, and stood before the window. Early afternoon sunlight streamed upon his face, which gleamed with sweat. He said tiredly, 'You don't understand, Bill. Lomax isn't playing it that way. Your name hasn't even come up. He's working through the Driscoll girl.'

'He's what?' Stoner asked blankly.

'You almost have to admire him,' Finch said. 'Somehow he knew damn well I knew all about it. So he came in yesterday, off-hand, you know, and told me he was going to have to fire the Driscoll girl and warned me there might be a stink.'

'No,' Stoner said. His hands ached where they gripped the leather arms of the easy chair.

Finch continued, 'According to Lomax, there have been complaints, from students mostly, and a few townspeople. It seems that men have been seen going in and out of her apartment at all hours—flagrant misbehavior—that sort of thing. Oh, he did it beautifully; he has no personal objection—he rather admires the girl, as a matter of fact—but he has the reputation of the department and the University to think of. We commiserated upon the necessities of bowing to the dictates of middle-class morality, agreed that the community of scholars ought to be a haven for the rebel against the Protestant ethic, and concluded that practically speaking we were helpless. He said he hoped he could let it ride until the end of the semester but doubted if he could. And all the time the son-of-a-bitch knew we understood each other perfectly.'

A tightness in his throat made it impossible for Stoner to speak. He swallowed twice and tested his voice; it was steady and flat. 'What he wants is perfectly clear, of course.'

'I'm afraid it is,' Finch said.

'I knew he hated me,' Stoner said distantly. 'But I never realized—I never dreamed he would—'

'Neither did I,' Finch said. He walked back to his desk and sat down heavily. 'And I can't do a thing, Bill. I'm helpless. If Lomax wants complainers, they'll appear; if he wants witnesses, they will appear. He has quite a following, you know. And if word ever gets to the president—' He shook his head.

'What do you imagine will happen if I refuse to resign? If we just refuse to be scared?'

'He'll crucify the girl,' Finch said flatly. 'And as if by accident you'll be dragged into it. It's very neat.'

'Then,' Stoner said, 'it appears there is nothing to be done.'

'Bill,' Finch said, and then was silent. He rested his head on his closed fists. He said dully, 'There is a chance. There is just one. I think I can hold him off if you—if the Driscoll girl will just—'

'No,' Stoner said. 'I don't think I can do it. Literally, I don't think I can do it.'

'God damn it!' Finch's voice was anguished. 'He's counting on that! Think for a minute. What would you do? It's April; almost May; what kind of job could you get this time of year—if you could get one at all?'

'I don't know,' Stoner said. 'Something . . .'

'And what about Edith? Do you think she's going to give in, give you a divorce without a fight? And Grace? What would it do to her, in this town, if you just took off? And Katherine? What kind of life would you have? What would it do to both of you?'

Stoner did not speak. An emptiness was beginning some-where within him; he felt a withering, a falling away. He said at last, 'Can you give me a week?—I've got to think. A week?'

Finch nodded. 'I can hold him off that long at least. But not much longer. I'm sorry, Bill. You know that.'

'Yes.' He got up from the chair and stood for a moment, testing the heavy numbness of his legs. 'I'll let you know. I'll let you know when I can.'

He went out of the office into the darkness of the long corridor and walked heavily into the sunlight, into the open world that was like a prison wherever he turned.

Years afterward, at odd moments, he would look back upon those days that followed his conversation with Gordon Finch and would be unable to recall them with any clarity at all. It was as if he were a dead man animated by nothing more than a habit of stubborn will. Yet he was oddly aware of himself and of the places, persons, and events which moved past him in these few days; and he knew that he presented to the public regard an appearance which belied his condition. He taught his classes, he greeted his colleagues, he attended the meetings he had to attend—and not one of the people he met from day to day knew that anything was wrong.

But from the moment he walked out of Gordon Finch's office, he knew, somewhere within the numbness that grew from a small center of his being, that a part of his life was over, that a part of him was so near death that he could watch the approach almost with calm. He was vaguely conscious that he walked across the campus in the bright crisp heat of an early spring afternoon; the dogwood trees along the sidewalks and in the front yards were in full bloom, and they trembled like soft clouds, translucent and tenuous, before his gaze; the sweet scent of dying lilac blossoms drenched the air.

And when he got to Katherine's apartment he was feverishly and callously gay. He brushed aside her questions about his latest encounter with the dean; he forced her to laugh; and he watched with an immeasurable sadness their last effort of gaiety, which was like a dance that life makes upon the body of death.

But finally they had to talk, he knew; though the words they said were like a performance of something they had rehearsed again and again in the privacies of their knowledge. They revealed that knowledge by grammatical usage: they progressed from the perfect—'We have been happy, haven't we?'—to the past—'We *were* happy—happier than

220

anyone, I think'—and at last came to the necessity of discourse.

Several days after the conversation with Finch, in a moment of quiet that interrupted the half-hysterical gaiety they had chosen as that convention most appropriate to see them through their last days together, Katherine said, 'We don't have much time, do we?'

'No,' Stoner said quietly.

'How much longer?' Katherine asked.

'A few days, two or three.'

Katherine nodded. 'I used to think I wouldn't be able to endure it. But I'm just numb. I don't feel anything.'

'I know,' Stoner said. They were silent for a moment. 'You know if there were anything—*anything* I could do, I'd—'

'Don't,' she said. 'Of course I know.'

He leaned back on the couch and looked at the low, dim ceiling that had been the sky of their world. He said calmly, 'If I threw it all away—if I gave it up, just walked out—you would go with me, wouldn't you?'

'Yes,' she said.

'But you know I won't do that, don't you?'

'Yes, I know.'

'Because then,' Stoner explained to himself, 'none of it would mean anything—nothing we have done, nothing we have been. I almost certainly wouldn't be able to teach, and you—you would become something else. We both would become something else, something other than ourselves. We would be—nothing.'

'Nothing,' she said.

'And we have come out of this, at least, with ourselves. We know that we are—what we are.'

'Yes,' Katherine said.

'Because in the long run,' Stoner said, 'it isn't Edith or

even Grace, or the certainty of losing Grace, that keeps me here; it isn't the scandal or the hurt to you or me; it isn't the hardship we would have to go through, or even the loss of love we might have to face. It's simply the destruction of ourselves, of what we do.'

'I know,' Katherine said.

'So we are of the world, after all; we should have known that. We did know it, I believe; but we had to withdraw a little, pretend a little, so that we could—'

'I know,' Katherine said. 'I've known it all along, I guess. Even with the pretending, I've known that sometime, sometime, we would . . . I've known.' She halted and looked at him steadily. Her eyes became suddenly bright with tears. 'But damn it all, Bill! Damn it all!'

They said no more. They embraced so that neither might see the other's face, and made love so that they would not speak. They coupled with the old tender sensuality of knowing each other well and with the new intense passion of loss. Afterward, in the black night of the little room, they lay still unspeaking, their bodies touching lightly. After a long while Katherine's breath came steadily, as if in sleep. Stoner got up quietly, dressed in the dark, and went out of the room without awakening her. He walked the still, empty streets of Columbia until the first gray light began in the east; then he made his way to the University campus. He sat on the stone steps in front of Jesse Hall and watched the light from the east creep upon the great stone columns in the center of the quad. He thought of the fire that, before he was born, had gutted and ruined the old building; and he was distantly saddened by the view of what remained. When it was light he let himself into the hall and went to his office, where he waited until his first class began.

He didn't see Katherine Driscoll again. After he left her,

during the night, she got up, packed all her belongings, cartoned her books, and left word with the manager of the apartment house where to send them. She mailed the English office her grades, her instructions to dismiss her classes for the week and a half that remained of the semester, and her resignation. And she was on the train, on her way out of Columbia, by two o'clock that afternoon.

She must have been planning her departure for some time, Stoner realized; and he was grateful that he had not known and that she left him no final note to say what could not be said.

14

That summer he did not teach; and he had the first illness of his life. It was a fever of high intensity and obscure origin, which lasted only a week; but it drained him of his strength, he became very gaunt, and suffered in its aftermath a partial loss of hearing. For the entire summer he was so weak and listless that he could walk only a few steps without becoming exhausted; he spent nearly all that time in the small enclosed porch at the back of the house, lying on the day bed or sitting in the old easy chair he had had brought up from the basement. He stared out the windows or at the slatted ceiling, and stirred himself now and then to go into the kitchen to get a bite of food.

He had hardly the energy to converse with Edith or even with Grace—though sometimes Edith came into the back room, spoke to him distractedly for a few minutes, and then left him alone as abruptly as she had intruded upon him.

Once, in the middle of summer, she spoke of Katherine.

'I just heard, a day or so ago,' she said. 'So your little coed has gone, has she?'

With an effort he brought his attention away from the window and turned to Edith. 'Yes,' he said mildly.

'What was her name?' Edith asked. 'I never can remember her name.'

'Katherine,' he said. 'Katherine Driscoll.'

'Oh, yes,' Edith said. 'Katherine Driscoll. Well, you see? I told you, didn't I? I told you these things weren't important.'

He nodded absently. Outside, in the old elm that crowded the back-yard fence, a large black-and-white bird—a magpie—had started to chatter. He listened to the sound of its calling and watched with remote fascination the open beak as it strained out its lonely cry.

He aged rapidly that summer, so that when he went back to his classes in the fall there were few who did not recognize him with a start of surprise. His face, gone gaunt and bony, was deeply lined; heavy patches of gray ran through his hair; and he was heavily stooped, as if he carried an invisible burden. His voice had grown a little grating and abrupt, and he had a tendency to stare at one with his head lowered, so that his clear gray eyes were sharp and querulous beneath his tangled eyebrows. He seldom spoke to anyone except his students, and he responded to questions and greetings always impatiently and sometimes harshly.

He did his work with a doggedness and resolve that amused his older colleagues and enraged the younger instructors, who, like himself, taught only freshman composition; he spent hours marking and correcting freshman themes, he had student conferences every day, and he attended faithfully all departmental meetings. He did not speak often at these meetings, but when he did he spoke without tact or diplomacy, so that among his colleagues he developed a reputation for crustiness and ill temper. But with his young students he was gentle and patient, though he demanded of them more work than they were willing to give, with an impersonal firmness that was hard for many of them to understand.

It was a commonplace among his colleagues—especially the younger ones—that he was a 'dedicated' teacher, a term they used half in envy and half in contempt, one whose dedication blinded him to anything that went on outside the classroom or, at the most, outside the halls of the University. There were mild jokes: after a departmental meeting at which Stoner had spoken bluntly about some recent experiments in the teaching of grammar, a young instructor remarked that 'To Stoner, copulation is restricted to verbs,' and was surprised at the quality of laughter and meaningful looks exchanged by some of the older men. Someone else once said, 'Old Stoner thinks that WPA stands for Wrong Pronoun Antecedent,' and was gratified to learn that his witticism gained some currency.

But William Stoner knew of the world in a way that few of his younger colleagues could understand. Deep in him, beneath his memory, was the knowledge of hardship and hunger and endurance and pain. Though he seldom thought of his early years on the Booneville farm, there was always near his consciousness the blood knowledge of his inheritance, given him by forefathers whose lives were obscure and hard and stoical and whose common ethic was to present to an oppressive world faces that were expressionless and hard and bleak.

And though he looked upon them with apparent impassivity, he was aware of the times in which he lived. During that decade when many men's faces found a permanent hardness and bleakness, as if they looked upon an abyss, William Stoner, to whom that expression was as familiar as the air he walked in, saw the signs of a general despair he had known since he was a boy. He saw good men go down into a slow decline of hopelessness, broken as their vision of a decent life was broken; he saw them walking aimlessly upon the streets, their eyes empty like shards of broken glass; he saw them walk up to back doors, with the bitter pride of men who go to their executions, and beg for the bread that would allow them to beg again; and he saw men, who had once walked erect in their own identities, look at him with envy and hatred for the poor security he enjoyed as a tenured empoyee of an institution that somehow could not fail. He did not give voice to this awareness; but the knowledge of common misery touched him and changed him in ways that were hidden deep from the public view, and a quiet sadness for the common plight was never far beneath any moment of his living.

He was aware, too, of the stirrings in Europe like a distant nightmare; and in July 1936, when Franco rebelled against the Spanish government and Hitler fanned that rebellion into a major war, Stoner, like many others, was sickened by the vision of the nightmare breaking out of the dream into the world. When the fall semester began that year the younger instructors could talk of little else; several of them proclaimed their intention of joining a volunteer unit and fighting for the loyalists or driving ambulances. By the close of the first semester a few of them had actually taken the step and submitted hasty resignations. Stoner thought of Dave Masters, and the old loss was brought back to him with a renewed intensity; he thought, too, of Archer Sloane and remembered, from nearly twenty years before, the slow anguish that had grown upon that ironic face and the erosive despair that had dissipated that hard self—and he thought that he knew now, in a small way, something of the sense of waste that Sloane had apprehended. He foresaw the years that stretched ahead, and knew that the worst was to come.

As Archer Sloane had done, he realized the futility and waste of committing one's self wholly to the irrational and dark forces that impelled the world toward its unknown end; as Archer Sloane had not done, Stoner withdrew a little distance to pity and love, so that he was not caught in the rushing that he observed. And as in other moments of crisis and despair, he looked again to the cautious faith that was embodied in the institution of the University. He told himself that it was not much; but he knew that it was all he had.

In the summer of 1937 he felt a renewal of the old passion for study and learning; and with the curious and disembodied vigor of the scholar that is the condition of neither youth nor age, he returned to the only life that had not betrayed him. He discovered that he had not gone far from that life even in his despair.

His schedule that fall was particularly bad. His four classes of freshman composition were spaced at widely separated hours six days a week. During all his years as chairman, Lomax had not once failed to give Stoner a teaching schedule that even the newest instructor would have accepted with bad grace.

On the first class day of that academic year, in the early morning, Stoner sat in his office and looked again at his neatly typed schedule. He had been up late the night before reading a new study of the survival of the medieval tradition into the Renaissance, and the excitement he had felt carried over to the morning. He looked at his schedule, and a dull anger rose within him. He stared at the wall in front of him for several moments, glanced at his schedule again, and nodded to himself. He dropped the schedule and the attached syllabus into a wastebasket and went to his filing cabinet in a corner of the room. He pulled out the top drawer, looked absently at the brown folders there, and withdrew one. He flipped through the papers in the folder, whistling silently as he did so. Then he closed the drawer and with the folder under one arm went out of his office and across the campus to his first class.

The building was an old one, with wooden floors, and

it was used as a classroom only in emergencies; the room to which he had been assigned was too small for the number of students enrolled, so that several of the boys had to sit on the window-sills or stand. When Stoner came in they looked at him with the discomfort of uncertainty; he might be friend or foe, and they did not know which was worse.

He apologized to the students for the room, made a small joke at the expense of the registrar, and assured those who were standing that there would be chairs for them tomorrow. Then he put his folder on the battered lectern that rested unevenly on the desk and surveyed the faces before him.

He hesitated for a moment. Then he said, 'Those of you who have purchased your texts for this course may return them to the bookstore and get a refund. We shall not be using the text described in the syllabus—which, I take it, you all received when you signed up for the course. Neither will we be using the syllabus. I intend in this course to take a different approach to the subject, an approach which will necessitate your buying two new texts.'

He turned his back to the students and picked up a piece of chalk from the trough beneath the scuffed blackboard; he held the chalk poised for a moment and listened to the muted sigh and rustle of the students as they settled at their desks, enduring the routine that suddenly became familiar to them.

Stoner said, 'Our texts will be'—and he enunciated the words slowly as he wrote them down—'*Medieval English Verse and Prose*, edited by Loomis and Willard; and *English Literary Criticism: The Medieval Phase*, by J. W. H. Atkins.' He turned to the class. 'You will find that the bookstore has not yet received these books—it may be as much as two weeks before they are in. In the meantime I will give you some background information upon the matter and purpose of this course, and I shall make a few library assignments to keep you occupied.'

He paused. Many of the students were bent over their desks, assiduously noting what he said; a few were looking at him steadily, with small smiles that wanted to be intelligent and understanding; and a few were staring at him in open amazement.

'The primary matter of this course,' Stoner said, 'will be found in the Loomis and Willard anthology; we shall study examples of medieval verse and prose for three purposes—first, as literary works significant in themselves; second, as a demonstration of the beginnings of literary style and method in the English tradition; and third, as rhetorical and grammatical solutions to problems of discourse that even today may be of some practical value and application.'

By this time nearly all the students had stopped taking notes and had raised their heads; even the intelligent smiles had become a trifle strained; and a few hands were waving in the air. Stoner pointed to one whose hand remained steady and high, a tall young man with dark hair and glasses.

'Sir, is this General English One, Section Four?'

Stoner smiled at the young man. 'What is your name, please?'

The boy swallowed. 'Jessup, sir. Frank Jessup.'

Stoner nodded. 'Mr Jessup. Yes, Mr Jessup, this is General English One, Section Four; and my name is Stoner—facts which, no doubt, I should have mentioned at the beginning of the period. Did you have another question?'

The boy swallowed again. 'No, sir.'

Stoner nodded and looked benevolently around the room. 'Does anyone else have a question?'

The faces stared back at him; there were no smiles, and a few mouths hung open.

'Very well,' Stoner said. 'I shall continue. As I said at the beginning of this hour, one purpose of this course is to study certain works of the period roughly between twelve and fifteen hundred. Certain accidents of history will stand in our way; there will be linguistic difficulties as well as philosophical, social as well as religious, theoretical as well as practical. Indeed, all of our past education will in some ways hinder us; for our habits of thinking about the nature of experience have determined our own expectations as radically as the habits of medieval man determined his. As a preliminary, let us examine some of those habits of mind under which medieval man lived and thought and wrote . . .'

That first meeting he did not keep the students for the entire hour. After less than half the period he brought his preliminary discussion to a close and gave them a weekend assignment.

'I should like for each of you to write a brief essay, no more than three pages, upon Aristotle's conception of the *topoi*—or, in its rather crude English translation, topic. You will find an extended discussion of the "topic" in Book Two of *The Rhetoric* of Aristotle, and in Lane Cooper's edition there is an introductory essay that you will find most helpful. The essay will be due on—Monday. And that, I think, will be all for today.'

For a moment after he dismissed the class he gazed at the students, who did not move, with some concern. Then he nodded briefly to them and walked out of the classroom, the brown folder under his arm.

On Monday fewer than half the students had finished their papers; he dismissed those who handed their essays in and spent the rest of the hour with the remaining students, rehearsing the subject he had assigned, going over it again and again, until he was sure they had it and could complete the assigned essay by Wednesday.

On Tuesday he noticed in the corridors of Jesse Hall, outside Lomax's office, a group of students; he recognized them as members of his first class. As he passed, the students turned away from him and looked at the floor or the ceiling or at the door of Lomax's office. He smiled to himself and went to his office and waited for the telephone call that he knew would come.

It came at two o'clock that afternoon. He picked up the phone, answered, and heard the voice of Lomax's secretary, icy and polite. 'Professor Stoner? Professor Lomax would like you to see Professor Ehrhardt this afternoon, as soon as possible. Professor Ehrhardt will be expecting you.'

'Will Lomax be there?' Stoner asked.

There was a shocked pause. The voice said uncertainly, 'I—believe not—a previous appointment. But Professor Ehrhardt is empowered to—'

'You tell Lomax he ought to be there. You tell him I'll be in Ehrhardt's office in ten minutes.'

Joel Ehrhardt was a balding young man in his early thirties. He had been brought into the department three years before by Lomax; and when it was discovered that he was a pleasant and serious young man with no special talent and no gift for teaching, he had been put in charge of the freshman English program. His office was in a small enclosure at the far end of the large common room where twenty-odd young instructors had their desks, and Stoner had to walk the length of the room to get there. As he made his way among the desks, some of the instructors looked up at him, grinned openly, and watched his progress across the room. Stoner opened the door without knocking, went into the office, and sat down in the chair opposite Ehrhardt's desk. Lomax was not there.

'You wanted to see me?' Stoner asked.

Ehrhardt, who had a very fair skin, blushed slightly. He fixed a smile on his face, said enthusiastically, 'It's good of you to drop by, Bill,' and fumbled for a moment with a match, trying to light his pipe. It wouldn't draw properly. 'This damned humidity,' he said morosely. 'It keeps the tobacco too wet.'

'Lomax won't be here, I take it,' Stoner said.

'No,' Ehrhardt said, putting the pipe on his desk. 'Actually, though, it was Professor Lomax who asked me to talk to you, so in a way'—he laughed nervously—'I'm really sort of a messenger boy.'

'What message were you asked to deliver?' Stoner asked dryly.

'Well, as I understand it, there have been a few complaints. Students—*you* know.' He shook his head commiseratingly. 'Some of them seem to think—well, they don't really seem to understand what's going on in your eight o'clock class. Professor Lomax thought—well, actually, I suppose he's questioning the wisdom of approaching the problems of freshman composition through the—the study of—'

'Medieval language and literature,' Stoner said.

'Yes,' Ehrhardt said. 'Actually, I think I understand what you're trying to do—shock them a bit, shake them up, try a new approach, get them to thinking. Right?'

Stoner nodded gravely. 'There has been a great deal of talk in our freshman comp meetings lately about new methods, experimentation.'

'Exactly,' Ehrhardt said. 'No one has more sympathy than I for experimentation, for—but perhaps sometimes, out of the very best motives, we go too far.' He laughed and shook

233

his head. 'I certainly know I do; I'd be the first to confess it. But I—or Professor Lomax—well, perhaps some sort of compromise, some partial return to the syllabus, a use of the assigned texts—you understand.'

Stoner pursed his lips and looked at the ceiling; resting his elbows on the arms of the chair, he placed the tips of his fingers together and let his chin rest on his thumb-tips. Finally, but decisively, he said, 'No, I don't believe the—experiment—has had a fair chance. Tell Lomax I intend to carry it through to the end of the semester. Would you do that for me?'

Ehrhardt's face was red. He said tightly, 'I will. But I imagine—I'm sure Professor Lomax will be most—disappointed. Most disappointed indeed.'

Stoner said, 'Oh, at first he may be. But he'll get over it. I'm sure Professor Lomax wouldn't want to interfere with the way a senior professor sees fit to teach one of his classes. He may disagree with the judgment of that professor, but it would be most unethical for him to attempt to impose his own judgment—and, incidentally, a little dangerous. Don't you agree?'

Ehrhardt picked up his pipe, gripped its bowl tightly, and contemplated it fiercely. 'I'll—tell Professor Lomax of your decision.'

'I'd be grateful if you would,' Stoner said. He rose from his chair, walked to the door, paused as if reminded of something, and turned to Ehrhardt. He said casually, 'Oh, another thing. I've been doing a little thinking about next semester. If my experiment works out, next semester I might try something else. I've been considering the possibility of getting at some of the problems of composition by examining the survival of the classical and medieval Latin tradition in some of Shakespeare's plays. It may sound a little specialized, but I think I can bring it down to a workable level. You might pass my little idea along to Lomax—ask him to turn it over in his mind. Maybe in a few weeks, you and I can—'

Ehrhardt slumped in his chair. He dropped his pipe on the table and said wearily, 'All right, Bill. I'll tell him. I'll—thanks for dropping by.'

Stoner nodded. He opened the door, went out, closed it carefully behind him, and walked across the long room. When one of the young instructors looked up at him inquiringly, he winked broadly, nodded, and—finally—let the smile come over his face.

He went to his office, sat at his desk, and waited, looking out the open doorway. After a few minutes he heard a door slam down the hall, heard the uneven sound of footsteps, and saw Lomax go past his office as swiftly as his limp would carry him.

Stoner did not move from his watch. Within half an hour he heard Lomax's slow, shuffling ascent of the stairway and saw him go once more past his office. He waited until he heard the door down the hall close; then he nodded to himself, got up, and went home.

It was some weeks later that Stoner learned from Finch himself what happened that afternoon when Lomax stormed into his office. Lomax complained bitterly about Stoner's behavior, described how he was teaching what amounted to his senior course in Middle English to his freshman class, and demanded that Finch take disciplinary measures. There was a moment of silence. Finch started to say something, and then he burst out laughing. He laughed for a long time, every now and then trying to say something that was pushed back by laughter. Finally he quieted, apologized to Lomax for his outburst, and said, 'He's got you, Holly; don't you see that? He's not about to let go, and there's not a damn thing you can do. You want *me* to do the job for you? How do you think that would look—a dean meddling in how a senior member of the department teaches his classes, *and* meddling at the instigation of the department chairman himself? No, sir. You take care of it yourself, the best way you can. But you really don't have much choice, do you?'

Two weeks after that conversation Stoner received a memo from Lomax's office which informed him that his schedule for the next semester was changed, that he would teach his old graduate seminar on the Latin Tradition and Renaissance Literature, a senior and graduate course in Middle English language and literature, a sophomore literature survey, and one section of freshman composition.

It was a triumph in a way, but one of which he always remained amusedly contemptuous, as if it were a victory won by boredom and indifference.

15

And that was one of the legends that began to attach to his name, legends that grew more detailed and elaborate year by year, progressing like myth from personal fact to ritual truth.

In his late forties, he looked years older. His hair, thick and unruly as it had been in his youth, was almost entirely white; his face was deeply lined and his eyes were sunken in their sockets; and the deafness that had come upon him the summer after the end of his affair with Katherine Driscoll had worsened slightly year by year, so that when he listened to someone, his head cocked to one side and his eyes intent, he appeared to be remotely contemplating a puzzling species that he could not quite identify.

That deafness was of a curious nature. Though he sometimes had difficulty understanding one who spoke directly to him, he was often able to hear with perfect clarity a murmured conversation held across a noisy room. It was by this trick of deafness that he gradually began to know that he was considered, in the phrase current in his own youth, a 'campus character.'

Thus he overheard, again and again, the embellished tale of his teaching Middle English to a group of new freshmen and of the capitulation of Hollis Lomax. 'And when the freshman class of thirty-seven took their junior English exams, you know what class had the highest score?' a reluctant young instructor of freshman English asked. 'Sure. Old Stoner's Middle English bunch. And we keep on using exercises and handbooks!'

Stoner had to admit that he had become, in the regard of the young instructors and the older students, who seemed to come and go before he could firmly attach names to their faces, an almost mythic figure, however shifting and various the function of that figure was.

Sometimes he was villain. In one version that attempted to explain the long feud between himself and Lomax, he had seduced and then cast aside a young graduate student for whom Lomax had had a pure and honorable passion. Sometimes he was the fool: in another version of the same feud, he refused to speak to Lomax because once Lomax had been unwilling to write a letter of recommendation for one of Stoner's graduate students. And sometimes he was hero: in a final and not often accepted version he was hated by Lomax and frozen in his rank because he had once caught Lomax giving to a favored student a copy of a final examination in one of Stoner's courses.

The legend was defined, however, by his manner in class. Over the years it had grown more and more absent and yet more and more intense. He began his lectures and discussions fumblingly and awkwardly, yet very quickly became so immersed in his subject that he seemed unaware of anything or anyone around him. Once a meeting of several members of the board of trustees and the president of the University was scheduled in the conference room where Stoner held his seminar in the Latin Tradition; he had been informed of the meeting but had forgotten about it and held his seminar at the usual time and place. Halfway through the period a timid knock sounded at the door; Stoner, engrossed in translating extemporaneously a pertinent Latin passage, did not notice. After a few moments the door opened and a small plump middle-aged man with rimless glasses tiptoed in and lightly tapped Stoner on the shoulder. Without looking up, Stoner waved him away. The man retreated; there was a whispered conference with several others outside the open door. Stoner continued the translation. Then four men, led by the president of the University, a tall heavy man with an imposing chest and florid face, strode in and halted like a squad beside Stoner's desk. The president frowned and cleared his throat loudly. Without a break or a pause in his extemporaneous translation, Stoner looked up and spoke the next line of the poem mildly to the president and his entourage: "'Begone, begone, you bloody whoreson Gauls!'" And still without a break returned his eyes to his book and continued to speak, while the group gasped and stumbled backward, turned, and fled from the room.

Fed by such events, the legend grew until there were anecdotes to give substance to nearly all of Stoner's more typical activities, and grew until it reached his life outside the University. It finally included even Edith, who was seen with him so rarely at University functions that she was a faintly mysterious figure who flitted across the collective imagination like a ghost: she drank secretly, out of some obscure and distant sorrow; she was dying slowly of a rare and always fatal disease; she was a brilliantly talented artist who had given up her career to devote herself to Stoner. At public functions her smile flashed out of her narrow face so quickly and nervously, her eyes glinted so brightly, and she spoke so shrilly and disconnectedly that everyone was sure that her appearance masked a reality, that a self hid behind the façade that no one could believe.

After his illness, and out of an indifference that became a way of living, William Stoner began to spend more and more of his time in the house that he and Edith had bought many years ago. At first Edith was so disconcerted by his presence that she was silent, as if puzzled about something. Then, when she was convinced that his presence, afternoon after afternoon, night after night, weekend after weekend, was to be a permanent condition, she waged an old battle with new intensity. Upon the most trivial provocation she wept forlornly and wandered through the rooms; Stoner looked at her impassively and murmured a few absent words of sympathy. She locked herself in her room and did not emerge for hours at a time; Stoner prepared the meals that she would otherwise have prepared and didn't seem to have noticed her absence when she finally emerged from her room, pale and hollow of cheek and eye. She derided him upon the slightest occasion, and he hardly seemed to hear her; she screamed imprecations upon him, and he listened with polite interest. When he was immersed in a book, she chose that moment to go into the living room and pound with frenzy upon the piano that she seldom otherwise played; and when he spoke quietly to his daughter, Edith would burst into anger at either or both of them. And Stoner looked upon it all—the rage, the woe, the screams, and the hateful silences—as if it were happening to two other people, in whom, by an effort of the will, he could summon only the most perfunctory interest.

And at last—wearily, almost gratefully—Edith accepted her defeat. The rages decreased in intensity until they became as perfunctory as Stoner's interest in them; and the long silences became withdrawals into a privacy at which Stoner no longer wondered, rather than offenses upon an indifferent position.

In her fortieth year, Edith Stoner was as thin as she had been as a girl, but with a hardness, a brittleness, that came from an unbending carriage, that made every movement seem reluctant and grudging. The bones of her face had sharpened, and the thin pale skin was stretched upon them as upon a framework, so that the lines upon the skin were taut and sharp. She was very pale, and she used a great deal of powder and paint in such a way that it appeared she daily composed her own features upon a blank mask. Beneath the dry hard skin, her hands seemed all bone; and they moved ceaselessly, twisting and plucking and clenching even in her quietest moments.

Always withdrawn, she grew in these middle years increasingly remote and absent. After the brief period of her last assault upon Stoner, which flared with a final, desperate intensity, she wandered like a ghost into the privacy of herself, a place from which she never fully emerged. She began to speak to herself, with the kind of soft reasonableness that one uses with a child; she did so openly and without self-consciousness, as if it were the most natural thing she could do. Of the scattered artistic endeavors with which she had occupied herself intermittently during her marriage, she finally settled upon sculpture as the most 'satisfying.' She modeled clay mostly, though she occasionally worked with the softer stones; busts and figures and compositions of all sorts were scattered about the house. She was very modern: the busts she modeled were minimally featured spheres, the figures were blobs of clay with elongated appendages, and the compositions were random geometric gatherings of cubes and spheres and rods. Sometimes, passing her studio—the room that had once been his study—Stoner would pause and listen to her work. She gave herself directions, as if to a child: 'Now, you must put that here—not too much—here, right beside the little gouge. Oh, look, it's falling off. It wasn't wet enough, was it? Well, we can fix that, can't we? Just a little more water, and—there. You see?'

She got in the habit of talking to her husband and daughter in the third person, as if they were someone other than those to whom she spoke. She would say to Stoner: 'Willy had better finish his coffee; it's almost nine o'clock, and he wouldn't want to be late to class.' Or she would say to her daughter: 'Grace really isn't practicing her piano enough. An hour a day at least, it ought to be two. What's going to happen to that talent? A shame, a shame.'

What this withdrawal meant to Grace, Stoner did not know; for in her own way she had become as remote and withdrawn as her mother. She had got the habit of silence; and though she reserved a shy, soft smile for her father, she would not talk to him. During the summer of his illness she had, when she could do so unobserved, slipped into his little room and sat beside him and looked with him out the window, apparently content only to be with him; but even then she had been silent and had become restless when he attempted to draw her out of herself.

That summer of his illness she was twelve years old, a tall, thin girl with a delicate face and hair that was more blond than red. In the fall, during Edith's last violent assault upon her husband, her marriage, herself, and what she thought she had become, Grace had become almost motionless, as if she felt that any movement might throw her into an abyss from which she would not be able to clamber. In an aftermath of the violence, Edith decided, with the kind of sure recklessness of which she was capable, that Grace was quiet because she was unhappy and that she was unhappy because she was not popular with her schoolmates. She transferred the fading violence of her assault upon Stoner to an assault upon what she called Grace's 'social life.' Once again she took an 'interest'; she dressed her daughter brightly and fashionably in clothes whose frilliness intensified her thinness, she had parties and played the piano and insisted brightly that everyone dance, she nagged at Grace to smile at everyone, to talk, to make jokes, to laugh.

This assault lasted for less than a month; then Edith dropped her campaign and began the long slow journey to where she obscurely was going. But the effects of the assault upon Grace were out of proportion to its duration.

After the assault, she spent nearly all her free time alone in her room, listening to the small radio her father had given her on her twelfth birthday. She lay motionless on her unmade bed, or sat motionless at her desk, and listened to the sounds that blared thinly from the scrollwork of the squat, ugly instrument on her bedside table, as if the voices, music, and laughter she heard were all that remained of her identity and as if even that were fading distantly into silence, beyond her recall.

And she grew fat. Between that winter and her thirteenth birthday she gained nearly fifty pounds; her face grew puffy and dry like rising dough, and her limbs became soft and slow and clumsy. She ate little more than she had eaten before, though she became very fond of sweets and kept a box of candy always in her room; it was as if something inside her had gone loose and soft and hopeless, as if at last a shapelessness within her had struggled and burst loose and now persuaded her flesh to specify that dark and secret existence.

Stoner looked upon the transformation with a sadness that belied the indifferent face he presented to the world. He did not allow himself the easy luxury of guilt; given his own nature and the circumstance of his life with Edith, there was nothing that he could have done. And that knowledge intensified his sadness as no guilt could have, and made his love for his daughter more searching and more deep.

She was, he knew—and had known very early, he supposed—one of those rare and always lovely humans whose moral nature was so delicate that it must be nourished and cared for that it might be fulfilled. Alien to the world, it had to live where it could not be at home; avid for tenderness and quiet, it had to feed upon indifference and callousness and noise. It was a nature that, even in the strange and inimical place where it had to live, had not the savagery to fight off the brutal forces that opposed it and could only withdraw to a quietness where it was forlorn and small and gently still.

When she was seventeen years old, during the first part of her senior year in high school, another transformation came upon her. It was as if her nature had found its hiding place and she was able at last to present an appearance to the world. As rapidly as she had gained it, she lost the weight she had put on three years before; and to those who had known her she seemed one whose transformation partook of magic, as if she had emerged from a chrysalis into an air for which she had been designed. She was almost beautiful; her body, which had been very thin and then suddenly very fat, was delicately limbed and soft, and it walked with a light grace. It was a passive beauty that she had, almost a placid one; her face was nearly without expression, like a mask; her light blue eyes looked directly at one, without curiosity and without any apprehension that one might see beyond them; her voice was very soft, a little flat, and she spoke rarely.

Quite suddenly she became, in Edith's word, 'popular.' The telephone rang frequently for her, and she sat in the living room, nodding now and then, responding softly and briefly to the voice; cars drove up in the dusky afternoons and carried her away, anonymous in the shouting and laughter. Sometimes Stoner stood at the front window and watched the automobiles screech away in clouds of dust, and he felt a small concern and a little awe; he had never owned a car and had never learned to drive one.

And Edith was pleased. 'You see?' she said in absent triumph, as if more than three years had not passed since her frenzied attack upon the problem of Grace's 'popularity.' 'You see? I was right. All she needed was a little push. And Willy didn't approve. Oh, I could tell. Willy never approves.'

For a number of years, Stoner had, every month, put aside a few dollars so that Grace could, when the time came, go away from Columbia to a college, perhaps an eastern one, some distance away. Edith had known of these plans, and she had seemed to approve; but when the time came, she would not hear of it.

'Oh, no!' she said. 'I couldn't bear it! My baby! And she *has* done so well here this last year. So popular, and so happy. She would have to adjust, and—baby, Gracie, baby'—she turned to her daughter—'Gracie doesn't *really* want to go away from her mommy. Does she? Leave her all alone?'

Grace looked at her mother silently for a moment. She turned very briefly to her father and shook her head. She said to her mother, 'If you want me to stay, of course I will.'

'Grace,' Stoner said. 'Listen to me. If you want to go— please, if you really want to go—'

She would not look at him again. 'It doesn't matter,' she said.

Before Stoner could say anything else, Edith began talking about how they could spend the money her father had saved on a new wardrobe, a really nice one, perhaps even a little car so that she and her friends could . . . And Grace smiled her slow small smile and nodded and every now and then said a word, as if it were expected of her.

It was settled; and Stoner never knew what Grace felt, whether she stayed because she wanted to, or because her mother wanted her to, or out of a vast indifference to her own fate. She would enter the University of Missouri as a freshman that fall, go there for at least two years, after which, if she wanted, she would be allowed to go away, out of the state, to finish her college work. Stoner told himself that it was better this way, better for Grace to endure the prison she hardly knew she was in for two more years, than to be torn again upon the rack of Edith's helpless will.

So nothing changed. Grace got her wardrobe, refused her mother's offer of a little car, and entered the University of Missouri as a freshman student. The telephone continued to ring, the same faces (or ones much like them) continued to appear laughing and shouting at the front door, and the same automobiles roared away in the dusk. Grace was away from home even more frequently than she had been in high school, and Edith was pleased at what she thought to be her daughter's growing popularity. 'She's like her mother,' she said. 'Before she was married she was *very* popular. All the boys . . . Papa used to get so mad at them, but he was secretly very proud, I could tell.'

'Yes, Edith,' Stoner said gently, and he felt his heart contract.

It was a difficult semester for Stoner; it had come his turn to administer the university-wide junior English examination, and he was at the same time engaged in directing two particularly difficult doctoral dissertations, both of which required a great deal of extra reading on his part. So he was

246

away from home more frequently than had been his habit for the last few years.

One evening, near the end of November, he came home even later than usual. The lights were off in the living room, and the house was quiet; he supposed that Grace and Edith were in bed. He took some papers he had brought with him to his little back room, intending to read a few of them after he got into bed. He went into the kitchen to get a sandwich and a glass of milk; he had sliced the bread and opened the refrigerator door when suddenly he heard, sharp and clean as a knife, a prolonged scream from somewhere downstairs. He ran into the living room; the scream came again, now short and somehow angry in its intensity, from Edith's studio. Swiftly he went across the room and opened the door.

Edith was sitting sprawled on the floor, as if she had fallen there; her eyes were wild, and her mouth was open, ready to emit another scream. Grace sat across the room from her on an upholstered chair, her knees crossed, and looked almost calmly at her mother. A single desk lamp, on Edith's work table, was burning, so that the room was filled with harsh brightness and deep shadows.

'What is it?' Stoner asked. 'What's happened?'

Edith's head swung around to face him as if it were on a loose pivot; her eyes were vacant. She said with a curious petulance, 'Oh, Willy. Oh, Willy.' She continued to look at him, her head shaking weakly.

He turned to Grace, whose look of calm did not change. She said conversationally, 'I'm pregnant, Father.'

And the scream came again, piercing and inexpressibly angry; they both turned to Edith, who looked back and forth, from one to the other, the eyes absent and cool above the screaming mouth. Stoner went across the room, stooped behind her, and lifted her upright; she was loose in his arms, and he had to support her weight.

'Edith!' he said sharply. 'Be quiet.'

She stiffened and pulled away from him. On trembling legs she stalked across the room and stood above Grace, who had not moved.

'You!' she spat. 'Oh, my God. Oh, Gracie. How could you—oh, my God. Like your father. Your father's blood. Oh, yes. Filth. Filth—'

'Edith!' Stoner spoke more sharply and strode over to her. He placed his hands firmly on her upper arms and turned her away from Grace. 'Go to the bathroom and throw some cold water on your face. Then go up to your room and lie down.'

'Oh, Willy,' Edith said pleadingly. 'My own little baby. My very own. How could this happen? How could she—'

'Go on,' Stoner said. 'I'll call you after a while.'

She tottered out of the room. Stoner looked after her without moving until he heard the tap water start in the bathroom. Then he turned to Grace, who remained looking up at him from the easy chair. He smiled at her briefly, walked across to Edith's work table, got a straight chair, brought it back, and placed it in front of Grace's chair, so that he could talk to her without looking down upon her upturned face.

'Now,' he said, 'why don't you tell me about it?'

She gave him her small soft smile. 'There isn't much to tell,' she said. 'I'm pregnant.'

'Are you sure?'

She nodded. 'I've been to a doctor. I just got the report this afternoon.'

'Well,' he said and awkwardly touched her hand. 'You aren't to worry. Everything will be all right.'

'Yes,' she said.

He asked gently, 'Do you want to tell me who the father is?'

'A student,' she said. 'At the University.'

'Had you rather not tell me?'

'Oh, no,' she said. 'It doesn't make any difference. His name is Frye. Ed Frye. He's a sophomore. I believe he was in your freshman comp class last year.'

'I don't remember him,' Stoner said. 'I don't remember him at all.'

'I'm sorry, Father,' Grace said. 'It was stupid. He was a little drunk, and we didn't take—precautions.'

Stoner looked away from her, at the floor.

'I'm sorry, Father. I've shocked you, haven't I?'

'No,' Stoner said. 'Surprised me, perhaps. We really haven't known each other very well these last few years, have we?'

She looked away and said uncomfortably, 'Well—I suppose not.'

'Do you—love this boy, Grace?'

'Oh, no,' she said. 'I really don't know him very well.'

He nodded. 'What do you want to do?'

'I don't know,' she said. 'It really doesn't matter. I don't want to be a bother.'

They sat without speaking for a long time. Finally Stoner said, 'Well, you aren't to worry. It will be all right. Whatever you decide—whatever you want to do, it will be all right.'

'Yes,' Grace said. She rose from the chair. Then she looked down at her father and said, 'You and I, we can talk now.'

'Yes,' Stoner said. 'We can talk.'

She went out of the studio, and Stoner waited until he heard her bedroom door close upstairs. Then, before he went to his own room, he went softly upstairs and opened the door to Edith's bedroom. Edith was fast asleep, sprawled fully clothed on her bed, the bedside light harsh upon her face. Stoner turned the light out and went downstairs.

The next morning at breakfast Edith was almost cheerful; she gave no sign of her hysteria of the night before, and she spoke as if the future were a hypothetical problem to be solved. After she learned the name of the boy she said brightly, 'Well, now. Do you think we ought to get in touch with the parents or should we talk to the boy first? Let's see—this is the last week in November. Let's say two weeks. We can make all the arrangements by then, maybe even a small church wedding. Gracie, what does your friend, what's his name—?'

'Edith,' Stoner said. 'Wait. You're taking too much for granted. Perhaps Grace and this young man don't want to get married. We need to talk it out with Grace.'

'What's there to talk about? Of course they'll want to get married. After all, they—they— Gracie, *tell* your father. Explain to him.'

Grace said to him, 'It doesn't matter, Father. It doesn't matter at all.'

And it didn't matter, Stoner realized; Grace's eyes were fixed beyond him, into a distance she could not see and which she contemplated without curiosity. He remained silent and let his wife and daughter make their plans.

It was decided that Grace's 'young man,' as Edith called him, as if his name were somehow forbidden, would be invited to the house and that he and Edith would 'talk.' She arranged the afternoon as if it were a scene in a drama, with exits and entrances and even a line or two of dialogue. Stoner was to excuse himself, Grace was to remain for a few moments more and then excuse herself, leaving Edith and the young man alone to talk. In half an hour Stoner was to return, then Grace was to return, by which time all arrangements were to be completed.

And it all worked out exactly as Edith planned. Later Stoner wondered, with amusement, what young Edward Frye thought when he knocked timidly on the door and was admitted to a room that seemed filled with mortal enemies. He was a tall, rather heavy young man, with blurred and faintly sullen features; he was caught in a numbing embarrassment and fear, and he would look at no one. When Stoner left the room he saw the young man sitting slumped in a chair, his forearms on his knees, staring at the floor; when, half an hour later, he came back into the room, the young man was in the same position, as if he had not moved before the barrage of Edith's birdlike cheerfulness.

But everything was settled. In a high, artificial, but genuinely cheerful voice Edith informed him that 'Grace's young man' came from a very good St Louis family, his father was a broker and had probably at one time had dealings with her *own* father, or at least her father's bank, that the 'young people' had decided on a wedding, 'as soon as possible, very informal,' that both were dropping out of school, at least for a year or two, that they would live in St Louis, 'a change of scenery, a new start,' that though they wouldn't be able to finish the semester they would go to school until the semester break, and they would be married on the afternoon of that day, which was a Friday. And wasn't it all sweet, really—no matter what.

The wedding took place in the cluttered study of a justice of the peace. Only William and Edith witnessed the ceremony; the justice's wife, a rumpled gray woman with a permanent frown, worked in the kitchen while the ceremony was performed and came out when it was over only to sign the papers as a witness. It was a cold, bleak afternoon; the date was December 12, 1941.

Five days before the marriage took place the Japanese had bombed Pearl Harbor; and William Stoner watched the ceremony with a mixture of feeling that he had not had before. Like many others who went through that time, he was gripped by what he could think of only as a numbness, though he knew it was a feeling compounded of emotions so deep and intense that they could not be acknowledged because they could not be lived with. It was the force of a public tragedy he felt, a horror and a woe so all-pervasive that private tragedies and personal misfortunes were removed to another state of being, yet were intensified by the very vastness in which they took place, as the poignancy of a lone grave might be intensified by a great desert surrounding it. With a pity that was almost impersonal he watched the sad little ritual of the marriage and was oddly moved by the passive, indifferent beauty of his daughter's face and by the sullen desperation on the face of the young man.

After the ceremony the two young people climbed joylessly into Frye's little roadster and left for St Louis, where they still had to face another set of parents and where they were to live. Stoner watched them drive away from the house, and he could think of his daughter only as a very small girl who had once sat beside him in a distant room and looked at him with solemn delight, as a lovely child who long ago had died.

Two months after the marriage Edward Frye enlisted in the Army; it was Grace's decision to remain in St Louis until the birth of her child. Within six months Frye was dead upon the beach of a small Pacific island, one of a number of raw recruits that had been sent out in a desperate effort to halt the Japanese advance. In June of 1942 Grace's child was born; it was a boy, and she named it after the father it had never seen and would not love.

Though Edith, when she went to St Louis that June to 'help out,' tried to persuade her daughter to return to Columbia, Grace would not do so; she had a small apartment, a small income from Frye's insurance, and her new parents-in-law, and she seemed happy.

'Changed somehow,' Edith said distractedly to Stoner. 'Not our little Gracie at all. She's been through a lot, and I guess she doesn't want to be reminded . . . She sent you her love.'

16

The years of the war blurred together, and Stoner went through them as he might have gone through a driving and nearly unendurable storm, his head down, his jaw locked, his mind fixed upon the next step and the next and the next. Yet for all his stoical endurance and his stolid movement through the days and weeks, he was an intensely divided man. One part of him recoiled in instinctive horror at the daily waste, the inundation of destruction and death that inexorably assaulted the mind and heart; once again he saw the faculty depleted, he saw the classrooms emptied of their young men, he saw the haunted looks upon those who remained behind, and saw in those looks the slow death of the heart, the bitter attrition of feeling and care.

Yet another part of him was drawn intensely toward that very holocaust from which he recoiled. He found within himself a capacity for violence he did not know he had: he yearned for involvement, he wished for the taste of death, the bitter joy of destruction, the feel of blood. He felt both shame and pride, and over it all a bitter disappointment, in himself and in the time and circumstance that made him possible.

Week by week, month by month, the names of the dead rolled out before him. Sometimes they were only names that he remembered as if from a distant past; sometimes he could evoke a face to go with a name; sometimes he could recall a voice, a word.

Through it all he continued to teach and study, though he sometimes felt that he hunched his back futilely against the driving storm and cupped his hands uselessly around the dim flicker of his last poor match.

Occasionally Grace returned to Columbia for a visit with her parents. The first time she brought her son, barely a year old; but his presence seemed obscurely to bother Edith, so thereafter she left him in St Louis with his paternal grandparents when she visited. Stoner would have liked to see more of his grandson, but he did not mention that wish; he had come to realize that Grace's removal from Columbia—perhaps even her pregnancy—was in reality a flight from a prison to which she now returned out of an ineradicable kindness and a gentle good will.

Though Edith did not suspect it or would not admit it, Grace had, Stoner knew, begun to drink with a quiet seriousness. He first knew it during the summer of the year after the war had ended. Grace had come to visit them for a few days; she seemed particularly worn; her eyes were shadowed, and her face was tense and pale. One evening after dinner Edith went to bed early, and Grace and Stoner sat together in the kitchen, drinking coffee. Stoner tried to talk to her, but she was restless and distraught. They sat in silence for many minutes; finally Grace looked at him intently, shrugged her shoulders, and sighed abruptly.

'Look,' she said, 'do you have any liquor in the house?'

'No,' he said, 'I'm afraid not. There may be a bottle of sherry in the cupboard, but—'

'I've got most desperately to have a drink. Do you mind if I call the drugstore and have them send a bottle over?'

'Of course not,' Stoner said. 'It's just that your mother and I don't usually—'

But she had got up and gone into the living room. She riffled through the pages of the phone book and dialed savagely. When she came back to the kitchen she passed the table, went to the cupboard, and pulled out the half-full bottle of sherry. She got a glass from the drainboard and filled it nearly to the brim with the light brown wine. Still standing, she drained the glass and wiped her lips, shuddering a little. 'It's gone sour,' she said. 'And I hate sherry.'

She brought the bottle and the glass back to the table, sat down, and placed them precisely in front of her. She half-filled the glass and looked at her father with an odd little smile.

'I drink a little more than I ought to,' she said. 'Poor Father. You didn't know that, did you?'

'No,' he said.

'Every week I tell myself, next week I won't drink quite so much; but I always drink a little more. I don't know why.'

'Are you unhappy?' Stoner asked.

'No,' she said. 'I believe I'm happy. Or almost happy anyway. It isn't that. It's—' She did not finish.

By the time she had drunk the last of the sherry the delivery boy from the drugstore had come with her whisky. She brought the bottle into the kitchen, opened it with a practiced gesture, and poured a stiff portion of it into the sherry glass.

They sat up very late, until the first gray crept upon the windows. Grace drank steadily, in small sips; and as the night wore on, the lines in her face eased, she grew calm and younger, and the two of them talked as they had not been able to talk for years.

'I suppose,' she said, 'I suppose I got pregnant deliberately, though I didn't know it at the time; I suppose I didn't even know how badly I wanted, how badly I *had* to get away from here. I knew enough not to get pregnant unless I wanted to, Lord knows. All those boys in high school, and'—she smiled crookedly at her father—'you and mamma, you didn't know, did you?'

'I suppose not,' he said.

'Mamma wanted me to be popular, and—well, I was popular, all right. It didn't mean anything, not anything at all.'

'I knew you were unhappy,' Stoner said with difficulty. 'But I never realized—I never knew—'

'I suppose I didn't either,' she said. 'I couldn't have. Poor Ed. He's the one that got the rotten deal. I used him, you know; oh, he was the father all right—but I used him. He was a nice boy, and always so ashamed—he couldn't stand it. He joined up six months before he had to, just to get away from it. I killed him, I suppose; he was such a nice boy, and we couldn't even like each other very much.'

They talked late into the night, as if they were old friends. And Stoner came to realize that she was, as she had said, almost happy with her despair; she would live her days out quietly, drinking a little more, year by year, numbing herself against the nothingness her life had become. He was glad she had that, at least; he was grateful that she could drink.

The years immediately following the end of the Second World War were the best years of his teaching; and they were in some ways the happiest years of his life. Veterans of that war descended upon the campus and transformed it, bringing to it a quality of life it had not had before, an intensity and turbulence that amounted to a transformation.

He worked harder than he had ever worked; the students, strange in their maturity, were intensely serious and contemptuous of triviality. Innocent of fashion or custom, they came to their studies as Stoner had dreamed that a student might—as if those studies were life itself and not specific means to specific ends. He knew that never, after these few years, would teaching be quite the same; and he committed himself to a happy state of exhaustion which he hoped might never end. He seldom thought of the past or the future, or of the disappointments and joys of either; he concentrated all the energies of which he was capable upon the moment of his work and hoped that he was at last defined by what he did.

Rarely during these years was he removed from this dedication to the moment of his work. Sometimes when his daughter came back to Columbia for a visit, as if wandering aimlessly from one room to another, he had a sense of loss that he could scarcely bear. At the age of twenty-five she looked ten years older; she drank with the steady diffidence of one utterly without hope; and it became clear that she was relinquishing more and more control of her child to the grandparents in St Louis.

Only once did he have news of Katherine Driscoll. In the early spring of 1949 he received a circular from the press of a large eastern university; it announced the publication of Katherine's book, and gave a few words about the author. She was teaching at a good liberal arts college in Massachusetts; she was unmarried. He got a copy of the book as soon as he could. When he held it in his hands his fingers seemed to come alive; they trembled so that he could scarcely open it. He turned the first few pages and saw the dedication: 'To W. S.'

His eyes blurred, and for a long time he sat without

moving. Then he shook his head, returned to the book, and did not put it down until he had read it through.

It was as good as he had thought it would be. The prose was graceful, and its passion was masked by a coolness and clarity of intelligence. It was herself he saw in what he read, he realized; and he marveled at how truly he could see her even now. Suddenly it was as if she were in the next room, and he had only moments before left her; his hands tingled, as if they had touched her. And the sense of his loss, that he had for so long dammed within him, flooded out, engulfed him, and he let himself be carried outward, beyond the control of his will; he did not wish to save himself. Then he smiled fondly, as if at a memory; it occurred to him that he was nearly sixty years old and that he ought to be beyond the force of such passion, of such love.

But he was not beyond it, he knew, and would never be. Beneath the numbness, the indifference, the removal, it was there, intense and steady; it had always been there. In his youth he had given it freely, without thought; he had given it to the knowledge that had been revealed to him—how many years ago?—by Archer Sloane; he had given it to Edith, in those first blind foolish days of his courtship and marriage; and he had given it to Katherine, as if it had never been given before. He had, in odd ways, given it to every moment of his life, and had perhaps given it most fully when he was unaware of his giving. It was a passion neither of the mind nor of the flesh; rather, it was a force that comprehended them both, as if they were but the matter of love, its specific substance. To a woman or to a poem, it said simply: Look! I am alive.

He could not think of himself as old. Sometimes, in the morning when he shaved, he looked at his image in the glass and felt no identity with the face that stared back at him in surprise, the eyes clear in a grotesque mask; it was as if he wore, for an obscure reason, an outrageous disguise, as if he could, if he wished, strip away the bushy white eyebrows, the rumpled white hair, the flesh that sagged around the sharp bones, the deep lines that pretended age.

Yet his age, he knew, was not pretense. He saw the sickness of the world and of his own country during the years after the great war; he saw hatred and suspicion become a kind of madness that swept across the land like a swift plague; he saw young men go again to war, marching eagerly to a senseless doom, as if in the echo of a nightmare. And the pity and sadness he felt were so old, so much a part of his age, that he seemed to himself nearly untouched.

The years went swiftly, and he was hardly aware of their passing. In the spring of 1954 he was sixty-three years old; and he suddenly realized that he had at the most four years of teaching left to him. He tried to see beyond that time; he could not see, and had no wish to do so.

That fall he received a note from Gordon Finch's secretary, asking him to drop by to see the dean whenever it was convenient. He was busy, and it was several days before he found a free afternoon.

Every time he saw Gordon Finch, Stoner was conscious of a small surprise at how little he had aged. A year younger than Stoner, he looked no more than fifty. He was wholly bald, his face was heavy and unlined, and it glowed with an almost cherubic health; his step was springy, and in these later years he had begun to affect a casualness of dress; he wore colorful shirts and odd jackets.

He seemed embarrassed that afternoon when Stoner came in to see him. They talked casually for a few moments; Finch asked him about Edith's health and mentioned that his own wife, Caroline, had been talking just the other day about how they all ought to get together again. Then he said, 'Time. My God, how it flies!'

Stoner nodded.

Finch sighed abruptly. 'Well,' he said, 'I guess we've got to talk about it. You'll be—sixty-five next year. I suppose we ought to be making some plans.'

Stoner shook his head. 'Not right away. I intend to take advantage of the two-year option, of course.'

'I figured you would,' Finch said and leaned back in his chair. 'Not me. I have three years to go and I'm getting out. I think sometimes about what I've missed, the places I haven't been to, and—hell, Bill, life's too short. Why don't you get out too? Think of all the time—'

'I wouldn't know what to do with it,' Stoner said. 'I've never learned.'

'Well, hell,' Finch said. 'This day and age, sixty-five's pretty young. There's time to learn things that—'

'It's Lomax, isn't it? He's putting the squeeze on you.'

Finch grinned. 'Sure. What did you expect?'

Stoner was silent for a moment. Then he said, 'You tell Lomax that I wouldn't talk to you about it. Tell him that I've become so cantankerous and ornery in my old age that you can't do a thing with me. That he's going to have to do it himself.'

Finch laughed and shook his head. 'By God, I will. After all these years, maybe you two old bastards will unbend a little.'

But the confrontation did not take place at once, and when it did—in the middle of the second semester, in March—it did not take the form that Stoner expected. Once again he was requested to appear at the dean's office; a time was specified, and urgency was hinted.

Stoner came in a few minutes late. Lomax was already

there; he sat stiffly in front of Finch's desk; there was an empty chair beside him. Stoner walked slowly across the room and sat down. He turned his head and looked at Lomax; Lomax stared imperturbably in front of him, one eyebrow lifted in a general disdain.

Finch stared at both of them for several moments, a little smile of amusement on his face.

'Well,' he said, 'we all know the matter before us. It is that of Professor Stoner's retirement.' He sketched the regulations—voluntary retirement was possible at sixty-five; under this option, Stoner could if he wished retire either at the end of the current academic year, or at the end of either semester of the following year. Or he could, if it were agreed upon by the chairman of the department, the dean of the college, and the professor concerned, extend his retirement age to sixty-seven, at which time retirement was mandatory. Unless, of course, the person concerned were given a Distinguished Professorship and awarded a Chair, in which event—

'A most remote likelihood, I believe we can agree,' Lomax said dryly.

Stoner nodded to Finch. 'Most remote.'

'I frankly believe,' Lomax said to Finch, 'it would be in the best interests of the department and college if Professor Stoner would take advantage of his opportunity to retire. There are certain curricular and personnel changes that I have long contemplated, which this retirement would make possible.'

Stoner said to Finch, 'I have no wish to retire before I have to, merely to accommodate a whim of Professor Lomax.'

Finch turned to Lomax. Lomax said, 'I'm sure that there is a great deal that Professor Stoner has not considered. He would have the leisure to do some of the writing that his'—he paused delicately—'his dedication to teaching has prevented him from doing. Surely the academic community would be edified if the fruit of his long experience were—'

Stoner interrupted, 'I have no desire to begin a literary career at this stage in my life.'

Lomax, without moving from his chair, seemed to bow to Finch. 'I'm sure our colleague is too modest. Within two years I myself will be forced by regulations to vacate the chairmanship of the department. I certainly intend to put my declining years to good use; indeed, I look forward to the leisure of my retirement.'

Stoner said, 'I hope to remain a member of the department, at least until that auspicious occasion.'

Lomax was silent for a moment. Then he said contemplatively to Finch, 'It has occurred to me several times during the past few years that Professor Stoner's efforts on behalf of the University have perhaps not been fully appreciated. It has occurred to me that a promotion to full professor might be a fitting climax to his retirement year. A dinner in honor of the occasion—a fitting ceremony. It should be most gratifying. Though it is late in the year, and though most of the promotions have already been declared, I am sure that, if I insisted, a promotion might be arranged for next year, in commemoration of an auspicious retirement.'

Suddenly the game that he had been playing with Lomax—and, in a curious way, enjoying—seemed trivial and mean. A tiredness came over him. He looked directly at Lomax and said wearily, 'Holly, after all these years, I thought you knew me better than that. I've never cared a damn for what you thought you could "give" me, or what you thought you could "do" to me, or whatever.' He paused; he was, indeed, more tired than he had thought. He continued with an effort, 'That isn't the point; it has never been the point. You're a good man, I suppose; certainly you're a good teacher. But in some ways you're an ignorant son-of-a-bitch.' He paused again. 'I don't know what you hoped for. But I won't retire—not at the end of this year, nor the end of the next.' He got up slowly and stood for a moment, gathering his strength. 'If you gentlemen will excuse me, I'm a little tired. I'll leave you to discuss whatever it is you have to discuss.'

He knew that it would not end there, but he did not care. When, at the last general faculty meeting of the year, Lomax, in his departmental report to the faculty, announced the retirement at the end of the next year of Professor William Stoner, Stoner got to his feet and informed the faculty that Professor Lomax was in error, that the retirement would not be effective until two years after the time that Lomax had announced. At the beginning of the fall semester the new president of the University invited Stoner to his home for afternoon tea and spoke expansively of the years of his service, of the well-earned rest, of the gratitude they all felt; Stoner put on his most crochety manner, called the president 'young man,' and pretended not to hear, so that at last the young man ended by shouting in the most placatory tone he could manage.

But his efforts, meager as they were, tired him more than he had expected, so that by Christmas vacation he was nearly exhausted. He told himself that he was, indeed, getting old, and that he would have to let up if he were to do a good job the rest of the year. During the ten days of Christmas vacation he rested, as if he might hoard his strength; and when he returned for the last weeks of the semester he worked with a vigor and energy that surprised him. The issue of his retirement seemed settled, and he did not bother to think of it again.

Late in February the tiredness came over him again, and he could not seem to shake it off; he spent a great deal of his time at home and did much of his paper work propped on the day bed in his little back room. In March he became aware of a dull general pain in his legs and arms; he told himself that he was tired, that he would be better when the warm spring days came, that he needed rest. By April the pain had become localized in the lower part of his body; occasionally he missed a class, and he found that it took most of his strength merely to walk from class to class. In early May the pain became intense, and he could no longer think of it as a minor nuisance. He made an appointment with a doctor at the University infirmary.

There were tests and examinations and questions, the import of which Stoner only vaguely understood. He was given a special diet, some pills for the pain, and was told to come back at the beginning of the next week for consultation, when the results of the tests would be completed and put together. He felt better, though the tiredness remained.

His doctor was a young man named Jamison, who had explained to Stoner that he was working for the University for a few years before he went into private practice. He had a pink, round face, wore rimless glasses, and had a kind of nervous awkwardness of manner that Stoner trusted.

Stoner was a few minutes early for his appointment, but the receptionist told him to go right in. He went down the long narrow hall of the infirmary to the little cubicle where Jamison had his office.

Jamison was waiting for him, and it was clear to Stoner that he had been waiting for some time; folders and X-rays and notes were laid out neatly on his desk. Jamison stood up, smiled abruptly and nervously, and extended his hand toward a chair in front of his desk.

'Professor Stoner,' he said. 'Sit down, sit down.'

Stoner sat.

Jamison frowned at the display on his desk, smoothed a sheet of paper, and let himself down on his chair. 'Well,' he said, 'there's some sort of obstruction in the lower intestinal tract, that's clear. Not much shows up on the X-rays, but that isn't unusual. Oh, a little cloudiness; but that doesn't necessarily mean anything.' He turned his chair, set an X-ray in a frame, switched on a light, and pointed vaguely. Stoner looked, but he could see nothing. Jamison switched off the light and turned back to his desk. He became very businesslike. 'Your blood count's down pretty low, but there doesn't seem to be any infection there; your sedimentation is subnormal and your blood pressure's down. There is some internal swelling that doesn't seem quite right, you've lost quite a bit of weight, and—well, with the symptoms you've shown and from what I can tell from these'—he waved at his desk—'I'd say there's only one thing to do.' He smiled fixedly and said with strained jocularity, 'We've just got to go in there and see what we can find out.'

Stoner nodded. 'It's cancer then.'

'Well,' Jamison said, 'that's a pretty big word. It can mean a lot of things. I'm pretty sure there's a tumor there, but—well, we can't be absolutely sure of anything until we go in there and look around.'

'How long have I had it?'

'Oh, there's no way of telling that. But it feels like—well, it's pretty large; it's been there some time.'

Stoner was silent for a moment. Then he said, 'How long would you estimate I have?'

Jamison said distractedly, 'Oh, now, look, Mr Stoner.' He attempted a laugh. 'We mustn't jump to conclusions. Why, there's always a chance—there's a chance it's only a tumor, non-malignant, you know. Or—or it could be a lot of things. We just can't know for sure until we—'

'Yes,' Stoner said. 'When would you want to operate?'

'As soon as possible,' Jamison said relievedly. 'Within the next two or three days.'

'That soon,' Stoner said, almost absently. Then he looked at Jamison steadily. 'Let me ask you a few questions, Doctor. I must tell you that I want you to answer them frankly.'

Jamison nodded.

'If it is only a tumor—non-malignant, as you say—would a couple of weeks make any great difference?'

'Well,' Jamison said reluctantly, 'there would be the pain; and—no, not a *great* deal of difference, I suppose.'

'Good,' Stoner said. 'And if it is as bad as you think it is—would a couple of weeks make a great difference *then*?'

After a long while Jamison said, almost bitterly, 'No, I suppose not.'

'Then,' Stoner said reasonably, 'I'll wait for a couple of weeks. There are a few things I need to clear up—some work I need to do.'

'I don't advise it, you understand,' Jamison said. 'I don't advise it at all.'

'Of course,' Stoner said. 'And, Doctor—you won't mention this to anyone, will you?'

'No,' Jamison said and added with a little warmth, 'of course not.' He suggested a few revisions of the diet he had earlier given him, prescribed more pills, and set a date for his entrance into the hospital.

Stoner felt nothing at all; it was as if what the doctor told him were a minor annoyance, an obstacle he would have somehow to work around in order to get done what he had to do. It occurred to him that it was rather late in the year for this to be happening; Lomax might have some difficulty in finding a replacement.

The pill he had taken in the doctor's office made him a little light-headed, and he found the sensation oddly pleasurable. His sense of time was displaced; he found himself standing in the long parqueted first-floor corridor of Jesse Hall. A low hum, like the distant thrumming of birds' wings, was in his ears; in the shadowed corridor a sourceless light seemed to glow and dim, pulsating like the beat of his heart; and his flesh, intimately aware of every move he made, tingled as he stepped forward with deliberate care into the mingled light and dark.

He stood at the stairs that led up to the second floor; the steps were marble, and in their precise centers were gentle troughs worn smooth by decades of footsteps going up and down. They had been almost new when—how many years ago?—he had first stood here and looked up, as he looked now, and wondered where they would lead him. He thought of time and of its gentle flowing. He put one foot carefully in the first smooth depression and lifted himself up.

Then he was in Gordon Finch's outer office. The girl said, 'Dean Finch was about to leave . . .' He nodded absently, smiled at her, and went into Finch's office.

'Gordon,' he said cordially, the smile still on his face. 'I won't keep you long.'

Finch returned the smile reflexively; his eyes were tired. 'Sure, Bill, sit down.'

'I won't keep you long,' he said again; he felt a curious power come into his voice. 'The fact is, I've changed my mind—about retiring, I mean. I know it's awkward; sorry to be so late letting you know, but—well, I think it's best all around. I'm quitting at the end of this semester.'

268

Finch's face floated before him, round in its amazement. 'What the hell,' he said. 'Has anyone been putting the screws on you?'

'Nothing like that,' Stoner said. 'It's my own decision. It's just that—I've discovered there *are* some things I'd like to do.' He added reasonably, 'And I do need a little rest.'

Finch was annoyed, and Stoner knew that he had cause to be. He thought he heard himself murmur another apology; he felt the smile remain foolishly on his face.

'Well,' Finch said, 'I guess it's not too late. I can start the papers through tomorrow. I suppose you know all you need to know about your annuity income, insurance, and things like that?'

'Oh, yes,' Stoner said. 'I've thought of all that. It's all right.'

Finch looked at his watch. 'I'm kind of late, Bill. Drop by in a day or so and we'll clear up the details. In the meantime—well, I suppose Lomax ought to know. I'll call him tonight.' He grinned. 'I'm afraid you've succeeded in pleasing him.'

'Yes,' Stoner said. 'I'm afraid I have.'

There was much to do in the two weeks that remained before he was to go into the hospital, but he decided that he would be able to do it. He canceled his classes for the next two days and called into conference all those students for whom he had the responsibility of directing independent research, theses, and dissertations. He wrote detailed instructions that would guide them to the completion of the work they had begun and left carbon copies of these instructions in Lomax's mailbox. He soothed those who were thrown into a panic by what they considered his desertion of them and reassured those who were fearful of committing themselves to a new adviser. He found that the pills he had been taking reduced the clarity of his intelligence as they relieved the pain; so in the daytime, when he talked to students, and in the evening, when he read the deluge of half-completed papers, theses, and dissertations, he took them only when the pain became so intense that it forced his attention away from his work.

Two days after his declaration of retirement, in the middle of a busy afternoon, he got a telephone call from Gordon Finch.

'Bill? Gordon. Look—there's a small problem I think I ought to talk to you about.'

'Yes?' he said impatiently.

'It's Lomax. He can't get it through his head that you aren't doing this on his account.'

'It doesn't matter,' Stoner said. 'Let him think what he wants.'

'Wait—that isn't all. He's making plans to go through with the dinner and everything. He says he gave his word.'

'Look, Gordon, I'm very busy just now. Can't you just put a stop to it somehow?'

'I tried to, but he's doing it through the department. If you want me to call him in I will; but you'll have to be here too. When he's like this I can't talk to him.'

'All right. When is this foolishness supposed to come off?'

There was a pause. 'A week from Friday. The last day of classes, just before exam week.'

'All right,' Stoner said wearily. 'I should have things cleared up by then, and it'll be easier than arguing it now. Just let it ride.'

'You ought to know this too; he wants me to announce your retirement as professor emeritus, though it can't be really official until next year.'

Stoner felt a laugh come up in his throat. 'What the hell,' he said. 'That's all right too.'

All that week he worked without consciousness of time. He worked straight through Friday, from eight o'clock in the morning until ten that night. He read a last page and made a last note, and leaned back in his chair; the light on his desk filled his eyes, and for a moment he did not know where he was. He looked around him and saw that he was in his office. The bookshelves were bulging with books haphazardly placed; there were stacks of papers in the corners; and his filing cabinets were open and disarranged. I ought to straighten things up, he thought; I ought to get my things in order.

'Next week,' he said to himself. 'Next week.'

He wondered if he could make it home. It seemed an effort to breathe. He narrowed his mind, forced it upon his arms and legs, made them respond. He got to his feet, and would not let himself sway. He turned the desk light off and stood until his eyes could see by the moonlight that came through his windows. Then he put one foot before the other and walked through the dark halls to the out-of-doors and through the quiet streets to his home.

The lights were on; Edith was still up. He gathered the last of his strength and made it up the front steps and into the living room. Then he knew he could go no farther; he was able to reach the couch and to sit down. After a moment he found the strength to reach into his vest pocket and take out his tube of pills. He put one in his mouth and swallowed it without water; then he took another. They were bitter, but the bitterness seemed almost pleasant.

He became aware that Edith had been walking about the room, going from one place to another; he hoped that she had not spoken to him. As the pain eased and as some of his strength returned, he realized that she had not; her face was set, her nostrils and mouth pinched, and she walked stiffly, angrily. He started to speak to her, but he decided that he could not trust his voice. He let himself wonder why she was angry; she had not been angry for a long time.

Finally she stopped moving about and faced him; her hands were fists and they hung at her sides. 'Well? Aren't you going to say anything?'

He cleared his throat and made his eyes focus. 'I'm sorry, Edith.' He heard his voice quiet but steady. 'I'm a little tired, I guess.'

'You weren't going to say anything at all, were you? Thoughtless. Didn't you think I had a right to know?'

For a moment he was puzzled. Then he nodded. If he had had more strength he would have been angry. 'How did you find out?'

'Never mind that. I suppose everyone knows except me. Oh, Willy, honestly.'

'I'm sorry, Edith, really, I am. I didn't want to worry you. I was going to tell you next week, just before I went in. It's nothing; you aren't to trouble yourself.'

'Nothing!' She laughed bitterly. 'They say it might be cancer. Don't you know what that means?'

He felt suddenly weightless, and he had to force himself not to clutch at something. 'Edith,' he said in a distant voice, 'let's talk about it tomorrow. Please. I'm tired now.'

She looked at him for a moment. 'Do you want me to help you to your room?' she asked crossly. 'You don't look like you'll make it by yourself.'

'I'm all right,' he said.

But before he got to his room he wished he had let her help him—and not only because he found himself weaker than he had expected.

He rested Saturday and Sunday, and Monday he was able to meet his classes. He went home early, and he was lying on the living-room couch gazing interestedly at the ceiling when the doorbell rang. He sat upright and started to rise, but the door opened. It was Gordon Finch. His face was pale, and his hands were unsteady.

'Come in, Gordon,' Stoner said.

'My God, Bill,' Finch said. 'Why didn't you tell me?'

Stoner laughed shortly. 'I might as well have advertised it in the newspapers,' he said. 'I thought I could do it quietly, without upsetting anyone.'

'I know, but—Jesus, if I had known.'

'There's nothing to get upset about. There's nothing definite yet—it's just an operation. Exploratory, I believe they call it. How did you find out anyway?'

'Jamison,' Finch said. 'He's my doctor too. He said he knew it wasn't ethical, but that I ought to know. He was right, Bill.'

'I know,' Stoner said. 'It doesn't matter. Has the word got around?'

Finch shook his head. 'Not yet.'

'Then keep your mouth shut about it. Please.'

'Sure, Bill,' Finch said. 'Now about this dinner party Friday—you don't have to go through with it, you know.'

'But I will,' Stoner said. He grinned. 'I figure I owe Lomax something.'

The ghost of a smile came upon Finch's face. 'You *have* turned into an ornery old son-of-a-bitch, haven't you?'

'I guess I have,' Stoner said.

The dinner was held in a small banquet room of the Student Union. At the last minute Edith decided that she wouldn't be able to sit through it, so he went alone. He went early and walked slowly across the campus, as if ambling casually on a spring afternoon. As he had anticipated, there was no one in the room; he got a waiter to remove his wife's name card and to reset the main table, so that there would not be an empty space. Then he sat down and waited for the guests to arrive.

He was seated between Gordon Finch and the president of the University; Lomax, who was to act as the master of ceremonies, was seated three chairs away. Lomax was smiling and chatting with those sitting around him; he did not look at Stoner.

The room filled quickly; members of the department who had not really spoken to him for years waved across the room to him; Stoner nodded. Finch said little, though he watched Stoner carefully; the youngish new president, whose name Stoner could never remember, spoke to him with an easy deference.

The food was served by young students in white coats; Stoner recognized several of them; he nodded and spoke to them. The guests looked sadly at their food and began to eat. A relaxed hum of conversation, broken by the cheery clatter of silverware and china, throbbed in the room; Stoner knew that his own presence was almost forgotten, so he was able to poke at his food, take a few ritual bites, and look around him. If he narrowed his eyes he could not see the faces; he saw colors and vague shapes moving before him, as in a frame, constructing moment by moment new patterns of contained flux. It was a pleasant sight, and if he held his attention upon it in a particular way, he was not aware of the pain.

Suddenly there was silence; he shook his head, as if coming out of a dream. Near the end of the narrow table Lomax was standing, tapping on a water glass with his knife. A handsome face, Stoner thought absently; still handsome. The years had made the long thin face even thinner, and the lines seemed marks of an increased sensitivity rather than of age. The smile was still intimately sardonic, and the voice as resonant and steady as it had ever been.

He was speaking; the words came to Stoner in snatches, as if the voice that made them boomed from the silence and then diminished into its source. '. . . the long years of dedicated service . . . richly deserved rest from the pressures . . . esteemed by his colleagues . . .' He heard the irony and knew that, in his own way, after all these years, Lomax was speaking to him.

A short determined burst of applause startled his reverie. Beside him, Gordon Finch was standing, speaking. Though he looked up and strained his ears, he could not hear what Finch said; Gordon's lips moved, he looked fixedly in front of him, there was applause, he sat down. On the other side of him, the president got to his feet and spoke in a voice that scurried from cajolery to threat, from humor to sadness, from regret to joy. He said that he hoped Stoner's retirement would be a beginning not an ending; he knew that the University would be the poorer for his absence; there was the importance of tradition, the necessity for change; and the gratitude, for years to come, in the hearts of all his students. Stoner could not make sense of what he said; but when the president finished, the room burst into loud applause and the faces smiled. As the applause dwindled someone in the audience shouted in a thin voice: 'Speech!' Someone else took up the call, and the word was murmured here and there.

Finch whispered in his ear, 'Do you want me to get you out of it?'

'No,' Stoner said. 'It's all right.'

He got to his feet, and realized that he had nothing to say. He was silent for a long time as he looked from face to face. He heard his voice issue flatly. 'I have taught . . .'

he said. He began again. 'I have taught at this University for nearly forty years. I do not know what I would have done if I had not been a teacher. If I had not taught, I might have—' He paused, as if distracted. Then he said, with a finality, 'I want to thank you all for letting me teach.'

He sat down. There was applause, friendly laughter. The room broke up and people milled about. Stoner felt his hand being shaken; he was aware that he smiled and that he nodded at whatever was said to him. The president pressed his hand, smiled heartily, told him that he must drop around, any afternoon, looked at his wrist watch, and hurried out. The room began to empty, and Stoner stood alone where he had risen and gathered his strength for the walk across the room. He waited until he felt something harden inside him, and then he walked around the table and out of the room, passing little knots of people who glanced at him curiously, as if he were already a stranger. Lomax was in one of the groups, but he did not turn as Stoner passed; and Stoner found that he was grateful that they had not had to speak to each other, after all this time.

The next day he entered the hospital and rested until Monday morning, when the operation was to be performed. He slept much of that time and had no particular interest in what was to happen to him. On Monday morning someone stuck a needle in his arm; he was only half conscious of being rolled through halls to a strange room that seemed to be all ceiling and light. He saw something descend toward his face and he closed his eyes.

He awoke to nausea; his head ached; there was a new sharp pain, not unpleasant, in his lower body. He retched, and felt better. He let his hand move over the heavy bandages that covered the middle part of his body. He slept,

276

wakened during the night and took a glass of water, and slept again until morning.

When he awoke, Jamison was standing beside his bed, his fingers on his left wrist.

'Well,' Jamison said, 'how are we feeling this morning?'

'All right, I think.' His throat was dry; he reached out, and Jamison handed him the glass of water. He drank and looked at Jamison, waiting.

'Well,' Jamison said at last, uncomfortably, 'we got the tumor. Big feller. In a day or two you'll be feeling much better.'

'I'll be able to leave here?' Stoner asked.

'You'll be up and around in two or three days,' Jamison said. 'The only thing is, it might be more convenient if you did stay around for a while. We couldn't get—all of it. We'll be using X-ray treatment, things like that. Of course, you could go back and forth, but—'

'No,' Stoner said and let his head fall back on the pillow. He was tired again. 'As soon as possible,' he said, 'I think I want to go home.'

17

'Oh, Willy,' she said. 'You're all eaten up inside.'

He was lying on the day bed in the little back room, gazing out the open window; it was late afternoon, and the sun, dipping beneath the horizon, sent a red glow upon the underside of a long rippling cloud that hung in the west above the tree-tops and the houses. A fly buzzed against the window screen; and the pungent aroma of trash burning in the neighbors' yards was caught in the still air.

'What?' Stoner said absently and turned to his wife.

'Inside,' Edith said. 'The doctor said it has spread all over. Oh, Willy, poor Willy.'

'Yes,' Stoner said. He could not make himself become very interested. 'Well, you aren't to worry. It's best not to think about it.'

She did not answer, and he turned again to the open window and watched the sky darken, until there was only a dull purplish streak upon the cloud in the distance.

He had been home for a little more than a week and had just that afternoon returned from a visit to the hospital where he had undergone what Jamison, with his strained smile, called a 'treatment.' Jamison had admired the speed with which his incision had healed, had said something about his having the constitution of a man of forty, and then had abruptly grown silent. Stoner had allowed himself to be poked and prodded, had let them strap him on a table, and had remained still while a huge machine hovered silently about him. It was foolishness, he knew, but he did not protest; it would have been unkind to do so. It was little enough to undergo, if it would distract them all from the knowledge they could not evade.

Gradually, he knew, this little room where he now lay and looked out the window would become his world; already he could feel the first vague beginnings of the pain that returned like the distant call of an old friend. He doubted that he would be asked to return to the hospital; he had heard in Jamison's voice this afternoon a finality, and Jamison had given him some pills to take in the event that there was 'discomfort.'

'You might write Grace,' he heard himself saying to Edith. 'She hasn't visited us in a long time.'

And he turned to see Edith nodding absently; her eyes had been, with his, gazing tranquilly upon the growing darkness outside the window.

During the next two weeks he felt himself weaken, at first gradually and then rapidly. The pain returned, with an intensity that he had not expected; he took his pills and felt the pain recede into a darkness, as if it were a cautious animal.

Grace came; and he found that, after all, he had little to say to her. She had been away from St Louis and had returned to find Edith's letter only the day before. She was worn and tense and there were dark shadows under her eyes; he wished that he could do something to ease her pain and knew that he could not.

'You look just fine, Daddy,' she said. 'Just fine. You're going to be all right.'

'Of course,' he said and smiled at her. 'How is young Ed? And how have you been?'

She said that she had been fine and that young Ed was fine, that he would be entering junior high school the coming fall. He looked at her with some bewilderment. 'Junior high?' he asked. Then he realized that it must be true. 'Of course,' he said. 'I forgot how big he must be by now.'

'He stays with his—with Mr and Mrs Frye a lot of the time,' she said. 'It's best for him that way.' She said something else, but his attention wandered. More and more frequently he found it difficult to keep his mind focused upon any one thing; it wandered where he could not predict, and he sometimes found himself speaking words whose source he did not understand.

'Poor Daddy,' he heard Grace say, and he brought his attention back to where he was. 'Poor Daddy, things haven't been easy for you, have they?'

He thought for a moment and then he said, 'No. But I suppose I didn't want them to be.'

'Mamma and I—we've both been disappointments to you, haven't we?'

He moved his hand upward, as if to touch her. 'Oh, no,' he said with a dim passion. 'You mustn't . . .' He wanted to say more, to explain; but he could not go on. He closed his eyes and felt his mind loosen. Images crowded there, and changed, as if upon a screen. He saw Edith as she had been that first evening they had met at old Claremont's house—the blue gown and the slender fingers and the fair, delicate face that smiled softly, the pale eyes that looked eagerly upon each moment as if it were a sweet surprise. 'Your mother . . .' he said. 'She was not always . . .' She was not always as she had been; and he thought now that he could perceive beneath the woman she had become the girl that she had been; he thought that he had always perceived it.

'You were a beautiful child,' he heard himself saying, and for a moment he did not know to whom he spoke. Light swam before his eyes, found shape, and became the face of his daughter, lined and somber and worn with care. He closed his eyes again. 'In the study. Remember? You used to sit with me when I worked. You were so still, and the light . . . the light . . .' The light of the desk lamp (he could see it now) had been absorbed by her studious small face that bent in childish absorption over a book or a picture, so that the smooth flesh glowed against the shadows of the room. He heard the small laughter echo in the distance. 'Of course,' he said and looked upon the present face of that child. 'Of course,' he said again, 'you were always there.'

'Hush,' she said softly, 'you must rest.'

And that was their farewell. The next day she came down to him and said she had to get back to St Louis for a few days and said something else he did not hear in a flat, controlled voice; her face was drawn, and her eyes were red and moist. Their gazes locked; she looked at him for a long moment, almost in disbelief; then she turned away. He knew that he would not see her again.

He had no wish to die; but there were moments, after Grace left, when he looked forward impatiently, as one might look to the moment of a journey that one does not particularly wish to take. And like any traveler, he felt that there were many things he had to do before he left; yet he could not think what they were.

He had become so weak that he could not walk; he spent his days and nights in the tiny back room. Edith brought him the books he wanted and arranged them on a table beside his narrow bed, so that he would not have to exert himself to reach them.

But he read little, though the presence of his books

comforted him. He had Edith open the curtains on all the windows and would not let her close them, even when the afternoon sun, intensely hot, slanted into the room.

Sometimes Edith came into the room and sat on the bed beside him and they talked. They talked of trivial things— of people they knew casually, of a new building going up on the campus, of an old one torn down; but what they said did not seem to matter. A new tranquillity had come between them. It was a quietness that was like the beginning of love; and almost without thinking, Stoner knew why it had come. They had forgiven themselves for the harm they had done each other, and they were rapt in a regard of what their life together might have been.

Almost without regret he looked at her now; in the soft light of late afternoon her face seemed young and unlined. If I had been stronger, he thought; if I had known more; if I could have understood. And finally, mercilessly, he thought: if I had loved her more. As if it were a long distance it had to go, his hand moved across the sheet that covered him and touched her hand. She did not move; and after a while he drifted into a kind of sleep.

Despite the sedatives he took, his mind, it seemed to him, remained clear; and he was grateful for that. But it was as if some will other than his own had taken possession of that mind, moving it in directions he could not understand; time passed, and he did not see its passing.

Gordon Finch visited him nearly every day, but he could not keep the sequence of these visits clear in his memory; sometimes he spoke to Gordon when he was not there, and was surprised at his voice in the empty room; sometimes in the middle of a conversation with him he paused and blinked, as if suddenly aware of Gordon's presence. Once, when Gordon tiptoed into the room, he turned to him with a kind of surprise and asked, 'Where's Dave?' And when he saw the shock of fear come over Gordon's face he shook his head weakly and said, 'I'm sorry, Gordon. I was nearly asleep; I'd been thinking about Dave Masters and—sometimes I say things I'm thinking without knowing it. It's these pills I have to take.'

Gordon smiled and nodded and made a joke; but Stoner knew that in that instant Gordon Finch had withdrawn from him in such a way that he could never return. He felt a keen regret that he had spoken so of Dave Masters, the defiant boy they both had loved, whose ghost had held them, all these years, in a friendship whose depth they had never quite realized.

Gordon told him of the regards that his colleagues sent him and spoke disconnectedly of University affairs that might interest him; but his eyes were restless, and the nervous smile flickered on his face.

Edith came into the room, and Gordon Finch lumbered to his feet, effusive and cordial in his relief at being interrupted.

'Edith,' he said, 'you sit down here.'

Edith shook her head and blinked at Stoner.

'Old Bill's looking better,' Finch said. 'By God, I think he's looking much better than he did last week.'

Edith turned to him as if noticing his presence for the first time.

'Oh, Gordon,' she said. 'He looks awful. Poor Willy. He won't be with us much longer.'

Gordon paled and took a step backward, as if he had been struck. 'My God, Edith!'

'Not much longer,' Edith said again, looking broodingly at her husband, who was smiling a little. 'What am I going to do, Gordon? What will I do without him?'

He closed his eyes and they disappeared; he heard Gordon

whisper something and heard their footsteps as they drew away from him.

What was so remarkable was that it was so easy. He had wanted to tell Gordon how easy it was, he had wanted to tell him that it did not bother him to talk about it or to think about it; but he had been unable to do so. Now it did not seem really to matter; he heard their voices in the kitchen, Gordon's low and urgent, Edith's grudging and clipped. What were they talking about?

. . . The pain came upon him with a suddenness and an urgency that took him unprepared, so that he almost cried out. He made his hands loosen upon the bedclothes and willed them to move steadily to the night table. He took several of the pills and put them in his mouth and swallowed some water. A cold sweat broke upon his forehead and he lay very still until the pain lessened.

He heard the voices again; he did not open his eyes. Was it Gordon? His hearing seemed to go outside his body and hover like a cloud above him, transmitting to him every delicacy of sound. But his mind could not exactly distinguish the words.

The voice—was it Gordon's?—was saying something about his life. And though he could not make out the words, could not even be sure that they were being said, his own mind, with the fierceness of a wounded animal, pounced upon that question. Mercilessly he saw his life as it must appear to another.

Dispassionately, reasonably, he contemplated the failure that his life must appear to be. He had wanted friendship and the closeness of friendship that might hold him in the race of mankind; he had had two friends, one of whom had died senselessly before he was known, the other of whom had now withdrawn so distantly into the ranks of the living that . . .

He had wanted the singleness and the still connective passion of marriage; he had had that, too, and he had not known what to do with it, and it had died. He had wanted love; and he had had love, and had relinquished it, had let it go into the chaos of potentiality. Katherine, he thought. 'Katherine.'

And he had wanted to be a teacher, and he had become one; yet he knew, he had always known, that for most of his life he had been an indifferent one. He had dreamed of a kind of integrity, of a kind of purity that was entire; he had found compromise and the assaulting diversion of triviality. He had conceived wisdom, and at the end of the long years he had found ignorance. And what else? he thought. What else?

What did you expect? he asked himself.

He opened his eyes. It was dark. Then he saw the sky outside, the deep blue-black of space, and the thin glow of moonlight through a cloud. It must be very late, he thought; it seemed only an instant ago that Gordon and Edith had stood beside him, in the bright afternoon. Or was it long ago? He could not tell.

He had known that his mind must weaken as his body wasted, but he had been unprepared for the suddenness. The flesh is strong, he thought; stronger than we imagine. It wants always to go on.

He heard voices and saw lights and felt the pain come and go. Edith's face hovered above him; he felt his face smile. Sometimes he heard his own voice speak, and he thought that it spoke rationally, though he could not be sure. He felt Edith's hands on him, moving him, bathing him. She has her child again, he thought; at last she has her child that she can care for. He wished that he could speak to her; he felt that he had something to say.

What did you expect? he thought.

Something heavy was pressing upon his eyelids. He felt them tremble and then he managed to get them open. It was light that he felt, the bright sunlight of an afternoon. He blinked and considered impassively the blue sky and the brilliant edge of the sun that he could see through his window. He decided that they were real. He moved a hand, and with the movement he felt a curious strength flow within him, as if from the air. He breathed deeply; there was no pain.

With each breath he took, it seemed to him that his strength increased; his flesh tingled, and he could feel the delicate weight of light and shade upon his face. He raised himself up from the bed, so that he was half sitting, his back supported by the wall against which the bed rested. Now he could see the out-of-doors.

He felt that he had awakened from a long sleep and was refreshed. It was late spring or early summer—more likely early summer, from the look of things. There was a richness and a sheen upon the leaves of the huge elm tree in his back yard; and the shade it cast had a deep coolness that he had known before. A thickness was in the air, a heaviness that crowded the sweet odors of grass and leaf and flower, mingling and holding them suspended. He breathed again, deeply; he heard the rasping of his breath and felt the sweetness of the summer gather in his lungs.

And he felt also, with that breath he took, a shifting somewhere deep inside him, a shifting that stopped something and fixed his head so that it would not move. Then it passed, and he thought, So this is what it is like.

It occurred to him that he ought to call Edith; and then he knew that he would not call her. The dying are selfish, he thought; they want their moments to themselves, like children.

He was breathing again, but there was a difference within him that he could not name. He felt that he was waiting for something, for some knowledge; but it seemed to him that he had all the time in the world.

He heard the distant sound of laughter, and he turned his head toward its source. A group of students had cut across his back-yard lawn; they were hurrying somewhere. He saw them distinctly; there were three couples. The girls were long-limbed and graceful in their light summer dresses, and the boys were looking at them with a joyous and bemused wonder. They walked lightly upon the grass, hardly touching it, leaving no trace of where they had been. He watched them as they went out of his sight, where he could not see; and for a long time after they had vanished the sound of their laughter came to him, far and unknowing in the quiet of the summer afternoon.

What did you expect? he thought again.

A kind of joy came upon him, as if borne in on a summer breeze. He dimly recalled that he had been thinking of failure—as if it mattered. It seemed to him now that such thoughts were mean, unworthy of what his life had been. Dim presences gathered at the edge of his consciousness; he could not see them, but he knew that they were there, gathering their forces toward a kind of palpability he could not see or hear. He was approaching them, he knew; but there was no need to hurry. He could ignore them if he wished; he had all the time there was.

There was a softness around him, and a languor crept upon his limbs. A sense of his own identity came upon him with a sudden force, and he felt the power of it. He was himself, and he knew what he had been.

His head turned. His bedside table was piled with books that he had not touched for a long time. He let his hand play over them for a moment; he marveled at the thinness of the fingers, at the intricate articulation of the joints as he flexed them. He felt the strength within them, and let them pull a book from the jumble on the tabletop. It was his own book that he sought, and when the hand held it he smiled at the familiar red cover that had for a long time been faded and scuffed.

It hardly mattered to him that the book was forgotten and that it served no use; and the question of its worth at any time seemed almost trivial. He did not have the illusion that he would find himself there, in that fading print; and yet, he knew, a small part of him that he could not deny *was* there, and would be there.

He opened the book; and as he did so it became not his own. He let his fingers riffle through the pages and felt a tingling, as if those pages were alive. The tingling came through his fingers and coursed through his flesh and bone; he was minutely aware of it, and he waited until it contained him, until the old excitement that was like terror fixed him where he lay. The sunlight, passing his window, shone upon the page, and he could not see what was written there.

The fingers loosened, and the book they had held moved slowly and then swiftly across the still body and fell into the silence of the room.